A **TOM MARI**

CW00514999

SLEEPING SOLDIERS

NEW YORK TIMES #1 BESTSELLER **TONY LEE** WRITING AS

JACK GATLAND

MEDIA

Published by Hooded Man Media.
Cover design by Ligraphics

First Edition: August 2022
Second Edition: August 2023

PRAISE FOR JACK GATLAND

'This is one of those books that will keep you up past your bedtime, as each chapter lures you into reading just one more.'

'This book was excellent! A great plot which kept you guessing until the end.'

'Couldn't put it down, fast paced with twists and turns.'

'The story was captivating, good plot, twists you never saw and really likeable characters. Can't wait for the next one!'

'I got sucked into this book from the very first page, thoroughly enjoyed it, can't wait for the next one.'

'Totally addictive. Thoroughly recommend.'

'Moves at a fast pace and carries you along with it.'

'Just couldn't put this book down, from the first page to the last one it kept you wondering what would happen next.'

There's a new Detective Inspector in town...

Before Tom Marlowe, there was DI Declan Walsh!

An EXCLUSIVE PREQUEL, completely free to anyone who joins the Jack Gatland Reader's Club!

Join at www.subscribepage.com/jackgatland

Also by Jack Gatland

For Mum, who inspired me to write.

For Tracy, who inspires me to write.

CONTENTS

PROLOGUE

THEN.

'PUT THE GUN DOWN!'

'She said that? Really?'

'Damn right she did. "Put the gun down". As if saying it would make me do the bloody thing.'

'And did you?'

Marshall Kirk smiled at the question, placing the binoculars down for a moment as he considered this.

'You know? I did put the bloody gun down,' he said with complete conviction.

Tom Marlowe leaned back in the chair, staring at his companion with an expression of severe mistrust. 'You bloody didn't,' he muttered.

Kirk nodded. 'I did, and it was the best thing I ever did. Sure, I was arrested and placed in a Gulag for three months, but the day the wall came down we met up for a drink. A year later we got married.'

Marlowe shook his head. 'Nowadays you could just find someone on the internet,' he smiled.

'Aye?' Kirk raised an eyebrow at this. 'And you've done that, have you?'

'Do you honestly think I have time?' Marlowe laughed. 'They've got me running around all over the place right now.'

Marshall Kirk considered this, nodding slowly, reaching for a packet of crisps and opening them. 'Working for Box does that,' he said, using the name people who worked in the Secret Service used for it. 'You should have stayed in the SAS.'

'I wasn't in the SAS,' Marlowe replied with a hint of professional insult. 'I was a Royal Marine Commando.'

'But we met on an SAS reconnaissance,' Kirk frowned as he poured a couple of crisps into his hand and threw them into his mouth. 'Were you AWOL or something?'

'I wasn't in the SAS when we did that, in the same way that you weren't either,' Marlowe held a hand out for a crisp.

Kirk considered this, and then gave a single, small crisp to him.

'Wow, thanks,' Marlowe replied, unimpressed, but eating it anyway, wincing as he realised it was prawn cocktail flavoured. He should have realised this error well in advance, of course, as the only crisps Marshall Kirk seemed to eat were bloody prawn cocktail flavour.

Chuckling, Kirk raised the binoculars to his eyes once more with one hand, mainly to avoid looking at Marlowe.

'I might have been in the SAS,' he crunched, using his free hand to shovel more crisps into his mouth. 'I could have been in the SAS, doing all that SAS stuff they do. *We* do.'

'Yes,' Marlowe smiled. 'I can definitely see that.'

They'd been teamed up on this stakeout for around three days now; sitting in an abandoned apartment on a cheap and brutal East London housing estate, using one of the back windows to spy on a mosque next door. It wasn't a Muslim hunt, but rather the *opposite*; a far-right organisation had been rumoured to be targeting the mosque in a coordinated bombing campaign and, as Frank Robertson, the public face and leader of the organisation, had links to far-right groups in both Hungary and Greece, it'd been decided that MI5 should monitor the building, threats from outside the country, even if it was through a British National, being their remit.

And, as it wasn't deemed that high a problem, they'd stuck the weeks-from-retirement Marshall Kirk there with the wet-behind-the-ears recruit Thomas Marlowe, probably to keep him out of the way until they could work out what to do with him next.

The crisps finished, Kirk made a ring with his index finger and thumb, pushing the middle of the flattened pack of prawn cocktail crisps into it, making a hollow. Then, with as much attention to detail as he'd given the op, Marshall pushed the rest of the packet into it, folding them over, making a solid ball of a crisp packet that didn't unravel.

'I don't understand why you do that,' Marlowe muttered. 'All goes in the same bin.'

'Yes, but mine takes up less space,' Kirk replied smugly, returning to the binoculars. 'It's more efficient.'

'Whatever. I'm getting some lunch,' Marlowe said as he rose from the chair he'd been sitting in for the last four hours. 'Saveloy and chips?'

'Have I ever deviated?' Kirk still watched through the

glasses. 'Pick what you like and never deviate. Change is dangerous. Change leads to chaos.'

'This from the guy who fell in love across the Berlin Wall,' Marlowe chuckled, grabbing his jacket and wallet. 'Back in a minute.'

Marshall Kirk grinned.

'A minute was all it took,' he said wistfully. 'That, a commanding tone, and a cracking pair of legs.'

———

IT WAS RAINING AS MARLOWE LEFT THE APARTMENT, HURRYING down the battered, urine-tainted stairs from the third floor to the car park. The two of them were situated to the east of the building, which was good, because he didn't have to smell that sickening, ammonia-like smell for longer than he had to; only on food trips or snack hunts so far. There was a small selection of shops just outside and across the car park: an off-licence with strengthened Perspex around the till, a betting shop, and a fish and chip shop that also doubled as a Chinese takeaway.

Marlowe had tried the Chinese takeaway on the first day they'd been stationed there.

They'd stuck to the fish and chips after that.

As he walked across the car park, nodding at the group of hooded teenagers that hung around outside the off license, Marlowe considered the conversation he'd just had. He hadn't lied to Marshall Kirk; he *had* been a Commando. In fact, he'd been a teenager himself and on his Commando training course during the seventh of July 2005, when terrorists had attacked London.

His own mother, a high-level operative in Military Intelligence at the time, was killed that day. Because of intelligence given by one of her assets, she hadn't had the time to delegate a mission to one of her team, and instead had shadowed one bomber onto a train, intending to eradicate him silently before he could do anything. Unfortunately, she reached him just after they left King's Cross Station, and pretty much at the exact moment he detonated his bomb, killing her and twenty-six others.

They didn't add her to the victim list because she wasn't officially there, but everyone important knew. Even Marlowe knew, eventually. And her best friend in the department, Emilia Wintergreen, a woman who was practically Marlowe's aunt in all but blood since he was a kid, had replaced her in the role, bringing Tom into the Secret Service from the Royal Marines as soon as she could.

He'd gone because it was an opportunity to gain revenge for his mother's death, but he soon realised that it was far more than that. *It was a sacrifice.* Not only did you hide your true identity away, but for long periods you had to pretend to be someone else. There were people undercover for years who'd gotten married, had families, still waiting for the call.

Sleeping soldiers, waiting to be awakened.

He'd commented about this. Maybe even complained about it, while on the aforementioned mission with the SAS a few months back. And now, most likely this comment had been passed up the pole, and because people in high-level offices probably believed Tom Marlowe was a *complainer*, he was stuck on babysitting duty in a shit-hole East London council apartment, on an estate which had somehow missed the boat of development money that was being flashed out in the months leading up to the 2012 Olympics.

The only highlight had been Marshall Kirk and his

stories. A man who, according to his own tales, had single-handedly kept the British Empire safe during the Cold War.

You know, *James Bond*, if he'd been from the Black Country.

The tales were mostly bollocks, but Marlowe had seen Kirk in action once, on that reconnaissance in Kosovo, and he knew that even though Kirk's tales were fanciful, they most likely had a nugget of truth held within. And, more importantly, Kirk could probably back up every single claim he'd made over the last three days, in that way that someone offering a "pub bet" could always manage the impossible act they were challenging, for the cost of a pint, when the mark invariably lost.

Or, in Marlowe's case, a week of saveloy and chip lunches.

The girl behind the counter was called Vas; he knew this because he'd said hello to her every time he'd come in to buy dinner. She'd nodded at him as he walked into the fish bar.

'Saveloy and chips, cod and chips, curry sauce,' she said, as if reading from a script.

'Please.' Marlowe passed a ten-pound note across to her. 'Feel free to give me the most burned saveloy you have.'

'Can't burn saveloys,' Vas said as she turned away from Marlowe, already shovelling chips onto some white paper wrapping. 'Well, unless the wrapping splits.'

'Find one like that, then.'

'You want vinegar?'

'Yeah, please.' Marlowe looked out of the window as he waited, glancing back at the estate. Two SUVs had pulled up in the street outside the main stairway, and, emerging from the front of the two, was a familiar face. A middle-aged, stocky Caucasian with the features and build of a fighter.

Because he was.

Frank Robertson looked around the estate disdainfully as, from the SUV behind him, three more track-suited men emerged. The driver of the second SUV, a tall, lanky man in jeans and a black bomber jacket, his hair buzz-cut as short as Frank's was, pointed up at a window on the estate.

And, as he did so, Marlowe felt his stomach flip-flop.

That was their apartment window.

Someone had informed on them.

Looking back at Vas, he saw her pass across the bag filled with his wrapped chip lunches, unable to look him in the face. Either she knew what was going on, or she'd been the one to grass on him.

So much for never sodding deviating.

'Here,' she said, turning away and refusing the note. 'No charge.'

Marlowe looked back outside; the group of track-suited men and Robertson had already left the SUVs by now, walking to the stairway and the stakeout apartment.

'If I find out it was you that told them, I'll kill you,' he said conversationally to Vas as he watched through the window, not looking at her or caring about her likely horrified reaction as he considered his next actions. His weapons were in a bag in the apartment, and even with Kirk beside him in there, it would still be five against two. 'I suggest you leave, never look back and keep running for the rest of your life.'

This stated, Marlowe threw the hoodie's hood up over his head, grabbed the money and the bag of takeaway food, and left the fish and chip shop.

To the left of him, watching the SUVs with the look of kids who were weighing up the risk of trying to steal one, the hooded teenagers had blazed up a joint, and were sharing it as they considered their own next actions. Veering towards them, Marlowe offered the ten-pound note.

'Got another?' he asked, nodding at the joint.

The first of the three smiled, pulling one out from behind his ear. 'You got a light?' he asked.

Marlowe shook his head, passing the note across, as the teenager lit the end of the bought-and-paid-for blunt, inhaling deep.

'Good shit,' he said, passing it across. 'You want more, bring chips as well next time.'

Marlowe nodded, smiling, taking the joint and continuing to walk towards the block in front of him, taking the steps of the stairs two at a time. He took a deep breath of the joint, blowing it all back out so that he didn't inhale too much, walking through it, letting the smell and the smoke seep into his hooded top. Then, walking to the front door of the apartment they'd been staying in, he listened.

There was a faint shout; a yelp of pain, a noise suddenly stopped. Someone was being hurt, and Marlowe knew who it was. Banging on the door, he took another deep toke of the joint, blowing it out the moment the door opened, and one of the track-suited goons stared at him, coughing as the smoke hit him.

'What the hell do you want?' he snapped, coughing, reaching with a hand to the back of his joggers, before pausing and thinking better of whatever action he was about to perform.

Marlowe knew what action he was about to perform.

Marlowe had counted on it.

'Delivery,' he kept his head down, muttering the word with the sullen arrogance of the teenagers down the stairs, hiding his face under the hood. 'Fish shop.'

'Give it here,' the doorman held out a hand. 'I'll take it.'

'Needs payment.' Marlowe looked down at the bag, as if checking something on the side. 'Eight-fifty.'

'Come back later.' The doorman, distracted by a crash behind him, went to close the door.

Marlowe took another drag of the joint and slammed the now burning tip of the cigarette into the doorman's right eye as he moved forward quickly, pushing past the doorman and into the corridor. As the man screamed loudly, clutching at his burned and destroyed eye, a second guard came out of the kitchen, directly into Marlowe's line of sight. Marlowe was already prepared though, and hurled the bag of chips at him, the guard instinctively raising his hands to catch it, momentarily taking him from the games board as Marlowe spun the half-blinded man around.

Hearing the screams, a third guard entered the hallway, a Glock 17 in his hand, raised and aimed already at the hooded intruder.

Instinctively, Marlowe pulled up the back of the half-blind doorman's tracksuit top, pulling out a similar weapon, one that had been tucked into the waistband of his hostage's joggers, as the third guard instinctively fired at him, accidentally hitting the doorman in the chest and neck. Marlowe had guessed the gun would be there when the doorman had reached for it, and he was grateful to have it in his hand as he fired back, taking out the shooter with a single headshot.

With his second shot, though, the gun clicked empty.

'One bullet?' Marlowe threw the gun at the guard who'd caught the chips; it bounced off his forehead as Marlowe, using the momentum to let the now dead, blinded doorman drop to the floor as he charged into the now-shouting-in-outrage guard. 'Who only puts one bullet in a gun?'

The track-suited guard now pulled a knife from his pocket; a box-cutter Stanley blade, it was a slashing rather than stabbing weapon, and as the guard slashed wildly with it, Marlowe used his forearm to block the guard's wrist while driving a vicious punch into the windpipe, the track-suited guard dropping the box-cutter and grabbing at his throat as Marlowe moved on, kicking out, sending the guard tumbling into the empty kitchen. Marlowe didn't need to worry about him finding a kitchen knife in there; the reason he'd bought lunch from a takeaway was because there was a distinct lack of utensils.

The guard, however, wasn't looking for knives; instead, he grabbed the toaster, yanking out the power cord and spinning around to throw it at Marlowe, or at least hit him with it. But Marlowe had already moved in, taking the box cutter's razor-sharp blade and using it correctly, slashing from left to right, opening his opponent's throat up in a vicious swing that covered Marlowe in a spray of hot, salty blood as the guard collapsed to the ground, the toaster slamming onto his now very-dead face. Which was a good thing, as Marlowe knew that would have hurt like hell if he were still alive.

Christ's sake, I only just bought this top, Marlowe thought to himself as, after rummaging in the guard's pockets and finding nothing but SUV keys, he wiped down his chest, ran to the door and picked up the other guard's discarded Glock 17, checking this time to make sure it had at least one bullet within.

Nodding with satisfaction at the half-filled magazine, he moved into the living room to find Robertson standing behind Marshall Kirk, a gun to his head, the tall, lanky bomber-jacketed driver to his side with a vicious-looking knife in his hand.

'Drop the gun or I kill him,' Robertson hissed. 'I mean it, plod.'

'Plod?' Marlowe rose out of his crouch, the gun lowering slightly, but still aimed at the two men. 'Do we look like sodding coppers?'

'If you're not plod then, who are you?' Robertson shook Marshall Kirk as he snarled. 'Because this old wanker won't tell us.'

Marlowe looked at Kirk; he had a nasty gash on his temple, likely from the knife being waved at him by the driver. He'd also been struck in the face a few times and, judging from Robertson's bloody knuckles, currently holding the gun to his head, the racist dickhole of a leader himself had done that personally.

'Did you bring my saveloy?' Kirk croaked, a smile loosening a globule of blood from his lip, running down his chin and dripping onto the carpet.

'I gave it to a guy out there,' Marlowe smiled. 'Best you didn't have it. Their cooking's really gone downhill.'

'Sorry,' Kirk groaned in pain as Robertson pulled him up, moving behind him, using Kirk as a shield.

'Yeah, me too,' Marlowe replied as he fired the Glock, the bullet striking Kirk in the shoulder, but carrying on through, hitting Robertson in the upper chest. As he instinctively let go of Kirk with a shout of intense pain, the old man falling to the floor, Robertson raised his gun--

To receive two more rounds in the head from Marlowe.

As Robertson fell to the floor, Marlowe turned to the last standing member of the group.

'You really want to do this?' he asked.

The driver looked down at his now-dead boss, then back at the man facing him, Glock in his hand ... and then finally to his own hand, holding nothing more than a short-range blade.

'No,' he said. 'I won't tell anyone—'

This turned out to be a feint, as the driver lunged forward in one last, desperate attack, but Marlowe, ready for this, fired the Glock one more time, the bullet striking between the driver's eyes, the back of his skull shattering open, spraying what was left of his brains over the cabinet behind him.

'Damn right you won't,' Marlowe muttered. 'Shouldn't have cut my mate.'

'Oh, I'm your mate now, am I?' Marshall Kirk moaned as he clutched at his shoulder. 'Funny bloody way to show it.'

'Shut your griping,' Marlowe pulled the protesting Kirk to his feet, sitting him on the arm of a sofa. 'Stay here. I need to grab our stuff. We need to get out before the police arrive.'

Kirk nodded as Marlowe pulled the surveillance equipment from the table beside the window, throwing the pieces carelessly into the two duffel bags they had underneath it. This done, he went through the pockets of the driver, pulling out his car keys.

'The chip shop grassed us up,' Kirk spoke it more as a statement than a question. 'Shame. I liked their saveloys.'

'Nobody likes saveloys,' Marlowe complained as he pulled Kirk back to his feet, the two duffels awkwardly hung over his other shoulder. 'They're like limp dicks.'

'Why do you smell of dope?' Kirk muttered. 'Were you getting blazed on the job?'

'Every day, Marshall,' Marlowe grinned. 'It's the only way I get through this.'

And this last comment out there, Tom Marlowe and Marshall Kirk left the apartment filled with dead far-right extremists, stumbling down the stairs to the car park where, after tossing the teenagers the keys to the second car, they took the nicer of the two SUVs and drove off into the London smog, back to Box and most likely another bloody bollocking.

———

1

INK BLOTS

NOW.

Marlowe leaned back in the leather chair, trying to find a position that was comfortable. The back of it was just that little too far behind him, the cushion under him was a little rounded, meaning he slid to the left or right, and the arms were just that little bit too high.

He knew this wasn't deliberate, and the chances were he'd just found himself to be in a bad mood on this day in particular, but considering where he was, and why he was there, he couldn't help wonder whether this was indeed some hell-scape chair, created by a department in the basement just to piss off spies in therapy.

No, this wasn't therapy. It was a re-evaluation.

Yes, that made everything sound better, and Marlowe tried once more to relax into the chair, before giving up and perching on the edge, hands on knees as he stared across the room at Doctor Fenchurch, the middle-aged psychiatrist watching him with a degree of amusement from behind her desk.

'Comfy now?' she asked.

'No, and you damn well know it,' Marlowe replied as politely as he could, resisting the urge to snap.

In response, Doctor Fenchurch just shrugged.

'Never needed to sit in it,' she replied. 'I've never been that side of the table before.'

'You should try it,' Marlowe smiled darkly. 'We could swap places.'

'Is that what you want, Thomas?' Doctor Fenchurch was writing on her notepad. 'To be in a position of power?'

'Is that what you believe the desk to be, Sonia?' Marlowe tried reverse tactics. 'A way to give yourself power?'

Doctor Fenchurch chuckled.

'Nice,' she said, relaxing a little. 'So, it's been a month since we saw each other. How have you been?'

'Bored,' Marlowe replied matter-of-factly. 'Just like I was last month. And the month before.'

'The month before, you were in hospital,' Doctor Fenchurch read from her notes.

'That's why I was bored.'

'How's your recovery going?'

'Honestly? I don't know,' Marlowe admitted. 'Until you rubber-stamp me, I can't do the course.'

'I didn't ask how your physical wellbeing was, I asked how your recovery was going.' Doctor Fenchurch clicked the top of her pen as she looked up. 'Your mental health.'

'My mental health would be a lot better if you'd rubber-stamp me and let me do the bloody course!' Marlowe snapped loudly, instantly regretting it, loosening his black tie a little, and popping the top button of his shirt. 'Sorry.

Haven't seen many people recently. Forgot what "indoor voice" sounds like.'

Doctor Fenchurch leant back in her chair, letting it rock backwards as she watched him.

'And the wounds?'

Marlowe paused at this. In all the talks, the mandatory, *go-if-you-want-to-continue-in-the-service* talks he'd had here, she'd never once mentioned the bullet wounds he'd received.

'What?' he asked, uncertain where this was going, and hoping a couple of seconds' delay would help him work it out.

Returning to the desk, the chair now upright, Doctor Fenchurch placed the pen down, placing her elbows on the desk as she linked her hands together.

'Real talk,' she said. 'You were shot while on an off-the-books' mission.'

'I was escorting a prisoner.'

'Who didn't exist on record, and who escaped from your custody on account of operative error?'

Marlowe simmered at this; the escape of Karl Schnitter, AKA the *Red Reaper,* a serial killer with a belief in right-eousness, hadn't escaped because of any *errors*. He'd escaped because someone in Westminster, someone who didn't like the small, off-the-books department of MI5 known as *Section D* and the links it had to Whitehall, had passed information to others in the shadows, allowing them to arrange Karl's release as long as he did something for them.

That Karl was also betrayed and tried to take out the people behind that before going to the CIA and gaining a new life, was irrelevant.

'Thomas?'

'We were set up,' Marlowe muttered, stroking his now-bearded chin. 'We were set up and you bloody well know it.'

'And how would I know that?'

'Because I've seen your file,' Marlowe, finally sick of this, replied. 'I know you worked for *Rattlestone*, when it was a mercenary black-bag alternative to the security services, and that you transferred into MI5 when the police closed it down, and Charles Baker made his play for Godhood.'

'I don't think our Prime Minister would take kindly to your opinion of his character,' Doctor Fenchurch replied coldly. 'And I'd like to know how the hell *you found my file.*'

At this, Marlowe finally smiled.

'Looks like I don't have to be that side of the desk to have any power after all,' he replied.

He could have told Doctor Fenchurch what she wanted to hear; how he'd spoken to Trix Preston in *Section D,* the resident cyber-hacking savant of his unit, and asked her to have a peek around Fenchurch's private files, see if there was anything he could use in them to fast-track his signing off. Or he could explain that he'd seen Rattlestone in action, seen how Francine Pearce, their onetime CEO had used them as her own, private black-bag operation before making a deal with the Government.

He could tell her how Rattlestone became *Phoenix Industries*, the rebranded Rattlestone mercs now working for Trisha Hawkins, Pearce's replacement, and a *gold-star bitch* if ever there was one.

And he could tell her with no doubt that it was Hawkins that not only set up the escape, gaining Schnitter's trust beforehand, while using him to frame a City of London police detective in the process, but who also arranged an ambush in the middle of a country road, where masked attackers had taken out the van Marlowe had been driving, killing his colleagues in cold blood, and leaving him for dead, shot in the leg and the chest.

Shot by the people Fenchurch had worked beside, who Fenchurch had declared fit for duty.

He'd been found in time, luckily for him, and placed in the Royal Berkshire Hospital under a fake name. And even now, months after the incident, he still didn't know who fired the weapons at him, who tried to kill him.

But he would.

Doctor Fenchurch pondered her reply, shuffling some sheets of A4 paper together as she played for time.

'I get that you think we were bad,' she said eventually. 'But mercenary units, off-the-books contractors, all that stuff, we all start with the best interests at heart. And some of us join for the right reasons.'

She waved around the room.

'If I wasn't one of the good ones, would I be here now?'

'I don't know,' Marlowe shrugged in response. 'Possibly. It depends who owes you favours.'

'Is that how you see the world, Thomas?' Doctor Fenchurch seemed saddened by the revelation. 'That it's black and white, good and bad, right and wrong?'

'I find it keeps me alive, yes,' Marlowe replied, wondering where this new thread would be going. 'Shades of grey are great and all that, but I prefer a moral compass that keeps me going straight.'

'Yet you went against orders.'

'No, not at all,' Marlowe smiled. 'I wasn't told *not* to deal with Karl Schnitter.'

'And an omission doesn't make a lie?'

'If you don't tell me to kill an enemy, how can you be

angry when I let the enemy live?' Marlowe shifted forward on the chair now. 'I do what I'm told, following orders. If I'm told to jump, I jump. I don't ask how high, or in which direction. Sometimes I don't have the luxury of time to ask such a question. I rely on the fact you'd have told me a height or direction if these details were important.'

He looked around the room again as he spoke, checking out the trinkets and ornaments on the shelves.

'You either backpacked, or you were in the field,' he said, nodding at the walls. 'You collect a memento from every location you visit. I'd say it's the latter because you keep them here rather than at home, which makes me think your family doesn't know about the missions, and explaining how a Tibetan prayer wheel happened to appear on your dresser is a question you'd rather not answer.'

'Again, do asking questions like this make you feel you're in control?' Doctor Fenchurch wasn't smiling as wide as she had earlier.

'Wasn't a question,' Marlowe risked the chair again, forcing himself to relax in it, ignoring the urge to shift around on the cushion. 'I was stating an observation. You tell field agents if they're well enough to go into the field, but at the same time you're a onetime field agent who left it.'

'Did you get that from my file?'

'No,' Marlowe smiled. 'But I got your love of spicy food from it.'

He reached into his jacket pocket, pulling out a small, red bottle.

'Here,' he said, placing it on the desk. 'Wiltshire Chilli Farm. The people who do *Regret*. This is their new one, not out in the stores yet, twelve million Scoville's. You'll love it.'

'You've tried it?'

'Christ no. I'm not a masochist,' Marlowe backed away from the desk, and the small bottle of chilli sauce. 'I wanted you to have it, because they gave me one, and I remembered.'

'Turning me into an asset will not help you get into the service again,' Doctor Fenchurch said as she took the bottle, clicking the lid open and taking a small sniff. 'Nice.'

'No underhand reasons,' Marlowe opened out his palms in surrender. 'I want to be back in, sure, but I'm also aware you wouldn't have any kind of agenda keeping me benched.'

Doctor Fenchurch secured the lid with a sigh, placing it back on the desk.

'I don't have an agenda,' she said. 'But there are people in Westminster that do. There are some in Whitehall that don't like you. Don't like what Section D stands for.'

At this, Marlowe laughed.

'All of Whitehall hates us,' he corrected. 'They get pissed off when they try to hack our servers.'

'Because they can't get through?'

'Because our computers expert launches DOS attacks on their own servers and brings them down,' Marlowe finished. 'One thing MI5 doesn't like is being schooled.'

'Technically, you're still part of MI5.'

'Then tell that to MI5,' Marlowe snapped, no longer smiling. 'Because as far as they're concerned, the "D" in Section D stands for "Disavowed", and we're nothing more than the screw-ups they can't fire.'

'And you don't think that's true?'

'I think they haven't managed to fire any of us yet.' Marlowe rose from the chair now, pacing the room. 'But that doesn't mean they haven't tried to end us.'

He punctuated this by tapping his chest where, under the shirt, was a bullet-shaped scar.

'You think MI5 did that?' Doctor Fenchurch asked.

'No, I think Rattlestone did.' Marlowe stopped pacing now, facing Doctor Fenchurch from across the room. 'And I think they all rejoined MI5 happily when the walls fell down.'

'That's paranoia.'

'Only when it's not true.'

There was a long moment of silence.

'Say, hypothetically, you're right,' Doctor Fenchurch eventually said. 'Say there are people in the security services that not only don't have your best interests at heart, but are working for their own agendas, rather than for Queen and Country and all that.'

'Okay.' Marlowe relaxed, his hands in his trouser pockets now. 'Go on.'

'Now, say there's someone, maybe a field agent who went against the grain, perhaps helped in things that embarrassed Whitehall, one who's making noise and causing them headaches. Are they going to be happy with him?'

'I suppose not.'

'And, when he's benched after an off-the-books Op goes wrong, are they going to go out of their way for him?' Doctor Fenchurch leant forward. 'Or are they going to do their best to make sure his air supply is cut and he's left out in the cold?'

Marlowe shuddered at the term *air supply is cut.* To have your air supply cut off was a terminology for being *burned.* And this, regardless of what television shows stated, wasn't fun. A "burn notice" was an official statement issued by intelligence agencies to other agencies. Sometimes allies, often enemies. It stated an asset or intelligence source they used was now unreliable for some usually unexplained reason, often fictional, and must from that point be officially disavowed in all aspects.

This was effectively a directive for the relevant agency or spy to disregard, to "burn" all information received from the agent currently in the crosshairs.

Once you were burned, once your air supply was cut off, you were *gone*. Any agency could gun you down, and your country would turn the other way and go "oops".

'Hypothetically,' Marlowe replied slowly. 'Have you heard something I should be aware of?'

'Don't rock boats right now.' Doctor Fenchurch rose, walking around the desk to face Marlowe. 'Being benched is good for you. You're not making noise. Which means certain Whitehall corridors can't hear you.'

'I'm not getting out into the field any time soon, am I?' Marlowe asked.

In response, Doctor Fenchurch shook her head.

'I could rubberstamp you right now and something else would come up,' she replied. 'They don't want you out there right now. Go home. Heal up. The country will carry on without you for a while.'

She straightened Marlowe's black tie, tightening it up once more.

'Go to the funeral,' she said. 'See old friends. Drink toasts to fallen soldiers and all that. Then go home and find a hobby to take up for the next two weeks. I'll speak to you after that.'

Knowing there was nothing more to say here, Marlowe nodded, turned away from Doctor Fenchurch, and walked to the door.

'I really am an excellent agent,' he said. 'No matter what those wankers in Whitehall think.'

'The fact they think about you at all confirms that,' Doctor Fenchurch smiled. 'Just keep away from all that spycraft stuff.'

She stopped, frowning.

'You *are* keeping away from all that spycraft stuff, aren't you?'

'Sure,' Marlowe lied. 'Nobody's speaking to me these days, anyway.'

Doctor Fenchurch stared at Marlowe for a long minute before nodding.

'I'll see you soon, Thomas.'

Smiling in return, an expression as fake as Fenchurch's had been, Marlowe left the office, walked over to the elevators and took the first one that arrived down to the lobby. The building he'd been in was a tall, glass and chrome monstrosity in London's Canary Wharf, and every other floor was filled with law firms or hedge fund corporations, all unaware of who the building's in-house performance coach truly worked for when she wasn't amping up commodities traders and legal partners.

Marlowe didn't know how many of these satellite offices there were, but he assumed there were a lot. He was a basic level spy, and he alone had two safe houses he could use and three "go bags" placed in locations around London, purely if needed.

But for Whitehall, outsourcing was the current buzzword. And that, if he was truly honest, worried Marlowe. That when he was finally cleared, there wouldn't be a job for him in Section D, as it'd all been farmed out to agencies like *Phoenix*.

Sighing, and forcing himself to be calm, he held out a hand, flagging down a passing taxi. Fenchurch had been right; there had been a funeral he needed to go to, starting in an hour. He didn't want to go, didn't want to admit it was even happening, but he owed everyone to be there.

And, as he gave an address to the driver and climbed into the cab, the slim man across the street placed his phone away as he watched Marlowe leave, waving down an unmarked black Mercedes that stopped beside him, and sliding into the back seat as it U-turned in the road, following Marlowe.

After all, you were only paranoid if they *weren't* out for you.

———

2

ASHES TO ASHES

MARLOWE REALLY HATED FUNERALS.

But sometimes you couldn't get out of them, and other times you wanted to go, because you felt you owed it to the person. And Marlowe owed Marshall Kirk a lot more than he could ever repay ... although that was going to be an impossibility now.

They'd said it was a heart attack, but Kirk was one of the healthiest people Marlowe had ever known. Even touching seventy, he still ran ultra-marathons, swearing off saveloys and chips after the last mission they'd been on, claiming that if he'd eaten healthier, the server at the counter of the chip shop (who turned out to be dating one of Frank Robertson's goons) wouldn't have met them, and therefore wouldn't have informed on them. After that utter shambles of a mission, he'd become a vegetarian, focused on non-processed foods and, when he retired five years ago, he looked healthier and younger than before he'd met Marlowe, which, to be brutally honest, pissed Marlowe off.

And then, just like that, Marshall Kirk was *gone*.

Everyone was sad and stated to the heavens that it was simply his time, but Marlowe didn't subscribe to that belief. Kirk had been murdered, and he was sure of it.

Marshall Kirk had visited Marlowe twice while he was in hospital, which was a feat in itself, considering he was there under an assumed identity. The first time, Marlowe had been stunned to see Kirk appear in the doorway, a bouquet of flowers and a teddy bear in his hands, a wide, shit-eating grin on his face. They'd talked for an hour or so, and during this, Marlowe had found the bug Kirk had secreted on the teddy. Kirk explained he'd have thought less of Marlowe if he hadn't, and they kept to small talk, mainly. Kirk now lived in a small house near East Finchley, but even though he reckoned he was fine with retirement, Marlowe saw his eyes light up when they talked about old cases.

The second time was right before Marlowe left the ward, but this time, it was a different Kirk who appeared; one who watched the door intently, one who was distracted, claiming a week of terrible nights as his reason, but Marlowe could see that something was weighing on his mentor's shoulders. Kirk, in turn shrugged off the worries and, after a few lewd and likely politically incorrect jokes, patted Marlowe on the shoulder and left.

Marlowe never saw him again.

But that second meeting had set off alarm bells in Marlowe's head and, while convalescing, he'd sent a message to Trix, asking her to check in on Kirk. She knew what he really meant, and within a week Marlowe had a detailed deep dive envelope arriving by Whitehall courier at his Battersea apartment, containing an encrypted USB, one that showed Marshall Kirk falling into old habits.

Old *spy* habits.

Marshall Kirk had retired. And the done thing, when being a spy, was to *stay* retired. Of course, if Whitehall decided your retirement for you, then you could scream blue murder and have at it, but Marshall had said he was happy to retire at sixty-five, said his ghosts had all been exorcised, and he was going to take life easy.

And then a year later, he was running forty-kilometre hill races in the Cairngorms.

Doctor Fenchurch had been closer than she thought when she asked if Marlowe was still playing with spycraft – he hadn't intended to until the USB arrived. And in these pages, Marlowe had seen his fit and healthy, *retired* friend contact old assets from his time as section chief of the St James office, which was a fancy way of saying "the bloke sent out to feed swans whenever the Russians wanted to swap information, or the CIA wanted to bitch about their President", as the "St James office" was a bench beside a bridge in St James's Park, near Buckingham Palace.

During the Cold War, when the British Secret Service were low on usable information on the Russians, they'd arrange pointless meetings there and, while chatting, subtly pick the pockets of the agents they were talking to, stealing wallets, receipts, anything that could give them something to work on, all while blaming the CIA.

And, when they did this to the CIA, they blamed the Russians.

Everyone knew who was really doing it, hell, even the British agents were coming home to find their pockets picked, but the plausible deniability was there for everyone to see. In fact, for several years, it was believed there were more spies from international agencies on the St James's Park Tin and Stone Bridge than there were tourists.

And Marshall Kirk had met his old friends and enemies there over the last couple of months.

The file wasn't complete, though; it was a Home Office folder based on intelligence gained from MI5 operatives stalking Kirk as he went about his business. The pages were mostly redacted too, but filled with second-hand reports of Kirk's meetings, with a couple of photos and even a half-blacked out transcript of a conversation he'd had with an ex-Stasi operative.

The result of the file, and what seemed to be the conclusion of "Operation follow Marshall Kirk" was that he was tipping over stones and rocks to see what came out from under them, but nobody could work out why he was doing this. The agents and assets he'd spoken to were also retired, many had been off grid for years, and even the files on them in the Security Archives had been rubber-stamped as inactive. It was as if Kirk was going to anyone and everyone not currently connected to an intelligence agency. And nobody knew why.

And a week after the last report in the file, Marshall Kirk had died.

Of a heart attack.

Bullshit.

Marlowe really hated funerals; it was a reminder of his own mortality, made more visible by the two bullet wound scars he now sported. He'd never been shot before. Stabbed, sure, and even poisoned, but never shot, although he'd been shot *at* many times in his career. And, when he'd lain on that tarmac road, bleeding out onto the ground, he'd waited for the flashback of his life that people always talked of. Instead, he had the "what ifs", as in *the life he could have lived if he hadn't taken this path*, the path taken if his mum hadn't died, and changed his career plan in a split second.

A family. Children.

A *life*.

And then he woke up in hospital, under a fake name, and with both bullets removed. Someone had got to him before he bled out and taken him to the hospital, giving a fake legend they knew Marlowe could keep to. And, as of right now, although Wintergreen, his boss, had claimed credit for the rescue, Marlowe still didn't know who'd really done this, a question that nagged at him daily.

There was the sudden sound of a church organ, and Marlowe was jerked back to the present, almost jumping out of the pew as, around him, everyone in the Anglican chapel stood. Joining them, Marlowe watched as they walked a coffin down the aisle, past him, the six pallbearers all looking like ex-military, which was probably correct. He didn't recognise any of them apart from one at the back; Anthony Farringdon had been a friend of Marshall Kirk's while alive, and was wearing his military blazer with pride, his white hair as spotless as ever, and parted on the right. Placing it down at the front, they stepped away from the coffin as the priest officiating the funeral began the service, and Farringdon glanced over at Marlowe, nodding briefly, the most he could give to the associate of a now passed friend. And then, like the others, he walked off, waiting until he was needed again.

Marlowe had been asked if he would speak at the funeral, perform a eulogy for his mentor, but he'd turned down the offer. He still felt a little vulnerable, and, more importantly, was quite happy to sit in the shadows. And, because of this, it was an attractive woman with short, blonde hair, Kirk's daughter Tessa, who spoke to the congregation.

Marlowe had never really spoken to Tessa in all the years he'd known Kirk, mainly as there was only a couple of years between them, and Kirk, on their first meeting had pointed out very clearly to Marlowe that if he ever tried anything with his daughter, he'd cut off a whole load of very important parts and fry them up in front of him, feeding them to Marlowe as he died of blood loss. It was quite a specific and gruesome visual, and Marlowe had wondered if this was something Kirk had done before, but the message was clear, so Tom Marlowe had made a point of keeping as far away from Tessa Kirk as humanly possible.

People were standing again, and Marlowe realised it was time for a hymn. Picking up his hymn book, he tried to work out where the lyrics were as a woman sitting on the pew behind him tapped him on the shoulder, passing across a tiny strip of paper, folded up.

Quietly and without acknowledging the offer, Marlowe took it, and, as everyone started singing the first verse of "Jerusalem", he opened it up and read the note.

YOU'RE BEING FOLLOWED
MARY'S CHAPEL AFTER FUNERAL

Marlowe folded the paper up and automatically placed it into his mouth, chewing down on it, pulping it up before spitting it into his hand and pressing it against the back of the hymnbook. Once it dried, it would fall off, but by then the books would be together somewhere else, and Marlowe would be far away. He looked behind once more, trying to casually see who gave him this, but the woman was gone, the space empty.

But, through the space, he could see another mourner

sitting at the back of the chapel, two empty rows of pews in front of him. He was in his fifties, slim and in a navy-blue suit.

And he was watching Marlowe.

Seeing Marlowe glance at him, however, the man rose silently, placing his hymnbook onto the pew and, with a nod to the altar, left through the main entrance, still ajar.

Marlowe turned around, thinking back to his previous actions that day. There had been a man across the street when he left Doctor Fenchurch, but he'd paid him little concern. Why would someone be following him, and why would someone warn him about it?

The woman had been old, in her sixties or seventies, with white hair cut short, and asymmetrical, with the buzz-cut side on her left. She'd been slight, with piercing green eyes that belied her age, and Marlowe knew for a fact he'd never met her before. She reminded him of Emilia Wintergreen, the white-haired head of Section D, and wondered for a moment whether this stranger held a similar position of authority.

In fact, Marlowe spent so long considering the options here that the funeral had ended before he realised, with him standing and sitting, singing and praying on an effective autopilot while the rest of his brain considered his options. The coffin was being taken out now and would be walked to the graveside that had been picked out, before being placed in and buried.

Marlowe wasn't sure if he could face watching that, and as the other mourners, many of whom Marlowe recognised as people connected to the security services, made their way out of the chapel and towards the spot reserved in East Finchley Cemetery for Marshall Kirk, Marlowe instead slid along the pew, emerging on the far left of the Nave, and near where St Mary's Chapel was.

It was pretty much just an alcove to the side, with a statue of Mary surrounded by candles. In front of it was a wrought-iron rack of tea-light candles which, for a small donation, you could buy and light in memory of someone lost.

Marlowe did this, placing a pound coin in the slot and lighting a tea-light candle, placing it in one row along the top.

'Here you go, mum,' he whispered. 'Hope you're okay there. Marshall's come to visit, so look after him. He'll be scared.'

There was a soft cough behind him, and Marlowe spun around to see the lady standing about ten feet back, watching around the chapel as she spoke.

'You're being tailed by MI5,' she said as a matter of fact. 'You need to lose him before we talk.'

'Talk about what?' Marlowe asked, moving forward.

'Stay there, and face the candles,' the woman commanded, and Marlowe did so. 'You don't think Kirk died of natural causes.'

'And how would you know that?'

'Because you had someone hack in and grab his file,' the woman replied. 'You're not as good as you think, Thomas. Or, rather, she wasn't as quiet as she thought. Either way, MI5 knows you took the file, and they're following you to see what else you know.'

'And what else should I know?' Marlowe faced the statue of Mary now, effectively talking to it. 'Because there's obviously something.'

'You already suspect it,' the woman stated calmly. 'Marshall Kirk was killed.'

Marlowe went to turn around but forced himself not to.

'I'm guessing you have another place for a meeting?' he asked. But after a couple of moments of no response, he turned around only to find the woman gone.

'Of course,' he muttered. 'Bloody spooks.'

On the pew she'd been standing beside was another thin strip of paper, however. And, when Marlowe looked at it, he saw an address and time.

NELLIE DEAN - SOHO - UPSTAIRS - 3PM

Reading the note, Marlowe folded it up once more. However, instead of chewing this, he held it over the flame of his tea light, letting it catch alight, allowing the flame to rise up the paper before dropping the charred remains onto the metal rail, beside the tea-lights, watching it until it was nothing but ash. Then, this done, he nodded to the candle and walked out of the chapel. If anyone had watched him, all they saw was a man who lit a candle in memory before rejoining the funeral mourners around the graveside, as the coffin of Marshall Kirk was lowered in.

The white-haired woman was missing now, but as Marlowe glanced back to the grey-bricked Anglican chapel, he saw the slim man in the navy-blue suit, standing beside the porch, watching the funeral continue from afar.

Marlowe forced himself to carry on his gaze past the man, not to give any clue as to seeing him, looking down at his watch as he returned to the graveside. The coffin was lowered, the funeral was winding up, and there was another hour before three. Avoiding the wake in a local pub in East Finchley, there was enough time to get into central London and lose a tail, with a little luck.

Marlowe straightened, rotated his neck to pull out any

kinks and, forcing himself to stay slow and steady, he walked out of the cemetery and towards Finchley Central Station, knowing without even looking that the slim man in the navy-blue suit was following.

But Marlowe wasn't worried, for Marlowe had a plan.

He just hoped it was one that could still work.

3

QUICK CHANGE

THE NORTHERN LINE TRAIN FROM FINCHLEY CENTRAL STATION had pulled into King's Cross Underground Station at half-past two, and although it was a little later than expected, Marlowe was okay with the delay, as it gave him another half an hour to lose the man following him.

He'd spied him on the underground train, a carriage down, sitting and ignoring everyone, reading a magazine he had either found on a seat or already had on his person, giving the public impression of a man without a care in the world. Which, in a way, Marlowe knew he was, as he likely knew Marlowe was a captive audience in the tunnels.

Arriving at King's Cross, Marlowe kept his speed slow, allowing the other travellers to walk past him as he exited the Underground Station and approached the barriers. Then, making a pantomime of not being able to find his ticket, he walked over to the guard, explaining how he dropped his ticket somewhere on the journey, keeping his tone in the awkward, apologetic way of the embarrassed yet slightly annoyed commuter.

The guard, as expected, couldn't magically provide the missing ticket and so quietly and patiently suggested that if he couldn't provide any kind of receipt for the lost item, Marlowe would have to use his credit card on the contactless device, paying for the journey that way.

At this, and noticing he'd effectively become the last to leave his carriage, Marlowe hunted once more for his ticket, eventually finding it with a triumphant smile. It had been a hunt that had taken up a good two minutes, including the conversation with the guard, and by this point all the other commuters and travellers had passed through the gates, including, reluctantly, the slim man, who'd been forced to take up an observation spot near the entrance.

Clocking him as he came through the barriers, Marlowe turned to the right as he exited out onto the main causeway, deliberately taking a longer route through the side of the station, emerging onto the junction of York Way and Euston Road, around twenty yards from where the man was still watching for him. Marlowe knew, however, that if this man *was* MI5, then there was every chance the CCTV cameras would watch for him as well, so he needed to move fast and think clever. And, as he headed for a McDonalds on the south side of Euston Road, he already saw the slim man take a call, looking directly across the road at him.

Great. They were watching him on cameras, too.

Next to the McDonalds was an Underground entrance, jutting out of the pavement and effectively blocking any view from the north side, so Marlowe used this to his advantage, sliding quickly into a Left Luggage store beside it, and making his way to the back of the shop. The lockers seen in movies, where spies and bank robbers could hide a duffle bag of guns or money, were a thing of the past in the UK, and no London stations had these anymore, which meant many agencies had to improvise. Marlowe had worked carefully over six months to create an asset in the store, one who held a small, black backpack for him in one locker for a small monthly fee, never asking questions.

'Manjit,' Marlowe smiled as he walked to the back. 'It's time.'

The Indian man in his forties behind the counter actively smiled with relief as he heard this.

'About time, Mister Heywood,' he replied, writing out a number and passing it to a colleague. 'I hadn't heard from you for a while. I was considering opening it.'

'If you had, I'd have known,' Marlowe smiled darkly. In fact, he wouldn't have known if the bag had been opened or not, but Manjit didn't know that. And as far as Manjit was concerned, Marlowe was a Government operative, scary and an enigma. After a couple of moments the colleague returned with a backpack, passing it to Manjit.

'We're clear now, yes?' he asked as he turned, passing the bag to Marlowe.

'Yes,' Marlowe smiled, hefting the bag. 'You've done the country a great service. One last thing though, I need to use your back door, too.'

'Of course.' Manjit spoke in Urdu to his companion and pointed at the small green door, with EMPLOYEE'S ONLY on it. 'Go that way.'

Marlowe fought the urge to correct the grammar on the sign, and, with a shake of Manjit's hand for the last time, he slipped through the door.

He was actually going to miss Manjit. In his business,

finding someone who understood what keeping quiet truly meant was a rarity.

Through the door, Marlowe stood in a corridor with another door at the very end, and a stairway behind him and to the side. He knew the corridor didn't go outside, but the door, usually locked, would place him into the McDonalds next to them. The stairway just went to the area they held the bags, and Marlowe had no need of that, so he ran to the door, crouching down and pulling out his lock pick set. The door had a chunky and easily pickable lock built into the round handle, and after it was unlocked and opened within a couple of seconds, Marlowe moved through quietly.

The area he was now entering backed onto the McDonalds kitchen area, and following it to the end, nodding at the kitchen staff who stared at him, pretending he was doing an inspection, complete with the occasional "good work" here and there, brought him out into the customer restrooms entranceway. Now outside the men's toilets, Marlowe quickly slipped inside and found an empty cubicle. Closing the cubicle door behind him, he placed the toilet lid down and rested the backpack onto it, opening up the zip.

Inside was a "go bag" of sorts, something purely to get him to his next location if he was in trouble. A blond wig and baseball cap, a white T-shirt and jeans, running shoes and a hoodie were pulled out and changed into, with Marlowe placing his black suit to the side as he did so. He pulled a pair of thick-rimmed glasses with clear lenses out, placing them on his face. They were specially made to reshape the upper portion of his head, so any security cameras using facial recognition would have issues linking the blond man in the glasses to agent Tom Marlowe. However, a visual examination would still reveal him as, unlike in comics, Clark Kent would have been identified as Superman in seconds, glasses and side parting or not. And his beard, although not long, was still obviously not the same colour as the hair on his head.

Now re-dressed, Marlowe took out the last few items he needed from his suit: his wallet, a pen, a Leatherman folding-knife and his phone, and placed them into his new clothes, taking the time to connect the phone to a new one in the bag via a cable, cloning his information across to a new SIM card. The old phone would be destroyed here so they wouldn't be able to follow him, and although this was probably an over-complication, Marlowe didn't want to risk anything. The cloning complete and the new SIM card now replacing his old, he sighed as he pulled up the toilet seat and dropped the phone into the water underneath, flushing for good measure.

With his suit in the backpack and his items passed across, Marlowe opened up the last part of the backpack, pulling out new ID, a driving license and a passport, placing them in his pockets where he could grab them quickly, before removing a wad of ten-pound notes and an SIG P226 from the bag. It was a common misconception that MI5 officers had guns, first because most MI5 agents were effectively office workers and observers, but also because the term "MI5" didn't really exist anymore. They were all the *Security Service*, even though they still used the individual terms in their various sub sections.

But even though Tom Marlowe publicly didn't have a gun, the fact of the matter was he was armed most of the time, and he knew without a doubt that the man following him would also hold a weapon. And now, with the SIG Sauer P226 in his hand, feeling the weight of the metal in his grip as he quickly checked to make sure it was loaded, he felt just that little bit more secure. Most of his peers preferred the Glock 17 now, but the SIG P266 had an advantage over the Glock in range firing, and it pretty much had what Marlowe needed out of the box. In fact, if he looked at it in motorcycle terms, a Glock 17 was like a Harley-Davidson, constantly able to be customised in a variety of ways thanks to the plastic outer casing, while the SIG P266 was like a Ducati, already coming with everything he needed.

Gun now tucked into the back of his jeans, Marlowe zipped up the backpack and slung it over his shoulder, picking up the wad of ten-pound notes and placing them in his wallet. Cards could be traced, and where he needed to go would be cash only for a while.

Walking out of the McDonalds toilets, Marlowe checked the restaurant for any signs of the slim man in the navy suit, but he wasn't anywhere in sight. That said, he was keeping out of view, or still next door trying to convince Manjit – likely playing dumb – to give him information on where Marlowe had gone.

The McDonalds had a corner entrance, which took him out even further from the doorway he'd originally entered, and so he took this, sliding to the right and heading south down Crestfield Street. It was a two-mile walk to Soho, and going on his watch, he had just under twenty minutes to make it, which was tight. He considered hiring a bike or an e-scooter, but they were both card-based, and again, cash was key right now. All he could do was hope for a passing cab rather than risk a tube train or bus complete with CCTV cameras.

By the time he passed Argyle Square he saw one approaching and hailed it down. Giving the address of the

Prince Edward Theatre, a location on Old Compton Street in Soho that was close enough to get to by foot from the meeting place, but at the time suitably far enough so that if asked, the driver wouldn't be able to give him up, Marlowe sat back in the seat and relaxed.

For about *three roads.*

They were heading south down Judd Street, past Brunswick Square Gardens, when he noticed the black Mercedes following them. It was the same plates as one he'd seen at Canary Wharf, when he'd climbed into a cab earlier that day, and there was no way that was a coincidence.

They knew where he was going.

Pulling off the backpack, he stared down at it. It had been in King's Cross for months, and there was every chance he could have been compromised during that time. All the running, the subterfuge would have meant nothing if all they had to do was follow his tracker's signal.

Pulling out his iPhone, the one he'd cloned everything onto, he quickly swiped through the apps, opening one with a single eye for a logo. This was an app created by a friend, and it transformed the magnetometer in the iPhone into a bug detector.

He'd had it hammered into him repeatedly, that every speaker, microphone, mobile phone and surveillance device had built into the device itself a magnetic field. Because of the *compass* app, iPhones were equipped with magnetometers; this way the "compass" actually worked and could help someone lost in the woods. The app, linked to this data, could read the information captured by the magnetometer and locate any magnetic field emitted. It was basic, and nowhere near as good as any standard issue kit, but it was hopefully enough to do what Marlowe needed to achieve right now.

Scanning his backpack, Marlowe paused at his right-hand strap. The iPhone's screen was showing a strong magnetic pulse from it, so he placed it down, pulled out his Leatherman and, with the blade, he gently cut along the seam of the padded strap. Reaching into it, he used the tweezers to remove a small, simple looking piece of wire connected to a tiny battery.

As basic as it looked, this was the transmitter that had told MI5, or whomever it was following him, that he was in the cab.

'Oh, very clever,' he muttered, placing the Leatherman away and, with the transmitter in his hand, he slung the backpack over his shoulder. The counter on the cab's dashboard said he'd spent just under ten pounds, and so he leant forward, pulling out some notes.

'Hey,' he said, leaning as close as he could to the glass screen. 'I need a favour, and it's a bit odd.'

'Go on,' the cabbie, probably used to questions like this, replied.

Marlowe pushed four notes through the hole.

'I'm on a YouTube treasure hunt,' he lied, smiling. 'The black car behind me is the film crew, but I need to get rid of them. Like evasion.'

'Okay,' the cabbie took the money. 'What do you want me to do?'

'That's payment for the trip, and a large tip.' Marlowe forced a smile. 'I need to drop out at the next opportunity, and I need you to head west towards Paddington. Give it a few minutes, and when you hit twenty quid, stop the counter, keep the tip.'

'Sure, it's your money,' the cabbie said, looking in his mirror. 'They mates of yours, then?'

'Kinda,' Marlowe replied. 'One's my ex's new partner, so I'd love to screw him over.'

The cabbie grinned at this, and Marlowe knew he had him. One thing people love to do is help an underdog, especially against someone they're predisposed not to like. So, as they reached the junction of Bernard Street and Woburn Place, the cabbie slammed his foot down, just making it through the lights before they changed to red, the black Mercedes now halted at the crossing. This done, the moment the cab turned the corner of Russell Square and now out of sight, the cabbie pulled sharply to the side, the door unlocking.

'Good luck,' he said as Marlowe leaped out with a nod of thanks, running to the entrance of Russell Square, ducking into the foliage as the cab, still with the transmitter in drove off, heading south down Montague Street. A moment later and at speed, the black Mercedes followed around the corner, slowing down when they saw their target ahead, passing obliviously by Marlowe as he crouched lower.

Alone in the park Marlowe considered his options. There was every chance they had a second transmitter on him, but at the same time this had likely been placed as a failsafe, and they probably never expected to use it. The device hadn't been service standard, either, which made Marlowe wonder whether his tag was MI5 after all. Either way, though, they'd seen his disguise, as they'd likely been following him when he got into the cab.

Annoyed at this and tossing the blond wig and glasses into a bin, Marlowe took off the hoodie, turning it inside out to change the colour and tying it around his waist. Now, in his white T-shirt and throwing his sunglasses on under the cap, slinging the bag once more over his shoulder, he walked across Russell Square heading for Holborn and another cab to Soho.

If they find me now, he thought to himself as he hailed down another black cab, *I'll bloody lead them to wherever they want.*

———

IT WAS ANOTHER TEN MINUTES BEFORE THE CAB ARRIVED AT THE Nellie Dean pub on Dean Street, and Marlowe still asked the driver to loop around, just to make sure, claiming he was seeing his girlfriend, but that her previous boyfriend might look for them. Once more with the driver on his side, he got out of the cab at the junction of Carlisle Street, crossed the road and made his way up the narrow, rickety stairs of the pub, entering the usually quiet, upstairs dining area.

The woman from the funeral with the white hair was sitting at a table by the window, watching out of it.

She smiled as she saw Marlowe enter.

'Are we cosplaying teenagers now?' she asked.

Ignoring the jibe, Marlowe sat down.

'I have people bugging my go bags,' he said, showing the slit on his strap. 'I can't work out if it's my people or not. So rather than the small talk, how about you tell me what's going on here?'

The woman nodded and pushed over a glass of sparkling water.

'Here,' she said. 'On me. I thought you'd be thirsty after all your running.'

'Thanks,' Marlowe muttered sarcastically. 'Whenever you want to start?'

The woman considered the question, as if working out where best to begin.

'My name is Bridget Summers, and I worked with Marshall Kirk,' she said. 'And he told me, if he was ever murdered, to seek your help.'

4

PUB LUNCH

Marlowe took a long sip of his water before replying.

'Okay, so you're going to have to tell me what the hell is going on,' he said carefully. 'I don't know who you are, I'm finding tracking devices in my things and I'm being followed by God knows who, all for being friends with Marshall Kirk.'

Bridget nodded at this.

'Understandable,' she said, leaning back on her chair and tapping her index finger rhythmically against her lips, as if working out how to start. 'What do you know about *Project Rubicon?*'

'Nothing,' Marlowe replied honestly. 'Apart from the fact it was the river Caesar crossed, hence the phrase "crossing the Rubicon", as in reaching the point of no return. I'm guessing it was something Marshall was involved in?'

'In a way, yes,' Bridget nodded. 'It's back in the late eighties. Marshall Kirk had only been in the service a few years and was full of piss and vinegar. And I was part of the team that supported him, mainly on the desks.'

'Kirk was always full of piss and vinegar,' Marlowe chuckled. 'I'm guessing Rubicon was a late eighties op, so probably against the Soviet Bloc at the time?'

Bridget didn't reply, simply nodding as she sipped at her own drink, a white wine of some kind. After swallowing, she looked out of the window as she continued.

'Mid-eighties, we were all about the Cold War,' she said. 'Nuclear threat was imminent, the Berlin Wall was still an issue, and the Russians were the villains in pretty much every film and TV show, while in the real world they were planting sleeper agents across the globe.'

'I heard about a few of those,' Marlowe replied. 'But they were closed down, weren't they?'

Bridget shrugged.

'So we were told,' she said. 'By the mid-eighties, Mikhail Gorbachev had arrived, replacing Chernenko, who'd been the last in a long line of party faithful. And, unfortunately for him, but fortunately for the rest of the world, Chernobyl happened.'

Marlowe didn't reply to this; the Chernobyl nuclear disaster, created when a reactor in Russian-controlled Ukraine went into meltdown in 1986, creating a twenty-mile fallout exclusion zone, was a global disaster that still existed to this day.

'And that started the end of the Cold War,' he replied. 'Gorbachev realised he needed to gain outside help, and started meeting with Western leaders, pushing for significant reform. His two policies of *Glasnost* and *Perestroika* were created to bring economic stability to the USSR, but Marxist–Leninist hardliners went against him, there was a revolutionary wave across Central and Eastern Europe that ended the Russian control over places like Poland, Hungary and the Berlin Wall. By '91, the Soviet Union dissolved against his wishes, and he resigned.'

'Exactly,' Bridget smiled. 'Under Yeltsin, Russia flailed even more, and for a decade it became far less a threat than it ever was. And, with the Cold War effectively ended, many sleeper agents returned home, their service no longer needed. Or they renounced their motherland for their new lives.'

'And Rubicon was this?'

'No, Rubicon was before the fall. It was in the early days, after Chernobyl but before Berlin. It was an operation to not only flush out sleepers, but to turn them to our side and send them home, once more as sleeper agents, but for us,' Bridget explained. 'We worked with members of the Eastern Bloc, people like Gorbachev, disillusioned with the world as it was. Did Kirk ever tell you about Primakov?'

'Not that I can remember,' Marlowe shook his head. 'Although I've heard of a Russian spy named Vladimir Primakov?'

'Same man.' Bridget sipped her wine. 'Ended up requesting asylum in the UK when Putin came to power in 1999. But, at the time, he was connected to the Stasi in Berlin, and ran the corridor of spies.'

'I thought Berlin had a bridge of spies?'

'Only in the movies, dear.'

Bridget glanced again out of the window and for a moment her focus was distracted before she looked back at Marlowe.

'Rubicon was an Op to remove people who'd crossed the line, who wouldn't go back. On both sides. We had some sleepers in Russia and East Berlin too, who'd gone native.'

'By remove, I'm guessing you mean ...' Marlowe mimed a gun with his index finger.

'Only the ones deemed as a threat, if they couldn't be turned,' Bridget shrugged. 'Others were set up for crimes they didn't commit, deported, thrown in prison, take your pick. Anyone we didn't deem as a threat right then was placed on the list and observed. And, after Gorbachev resigned, the Op was deemed a success, and the list was mothballed.'

'Until now.'

'Until now,' Bridget agreed. 'Marshall had a visitor about four months back. Primakov. He'd been living in Manchester, owned a restaurant or something. He was spooked, said he'd heard that Putin had reactivated some of the old Soviet operations, including sleepers. And at the moment, Putin is probably the worst person to run Russia, as he wants it to return to where it was, regardless of the cost.'

Marlowe nodded at this. Putin may have been in Moscow, but his reach went much further. Anyone in Salisbury knew this, after a Russian double-agent was poisoned in the UK town by Russian agents, men who cared so little for the collateral damage they poisoned several civilians, with one even dying from the nerve agent the agents had tossed away. They'd returned to Russia as heroes, but Putin had denied anything to do with this, all the while using this to threaten any other dissident who walked away from their "motherland".

If Putin was reactivating sleeper agents, these would be people in their sixties and seventies, whose children, born in the UK, would now be the same age as Marlowe himself was, give or take a few years. And if someone else was taking Rubicon's data, they could find the same people on the list and turn them – or *worse*.

'Where's Primakov now?'

'Dead,' Bridget replied matter-of-factly. 'Three days after he spoke to Kirk. Car accident in Paris.'

'And that's when Marshall started investigating?'

'Investigating is a bit strong for what he was doing.' Something still distracted Bridget outside. 'More buggering around where he shouldn't be poking. Are you sure you weren't followed?'

Marlowe leant across, following Bridget's gaze out of the window. Outside, on the crossroads of Dean Street and Carlisle Street was a young woman, in a grey suit, long brown hair pulled back, talking into a phone. Marlowe didn't recognise her, but that didn't mean she wasn't part of the company.

'Haven't seen her before, but that doesn't mean she hasn't seen me,' he replied. 'I can't be certain.'

'We should wrap this up,' Bridget carried on, now amped up and nervous. 'Marshall contacted a couple of his friends, old spies, that sort of thing, seeing if they'd heard anything.'

'I read a report on this,' Marlowe admitted. 'I gained it from a friend with Whitehall connections. They didn't know why Marshall was kicking over stones or talking to foreign assets.'

'Nobody did, but it didn't stop someone from getting to him,' Bridget hissed. 'He was killed, Thomas. He was murdered, just like Primakov.'

'How can you be sure?'

'Because we didn't bury Marshall Kirk today,' Bridget replied, ignoring Marlowe's surprised expression. 'It was an empty casket. Marshall Kirk disappeared, and the day after, the security service announced the heart attack story.'

'MI5 killed him?' Marlowe looked out of the window again, Bridget's paranoia now contagious.

The brunette woman was still across the road, and still on the phone.

'MI5, CIA, Mossad, take your pick,' Bridget replied. 'Could be anyone. Maybe even a sleeper, brought to life and working deep within our own intelligence community.'

Marlowe wanted to scoff at this, to tell Bridget she'd watched too many spy movies, but there was something here that rang true.

'So, what do you want me to do?' he asked. 'What were Marshall's wishes?'

'He said, if he was murdered, I needed to come to you, as you'd finish what he started,' she said.

'That's not really going to help me get back into MI5.' Marlowe gave a wry smile, and was about to continue when Bridget placed a hand on his wrist.

'Dear boy,' she said, almost sadly. 'Do you still believe they're going to bring you back? They're trying to work out how to set you up for some terrible cock up they can pin on you, dump you on the street and forget about you.'

'You don't—'

'I've seen the memos.'

Marlowe thought back to his conversation with Fenchurch.

'When he's benched after an off-the-books Op goes wrong, are they going to go out of their way for him? Or are they going to do their best to make sure his air supply is cut and he's left out in the cold?'

'Bollocks,' he muttered, half to himself. 'So, what's the first step here?'

'Find an old analyst friend of ours, Raymond Sykes. He

was looking into things, but if they took Marshall down, Sykes could already be dead as well.'

She tapped a number into her phone, holding it up.

'Marshall said you were great with numbers,' she said. 'Memorise it. Only call me if you're in direst danger.'

Marlowe nodded, staring at the number on the screen for a couple of seconds, committing it to memory. One of the first things he'd learned from his mother was how to memorise numbers, especially phone numbers, so this came easily to him.

'And what will you do?' he asked, already rising.

'Try my best to bloody well stay alive.' Bridget was already walking to the back of the upstairs bar, where a small door led to another *employees only* area. Marlowe almost went to follow her, but the woman outside was too much of a risk to take. Marlowe, currently, could bluff his way out of this. He hadn't been in contact with Marshall; he'd checked in on him, but only through official paperwork. At best, he'd have a slapped wrist. They had nothing to place on him in connection with Bridget yet, and there was a thought, a stupid, crazy one, that actually said *you should go with them, see if they give you anything you can use.*

Leaving Bridget and returning down the stairs, Marlowe made his way to the bathrooms, entering a cubicle and closing the door behind him. Pulling a ziplock bag out of his backpack, he wiped down and stashed the SIG P266 into it, attaching it to the back of the cistern. He knew a deep clean would discover it, but even if they did, his prints were wiped, and it had been picked up off the black market, with no chain of sale. And if they didn't look for it, if they assumed he simply didn't have a signed-for sidearm, they might ignore the toilets completely, and he could come back for it later.

And, if there really was nobody outside, and this was all paranoia, ramped up to the max, he could simply return later in the day and pick it up again, none the worse for it.

Gun secured, Marlowe took a deep breath and emerged out into the bar. There were no faces he recognised, and nobody seemed to be interested in him, so he released his breath and walked out onto the street.

The brunette woman, seeing him, placed the phone back in her pocket as she walked over.

'Marlowe,' she said by introduction. 'Don't run. We've got you surrounded.'

'Why would I run?' Marlowe smiled, bluffing this out. 'You beat me, fair and square. Tell Doctor Fenchurch she won.'

This blindsided the woman for a moment as she tried to work out what Marlowe meant by this.

'It's a training exercise, right?' Marlowe smiled. 'I mean, you were waiting for me the moment I left the building. And you were quite blatant. I assumed you wanted to see if I was field-ready, so I pulled out all the stops.'

By now two more men, both situated outside the pub walked over, the first placing an arm around Marlowe purely to remove the backpack.

'Nice move, by the way, placing the transmitter into the strap,' Marlowe nodded. 'Classic tradecraft.'

'Who were you meeting with?' asked the brunette. She waved down the road, and Marlowe saw the black Mercedes that had been following him move out into the traffic, driving towards them.

'You,' Marlowe lied. 'I knew you'd find me, so I came to a place I could get some lunch. They do amazing pies up there.

But by the time I arrived, you'd already found me. And good on you for that.'

'Get in,' the woman hissed as, beside Marlowe, the back door to the car opened from within.

'Sure,' Marlowe smiled, not moving. 'And where are we going?'

'Get in.'

'Sure,' Marlowe repeated. 'Once you tell me where we're going.'

The woman wanted to scream; Marlowe could see it. She was only a couple of years younger than he was and spoke with the plummy accent of an Oxbridge student.

'Also, tell me your name,' he added. 'So I can commend you all to your Section Chief.'

'Mister Marlowe, get in the car before we force you in.'

At this, Marlowe faked a mock surprise.

'What, in the middle of this busy street?' he looked around, noting the many tourists and workers walking around. 'That wouldn't be bright.'

He leant over, peering into the back of the car. In it, against the other door and glaring balefully at him, was the slim man in the navy suit.

'Oh, hello!' he said with delight. 'I hope I didn't put you too far out.'

He straightened as the barrel of a gun was placed against the base of his spine.

'Get in the damned car,' the lead muscle, the one that had taken his backpack, whispered. 'Or I'll make sure you spend the rest of your life in a wheelchair—'

It was instinctive; Marlowe spun as the lead muscle said this, grabbing the gun with his left hand and pulling down and around, yanking it out of the lead muscle's hand and spinning it around to aim at him. He saw the other agent reach for his jacket, so shook his head.

'Don't,' he said, ejecting the magazine and round from the top chamber before spinning the gun around and passing it back. 'I don't like threats.'

He wasn't sure, but Marlowe thought he saw a little admiration in the brunette woman's face as the lead muscle snatched the gun back.

'Just get in the bloody car, Marlowe,' the slim man said out of the car door. 'Whitehall wants to speak to you.'

'That's all you had to say,' Marlowe replied cheerfully, sliding into the Mercedes, the brunette woman following him. 'Always happy to speak to Whitehall.'

And, as the now chastised agents left the corner for their own vehicle, the black Mercedes turned into Soho Square, heading for Westminster.

5

DE-BRIEF

WHEN A SPY IS BROUGHT IN FROM THE COLD, THERE ARE TWO ways it happens.

The first is all smiles and cups of tea, friendly faces sitting you down in a comfortable debriefing room and being treated like a welcome friend, returned from the frozen wastes. This way, the debrief is relaxed and warm.

The other way is a little worse.

Usually it involves sedation, hoods thrown over the head, flex-cuffs and dark basements, where instead of polite questions interspersed with cups of tea and biscuits, the interrogation was usually violent, bloody and to the point.

Currently, Marlowe didn't yet know which of those this was likely to be, although the lack of a hood was promising.

That said, Whitehall had a *lot* of basements.

'Nice car,' Marlowe said, stroking the seat. 'Leather, right? This the new hybrid?'

Nobody answered.

Marlowe looked at the brunette beside him.

'I'm Thomas,' he said. 'My friends call me Tom.'

Again, no answer.

Marlowe looked to the slim agent to his left.

'*You* can call me Mister Marlowe,' he stated.

'You're in a lot of trouble, *Mister* Marlowe,' the agent replied coldly.

'Yeah? Please, tell me why?' Marlowe smiled, hiding the concern he currently had. 'I'd love to know, because as far as I'm concerned, I've done nothing, and I thought this was a training exercise.'

He leant closer.

'Because if it wasn't, and you weren't deliberately giving me a chance to see you when I left the office, that's a little disappointing,' he whispered. 'And says a lot about your abilities.'

By now the car was driving down Whitehall, and Marlowe watched carefully out of the window, trying to work out where their destination was. If it was one of the various side roads, then it meant civil service offices, and there was a chance he'd be walking out of this a free man, if a little chastised.

However, the car didn't stop along Whitehall, and carried on past the Houses of Parliament, down Millbank, and towards Thames House, MI5's London headquarters, looking out over the Thames from London's south bank. This wasn't the green and cream building seen in James Bond movies; that was MI6's God-awful monstrosity. This was an unassuming white-brick building, nestled in among many others, keeping to itself and doing what all spies aimed to do – not stand out at all.

Of course, they weren't coming in through the front doors, and the Mercedes turned right down Horseferry Road, and then left into Thorney Street, pulling up at a set of metal bollards that, at their arrival, dropped into the pavement, the gate behind them rising up, allowing the car through into the car park, and the lower levels.

The *basement* levels.

The brunette must have noticed Marlowe's change of expression because she patted him in mock reassurance.

'Don't worry,' she said. 'They'll only taser you in the balls a couple of times before they shoot you in the back of the head.'

She punctuated this with a wink and finger gun motion. Marlowe smiled back, outwardly expressing zero cares, while secretly hammering through the skeletons in his cupboard.

Fact. They'd been following him since Doctor Fenchurch.

Fact. He'd recently stolen a file and read it.

Fact. He'd met with Bridget, but as far as he knew, they couldn't prove this.

That was it. Nothing more. Anything else he'd done had been rubber-stamped by Emilia Wintergreen, his current Control. At best, all they could do would be arrest him for breaking the Official Secrets Act when he stole the files, and as he hadn't done anything with them, he might have leeway to ask for mercy.

The car stopped, and both the brunette and the slim man climbed out, the latter holding up a hand to wave Marlowe out his side of the car. Doing this, Marlowe saw two more MI5 agents, this time people he did recognise – not well, but enough to know this was at least genuine – who, nodding at him, motioned for him to follow them.

There was an elevator at the end of the hall, in which people would travel up to the upper floors of the building. And, to the right of those were rather ornate stairs that also went upwards.

They didn't go anywhere near those. And that was concerning.

'Look, what the hell is this?' Marlowe asked. 'I did what you asked, and I played nice.'

'You're here to see Malcolm Harris,' the slim man said, holding open a door to a set of stairs that went *down*. 'He's down here.'

Marlowe swallowed as the brunette moved in, gently pushing him forward as he walked through the entrance and down the stairs. Malcolm Harris was one of the rising stars of MI5. In his forties and Oxbridge educated, Harris was a Section Chief with ambition, and a man who didn't care who he stood on to get there. To have a meeting with him wasn't great unless he liked you. If that was the case, you could pretty much write your own ticket in the service.

But, to have a meeting with him in the basement ...

There was a door at the end of the corridor, with an access doorway to the left, and what looked like a storeroom on the right. An armed guard, in a white shirt and black tie under a black stab vest, Heckler & Koch - or HK - MP5 held at the ready, watched them approach, hammered twice on the door and opened it, nodding for the slim agent, brunette and Marlowe to enter the room.

It was as Marlowe expected: dark, bare, and imposing. There was a table in the middle of the room, a chair on either side, and a standing lamp, the light adjusted to aim at one chair beside it. There was a fluorescent light on the ceiling but having that on as well was obviously too much light for the room, and currently, apart from the lamp, it was thrown into darkness.

Sitting on the chair facing the lit up one was a man in his forties, his brown hair slicked back in a side parting, his suit grey and bespoke, his burgundy tie probably worth more alone than Marlowe's funeral suit.

'Mister Harris,' Marlowe said, moving to the table. 'Could we swap seats? I think the lamp might be a bit bright.'

'Funny,' Harris replied. 'Anything else you'd like to add before we start?'

'Yeah, actually.' Marlowe jabbed a thumb at the brunette and the suited slim man. 'What are their names? I feel like we're really bonding.'

'Curtis and Shaw.' Harris smiled, but there was no warmth to it. 'I'll leave it up to you to work out which is which.'

Marlowe turned to face the two agents.

'Shaw has to be you,' he said to the brunette, who nodded.

'Just sit the hell down,' the now identified Curtis snapped.

'Rude,' Marlowe replied before turning and sitting down facing Harris, forcing himself not to squint at the lamp. 'For the record, Mister Curtis is rude.'

'There is no record, Marlowe.'

Marlowe didn't allow himself to give any emotion to this statement. "No record" meant this wasn't being recorded. And there weren't many *good* reasons why this would be.

'Why did you run?' Harris asked.

'I didn't.' Marlowe began his rehearsed lie. 'I assumed it was a test.'

'And how did you work that out?'

Marlowe shrugged at the question.

'I came out of Doctor Fenchurch's office, and Mister Curtis was across the road, watching. I got into a cab, and he followed in a Government issue Merc. I went to a funeral, and during it I saw him enter the back of the cemetery chapel.'

He leant forward, cupping his hand to the side of his mouth.

'Between us, he's a pretty shitty spy,' he stage-whispered.

'And after the funeral?' Harris ignored the jibe.

'By then, I assumed he wanted to be seen,' Marlowe continued. 'I mean, you'd have to think that if your tail was so bad at hiding, right? I guessed this was some test to see if I was field ready. Maybe even set by Doctor Fenchurch. And, when he made a real poor job of not being seen on the train, I decided to see how far I could go.'

He winked at Harris.

'Nice touch with the tracker in the strap, by the way,' he said. 'Anyway, I got to Soho but by then I was bored, it was a long day after all, and so I waited to be found. And that's when Miss Shaw stood out in the open for me to see.'

'I did no such thing,' Shaw spoke in anger.

'So, what, standing on a street corner, staring at my window while on a phone is MI5 standard surveillance technique now?' Marlowe shook his head, looking back at Harris. 'You need to do better because it looks like you can't get the staff. Hey, I'm hoping to come off sick leave soon. You could speak to my boss, see if she can lend me to you—'

He'd been expecting a smack to the cheek, or maybe something worse, but the butt of a Glock 17 slamming into the side of his skull, sending him sprawling to the floor, his vision a field of sparkling, spinning lights, was a definite surprise.

Looking up, he stared balefully at Shaw, now putting her gun away, her face still dispassionate.

'Do that again, and I'll make you eat it,' Marlowe hissed. 'Tell me why the hell I'm part of this clown show, or I walk.'

It was bravado, but Marlowe was angry now. And, as he

sat back in the chair, knocking the light to the side so it no longer shined at him, he glared at Harris, who simply watched him, no emotion to his face.

'Marshall Kirk.'

Here we go.

'Go on,' Marlowe replied. 'What about him?'

'You illegally gained a file we had on him,' Harris stated, placing his hands on the desk. 'Do you deny this?'

'Kirk was murdered.' Marlowe sat straighter in the chair. 'The report we gave out said it was natural causes. I wanted to know why you were lying to us all.'

The accusation was general, but he threw it at Harris in particular.

'We?'

'The Service. Unless you're telling me I'm not part of that anymore?'

Harris considered this before replying.

'Marshall Kirk was an old man.'

'Marshall Kirk was fitter than both of us combined, and you damn well know it,' Marlowe snapped. 'He didn't die of a heart attack. He was killed. I wanted to know what he'd been doing that led to this, and nobody would tell me as I was off sick. So, I did what any spy would do. Using the skills you, or rather people just like you, taught me.'

Harris nodded, watching Marlowe carefully for a few moments.

'And what had he been doing?' he eventually enquired.

'Some kind of greatest hits tour with a lot of old, retired spies,' Marlowe rubbed at the side of his head, seeing blood on his fingers as he looked at them. 'And before you ask why, all I have is what you had. I don't know what the hell he was doing, but I wanted to find out.'

Harris looked at Curtis and nodded. Curtis leant forward, placing a photo on the table.

'Vladimir Primakov.' Harris tapped the image with his finger. 'Ex-KGB, ex-German Stasi. Kirk's opposite number for a lot of the Cold War. Speaks to Kirk a week and a half ago, and three days later someone cuts his brakes in Paris. Have you been to France, recently, Mister Marlowe?'

'You think I did this?' Marlowe was still trying to work out the conversation here. He knew he was being set up for something, but he couldn't quite work out what it was.

Harris didn't reply, leaning back on his metal chair.

'Why did you want Primakov dead, Tom?'

'I've never met the man. I don't know him.'

Harris took his gaze off Marlowe, scanning the room, nodding.

'Why did you want Marshall Kirk dead, then?'

Marlowe frowned.

He really didn't like the way this was going.

'Marshall was my mentor, my friend,' he said cautiously, aware his every word was being scrutinised. 'I had no reason to want him dead. I was at his funeral today, for Christ's sake.'

'A funeral he wasn't at,' Curtis muttered from Marlowe's side. 'Because we have his body in the building.'

'A body that really wasn't fit for an open casket,' Shaw added. 'After what you did to him.'

'Wait, what?' Marlowe half-rose out of his chair at this and was slammed back into it by Curtis.

'Marshall Kirk was shot in the back of the head twice, at close range and from a raised position. You know what that means, right?' Harris asked, and Marlowe nodded.

Marshall Kirk had been on his knees when he was killed.

'He was then covered in accelerant and set on fire, left in a warehouse car park at three in the morning,' Harris continued. 'Here's the interesting thing. He was shot with a SIG Sauer P226 pistol. You have one of those, right?'

Marlowe felt his stomach flip-flop.

'You know I do,' he said. 'You would have seen it when you took my backpack and added a tracker.'

'But it wasn't in your backpack when we took you in,' Curtis replied. 'Did you lose it?'

Marlowe didn't want to answer.

'Was this the gun that killed Marshall Kirk?' Harris continued.

'I don't know,' Marlowe admitted.

At this, Harris raised his eyebrows.

'You don't *know*—' he started, his voice mocking and patronising, but Marlowe raised a hand, stopping him.

'You took my bag away to add the tracker, right?' he said. 'That means it was in other people's hands for an extended amount of time. Anything could have been done then, including using my gun.'

'Oh, so it *might* have been used, but not by you?' Harris smiled. 'How convenient.'

'Not really,' Marlowe sighed, leaning back on the chair. 'If you'd left the bag alone, this would have been far easier to prove.'

'Oh, we can prove it now,' Harris continued with his irritating smile. 'We have your gun. Nice hide with the bag and the toilet, but anyone who's seen *The Godfather* knows how that goes.'

He leant even further across the table now, his fingers knitted together as he rested his chin on his hands.

'What do you think our forensic boys will find?' he asked softly.

'That I didn't kill Marshall,' Marlowe repeated.

Harris looked at Curtis and nodded again. Curtis placed a new picture on the table. This time it was one Marlowe recognised.

'Bridget Summers,' Harris stated, giving Marlowe space again. 'Used to be an MI5 analyst in GCHQ but decided five years ago to defect to the Russians. Have you ever met her?'

Marlowe nodded. He couldn't lie his way out of this one. Curtis had seen them at the funeral.

'She was at the funeral,' he said.

'Yes, she met with you, didn't she.' Harris leaned back. 'A Russian asset, meeting with Marshall Kirk's protégé. Doesn't look good for you. None of this does, actually. I think you're spending your foreseeable future in a black-ops lockup—'

'She said she was on Kirk's side,' Marlowe protested. 'That there was a conspiracy; that Cold War spies were dying.'

At this, Harris looked at Shaw.

'Take the guards outside and get a van ready,' he said. 'Mister Marlowe's going on a journey.'

'Sir, I don't feel comfortable leaving you unguarded,' Shaw replied.

'Then send some new ones to guard us.'

Shaw nodded at this and left, as Harris looked back at his captive.

'Go on,' he said.

'She told me it was something to do with a Cold War operation called Rubicon,' Marlowe replied. 'I've never heard of it, but I know Marshall was checking in with a lot of Cold War spies before he died, so I reckon there's a piece of truth to it.'

At the word *Rubicon*, Marlowe had seen a shift in Harris's demeanour.

'Rubicon.'

'Yes, Rubicon,' Marlowe repeated. 'Check your records.'

'Did you talk to Kirk about this?'

'I told you, he was dead.'

'Did you speak about it before you executed him?'

'I told you, I didn't kill him.'

'What about his daughter?' Harris changed direction. 'Daughter of an ex-Stasi agent and Marshall Kirk. Was she on the list? Is this why you shot him?'

'I haven't seen her for years.'

'But yet she was at today's funeral.'

Marlowe silently cursed.

'I saw her there, sure,' he quickly corrected. 'But I didn't speak to her. I didn't attend the wake.'

'Why?' Harris asked. 'Because you knew the body wasn't there? That it was on a car park floor, smouldering?'

'No, because I'd seen your gorilla there, and I assumed I was being tested.'

Harris folded his arms, leaning back.

'Admit it, you're working with Summers,' he said calmly.

'I barely know the woman!'

'Did *she* kill Kirk on your orders?'

'No!'

Harris clicked his tongue for a couple of seconds as he considered this news, then rose from his chair and nodded for Curtis to walk to the back of the room, where they could speak in silence. As they faced each other, speaking softly so Marlowe couldn't hear them, almost out of the light, Marlowe watched intently.

Because there was something they didn't know, something not on his record.

Tom Marlowe had been bored in hospital, recovering from his wounds. And outside his door was the nurses' station. For hours a day he'd watch them, and slowly, over the weeks, he remembered how to lip read. It wasn't easy, a skill he'd learned in training but forgotten due to lack of usage, but it soon came back. Some shapes made by the lips when speaking looked very similar, like "th" and "f", making them harder to decipher, but as he progressed, he realised that as long as he knew the context, was in a quiet room and could see the facial expressions and body language, he had a ninety percent chance of getting a correct read.

And the read right now, watching Harris speak to Curtis, was chilling.

Wait until I'm gone, use your taser and remove him, Harris was saying. *Take him to a nice quiet place and retire him. And then do the same with the girl.*

Marlowe didn't know who "the girl" was, and he didn't need to know the context of the message.

To "retire" him meant to do the same as Marshall Kirk had received ...

Two rounds to the back of the head.

———

6

TUNNEL RATS

THE CONVERSATION FINISHED; HARRIS WALKED OVER TO Marlowe once more.

'I need to speak to my superiors,' he said. 'You'll be taken somewhere dark and quiet by Mister Curtis here, and we'll speak again.'

'I doubt that,' Marlowe replied carefully.

Without replying to this, Harris walked over to the door and opened it, leaving the room as he closed it behind him. Now alone in the room with Marlowe, Curtis walked up to his side, pulling out more flex-cuffs.

'Stand up,' he commanded. 'Turn to your left and place your hands behind your back.'

Marlowe did this, focusing on the wall in front. When he'd knocked the lamp earlier, it had shifted its angle slightly, and now cast his own shadow against the wall. And, more importantly, it cast the shadow of Curtis as well, as Marlowe watched him pull what looked like a gun from his jacket, aiming it at him—

Marlowe dropped and spun, grabbing the yellow X26

taser with both hands and wrenching it around quickly, aimed at Curtis's own chest as the agent pulled at the trigger instinctively, shocking himself as the tines embedded into his shirt, the charge entering him through them as he fell, shuddering, to the floor. The whole thing had taken less than a second, and the electricity coursing through Curtis had locked his body, stopping him from shouting out. Now down and finally unconscious, Curtis lay prone on the floor of the interrogation room as Marlowe knelt over him, already going through his pockets.

A phone. Gun. Wallet, ID, and a few other items including a vicious little folding knife. Taking these, Marlowe looked back at the door, considering his next move.

Because he was trapped in an MI5 basement, and the moment he left the room, the entire force of the British security service would be after him.

Marlowe considered what to do for a few moments as he gagged the unconscious Curtis, making sure the man could still breathe, using the flex-cuffs aimed for his own wrists to secure the agent to the table leg. It wouldn't keep him secured long, but the table was heavy and metal, and to overturn it from the angle he was at would take time.

On a plus point, Marlowe now had a phone, and there was a signal. That said, there weren't many people he could call, especially without throwing them under the bus in the process. He couldn't ask for help from his colleagues in Section D, as they'd already be under suspicion, so he had to think fast, and more importantly, he had to work alone.

They'd brought his backpack in with them, so he grabbed it, pulling out the suit he'd worn for the funeral, rolled up in the bottom. Agents were often plain-clothed, but here in the offices, suits and shirts were expected at the bare minimum.

The "T-shirt and jeans" look he currently sported would stick out like a sore thumb the moment he left the cell. Luckily, he had something that fitted this, as Curtis was way too slim for Marlowe's more muscled frame to fit into his clothing.

Now dressed in a suit and shirt, and with nothing else worth taking from the backpack, he placed it under the chair, out of the way, and examined the gun. It was a Glock 17, standard issue. He preferred the heavier SIGs, but a gun was a gun, and there really wasn't much between them. Curtis had one spare mag in his trouser pocket, and Marlowe placed that in his own trouser pocket as he slid the gun into the back of his waistband, considering his next moves. He was in the basement of Thames House, and to escape out of the building involved three different options.

First, he could brazenly walk out the door, but Shaw was still out there getting a van for him, and there were at least a dozen armed guards between him and the outside. And even then, he wasn't free, as there'd likely be armed guards out there too, able to take him down before he even reached the kerb.

Second, he could make his way to the roof and run across the tops of the buildings. A friend of his, Detective Inspector Declan Walsh, had done the same when he'd been falsely accused of terrorism a while back, but Temple Inn, in the City of London wasn't as closely guarded as Thames House. Being so close to Westminster, there were snipers always placed out of sight on the roofs, and emerging out onto one, gun in hand and at speed, was likely to have his escape cut violently and painfully short.

Or, third and finally, there was *down*.

It was an open secret there were tunnels under White-hall. The Cabinet War Room, the Admiralty Citadel, even

Pindar, the Defence Crisis Management Centre, a bunker deep beneath the Ministry of Defence in Whitehall were well known to the press. But the most notorious was *Q-Whitehall*, the name given to a communications facility under Whitehall itself, one that involved a network of tunnels, secret and unavailable to the public. Well, that was until journalist Duncan Campbell got into them with a bike in 1980, writing an article about it for the *New Statesman*.

The tunnels existed, but were barely used these days.

That didn't mean they *couldn't* be used, though.

Marlowe had been shown a tunnel, years earlier, that ran from MI5 at Thames House, under St John's Gardens, and ending at Great Minster House, on the Horseferry Road. It wasn't on any of the usual maps, and the man who'd shown it to him, Anthony Farringdon, had only known of it himself because of his years running security for the Houses of Parliament, which also had a secret entrance in case of attack, leading to a spur of Q-Whitehall running under the junction of Parliament Square and Great George Street.

Because of this knowledge, Marlowe knew that once in the tunnels, he could travel any of the Q-Whitehall routes all the way to Trafalgar Square if he so wanted, with exits even onto the Bakerloo Line tube tunnels at Charing Cross. And from there he could slip into the deep-level BT tunnels, giving him the option of getting to Paddington in the west, to Bethnal Green in the east.

The only problem was to get *to* them.

This would involve going up a floor, walking to the west of the building and following a back staircase into a now-disused server room, the entrance hidden – and likely forgotten – by any of the new people.

New people.

Shaw had taken the guards with her. The guards outside hadn't been there when Marlowe arrived.

Quickly, Marlowe grabbed Curtis's ID and taser – taking out the cartridge – and, after finding a spare in the jacket pocket, reloaded the weapon. Then, clipping the ID to his own jacket, he angled the still unconscious body so that the head was under the table and ran to the door, yanking it open.

There was a guard on duty at the door. He was a freshly arrived one, and his eyes widened as the bearded agent with the taser in his hand waved at him.

'Bugger tried to escape,' he said. 'Keep him covered while I call Harris.'

The armed guard entered, raising his rifle at the downed man – only to spasm up as Marlowe fired the second charge from the taser into his shoulder.

'Sorry,' Marlowe muttered apologetically, tossing the taser to the floor. Closing the door, Marlowe quietly moved onto the guard, pulling off his clothes as quickly as possible. Shaw could return at any moment, and Marlowe needed to be as far away from here as possible.

Pulling off his jacket, he thanked whoever was looking after him for the black trousers and white shirt the armed guard was wearing, as it meant Marlowe, in his funeral attire didn't need to totally strip his victim. Instead, Marlowe pulled his funeral black tie as a loop over his head, disliking the clip-on tie the guard wore, straightened his collar and secured the black stab vest over the top, rolling up the sleeves to match the fallen guard as he placed the police cap on his head, attaching the HK MP5 with retractable stock, to the front. The guard had a side holster with a Glock 17 the same as Curtis, so Marlowe removed the magazine from it and threw the extra ammunition into his pocket with the other cartridge.

Now looking more like an armed police officer than an on-the-run spy, Marlowe opened the door and looked outside.

The corridor was empty, and Marlowe wasted no time in opening the storeroom on the other side. They hadn't removed his lock-pick set when they sat him down, and he used this quickly to unlock the door, dump the guard inside, and re-lock it behind him. Then, once he'd closed the other door, he pressed on his radio, attached to the jacket on his left lapel.

'*Prisoner escaped!*' he shouted! '*Agent down and restrained! Prisoner heading to the car park! Is armed! I repeat, is armed! Wearing a T-shirt, jeans and a hoodie!*'

This done, he opened the door at the end of the corridor, and the stairs which would take him up, most likely, to a back corridor leading to the lobby. Taking them two at a time, he made a point of backing against the wall once he hit the ground floor, allowing the door to crash open, hiding him as three MI5 agents and two guards, all armed, ran down the stairs.

Marlowe was happy with this; *so far, so good.* They'd find a restrained Curtis, his Glock 17 removed, and with nobody else in the room, they'd assume the guard who'd been at the door was the one giving chase in the opposite direction. Now alone, Marlowe slid through the door, walking swiftly down the corridor that would lead him to the main lobby.

He could try to gain a car, or just walk out, but he was still too visible, even dressed like he was. You still swiped an ID card to get in and out, and currently he was using Curtis's card, purely for the higher-level security it probably had.

And the moment they realised Curtis was down, any use of the card would be better than a tracking device at working out where Marlowe was heading.

No, the best plan was still to get into the tunnels and run like hell.

The ground floor was chaos; armed units running in all directions, so Marlowe joined in, running at a jog towards the lobby. A casual, strolling guard in the middle of panic would stand out after all.

'Hey!' another armed officer with Sergeant stripes shouted over to him. 'What are you doing?'

Marlowe considered ignoring him – he had to get out fast, as the diversion would only last as long as it took for them to get to the car park and secure it. With no Marlowe there, they would know they'd been conned. But he knew walking away from a confrontation was just as bad.

There was a woman in the reception area, standing in confusion as the surrounding people ran about, and Marlowe made a beeline towards her.

'Escort duty,' he shouted over at the Sergeant who, noticing the woman, nodded and carried on through the lobby.

Breathing a silent sigh of relief, Marlowe stopped beside the woman.

'Come with me, Ma'am,' he said, grabbing her arm and pulling her towards the back. Again, he knew this would look quite normal amongst the chaos.

'Marlowe?' Tessa Kirk asked, even more confused now.

Marlowe said nothing as he looked across at her, escorting her out of the reception area and down a back corridor. Only now, out of sight of the others, did he feel it was safe enough to speak.

'Why are you here, Tessa?' he asked softly, keeping his face away from any CCTV cameras.

'I was told to come in,' Tessa snapped. 'Not really given a chance to say no. They turned up in the middle of the wake, looking for one of dad's old friends. I was brought in to see a man named—'

'Harris?' Marlowe asked, opening a side door and leading Tessa down some stairs, back towards the basement level, albeit a more easily accessible one than the area he'd previously been in.

'That's right,' Tessa frowned. 'Why are you dressed as a guard, Tom? I thought you were on leave. Did you get demoted?'

Marlowe stopped at a door now, crouching over and using his lock pick to open it.

'You're in danger,' he said. 'Marshall didn't die of a heart attack. Harris knows more than he's saying, and I think they're wanting to use you as bait for Bridget Summers.'

'Bridget? The woman who used to work with my dad?' Tessa entered through the door as Marlowe opened it. 'I haven't heard her name mentioned for years! What's she got to do with this?'

'Harris is claiming she and I killed Marshall.'

'Oh, come on!' Tessa exclaimed, stopping as Marlowe re-locked the door on the other side. 'That's insane! We both know you ...'

She trailed off as she properly scanned the clothing Marlowe wore and the lock picks in his hand.

'Shit,' she muttered. 'You're really telling the truth, aren't you?'

Marlowe gave a tight smile as he nodded, pulling Tessa after him down the rounded tunnel.

'This is a spur off Q-Whitehall,' he said. 'We're using these tunnels to escape.'

'No, I should go back,' Tessa pulled away. 'This isn't my world. I need to—'

'Harris was telling his agent to take me somewhere and kill me,' Marlowe replied calmly. 'He then said to "do the same with the girl". I'm guessing that was you.'

He pulled at her arm again, and this time Tessa complied, following Marlowe as they ran down the tunnel.

'So, what's the plan?' she asked. Marlowe marvelled at her ability to compartmentalise immediately, but considering she was the daughter of Marshall Kirk, he didn't really expect much else.

'I'm pretty much free-forming it at the moment,' he said as they turned right down a tunnel, thick cables attached to the sides, and with a handmade sign above reading "Tunnel G." 'If we can get some space, I can get to a safe house and think. Bridget wanted me to speak to a man. Raymond something.'

'Raymond Sykes?'

'Yes!' Marlowe smiled. 'That's the one. I memorised a number to call.'

'You remember his phone number, but not his name?' Tessa was amused by this.

'I'm better with numbers,' Marlowe replied as he paused at a crossroads, checking the signage. There were faint noises behind them, and Marlowe knew that not only had his ruse likely been discovered, but they were now hot on his heels. He wondered why his radio hadn't alerted him of this, but realised that in the tunnels, they probably didn't work.

Which also helped him.

Turning right, he walked a couple of steps before pausing,

motioning for Tessa to wait and then returned to the cross-roads, looking north as he took the police cap off his head and hurled it down the tunnel like a frisbee, gaining a good thirty yards of distance as it skidded on the floor. Then, turning back to Tessa, he ran, grabbing her and pulling her beside him.

'That should make them think we're heading to the Charing Cross tunnels,' he said.

'And we're not?'

'No,' Marlowe slowed once they were around a bend in the tunnel. 'There's a service door that exits these at the base of the *Boudicca's Rebellion* statue on the Embankment. We'll walk out, lock it behind us and find a cab.'

'An armed copper in a cab,' Tessa shook her head. 'They won't believe us.'

'I won't be armed by then,' Marlowe said as he unclipped the HK MP5, placing it gently on the floor before pulling off the black stab vest. 'I'll just be a normal guy.'

'You could never be a normal guy,' Tessa muttered, and Marlowe thought he could detect amusement in her voice.

'Do you have somewhere you can go?' he asked, turning off the radio and leaving it on the jacket as well. The last thing he wanted was anything that could track him. 'Someone off the grid, where you can stay for a couple of days while I fix this?'

Tessa stopped.

'How did my dad die?' she enquired quietly. 'If it wasn't a heart attack?'

'Tess—'

'How, Tom?'

Marlowe sighed.

'I can't be sure, but they're trying to set me and Summers

up for his death, and I was told he was shot in the back of the head,' he replied, deciding to omit the part about the body being burned. 'I swear, I'll make sure he gets justice.'

'*We'll* make sure.' Tessa shook her head.

'As you said earlier, this isn't your world.' Marlowe arrived at the last door now; under it he could see shafts of light and the faint noise of London as he worked with his lock picks.

'Yeah, well, now it is,' Tessa snapped. 'My dad was a spy, mum was a Stasi operative before the Berlin Wall came down, and I've been a part of this life since I was born. You're helping me, not the other way around.'

Marlowe wanted to reply, to correct her, to shout Tessa down, but deep down, he was happy about this. *Being on the run sucked. And she was right.*

'Toss your phone and your smartwatch,' he said. 'Anything they can locate you with gets left here. They'll find it in minutes anyway, so we need to move fast.'

'Already done,' Tessa pointed at a small pile on the ground. 'I did it while you played with the door.'

'Good,' Marlowe nodded. 'Then let's get the hell out of here before my people kill us.'

7

SAVED HOUSE

MARLOWE DIDN'T WANT TO THINK ABOUT WHAT WAS HAPPENING in MI5 after their escape, and the last thing he could do was check in with any of his old colleagues.

Instead, they'd walked down the lower part of the Embankment, having emerged from a door halfway up the staircase leading to it from Westminster Bridge, the sight of two people appearing from the door almost totally ignored because of the amount of tourists walking back and forth, watching the Thames rather than the service doors.

Their exit clear, Marlowe and Tessa had continued down the walkway, past the *Monument to the RAF* and returning to street level opposite Whitehall Gardens, crossing the Thames at Hungerford Bridge, intending to get onto the Southbank and merge into the crowds, now nothing more than a man in black trousers, white shirt and tie, and a woman in a black suit. Finding themselves around office workers who were finishing for the day, they matched in with half of the surrounding people.

During the walk, Marlowe had planned. He knew of a

safe house in Essex, and all they had to do was get there. He still had his cash, a secreted Glock under his shirt and a phone number in his head. All he had to do was survive until he could fix things.

Tessa, however, was a different matter. She was a civilian, and even though she was Marshall's daughter, she really shouldn't be in this mess. He had to work out a way to get her to safety, find someone who still spoke to him, who could get her out of this chaos, preferably without Tessa being violent in the process.

Of course, that was easier said than done.

At Southbank, he'd stolen a phone off a table in the bar area outside the BFI and dialled Trix on it. After three rings, it answered.

'Don't call me again, you goddamned *bastard*,' Trix hissed down the phone. 'I've heard what you did. You should be hanged in chains on the Great Road like the old traitors. Left up and removed at dawn.'

'Trix—' Marlowe had replied, but Trix had already slammed the phone down, after yelling *'Piss off, you traitor!'* down the line. He listened a little longer; there was an ever so slight *click* on the line, proving that MI5 were monitoring the lines of his Section D colleagues.

'Sounds like your friends aren't really your friends anymore,' Tessa said, as Marlowe tossed the phone into a nearby bin. He could have returned it to the phone's owner, pretended he'd seen it on the floor, but in about ten minutes the area would likely be swooped on by a dozen agents, and if the phone was stolen, the poor bugger wouldn't be dragged off as an accessory.

'It's a message,' he said. 'One she hopes I can work out.'

'And how is a comment hoping you'll die a message?'

'The Caxton Gibbet,' Marlowe explained as they walked away from the crowds, heading towards the main road and a black cab stand. 'It stands on the ancient thoroughfare known as Ermine Street, but also called "the Great Road". It's at the junction of the A1198 and the A428.'

'You seem to know scarily too much about this,' Tessa commented.

'Trix does,' Marlowe smiled. 'She saw it outside a services once and looked into it. We'd promised to go back and see it. Used to be a pub there named after it before it was destroyed for the service station to be built.'

'So "removed at dawn" means "meet there at dawn" instead?'

'Hopefully,' Marlowe nodded. 'First, we have to survive until then. I did what I needed to do, and I didn't tell her anything. She'll be questioned, released and then she'll work out what we need while we get somewhere safe.'

'And how do we do that?' Tessa was watching behind them as they walked. 'Because any minute now, we're going to get swamped. They'll be watching the cameras.'

Marlowe was observing the cars, and then smiled as he waved at a battered-looking grey Lexus.

'We get a cab,' he said as the car, driven by a young Turkish man, stopped beside them. 'How much to Liverpool Street, mate? Cash?'

The cab driver considered this and gave a number, and Marlowe nodded, opening the door.

'Unlicensed cabs are our friend,' he said. 'He won't want any attention, and our trip won't be logged anywhere.'

Tessa smiled, nodding as she worked out Marlowe's plan.

'And any CCTV finding us sees us deliberately walk south of the river for a cab, so they'll be watching stations like

London Bridge and Waterloo,' she said as she climbed into the car. 'Dad would have been proud of you.'

Marlowe flushed at the compliment, but then remembered that Marshall Kirk was dead, and the moment faded quickly.

Looking around, one last check to see if they were being followed, he clambered into the Lexus, and it drove off down the street.

———

IN FACT, THE ROUTE TO LIVERPOOL STREET TOOK ANOTHER half an hour, a route that took them across Blackfriars and through Smithfield Market, but they arrived at the station with no issues, and Marlowe even added another twenty to buy the flat cap the driver had on his passenger seat. This now on, and with Tessa pulling a scarf out of her pocket and pulling it around her head, hiding the bulk of her short blonde style, the two of them quickly walked to a machine in the centre of the station and, with cash, bought two returns to Harlow in Essex. The train was leaving in three minutes, so they hurried to the platform and slid through the doors of the carriage moments before it set off, Marlowe chuckling at his good fortune. Even if they were being followed, there was no way anyone followed them onto the train, and for the first time in a while, he relaxed.

'So, now we're in the clear a little, do you want to explain why you kidnapped me in more detail?' Tessa asked, sitting across from him, a small table between them both.

Marlowe rested his arms on it and considered his answer. And, as the train continued on, he told Tessa everything he knew about her father's last days, and what Bridget had told him about Rubicon.

After all, they had time to kill.

———

FROM HARLOW, THEY'D GRABBED A TAXI FROM THE STATION into the country lanes between Harlow and Epping. It had been a circular, winding route, but at the same time, Marlowe was more relaxed here; the simple fact of being outside London and its multitude of CCTV cameras was enough to lower his blood pressure significantly.

Tessa had sat silently beside him throughout the drive. In fact, she'd not really spoken since he'd told her everything. To be honest, he'd expected this; Tessa was Marshall's daughter in every way, even to the ability to compartmentalise emotions. Which would probably keep her alive, although that life expectancy would drop fast the longer she was with him. Which meant that as well as working out what he needed to do to keep himself alive, he needed to work out how to get Tessa to safety. And, from past experience with her, and from the stories Marshall would tell, he knew she wouldn't accept that willingly.

'Actually, can we make a stop first?' Marlowe suddenly asked. 'I have a real need for fish and chips.'

The driver smiled, nodding. And, with Tessa frowning at him, Marlowe relaxed back into the seat.

It was going to be a long night, and they needed to eat, at least.

———

THE HOUSE THEY'D EVENTUALLY ARRIVED AT WAS A THREE-
bedroom detached house at the end of a sparse cul-de-sac.
Walking up the path, Marlowe dived into a rockery,
rummaging around until he found an old, rusty key.

'For emergencies,' he said.

'Whose house is this?' Tessa looked up at it. 'And will they
try to shoot us?'

'Technically, it's mine,' Marlowe explained, walking up
the drive. 'That is, it was mum's house before she died. I never
moved in, as I felt it was a little creepy. So, I have a cleaner
maintain it as an Airbnb and holiday home, and I stay when I
need some space.'

'Surely MI5 will know about this,' Tessa said as they
walked around the side of the house, Marlowe using the large
key to open a gate. 'They'll check here as soon as they lose
you.'

'It'll definitely be looked into, but not immediately,'
Marlowe smiled as they walked through the gate, locking it
one-handedly behind them before walking out onto the
large, mildly overgrown garden. 'But we're not going to the
house.'

In fact, Marlowe continued walking across the grass to the
back of the garden where, under a tree was a large shed. The
key that opened the gate also unlocked the shed door, and he
ushered Tessa inside, again locking it from the inside.

The shed was a twelve-foot by eight-foot space, with a
table on one side, a massive rug on the floor and a selection
of garden equipment scattered around. A couple of cobwebs
were in the corners, and through the dirty, single window
Tessa could see the back door of the house.

'Not exactly the Ritz, but I suppose we won't get rained
on,' she said.

Marlowe, hearing this, chuckled as he kicked aside the rug, revealing a trapdoor in the floor. Grabbing the handle, he pulled it up, revealing a small hatch with a ladder.

'We're not staying here, either,' he said, motioning for her to start down the metal rungs of the ladder. 'At the bottom is a light switch. Turn it on when you get down there. I need to make sure the rug settles back down on the hatch when I close it.'

More curious than concerned, Tessa started down the ladder, and a moment later, light lit up underground as Marlowe clambered into the hole, holding the bag of fish and chips in one hand as he pulled the rug back onto the hatch with the other, lowering it and the hatch above him as he climbed down into a metal tunnel, leading to a door.

'What the hell is this?' Tessa banged on the wall, hearing a solid thunk as she did so. Marlowe opened the door, and they walked into a large area, easily half the size of the garden.

On one wall, held up by some kind of pin board, was a large and deadly amount of weaponry, with boxes and holdalls under it, all bulging with another, yet unseen armoury. Ahead of them was a computer and bank of monitors, now coming to life as Marlowe turned them on, to the right were two cots, in a pull-down bunk-bed style, and a door to the side of it read *WC*. Against the wall to the back of them were shelves of tins and boxes, all food.

'Jesus,' Tessa walked over to the guns. 'You have a Batcave. If Batman killed people, that is.'

'Mum bought the house in the late nineties,' Marlowe explained. 'The guy before us was an old fellow, lived here for decades. During the sixties, he'd worried about Russian missiles, so he built a fallout shelter in the garden. Over the next twenty years, he added to it. But it was rickety as hell, and he'd never asked for planning permission. So, when we bought it, he told us about the "secret nuclear bunker" he'd made, but it was done in a *wink wink* way, as he explained she'd have to fill it in before it became a sinkhole, wiping out the garden. He took ten grand off the price because of this, but all this was actually why she bought the bloody place.'

Marlowe looked around the place.

'It was held up by plywood walls and beams,' he explained, placing the bag of food on a table. 'Place was a death trap and looked like a Western mine. Mum had a couple of friends who worked on battleships, and they helped shore this all up after 9/11 happened, as everyone was getting paranoid again. Welded steel frames and panels. We placed a chemical toilet in, and concreted around everything once it was done, so it was secure.'

He looked back at the screens as they sparked to life.

'Nobody knows it exists, not even Whitehall,' he explained. 'Mum never finished it, and I took on the last touches a few years after her death. I felt I needed something for a rainy day. There was some guy on YouTube doing something similar, and it looked cool.'

On the screen were CCTV cameras now, half outside the house, the others in corners of rooms.

'They'll come in, and we'll see and hear everything,' Marlowe pulled out a black plastic hard-case, opening it up. Inside was a phone connected to a laptop, a box of money in various denominations, and a handful of passports. 'They won't know we're here, and we can hide out until tomorrow morning. I have a car nearby we can use to get to Trix.'

'Hence the fish and chips,' Tessa nodded. 'We're staying a while.'

Marlowe pointed at the shelves.

'I have some microwaveable food, long-term stuff, but it's pure survival,' he explained. 'Tastes like cardboard. Mushed cardboard.'

'I get it.' Tessa was already opening up one of the paper wrappers, eating a chip. 'Dad had me try survival rations once. I think I was going on about following in his footsteps, and he wanted to quickly turn me off that idea.'

'Did it work?'

Tessa smiled, blowing on a chip to cool it.

'Am I in the army?'

Marlowe didn't reply, opening up the laptop connected to the phone, already tapping out a message in some kind of internet relay chat app.

'We use a Starlink array for internet here,' he explained. 'And I had some techie friends boost the security. So, anything we do or say on this bounces around a dozen different IPs on every continent before they can even start to narrow down where we are. Same with phone calls. I'm sending Trix what I know so far through a forgotten IRC message board only we can find. She'll have algorithms set that scrape data from particular areas of the dark web, so she'll get it in a matter of minutes.'

Having finished a message, discussing everything he knew about Bridget, Rubicon and the events of the day, he pressed send, and Tessa saw it turn into random text and ASCII code.

'Nobody reads the board but better to be sure,' he smiled, turning on the phone, connecting it to the laptop as it booted up. Once the Lock Screen was bypassed, Marlowe typed in a number, pressing connect, and turning on the speaker.

After a moment of ringing, a man answered.

'Yes?' a nervous, worried voice spoke.

'Raymond?' Marlowe asked. 'Bridget Summers told me to call you. My name is—'

'Hello, Tom,' the voice continued. 'I met you with your mother once. You were about to join the army, so you probably don't remember. And Marshall had always said you were his backup plan.'

Marlowe glanced at Tessa; she was looking up from the chips she'd been demolishing.

'We're on an encrypted line, and I have Tessa Kirk with me,' Marlowe continued.

'Oh, dear girl, I'm so sorry I couldn't make the funeral today,' Raymond Sykes continued.

'It's fine,' she said, shrugging at Marlowe, giving the impression that, although this man knew her, she had no idea who he was. But, with Marshall's life being as secretive as it was, this was hardly surprising. 'But we don't have long to talk, and we're a little in the dark here.'

'Of course,' Raymond replied down the line. 'How much do you know?'

Quickly and succinctly, Marlowe explained what he already knew, primarily from Bridget's conversation.

'Okay, we definitely need to talk,' Raymond replied. 'But not on here. I know we're encrypted, but this is an "explain in person" kind of thing. Do you know Cambridge? If so, meet me at the Corpus Clock tomorrow at noon. It's quite a common tourist area, so nobody will think it strange, and there are enough exits for you.'

'Raymond, can you at least give me an idea of what I'm looking at here?' Marlowe asked. 'All I know is some old Op called Rubicon is throwing MI5 into full panic mode.'

'It's not MI5,' Raymond explained. 'It's the people in it.

We found proof someone in MI5 is killing anyone connected to Rubicon. Chances are, you've met them already.'

'Why though?' Tessa was frowning as she spoke. 'Surely they'd want this discovered as much as my dad did?'

'Not if they're the sleeper agent you're hunting,' Raymond explained. 'I need to go. Tomorrow, at noon. Wear something red.'

And with that, the call disconnected. Marlowe stared at the phone.

Someone in MI5 was a sleeper agent for the Russians. And, worse than that, it was possibly someone he'd already met.

Could it be Harris?

Without thinking, Marlowe had already walked over to the pin board and pulled down a new SIG P266 to replace his stolen one, discarding the Glock from his waistband as he started to quickly dismantle his new weapon, checking the springs, making sure it hadn't gummed up in the time it'd been down here.

'Are you okay?' Tessa asked, watching him.

'Not really,' he said, looking back. 'Your father may have been killed by one of his own.'

'I heard,' Tessa nodded. 'What do we do about it?'

'You're going somewhere safe for the moment,' Marlowe replied, holding a hand up. 'Look, I'm good. I was a Royal Marine Commando who then trained with the SAS, but these guys almost took me out. I can't be worrying about you while I look into this.'

'Oh, so you'd be worrying about poor little me?' Tessa took the discarded Glock, aiming it at Marlowe. 'And what makes you think—'

Without thinking, Marlowe moved in, grabbing and twisting, disarming Tessa as he turned the gun on her.

'I think because I have the experience,' he said, waggling the gun, aimed at her face.

'But you don't see all the angles,' Tessa smiled, nodding downwards.

As Marlowe glanced at his chest, he saw the SIG, now in Tessa's other hand, and aimed at his stomach.

'Okay, that's nice,' he said, lowering the gun. 'Your dad teach you that?'

Tessa smiled and went to reply, but there was a flashing red light above the monitor that distracted them both.

'What's that?' Tessa asked, as Marlowe ran over to the computer.

'Perimeter alarm,' he said, bringing up CCTV images. 'They've arrived.'

8

UNDERGROUND, OVERGROUND

MARLOWE FLICKED A SWITCH; THE LIGHTS IN THE BUNKER lowered, and a quick glance to the corridor showed the lights at the base of the ladder were turned off.

'In case they see a sliver of light,' he said as he scrolled through the footage. At the front of the house, a black SUV had stopped, and out of it moved four black-overalled figures. It was a black-ops team, and they were armed for a fight, each with guns strapped to their thighs and assault rifles in their hands.

'Recognise any of them?' Tessa asked, and Marlowe pointed to a woman opening the front gate.

'That's Shaw,' he said. 'Don't recognise the other three, and Curtis and Harris aren't there.'

'Maybe they're the second team?' Tessa continued. 'Coming in from the back? That's how dad always did it.'

Cursing, Marlowe switched cameras; Tessa was right. In the country lane at the back of the property, a second black SUV had appeared. And, out of this emerged five more agents, the lead being Curtis.

'Damn,' Marlowe hissed. 'If they're coming through the back, they'll pass right by the shed.'

'Well, now we'll see whether or not you placed the rug down properly,' Tessa smiled, already walking over to the pin board, and pulling a shotgun from the rack. 'Eat your chips before they get cold. Is there another way out of here?'

'Yeah, comes out a hundred feet south, on the edge of the next field,' Marlowe nodded, already grabbing a holdall and filling it with money, fake credit cards and passports. Moving to a shelf, he pulled down a handful of pay-as-you-go phones as well, tossing them in. Once this was done, he pulled up another duffle from the bottom of the weaponry wall, throwing assault rifles, pistols, and ammunition into it with wild abandon.

'Pass me that case,' he said, pointing at a box that looked no larger than a sheath of A4 paper. 'We might need some bugs.'

Throwing this into the second duffel and zipping it up, Marlowe looked up at the screens. On them, he could see Shaw and her team already in the house, checking room by room, while Curtis and the others had stopped outside the shed, talking. One of them was holding up some kind of transmitter.

'Shit,' he said, suddenly patting himself down. 'They found us because they're tracking us. Quick, check yourself. Did they put anything on you? In your pockets?'

'No,' Tessa started checking her pockets. 'These have little space for things in these suits, anyway—'

She stopped as Marlowe pulled out a scanner, turning it on. Walking over to Tessa, he passed it over her, pausing as it squealed at the back of her neck.

'They stuck it under your collar,' he said, flipping up the

jacket's collar and pulling a small tracker, the red light flashing off the fabric. Quickly, he placed it on the table and, with the butt of the SIG P266 slammed down onto it, shattering the device.

Looking up at the screen, he saw Curtis and his agents looking around in anger.

'They know we're around, but not where,' he said. 'The metal walls have caused confusion, but it won't last long, and the buggers are thorough.'

'I'm sorry,' Tessa hissed, staring at the broken tracker. 'Dad would be furious at me.'

'Your dad's done similar in the past, don't worry about it,' Marlowe was already slinging the heavier of the bags over his shoulder, pointing at the other. 'And between us? They found me earlier today in the same bloody manner. We don't dwell on the past, we push through the present. Grab that and follow me.'

'We could wait it out,' Tessa suggested. 'They don't know we're in here.'

On the screen, Curtis and the others were examining the shed door.

'Not an option,' he said. 'Go. Now.'

As Tessa ran to a grille beside the cots, pulling it off and clambering through it on all fours, Marlowe ran to the computer, typing in a string of commands as he looked around. The moment he left, the motion detector would click on, and as Curtis, Shaw or anyone else opened the hatch, it'd set off a series of claymores down here, which in turn would ignite the thermite. The whole place would be a blaze in a matter of moments.

'Damn it,' Marlowe muttered, munching on the remains

of a battered sausage as he followed Tessa through the grate. 'I really liked this place.'

MARLOWE HADN'T BEEN UNDERESTIMATING THE DISTANCE; THE hatch that emerged from the tunnel into an Epping woodlands was only a hundred feet from the entrance, and it'd only taken a minute to crawl along it. In fact, they were almost out when there was an immense explosion, and a blast of heat came up the tunnel behind them. Marlowe kept crawling; he knew the flames would keep Curtis at bay, and it'd still be a little while before they found the exit route, but the explosion would likely alert them to an escape attempt, and now MI5 agents would start looking at maps and drawing circles, working out possible escape routes, rates of speed, and exits.

The hatch opened into a clearing, and on the other side of the fence and hedge, Marlowe could see flames licking up. It was probably the shed, now ablaze.

Clambering out of the metal hatch, placing it back down and recovering the dirt and leaves above it, Marlowe waved at Tessa to follow him as he ran east, into the woods.

'We don't have much of a lead,' he said. 'They'll know we're—'

He stopped as he heard shouts behind him, and glancing back he could see the five agents, including Curtis, slowly making their way into the woods blindly, HK MP5s in their hands.

'Dammit! We have to circle,' he whispered, pulling Tessa low. 'I can't lead them to the barn.'

Moving deeper into the trees, Marlowe deliberately

snapped a branch with his foot, and a few yards further, broke another with his hand.

'Are you actually leading them towards us?' Tessa hissed, but as she spoke, Marlowe was already pulling out a flash-bang grenade and a length of wire, placing it across the path before running on.

'That's a terrible trap,' she shook her head. 'Dad would have—'

'Understood,' Marlowe smiled as he pulled her down. 'We can't kill any of them, even if they want to off us. That'd get everyone after us, and they're just doing their jobs, so we need to just slow them.'

He pointed into the woods; the MI5 agents had found the flash bang tripwire, and Curtis was waving them off to the left and right.

'They now realise there's a chance they could trip something, which makes them cautious about everything they see as they continue, because they don't want to get hurt,' Marlowe said as he rummaged on the ground for a branch. 'So, now they're spreading out to try to not only stop multiple people getting injured if someone trips a trap, but also to gain more ground.'

He forced a smile.

'Which is a great idea, but it leaves them in the woods, in the evening, alone, while the other group checks the house.'

'So, we take them out one by one?' Tessa looked incredulous.

'No, only one's needed,' Marlowe was already sneaking forwards, through the woods now, his voice low as he approached Curtis from behind. The agent was pulling out his radio, looking around, but missing Marlowe, now behind a tree.

'Anything?' he hissed into the radio, and the lack of any response seemed to anger him more than if someone had replied. Tossing the radio to the ground in impotent rage, he sighed, leant over to pick it up—

And fell to the floor as Marlowe slammed the branch against his head, sending him stumbling to the floor.

'Sorry for tasering you,' Marlowe said as he smacked down again, knocking the MP5 from Curtis's hand. 'But you were going to shoot me.'

Curtis went to shout again, but the sound didn't come as Marlowe rammed the end of the branch into his gut, knocking the wind from him.

'And I'm sorry for this,' Marlowe added as he swung hard at Curtis's shin with the branch, connecting hard.

Curtis screamed loudly, a piercing, high-pitched noise that sounded oddly feminine in the night, cut short as Marlowe hammed the end of the branch against the back of Curtis's head, stunning him, before grabbing his rifle and radio, sprinting deep into the woods.

'Come on!' he said, pulling Tessa further away, turning the radio on low as he listened. There was panicked chatter on the airwaves and Marlowe smiled.

'Take down the leader and the soldiers don't know what to do,' he said, veering her to the left. 'They don't have someone giving orders. They'll try to wake Curtis, make sure he's okay. He won't be able to walk-- I didn't break his shin, but it's bruised, and he'll be in pain for a bit--so they'll call for Shaw. They'll call in whoever the medic is. This'll add a few minutes before they even start after us again. They're scared of traps, and they've seen what happens when we take someone out, so they'll be more hesitant than ever. And that's all we need.'

They'd made a lot of space between them and their pursuers by now, and Marlowe slowed a little as they exited the woods and appeared beside a small barn in a clearing. It was a double-doored one, and a padlock was on the front. Marlowe didn't have a key this time, but a solid blow from the butt of the MP5 soon removed this problem, as they opened the doors to reveal a car hidden under a large painter's cloth.

'Whose is this?' Tessa asked, glancing back at the doors.

'It's mine,' Marlowe said, pulling off the cloth to reveal a Burgundy 2015 Jaguar XJ. 'I won it in a poker game. Don't ask. All you need to know is the keys are under the front passenger wheel. Open up the bonnet.'

Searching for the keys and finding them, Tessa opened the driver's side door, popping the bonnet for Marlowe to raise it and reconnect the battery. Closing the bonnet back down, he moved around to the back of the Jaguar and put the bags in the boot. He walked back to the door, looking out into the edge of the forest.

'There's a country lane three hundred yards down this,' he said. 'Far enough to not be in their radius yet. We get on that, we can get to the M11 in minutes. Then we'll get some distance, find a place to settle down, and wait for a few hours before we go to the Caxton Gibbet.'

Tessa had already walked over to the passenger side, getting in.

'How do you know they won't track this with their ANPR cameras?' she stopped, looking back.

'Because it's not in my name,' Marlowe turned the engine over, smiling as it purred into life. 'And it's not classed as stolen, so it won't raise any red flags. We should be good for a while, at least.'

And, with the doors open and the car slowly pulling out

of the barn, Marlowe gently pressed on the accelerator, taking the Jaguar out towards the country lane and the eventual M11 motorway, which would in time lead him to Caxton for his conversation with Trix. After that, he'd then find Raymond at Cambridge, hopefully with some answers.

He couldn't see any torches in the woods, and the radio chatter had stopped. Marlowe assumed the other MI5 agents had realised the radio was gone, and that he'd be listening, so they'd either changed channels or, more likely, given up on them altogether, which meant they'd stay more in a group.

Which again was good for Marlowe and Tessa, as they drove off towards the motorway.

———

THEY MADE IT TO THE M11 AND THE EPPING JUNCTION WITH NO issues, heading northwards, and merging with the early evening traffic. By eight pm they'd pulled off the motorway a good thirty miles north of where the house, barn and bunker had been, finding a small, out-of-the-way country pub to park at and spend the evening in relevant safety. As long as they kept to themselves, didn't make a scene and didn't pay by card, there was no way they could be found for the moment, as the agents hunting them didn't know what direction they took once they hit the road.

They would have found the barn by now, and the mud would have shown the tyre tracks, but even if they worked out the direction on the country lane, the amount of crossroads and side roads they'd passed made it an absolute haystack for MI5 to find this needle, let alone the fact they had no idea what car it even was.

They'd pressure the police into putting out Marlowe's

photo, but to do this would mean they were taking owner-
ship of the issue, and that meant explaining to Whitehall
and Westminster. And as much as current Prime Minister
Charles Baker was an insufferable jerk, he'd worked in the
past with Section D and with Tom Marlowe, so they couldn't
risk him taking a closer look, and realising it was all
bollocks.

*No, they wouldn't make this public. They'd keep it to them-
selves, hope for a CCTV pickup somewhere, at a moment when the
fugitives became careless.*

That was probably the biggest issue here; while Marlowe
or Tessa were at country pubs or villages, they were off the
grid while paying cash. However, once they hit Cambridge
the following day, the whole place was covered in security
cameras, and it would be harder to slip around unseen.

Of course, once he'd seen Raymond, Marlowe could get
out of the city as quickly as possible, but it still left him
exposed, and he didn't like that. Far better to find another
way. And the only one he could think of was to dump Tessa.

No, "dump" wasn't the right word. In the field, there'd
been times when he had to move alone, and leave an asset
behind, "dumping" them somewhere safe. Tessa hadn't asked
for this, and she sure as hell hadn't asked to be dragged by
Marlowe, but her dad was dead and she wanted answers.
And, unfortunately, she was just as much of a stubborn sod
as he was.

'So, what's the plan?' she asked, as if reading his thoughts.

'I'm going to finish my mixed grill and pint of craft ale,
and then we'll head towards Caxton Gibbet,' Marlowe replied
with a smile. 'We'll find somewhere to catch a couple of
hours' kip before dawn, and hopefully by morning proper,
we'll have a solid plan.'

Tessa nodded as she sipped at her own drink, watching the other patrons of the bar.

'We buried dad today,' she breathed. 'Literally earlier today. Like six hours or so ago. But it feels like a lifetime.'

She placed the glass down, staring at it.

'Is this how life is for you?' she spoke the question and Marlowe paused, his fork halfway to his mouth as she continued. 'Jumping from one life and death situation to the next?'

'Pretty much,' Marlowe admitted before eating the mouthful of meat on his fork.

'Was it the same for dad? When he was in the service?'

'I don't know,' Marlowe placed the cutlery down for a moment. 'We were different times, different worlds. He grew up amid Cold War paranoia. Real *Tinker, Tailor, Soldier, Spy* stuff. By the time I turned up, the enemy wasn't as subtle anymore, and the threats were bigger, more violent, and usually with an immediacy I don't think Marshall ever worried about, apart from maybe in his final years.'

He smiled.

'Did he ever tell you about the time we were sold out to nationalists by a fish and chips shop?'

Tessa almost spat her drink back into the glass.

'No,' she half-choked.

Picking up his knife and fork once more, and explaining through bites of his dinner, Marlowe told her.

9

GALLOWS HILL

It was still dark as the Jaguar pulled up in Caxton Gibbet Service Station.

After they'd finished their meals and drinks, Marlowe and Tessa had driven a few more miles north, pulling into a trucker lay-by on a country lane. There, they'd put the seats back, pulled their jackets around them and tried to catch a couple of hours' sleep.

It'd been difficult; the September night was cool, and the layers they had on, pretty much everything they'd taken with them when they escaped, weren't enough. Marlowe silently berated himself for not even having a car blanket in the boot, but he'd never expected to be on the run from his own people, so he felt it evened things out a little.

The noise hadn't helped either, with late night lorries and early morning delivery trucks passing through at speed, rocking the car when they whooshed past close to the lay-by. After a couple of hours of restless sleep, Marlowe had given up, lying back in the chair and staring at the roof of the car as he tried to work out a plan for the following day. At some point he must have dropped back off to sleep, as he woke around four in the morning as Tessa, who'd slept solidly through the night was nudging him awake. Wiping the sleep from his eyes, he'd reset his seat back up, started the car and, blasting some hot air into the cold cabin, they'd started their journey to the gibbet.

Once there, Marlowe deliberately drove towards the rear of the car park, but not *right* to the back, as although he didn't want to appear on any of the CCTV cameras around the service station and accompanying McDonalds, he *really* didn't want someone wondering what was going on at five in the morning at the back of their drive-in, and either coming to have a look, or worse, call the police on it.

Trix was waiting for them, standing with her hands in her pockets beside a familiar grey van, around two-thirds of the way across the car park when they arrived. Climbing out of the car, Marlowe smiled, glancing quickly around to make sure they weren't likely to be interrupted.

'Thanks for coming,' he said as, behind him, he heard Tessa leave the car as well. 'Did you come alone?'

'What do you think?' Trix replied, her voice showing both tiredness and irritation. 'Do you really believe I wanted MI5 to know I was coming to have a chat with you?'

'Yeah, fair point,' Marlowe conceded.

'Took your time anyway,' Trix was still irritated. 'I said to be here by dawn.'

'I am.' Marlowe pointed at the lightening grey sky. 'The sun isn't up.'

'I think you'll find my version of dawn and your version differ greatly,' Trix sniffed.

Marlowe accepted this, taking a step closer.

'So, what's the situation?'

'Well, MI5 are pissed at you for the fact you made one of their own look bad, and escaping from the middle of Thames House wasn't good optics,' Trix started. 'I mean, taking a guard's weapons and uniform didn't exactly help your case, and neither did kidnapping Miss Kirk here.'

Trix smiled at Tessa.

'I was a fan of your father,' she said. 'I only met him a couple of times, but he seemed to be a good man. Almost beat me in a drinking match once, so that goes a long way.'

'Thank you,' Tessa replied gratefully.

'There wasn't much I could do about the escape,' Marlowe cracked his neck, still stiff from the night in the car. 'It was that or be executed in a forest.'

'Yeah, that'll usually do it,' Trix nodded. 'So, there's this Section Chief called Harris in MI5, who's losing his mind about you.'

'We've met.'

'I don't know much about him, but it looks like he was brought in from MI6 about six months ago,' Trix continued. 'From what I can work out, he was working in the Berlin office for about four years, but then moved back after Brexit. He's very much a gung-ho nationalist, which means he's probably on the fast track to director level, you know, with the Conservative party loving that sort of thing.'

She shuddered.

'He also has this really intense gaze,' she added. 'Creepy as hell.'

Marlowe didn't reply to this, but he knew what Trix meant.

'He seems to have taken this personally, as he spent a chunk of yesterday trying to close Section D down,' Trix carried on. 'Luckily, we have bigger friends in Westminster than he does.'

'Sorry.'

Trix shook her head.

'You're in deep shit, Tom,' she said. 'I've been able to find some things, but I'm still in the dark. All I have is the post you sent me.'

'Was it enough?'

'I've taken down dictators with less,' Trix scoffed.

'What about the others?' Marlowe, amused at the bravado, continued.

'Well, Shaw, she's a standard agent, been working almost a decade for the service.' Trix was looking up as she spoke, and Marlowe knew this was her way of retrieving information locked away in her brain. 'Worked her way up from analyst at GCHQ, she worked with a Special Branch for a while on security details, and was head hunted by Harris a couple of years back. Curtis, meanwhile, is a bit of an enigma.'

'How come?'

'His record's pretty redacted,' Trix shrugged. 'Looks like he was undercover in a variety of places, so he was a field agent, but apart from that, all I can tell you is he returned to Thames House about four months back.'

'At Harris's request?'

'No, just the usual rotation.'

Marlowe considered this new information. Shaw and Harris had a connection, if he had personally requested her into the Service, but her record sounded long and spotless, while he'd been in Germany. At the same time, Curtis had effectively appeared out of nowhere. Which meant there was every chance that Harris or Curtis could be the double agent Raymond had warned about.

'Did you find anything about Rubicon?' it was Tessa who asked now.

Trix shook her head.

'To be honest, not a lot,' she admitted. 'I've looked around, checked about, found a few dark web places, and all I can see is the occasional conspiracy theory popping up. Something about a secret spreadsheet with agent names and contact numbers on it. Like a NOC list, but for traitors.'

Marlowe whistled softly at this. A *Non-Official Cover list*, or "NOC", pronounced "knock" list, was a list of operatives without official ties to the government for which they worked, who would often assume covert roles in organisations. It was basically a spy contacts list, showing their codenames and real names.

Something like this but filled with sleeper agents would be fatal in the wrong hands. Even if the phone numbers were decades out of date, they could still find the people. MI5 were good at that. Too good, even.

'Your friend Bridget seemed to be on the nose when she said people were dying, though,' Trix continued, bringing Marlowe back to the moment. 'I found one Russian agent who died—'

'Primakov?'

Trix nodded.

'I obviously found your father, Miss Kirk, but I also found a French agent from the Paris *Direction Générale de la Sécurité Extérieure,* who had a skiing accident in the Pyrenees four months ago, even though she apparently absolutely hated skiing. And a CIA agent Brad Haynes, who, the day after this happened, upped sticks and disappeared into thin air.'

'I heard Kirk mention Haynes once,' Marlowe mused. 'He tried to drown him on his boat, or something.'

Trix paused, as if annoyed she couldn't conclusively solve a problem.

'Well, whether he's been killed or taken, or whether he's clever enough to keep out of the way, I don't know, but digging deeper, all these people seem to have had a very close connection back in the day.'

'How do you mean?'

'I mean, all of them were based in Embassies around London in the eighties and early nineties, which means the chances were they passed information left, right, and centre daily. Proper *Spycatcher* stuff... if you've ever read the book.'

She leaned against the van, sighing, and Marlowe felt bad for bringing her into this. While they'd napped and eaten pub food, she'd likely worked into the early hours of the morning, trying to find all this out.

'So, is there something to this?' he enquired.

'Possibly,' Trix pushed herself away from the van, forcing herself back into alertness. 'There are a few places I found, which talked about sleeper agents being sneaked into various places; in the eighties, America had an enormous problem with sleeper agents from Russia, and there's every chance we still have some in the UK, so if there *was* something going on, then yes, this is a problem. And if some of these people have got into the security services and still love the motherland, then this could be a bigger problem than we expected.'

'How come?' Tessa asked, and Marlowe noticed for the first time that she was shaking. Possibly from the cold, but more likely from the situation. No matter where she grew up, she shouldn't have been involved in this.

'Because they could now be in their twenties, thirties,

even their fifties, depending on when they came over,' Trix explained. 'And if they're in positions of possible power, it's just in time for Putin to try to destroy the world again.'

Marlowe shuddered at the thought.

'So, let me see if I've got this right,' he said. 'We had Rubicon, whatever this was, and then Russia collapsed after Glasnost, and, as they weren't that much of a threat anymore, we just put this list of potentially dangerous people away in a box like the Ark of the Covenant in that *Indiana Jones* movie. Now Putin has started baring his teeth more there's a very strong chance he's maybe reactivating sleepers?'

'Or they've still been contacting Russia constantly over the years,' Tessa suggested. 'Dad was always convinced that although we started having good relations, there were still dodgy back channels going on.'

'Jesus,' Marlowe muttered. 'An army of soldiers who activate the moment they receive orders. People who've spent three decades of their lives in a simple normality, and then the next day they're betraying their so-called country.'

'Possibly.'

Marlowe considered this for a moment before continuing, turning back to Trix.

'I spoke to Raymond last night, and he said there was a very strong chance people in high levels of Box were sleepers.'

'Makes sense,' Tessa said. 'You reactivate sleepers, the first thing they need to do is remove obstructions. And retired or not, anyone who was involved in Rubicon, or knew about it even, is a threat.'

She stopped.

'*Was* a threat, even.' As she spoke, Tessa's eyes glazed a little, most likely as she started remembering her father.

Seeing this, Trix pulled Marlowe to the side, leaving Tessa in her own memories.

'Wintergreen's told us all to go dark,' she whispered. 'We're to go off grid until she contacts us. I'm driving to a holiday cottage in the Chiltern Hills. A friend owes me, and he owns one, so I'm sticking my head under a rock. You should do the same.'

'I can't,' Marlowe replied. 'I need to see this through. Uncovering a sleeper agent is the only way I can prove my innocence and get back in.'

'Are you insane?' Trix's voice rose, and she had to force it back down again. 'They'll never have you back, Tom. You're burned. They cut your air supply off. If you go ahead and expose a sleeper agent, you'll be revealing the biggest MI5 self-own since Kim Philby, Guy Burgess and the Cambridge Five became public knowledge back in the fifties.'

'I know that, but Bridget Summers—'

'Is dead,' Trix leant in. 'That was the other bit of news I had for you. She died last night. Gas explosion in her house in Kentish Town. Took out the house next door, too, but they were luckily out when it happened.'

She shuddered, her voice dropping to a whisper.

'They peeled her burned corpse off the walls, Tom.'

Marlowe looked away, remembering the cautious old lady in the church.

'Damn,' he hissed. 'Then at the least, I need to get Raymond out.'

'Do what you need to and get lost,' Trix replied. 'I mean that, Tom. Get as lost as you can, because if you don't know where you are, maybe they won't either. And don't stop, because the moment you stand still, they can catch up with you.'

Marlowe turned, pacing for a moment, glancing back at Tessa watching him from a distance, unable to hear the conversation but obviously aware that something was going on here.

'Take her with you,' he said as he walked back to Trix. 'To the cottage.'

'You want me to baby-sit someone?' Trix was genuinely astonished at the audacity of this. 'Are you utterly insane? I'm supposed to be going dark, not placing a flashing target over my head and going "here I am, boys". You're an idiot.'

'I'm serious, Trix,' Marlowe leant closer, pleading. 'I dragged her into this by kidnapping her, but I can't do what I do best with her around. I'll always be worrying. Taking her into danger that's not her problem.'

Trix went to reply, her face darkening, but then she slumped her shoulders and nodded.

'What do you need?' she asked.

'I have a burner phone,' Marlowe pulled out one of the new phones he'd picked up at the bunker. On the screen was the number for it. 'Write it down and—'

'Already got it,' Trix lowered the phone, smiling. 'What, you think you're the only one who learned how to memorise numbers? Please.'

She walked to the Jaguar now, popping the boot and looking inside.

'Weapons and go bag?' she tapped on the holdalls.

Marlowe nodded.

'What I could salvage before they came for us,' he replied. 'I'm pretty much tapped out now.'

'I have a few things you can borrow,' Trix opened the sliding door on the side of her van, pulling out a rucksack.

'It's not much, I couldn't take anything new because they were watching. But you should be able to use some of it.'

As she passed the rucksack to Marlowe, Tessa walked over, frowning.

'Am I being involved in the plan, or what?' she snapped.

'You're going with Trix and helping her,' Marlowe said, nodding at Trix in thanks as he spoke. 'I'm seeing Raymond alone.'

'The hell you are!' Tessa growled. 'No offence to your friend here, but I don't need to be mollycoddled—'

'I've been told by my section head to go dark before I'm murdered for my silence,' Trix interrupted sharply. 'I'm setting up a defensive position for when they attack. Do you seriously think you're having a holiday if you come with me?'

She jabbed a thumb over at Marlowe, now placing the rucksack in the boot of his car.

'He works alone. Always has. It's how he was trained. And every moment you're with him means he can't do his job properly. And considering his job right now is saving his arse, and yours, I might add, then how about you cut him some slack?'

Tessa, hearing this, stopped and nodded reluctantly.

'Two days, Marlowe,' she replied. 'Then I'm coming to find you.'

Marlowe smiled.

'If I haven't finished this in two days, I'm probably dead,' he replied, walking over to the car. 'Stay safe, the pair of you.'

Getting into the Jaguar, Marlowe watched as Tessa reluctantly joined Trix in the grey van, before it started up and drove off into the dawn morning.

Leaning back in his seat Marlowe shut his eyes for a moment.

He was alone, but he wasn't friendless, and that was a start. However, Bridget Summers was dead, Marshall Kirk was dead, and the list of people who could help was diminishing quickly.

First, he needed to find Raymond Sykes and see what he knew.

Then, he needed to find Brad Haynes, formerly of the CIA, and one-time boat enthusiast. Because disappearing after a mysterious death either meant he'd been part of the assassination, or he thought he was next.

As he started his own engine and headed out onto the dual carriageway, Marlowe hoped the hell it was the latter.

10

GRASSHOPPER

MARLOWE HADN'T BEEN TO CAMBRIDGE FOR A FEW YEARS, BUT he knew the Corpus Clock. Created in the late 2000s, it was a large sculptural clock on the outside of the Taylor Library at Corpus Christi College, looking out over King's College and its surrounding Parade.

Marlowe knew of it because of Corpus Christi College. In the 1580s, his ancestor (well, a distant one on the family tree at least) Christopher Marlowe had gone there, and in 2012, Marlowe had taken a road trip to visit his rooms. After all, having the surname allowed you through several doors around here.

The clock itself was divisive, with half the people of Cambridge applauding it, while the other half were less complimentary, giving it the nickname *The Grasshopper Clock*, because of the large, metal grasshopper that sat upon the five-foot wide, twenty-four-carat gold-plated, stainless-steel disc.

It was a good place to stage a meeting, too. On the corner of King's Parade and Bene't Street, it was across the road from the Cambridge Chop House, a suitable location to sit and scope the clock while waiting for someone's arrival. And it was here, at eleven in the morning, Marlowe had taken a spot by the window, a red T-shirt now worn under a jacket.

It was the only red item Marlowe could find at short notice and had been bought from a gift shop near where he'd parked, the words "Cambridge University" surrounding the University's coat of arms, a cross of ermine fur between four gold lions walking, each with one fore-leg raised. On the centre of the cross was a closed book, its spine horizontal, with clasps and decoration, the clasps pointing downward.

It was quite nice for a T-shirt, but it gave no hiding space for weaponry, so Marlowe had pulled on a leather bomber jacket – left in his car's boot a few months earlier – and filled it with anything he could think of.

He'd also spent the morning prepping his escape if needed; checking the back wall of nearby St Bene't's Church, the college itself and The Eagle pub opposite. If he was chased, open public places weren't the best locations to be trapped in, and Marlowe favoured narrow alleys and buildings instead; places with multiple exits and staircases to escape into, each one causing his followers to doubt whether they were even going in the right direction, second-guessing themselves and slowing down in the process.

The biggest worry Marlowe had right now, though, was whether spending the last hour checking around to see if anyone was watching had actually *drawn* the attention of anyone, you know, *watching*. But there was nothing he could do except to see them before they saw him.

He was aware this was paranoia, but there were many situations in flux here. Raymond could have turned on him, or Bridget could have given him up before she died; even Trix and Tessa could have been caught in the last couple of hours, and ...

No, let's not go wild with the imagination, eh?

Marlowe looked at his watch and saw it was exactly twelve. And, in front of the Corpus Clock, an elderly man now stood, looking nervous as he glanced around. He had a tweed jacket with a leather messenger bag hanging from the shoulder, likely filled with books or papers, short, balding white hair, and glasses on. Everything about him screamed *academic*, and Marlowe placed his paper down, rising from his seat.

He didn't leave yet, though, as something didn't feel right. He guessed that Raymond Sykes would be nervous of the meeting, but he kept staring up the road, past the Chop House.

Perhaps he was looking for Marlowe?

No.

Marlowe had an itch at the base of his neck, and he knew never to discount this. The clock was a choke point, with three exits and entrances, a T-junction where anyone could come along from any of the directions. Raymond was still watching up the road, and tapped at his ear, jerking as if shocked.

Marlowe knew why; Raymond had an earpiece in, probably a microphone too. Tapping the ear was probably nerves, and someone had just shouted at him to *stop bloody playing with it*. Which was good in one respect, as it meant Raymond wasn't a trained MI5 field agent, but it was bad, as it likely meant there were half a dozen of actual trained agents in the surrounding area.

Marlowe considered running, classing the meeting as a bust and moving on, but Raymond Sykes was currently the only person in the world who could help him, and Marlowe needed to carry on, no matter the risk.

New plan, then.

Opening the door of the shop, Marlowe walked straight towards Raymond, passing him and then spinning around, jabbing his P226 into Raymond's spine with one hand as he yanked out the earpiece with the other, ripping it from the pack on Raymond's belt and tossing it aside as he already started moving the elderly man towards Bene't's Church.

'You selling me out, Raymond?' he hissed. 'That's not nice.'

'You killed Bridget!' Raymond was almost purple with indignant rage. 'You killed Marshall!'

'I didn't do either of these things,' Marlowe said, also removing the battery pack and discarding it in a black, metal rubbish bin as he led Raymond into the churchyard, walking him to the side of the church. He stopped at a wrought-iron gate along the side, which he opened quickly, led Raymond through and then closed behind him, locking a length of chain around the bars with a padlock, securing them, before attaching a small, wireless camera to the gate with a length of cable.

'Is it Harris?' he snapped. 'Out there?'

'That's the name they said.'

'They?'

'The agents that wired me up.'

'Just the earpiece and battery?'

Raymond nodded. 'Look, Tom, if you're going to kill me, I'd appreciate it if you did it quickly,' he said, his voice trembling as they walked to the back wall of the graveyard, turning left. They travelled along a valley between two walls; to the left of them was the church itself, while to the right was the imposing outer wall of Corpus Christi College.

'I'm not going to kill you,' Marlowe insisted, placing away his P226 as proof. 'I need you to tell me why the others *were* killed. I don't know what you've been told, but I'm on the run for murders I didn't commit, and as you said on the phone, there could be sleeper agents in MI5 working against me.'

He turned Raymond to face him now, as they stood before another wrought-iron gate, leading out onto Free School Lane.

'What if the *sleeper* was the one telling you I'd sold people out?' he suggested.

Raymond stared in shock at Marlowe, and in the distance they could hear annoyed shouting.

'Looks like they found the lock,' Marlowe smiled, listening. 'But that sounds Russian, maybe Ukrainian.'

He walked to the gate, peering left along the road. If the agents realised the gate by the side of the church was barred, they'd look to flank, which meant retracing their steps and following around the church itself, eventually coming down this street. Wasting no time, he opened the gate slightly, leaving it ajar.

His phone beeped, and, pulling Raymond to the side of the arch, he quickly opened an old, oak door, which led into a dark corridor within the college. He'd come by earlier and picked the lock, but there was every chance someone could have locked the door in the intervening time.

Lucky for them, nobody had.

'In,' he urged Raymond through the door, closing and bolting it behind him. If anyone made it to the arch, they'd find a locked door and a gate that was half open. With luck, they'd follow it and carry on past the college. And even if they didn't, he'd have enough time to speak to Raymond.

'Recognise this guy?' he asked, showing the image on his phone's screen. As the gate to the side of the church had been pulled at, a small device attached to the wireless camera had forced it to take a photo, instantly emailing it to him.

The image was of an angry blond man, built like a wrestler, in full combats, staring down at the padlock.

'I saw him when they put my wire on,' Raymond nodded. 'He's MI5?'

'Yes.'

'No, he's not, Raymond, that's Stepan Chechik,' Marlowe pushed Raymond along a corridor now, oak-panelled walls on either side. 'He was part of the SBU, the Ukrainian Secret Service, until they outed him as a Russian spy and he escaped to Sevastopol, in Crimea during the 2014 annexation by Russia.'

'That can't be!' Raymond protested. 'I wouldn't have—'

'I can pretty much guarantee he doesn't work for MI5,' Marlowe interrupted, pausing Raymond as he picked a lock on a large mahogany door. 'And hopefully, this proves I'm actually on your side, because I'm the one here who *didn't* bring Russians to an MI5 meet up.'

The door now opened, Marlowe pushed Raymond out into the sun again, this time crossing a small grass courtyard, heading north towards a main door, placed in the middle of the opposite frontage.

'I gave them my files,' Raymond said in slow realisation. 'Everything I'd learned over the years. Not all of them, of course, as Brad has some—'

'Brad Haynes?' Marlowe looked around as they walked across the green; to anyone looking, Raymond gave the impression of an eccentric university professor walking to chambers with his younger friend. Marlowe couldn't have blended in better if he wanted, but he knew he was still in danger. 'I thought he'd gone off the grid.'

'He did,' Raymond nodded. 'Somewhere in Maldon, in Essex.'

'How do you know this?'

'He provided a message,' Raymond explained. 'Sent a porcelain clown to us. Creepy little bugger with a red and white striped shirt under a blue jacket, and with "MALDON" written in sharpie on the bottom. God knows what it means, though, and the circus isn't in town.'

'Us?'

'Me and Bridget—' Raymond tripped on the edge of the grass, but kept his balance, pausing as he gathered his breath.

'Look, Tom, I'm sorry,' he said. 'I was taken by MI5 half an hour after you called. Not because of your call, but because I'd been trying to contact Bridget. I didn't know she was dead back then.'

They walked to the door, Marlowe opening it as they continued on.

'Harris spoke to me. Said that you'd gone rogue, kidnapped Tessa, and were holding her against her will. He showed me your psyche report.'

Marlowe felt a chill run down his spine.

'Doctor Fenchurch's one?'

Raymond nodded.

'She stated you'd gone off reservation, done a few off-books missions, your loyalty was under suspicion, and you were burned from active missions,' he said, pausing in a hall-way. 'It was real, wasn't it?'

'Yes and no,' Marlowe hurried Raymond along. Somewhere outside and in the distance, he could hear men shouting. 'I did jobs off the book, but as favours. All of Section D did them. And when I was injured, MI5 had a pop at me. Harris wants to close us down.'

'I don't think there's a *want* about it, dear boy,' Raymond said sadly. 'I think that's now past tense.'

'If I can show him to be a mole, or a sleeper agent, or even show him to be controlled by one, then I might have a chance to bring things back around and clear my name.' By now Marlowe was out of the building once more, pulling Raymond across the college's New Court, heading towards the chapel. 'I just need to know what you – what *Marshall* knew.'

Raymond sighed, pausing.

'It was Primakov who first saw the pattern,' he explained, his hands waving around as he spoke. 'Some small-level, forgotten and retired analysts in Kiev, ones that the Brits had turned back in the seventies, were found dead in their apartment. Carbon monoxide poisoning, they said. And then he learns Amélie Blanchet died on a ski slope, and that Brad disappeared the next day with some old key in his hands, one that Primakov reckoned he gave Blanchet. So, now the poor bugger thinks this is CIA wiping out anyone connected to Rubicon, maybe even trying to take the list, and so he speaks to Marshall and Bridget.'

'Primakov was Russian,' Marlowe frowned. 'How would he know about a UK-based NOC list?'

'He didn't know what it was, exactly,' Raymond shrugged. 'But he also didn't want to be part of the Soviet Union. He happily waited out his pension during the nineties, but when Putin returned to the old ways, he ran. So, I'd say he probably helped create the bloody thing. May even have been an asset for MI5 or the CIA, that'd be a laugh.'

Raymond's smile faded.

'Anyway, they'd stayed in contact over the years, and Primakov went to them looking for help. He'd hacked his way into some system, God knows how, but he saw that not only were people connected to Rubicon being murdered but also the Op itself was being erased from existence. He downloaded some background info from the source, though.'

'The list?'

Raymond shook his head.

'That's analogue,' he said. 'Likely on a tape drive on a machine, air-gapped from the internet. All we have, and all he had, were calculated guesses.'

'Any idea where this analogue machine is?'

Raymond shook his head.

'We had thoughts, ideas, and Marshall took some notes for safekeeping, but it would likely have been taken when he was ...' Raymond mimed a gunshot to the head. 'I know there's something in a black site in Canary Wharf somewhere, because that's where Primakov gained his data in the first place, but that's it.'

He snapped his fingers.

'One more thing,' he said. 'When he looked through the files, there was a date that kept popping up. September the fifth.'

'That's in three days,' Marlowe frowned. 'Do we know what it means?'

Raymond shook his head.

'Whomever is wiping details and killing spies, they want to make sure nobody's paying attention to this,' he leant in, his voice tight and nervous. 'And I've only found one event that matches that date. The arrival of the US President, to speak to Parliament as they return from recess. And guess who's running point on security?'

'Section Chief Harris.' Marlowe knew without a doubt he was correct but was distracted by a commotion at the gates to the college across the green. Behind the wrought-iron, the agents, led by Stepan Chechik, had arrived, and were waving weapons at the security guards.

'I'm really sorry about this,' Marlowe said as he pulled out his SIG P226. 'I need you to call for help. I'm then going to leave a mark, but it'll mean they think I took you under duress. Okay?'

Raymond looked at the gate, the guards backing off as the agents unlocked it, and set his jaw as he realised the obvious outcomes available.

'Help me!' he screamed out. 'He has a gun! He's insane!'

'Sorry,' Marlowe repeated as he slammed the hilt into Raymond's face, effectively pistol-whipping him to the floor. Then, turning and sprinting for the closest door, he ducked as bullets *spanged* around him. With luck, the agents, whoever they were, would class Raymond as a victim; the chances were they'd watched Marlowe walk up to him, tear off the earpiece and press a gun into Raymond's back, so the story had been set from the very beginning. As long as Raymond played the part of the asset almost killed, they'd leave him.

Hopefully.

Marlowe wasn't worried at this point about Raymond, though. Right now, he was more worried about himself. He'd been through the college earlier and had worked out three different escape routes if need be, but only one of them was close, and it was the worst of the three.

The door in the south-east corner led into a portico that carried on out into the Bursar's Garden. Unlike the courts, this was more chaotic, with the foliage left to grow wild, and with what looked to be an archaeology dig in the middle, the trench covered with a tarpaulin. Marlowe kept running in a south-easterly direction, passing the tarpaulin and heading towards a selection of trees against a back wall, a small garage built to the side.

Behind him, he could hear movement and he spun, dropping low and raising his SIG P226 as Chechik and his men entered the gardens, slowing as they realised the options for hiding, and the options for attacking from cover Marlowe had. Waving his arm silently, Chechik motioned for the others to spread out, to fan across both sides of the area.

We can't have that now, Marlowe thought to himself, lowering himself down.

He held his gun in two hands now for stability and, peeking out from the side of the garage, aimed it carefully at the tarpaulin. It might have looked like an archaeological dig, but half an hour earlier he'd placed a couple of things he found within the garden into the trench and now, firing once, aiming at the flash of red under the tarpaulin, he sent a round directly into the first of the three large propane bottles he'd hidden there.

The explosion was larger and more violent than he'd expected; Marlowe hadn't been sure if the bottles had even had propane in them still, and this was why he'd overloaded the trench. As it was, it seemed that all three were at least half, if not fully fuelled, and the spark of the bullet igniting the first bottle triggered a chain reaction that detonated all three in quick succession, a blast of hot air knocking Marlowe backwards, and sending Chechik's men to the ground, screaming with rage as pieces of torn, burning tarpaulin and plastic rained down on them.

Back on his feet, Marlowe ran to the back wall and the ladder he'd placed against it earlier that day. The reason he hadn't liked this option was the noise. By now, half a dozen car alarms were going off, the force of the blast rocking them enough to set off the sensors, and the police would be here soon.

Explosions did that.

Taking the rungs two at a time, Marlowe climbed the wall. It was a high one, a good fifteen to twenty feet to the top, and Marlowe shimmied up as fast as he could, swinging his leg over and sitting astride the wall, pulling the ladder up with him and dropping it to the street below. Now shimmying over and dropping the last few feet as well, Marlowe landed awkwardly in Botolph Lane, a narrow, one-lane alley that ran along the side of the college. There wasn't anything else on the other side that could assist his pursuers in climbing the wall quickly, and so Marlowe turned from the wall, running westwards down Pembroke Street, using the random side roads of Cambridge to hide his exit.

He knew a couple of streets away his car was parked in a doctor's space, the requisite card on his dashboard.

And, once in it, he could get away from Cambridge before they even realised he was gone.

11

CLOSE PURSUIT

MARLOWE ONLY STOPPED FOR BREATH THE MOMENT HE reached his Jaguar, opening the door and pulling out a bottle of water, drinking it down as he pulled off the jacket and T-shirt, tossing the latter onto the back seat of the car and pulling the white shirt back on, using the water to slick his hair back. He couldn't do much with his face, but he could at least bypass the second glance. A pair of sunglasses finished the look, And Marlowe pulled the holdalls and Trix's ruck-sack gift from the boot and placed them onto the front seat for quick access if needed, before climbing into the Jaguar, starting it up and moving out into the street.

His plan, however, wasn't to leave. That's what would be expected of him. Instead, he took a long, leisurely route around St Andrews Street, heading northwards as he aimed for the north end of the King's Parade. This had been where he'd seen Raymond looking towards as he stood beside the Corpus Clock, and this was where Marlowe had a pretty good bet that Stepan Chechik would likely be. He just hoped that he'd arrive in time to see the aftermath of the botched capture.

As it was, he timed it perfectly. As he pulled up beside St Mary's Church, he saw two vans and an SUV parked across the road at the top of Trinity Street. Ducking down in his seat and pulling a Zeiss 8x22 out of the rucksack, Marlowe aimed the monocular scope at the vans. Through it, he could see a visibly angry Stepan Chechik talking on the phone and waving his hands. Marlowe checked his watch; it was twelve thirty-four. Noting this down, Marlowe returned to watching. Chechik was finished with the call, and was shouting at two agents, both men who Marlowe had seen with him during the chase, both with wicked burns on their faces. They stood on either side of an angry Raymond Sykes, obviously playing up his injury, holding something white, maybe a cloth or ice pack, to his temple.

Marlowe felt bad for striking the analyst, but watching the conversation, it might have just saved the man's life.

Eventually, Chechik tired of the conversation, nodded and waved to the driver of one van. The back doors opened, and Raymond and the two agents beside him climbed into it.

Marlowe hoped they were giving him a lift home, but until he could find out for sure, he'd have to assume Raymond was under arrest and being taken somewhere isolated. Marlowe jotted down the number plate of the van as it drove off, but he didn't make a move yet.

He was waiting for Chechik.

As Marlowe saw it, they'd assume he was gone again and, as seen before, Marlowe was very good at going off the grid. They'd have to regroup, to flush him out again. It was probably why Raymond was still under guard. But until then, they'd stand down. And with a little luck, this meant they'd relax their guard a little.

Chechik climbed into the SUV, and Marlowe was grateful to see he did this alone. And, as Chechik pulled out into the street, Marlowe started the Jaguar and slowly followed him out of Cambridge.

It looked to all intents and purposes like Chechik was travelling back to London, because after a few country roads, he started heading southwards on the M11. Marlowe had kept three vehicles behind Chechik at all times; he'd been trained well in following operatives in cars, but he knew very well that Chechik would have been taught the same lessons and was probably watching his rear-view mirror constantly.

Or was he?

After a mission, especially one that failed, there was a heightened sense of adrenaline coursing through your body which, without a triumphant closure to release it in some kind of celebration, simply hung around, sapping your energy. The "come down", as people liked to call it. Your reactions would slow, you'd get tired. There was every chance Chechik wasn't even looking in his rear-view mirror, for to do that meant looking back at Cambridge, and failure. He might be heading to his destination and likely debrief as quickly as he could, just to get things over and done with.

So, if he really wanted to know what was going on, Marlowe needed to up the ante a little.

The M11 wasn't that busy this time in the afternoon, and so Marlowe spent the next five miles moving closer, to the point he was now directly behind Chechik, if at a small distance. He needed to have his own debrief with the Ukrainian, and they could do this in one of two ways. Either with Marlowe as the interrogator, and Chechik as his prisoner. Or, more likely and more uncomfortable for Marlowe, the other way around.

He was trying to work out how to make himself more obvious to Chechik when, approaching a junction just north of Duxworth, Chechik veered his SUV at the last minute into the slow lane, taking the junction. And Marlowe, following, had to do the same. A more common two-car tail could have let the first car continue on as the second, yet unnoticed car continued on, but alone, he had no option. So, he too steered sharply to the left, mounting the zig-zag rumble strips and crossing onto the slip road at the very last moment.

Marlowe chuckled as he did so. *If this didn't reveal him, then nothing would.*

Chechik indicated left and, after a moment, Marlowe followed, knowing this was the point of no return. There was absolutely no way Chechik wouldn't see him. Now he had to work out how to play the meeting.

As it was, Chechik arranged that for him. Dropping back, Marlowe noticed the SUV also slowing, as if making sure he hadn't lost his tail after all this. And, when the dual carriageway they were driving along showed the sign for a service station, the SUV took the slip road towards it, Marlowe following.

It wasn't so much as a service station as more of a fuel stop with a car park, with a separate diner at the far end. These had been the mainstays of the roads during Marlowe's youth, and he had many memories as a child of stopping at "Happy Eater" restaurants, in places like this diner was now. In fact, from the looks of the building, there was every chance this had been a "Happy Eater" once, no matter what the signage said.

Marlowe pulled into the car park, making sure he was a

couple of cars behind Chechik. He wanted the Ukrainian to think he was in the driving seat here; it was the only way this could work.

Unzipping the holdall beside him, Marlowe started searching through it, looking for something he could use, as, through his windscreen, he saw Chechik leave the SUV and walk to the diner. There wasn't a great deal he could use within, and even a second pass through the other holdall and quick scan of Trix's bag didn't give him anything he could really use in a situation like this that didn't end in a more *terminal* option, but there was a discarded EpiPen at the bottom of the first bag, a throwback to a girlfriend he'd dated a couple of years earlier, who'd been allergic to nuts.

It was old, only just within the expiration date, but it could be used.

Marlowe pulled a roll of duct tape out, wrapping some around the handle, hiding the pen's true identity. Then, taking one of the several vicious-looking blades Trix had left him, he exited the Jaguar carefully, making sure he wasn't seen from the window.

Working his way quietly to the scrubland beside his car, he looked for what he wanted, pulling a leather glove on and grabbing a handful of weeds and nettles, using them quickly before tossing them away and pulling off the glove. Then, carefully, he walked to Chechik's SUV, placing a small black device against the lock and clicking a button on it. The device flashed and after a moment linked to the vehicle's central locking, opening the car. Moving to the back passenger door, Marlowe opened it, placing some items on the back seat, making sure as he did so, shifting around the inside of the car and reaching to the dashboard that Chechik, in the diner couldn't see anything more than the fact his back door had been opened.

In fact, he *needed* Chechik to see that.

Then, the task finished, Marlowe re-locked the SUV and walked over to the diner.

Chechik was waiting for him as he entered, quietly waving to the seat opposite, no surprised expression on his face. He had one hand under the counter, and Marlowe knew this was for the gun he had aimed at his target.

'You are a terrible tail,' he said, his accent audible.

'Only when I want to be seen,' Marlowe smiled. 'You didn't see me watching you when you bundled Sykes off.'

He sat down on the chair opposite Chechik.

'I hope you don't hurt him too bad,' he continued to smile. 'He genuinely thought I'd killed people. Imagine that.'

He leant back on the plastic chair.

'And imagine this; the great Stepan Chechik, working with MI5,' he said, watching Chechik. 'Or are you working with someone within MI5, someone who might have the same *affiliations* as you?'

Chechik chuckled.

'Fisherman,' he stated. 'I am not biting fish for you.'

'Then what are you doing?' Marlowe asked. 'Because you're sure as hell not ordering food right now.'

'You could have killed me,' Chechik replied calmly. 'You could have waited until we were beside the gas and ignited them. We would be dead. You would be free.'

'I'd still be hunted, and I wouldn't know why it was you there, hunting me,' Marlowe shrugged. 'Look, Stepan. I only know you by reputation, but I know you're not a fan of us. You escaped the moment you could in 2014. So, you being here is off. You working for Harris is off.'

Marlowe watched Chechik's face as he said *Harris*. There was no response. Either Chechik didn't know the name, or he was a hell of a poker player.

'I was called in by mutual friend,' Chechik said slowly, shaking his head at the waitress as she moved to approach, waving her off for the moment. 'My men were also called in.'

'So not MI5?' Marlowe clicked his tongue against the top of his mouth. 'Russia want me dead too?'

'Why would they want that?'

'Because I'm asking about Rubicon,' Marlowe suggested. 'I want to speak to your superior. The *mutual friend* you talk of.'

At this, Chechik sighed, pulling out a couple of flex-cuff cable ties, placing them on the table.

'I thought you would be more fun,' he said. 'But you are just like French woman. Put these on or I will shoot you. And where I aim would not be fun.'

Marlowe nodded, pulling on the cable ties. He'd expected – no, he'd *hoped* for these, as much as he'd hoped Chechik had been watching him.

'French woman,' he said. 'You mean Amélie Blanchet.'

'I never asked name,' Chechik held his weapon to his side as he rose, motioning for Marlowe to do the same. 'Come, it is time for you to meet God.'

'God's your boss?'

'You will not be meeting boss,' Chechik sighed. 'Your insistence has changed the plans, so I will fulfil contract.'

Contract. So, this was a freelance job.

'Fine, God it is,' Marlowe smiled as he walked ahead, nodding one last time to the waitress, making sure she didn't notice his cuffed wrists as she walked past.

Marlowe had led Chechik to his SUV, the gun against his spine never wavering. Walking to the back door, he went to open it, but Chechik pushed him back.

'You think I am stupid?' he snapped. 'I watch you enter back seat. You think I let you in there?'

With the gun trained on Marlowe, Chechik opened the door and reached in, pulling out the blade Marlowe had placed in earlier.

'You were to use this on me, yes?' Chechik tutted. 'I thought you were professional. You drive. I sit behind.'

Getting into the driver's seat, Marlowe raised his secured hands.

'I can't drive like this,' he said.

'It is automatic,' Chechik chuckled. 'You need no hands.'

Marlowe fumbled with the seat controls, adjusting his seat, before knocking the steering wheel, catching the horn.

'Idiot!' Chechik said, the gun now passing between seats as he aimed it at Marlowe's head. 'You must—'

He didn't finish, as Marlowe, his hands now free of the cable, grabbed the arm, slamming it down with one hand as he stabbed the back of Chechik's forearm with the EpiPen. As Chechik's hand instantly spasmed, Marlowe spun around, gun now in his hand.

'You should have paid more attention,' he said, holding up a duct-taped second blade with his free hand. 'I may have got in the back, but I also played around in the front. You know, I thought killing someone as legendary as you would be harder.'

'What did you stab me with?' clutching his arm, and staring at the pinprick, Chechik was wide-eyed as the surrounding area began bubbling with small white boils, with a redness spreading.

'Ah, shit, it wasn't supposed to work that fast,' Marlowe said, waving the duct-taped EpiPen before tossing it aside. 'You've just been injected with our latest toy, a painful little bastard comprising five ccs of methyl-chloride benzamide, and a shit-ton of vicious little additions. You'll be dead in an hour if you don't get the antidote.'

It was all lies, made up on the spot; all Chechik had been injected with was epinephrine, which would speed up his heart rate temporarily and give him a numb, tingling feeling. Add to this a pen top wiped in stinging nettles, and the immediate, allergenic rash the contact would cause gave a really nice visual to the scene.

'It's our little thank you for Novichok,' Marlowe continued with a smile. 'After an hour, you lose control of your bodily functions, but your sense of smell doesn't go until well after you shit yourself.'

He held up two white circular tablets. They were nothing more than paracetamol, but Chechik didn't know that.

'But these will kill off the bulk of the symptoms,' he said. 'Not all of them, you'll still have an awful couple of weeks, but at least you'll be alive.'

He leant closer now, watching the sweating Ukrainian.

'So, tell me about the US President, and why you're killing anyone connected with Rubicon.'

Chechik shook his head.

'You are too late,' he whispered. 'It's already in play.'

'Harris?'

Chechik reached for the tablets.

'Please,' he said. 'I cannot die.'

'I'd also like you to live, Stepan,' Marlowe replied. 'I need you to prove my innocence. Where did you take Raymond?'

'A safe house in London. One of your secret little archives.'

'Why not Thames House?'

'Because your MI5 does not know. Nobody visits the physical location, as it's all online now.'

'So, someone is off books,' Marlowe nodded. 'Who's helping you kill old spies?'

Something changed in Chechik's expression, and suddenly he set his jaw, his teeth tight together.

'I will not betray the motherland,' he hissed through gritted teeth. 'I will not betray her.'

'No offence, Stepan, but I think she's been betraying you ever since Glasnost,' Marlowe joked, but stopped as he saw Chechik's eyes bulge. 'What are you—'

The foam flecked Chechik's lips as his eyes rolled back into his head, and his mouth opened, his tongue slack, and covered in pieces of shattered tooth enamel.

Oh shit, Marlowe realised. *He has a suicide capsule.*

'Chechik!' he leant over, shaking the Ukrainian. 'You bloody fool! I wasn't going to kill you—'

But it was too late. Chechik's eyes were glassy and vacant, the life having already left his body, slumping to the side in the SUV.

'Dammit,' Marlowe hissed, climbing out of the driver's seat and opening the back door, he reached in, pulling Chechik back up. A quick pulse check proved the worst. Stepan Chechik had killed himself rather than betray Russia.

Looking around the car park, Marlowe realised he needed to leave, and fast. Luckily, any spook who found the body would understand what had happened, and the average passer-by would assume from the spittle that he'd had some kind of seizure. However, anyone who then went into the diner and looked at the security footage would see him meeting Marlowe.

Sighing, and closing the door to the SUV, Marlowe pulled on his sunglasses, pulled out a barely passable fake ID for Special Branch, and went to have a chat with whoever ran the diner's cameras.

12

THE CLEANER

IT TOOK LITTLE TO MAKE SURE THE CAMERAS WERE DELETED. Marlowe had re-entered the diner and walked to the booth, looking for a "forgotten phone", and with no obvious device there, he'd politely and quietly asked to speak to the manager, showing his Special Branch ID. He explained how the device had the contact numbers of several Whitehall names, and he *had* to find it, or it was his career on the line.

Of course, the incredibly understanding manager, on discussing this loss had mentioned the security footage, and Marlowe had gratefully asked to check through it with him. And, while checking the footage from a CCTV camera in the diner's corner, they watched as Chechik and Marlowe met, spoke and left, Marlowe walking with his hands clasped, and with no phone in sight. After a couple of passes, Marlowe then "realised" he must have left the phone in the car, and with a fair amount of embarrassment, thanked everyone for their help, and left to return to it.

About thirty seconds after he left, a vicious little malware daemon file set up while he was there blue-toothed into the computer and deleted all footage from that day. Marlowe hoped nothing serious – well, apart from a dead body in the car park – happened that day, as all evidence would have been removed with this one hack.

It meant that Marlowe was back to being invisible, but any spook who arrived and then spoke to the diner's manager would work out quickly it was Marlowe who'd been deleting footage of a meeting with a pro-Russia, Ukrainian mercenary who was now not taking their calls, and a glance into the parking lot would find the reason. So, quickly and quietly, Marlowe set to work on fixing this issue as well.

Trix had left a small box of latex gloves in her rucksack, probably a throwback to her police days, but Marlowe accepted the gift, pulling on a pair of gloves to disguise his fingerprints as he quickly went through Chechik's pockets, pulling out his gun and his wallet. There was a small USB drive in his jeans, and Marlowe wondered whether this was the information Raymond had passed to Harris.

Opening the phone, Marlowe used Chechik's thumbprint to open the device, scrolling through it. However, this was not the time to start deep diving, so Marlowe closed the door, sliding into the driver's seat, and started the SUV. It was a Range Rover, a button to start, and very similar to the ones seen driving high-up members of the Cabinet around London. It was automatic and Marlowe easily pulled out into the road, leaving the service station and following the road for another half a mile. He turned into a small country lane and then left into another lane – not more than a track, in fact – a farm road that didn't look like it was used that much. Checking he wasn't being followed, Marlowe parked up outside a field's gate, making sure the Range Rover was off the road.

Alone, and with a far less chance of being interrupted than when he was in the car park, Marlowe took an antiseptic wipe from a pack in the glove compartment and wiped the dashboard and steering wheel down. He may have been wearing gloves now, but when he was playing the captive he wasn't, and there was every chance he rubbed up against something.

Now it was time to set the scene. He could have checked through Chechik's things first but, if he was interrupted, he'd have to explain why the dead man was spread out across the back seat. At least if Chechik's body was in the correct position, Marlowe could bluff it out; he was walking and had come across the car, or more likely, he could get to cover and not be there at all as the body was found.

With this in mind, Marlowe repositioned Chechik's body back into the driver's seat with a small amount of effort. A dead body was harder to move than a normal person and the term "dead weight" was right on the nose. It wasn't impossible, however, and apart from one stumble, where Marlowe almost dropped Chechik's body onto the floor, he slid him into the driver's seat with a sigh of relief, buckling the seatbelt as he did so.

This was mainly to confuse any investigators as his plan was to let the police, or any forensics examiners, see the cyanide tooth and make their own decisions. Perhaps Chechik accidentally bit down while driving? Perhaps he thought he was going to be executed and took the simple way out? The options were endless and, luckily for Marlowe, all aimed at the people following him. He knew Chechik would be found. The chances were whomever hired him had a tracker on the car, and when he didn't answer the phone or turn up, they'd track the SUV down and find it eventually – and the body within.

But the logic was sound. Spooks would work out Marlowe was connected.

Police, however, wouldn't.

If someone saw Chechik and the car later that day, perhaps a nosey farmer, or a dog walker passing by, they'd find a man dead with no other evidence around. Even MI5 would surmise Chechik met their killer here, whether or not it was Marlowe. And a suicide capsule meant suicide. The people in suits would more likely spend time working out why Stepan Chechik drove to a deserted track and killed himself. Eventually they'd realise he met burned spy Tom Marlowe, but then that was also in a diner down the road. This could still be plausibly denied as an assassination.

Looking around the lane, Marlowe reckoned there'd be an hour or two before people found the body. Add time for the spooks to arrive, and then for them to retrace his steps back to the diner and the unfortunate CCTV issue which screamed "spooks were here", and by then they'd know Marlowe was involved, but also that Marlowe was gone.

It wasn't a lot of time, but it was enough to do *something*.

As expected, Chechik was holding the bare essentials: a gun, a phone, a wallet with around a grand in twenty-pound notes, and an ID for SCO19, the armed unit of the police, stating Chechik as Peter Bradley, a *Counter Terrorist Specialist Firearms Officer,* or CTSFO, ranked as a Sergeant.

Marlowe grinned at the audacity of this while quietly applauding. CTSFO teams in the UK were often on standby, ready to respond to terrorist or major crime incidents in London, but also at the national level. This was the ID badge equivalent of the US's National Security Agency badge, where a simple wave and the mention of "terrorism" and "national security" were enough to open all doors. In addition, if his team were also identified as CTSFOs, then running around Cambridge with HK MP5s and 147s wasn't likely to gain a second glance.

But to have these was a high-level forgery. Few people dared to do this, as the principal people who'd be checking these would be equally positioned, genuine officers. With guns.

Or, these were real.

Marlowe didn't want to consider this option, that someone in Whitehall had rubber-stamped these IDs for Chechik and his men, knowing what they intended to do … but it was still an option.

Marlowe considered replacing the ID, as to find it missing would alert whoever was looking for him, but that horse had bolted, and there was every chance Marlowe could use this somehow.

Leaning back against the driver's door frame, Marlowe considered his next steps.

First, he had to clear his name, but this was an end goal more than the next thing to do.

Second, Brad Haynes was a logical step, as finding the CIA agent could fill in some blanks. Bridget Summers had worried he'd killed Amélie Blanchet and run, but Chechik's confession to her murder meant Brad was likely looking after himself here. Which meant he'd be difficult to find, but likely to help once he realised it was in his best interests. And if he had a key, he could have taken this from Amélie, or been given it, before she died. Maybe this key was the reason Chechik had killed her, even.

Third, he needed to find *Rubicon*.

This was going to be the hardest of the tasks, even harder than clearing his name; the list would be deep within a server, and until he could gain the list, he wouldn't be able to accurately work out who the moles in the security services were. It could be Curtis, Harris, both or even neither. Luckily for Marlowe, the server wouldn't have any remote access opportunities, but also wouldn't be in Central London. It was easier to find an out-of-the-way server farm, somewhere with a redundant backup protocol, where he could slip in and locate the file on site, than it was to return to Thames House.

Of course, this probably wasn't a one-man job, either. Which meant he needed a team. Trix would be a good start, but he'd sent her off into the Chiltern Hills about eight hours earlier. Tessa was with her, too, so bringing Trix in would involve a two-for-one deal, and Tessa's safety would be his concern once more.

But it was something that could wait. For all he knew, Marlowe could speak to Haynes later that day and suddenly have the CIA at his beck and call, although that wasn't as likely.

And walking into a server farm with the CIA would *definitely* kill his chances with Her Majesty's Secret Service.

And then there was four, his immediate next move.

He picked up Chechik's phone once more, now having the time to use the thumb to open it, taking his time to slowly check the device. He'd connected it to one of his burn phones and cloned it as he left the car park, but this wasn't like the movies. Anything encrypted would be harder to crack without the onboard app the phone would have, and even the best equipment often missed things. It was far better to use the item itself when possible.

He didn't expect much; spies weren't that stupid when it came to things like this, but a last number that called, or even a last number *he* called, even without contact details, was something Marlowe could use. Flicking through the phone, Marlowe saw there was also a map app, a phone sat-nav which had a couple of addresses marked down within the "recent journeys" tab. Checking his own phone, he saw one was the location he'd seen Chechik meet with the others back in Cambridge, but the most recent was unknown and, more importantly, still active.

This had been the sat-nav journey he'd been taking when Marlowe interrupted.

Checking the location against his own maps app, Marlowe saw Chechik had been heading back to London, and in particular, to a warehouse in Canary Wharf. Not the sparkly, chrome and glass business side, but the area to the south, before you reached Millwall Docks. It was still an area filled with building works and construction projects, but the docks and wharfs along there were isolated enough for a safe-house, or some kind of warehouse space.

He remembered a line Chechik had said. *A safe house in London. One of your secret little archives.* Could this also be where the backup could be found?

'I know there's something in a black site in Canary Wharf somewhere, because that's where Primakov gained his data in the first place.'

Raymond's statement also returned to the forefront of his thoughts. If the secret archive was where Raymond had been taken, there was a chance to kill two birds with one stone, but until he knew more, there was no point removing the academic from the jaws of whatever Government beast currently had him. In fact, if they thought Marlowe might be after him, wherever he was right now could actually be the safest place for Raymond Sykes.

No, this was a journey for later. For now, there was another task to perform. Because the number that Chechik had called while in Cambridge – an outgoing number for a mobile phone – was still in the memory.

So, Marlowe dialled it.

After a few rings, however, it went to voicemail. There was no message, just the incredibly familiar, computerised *"the person at x isn't available to take your call right now. Please leave a message after—"* answerphone message, which had been halted near the end as Marlowe disconnected the call and immediately redialled.

He'd received the same message the second time, but on the third call, the phone answered, and an irritated voice said, 'What?'

Marlowe paused.

He knew the voice.

'Hello Curtis,' he said. 'Small world.'

'Marlowe?' the voice of Curtis seemed surprised. 'How did you get this number?'

'I gained it from Stepan Chechik,' Marlowe replied calmly. 'In fact, I'm using his phone right now. You know Stepan, I'm sure.'

There was a pause on the line, and Marlowe wondered if this was while Curtis tried to gain a tracer on the line.

'Is he with you?' Curtis asked, his voice sounding more curious than angry. Probably trying to work out if his pet enforcer was playing for the other team now.

Marlowe looked at the dead Chechik beside him.

'He is, but he's busy,' he replied. 'I can get him to send a message.'

'Look, I don't know what your plan here is—' Curtis started, but Marlowe cut him off.

'My plan is discovering and then stopping your plan,' he replied, checking his watch.

Ten seconds before they could lock onto his position.

'I'll save you time and hassle,' Marlowe continued. 'I'm duplicating the SIM and the phone, so even if you do find me, I'll be long gone. But whatever you're doing, I'm onto you. And I won't let you continue.'

'I have no earthly clue what you're talking about,' Curtis said. 'This is—'

At this point the phone screeched in Marlowe's ear and, pulling it back, Marlowe saw the screen corrupting as lines of data slid up and down it.

He was being hacked.

As much as he wanted to find out more, this was worse than he could hope for; someone was trying to take hold of Chechik's phone, which, if successful, could even open the phone's camera, or Bluetooth connect to anything nearby.

Quickly jumping away from the car, Marlowe threw the phone onto a slab of concrete at the base of a gatepost, using a hastily grabbed rock to slam down hard on the screen, the high-pitched data scream instantly ceasing.

Looking around, Marlowe forced himself to relax. There was no way MI5 or Curtis could have done this remotely, so fast, but that wasn't the concern here. There was every chance the cyber-attack was aimed purely to set off some kind of detonator inside the phone. It would have been a small, shaped charge, not enough to do a ton of damage around him, but enough to blow his head off, if he'd been staring at it when it went off, or if he'd been holding it against his ear.

Marlowe shuddered, remembering that his decided way to disable the potential bomb was to hit it very hard with a rock. He could have been killed.

But why would Chechik have such a phone? Surely a willing member of a team wouldn't need to be controlled. Or was this a bomb given to an unsuspecting Stepan Chechik, ready to be used when the mission was over?

The one thing Marlowe knew for sure was this wasn't MI5 tech. He'd seen ideas, plans for things like this, designed by large military contractors and corporations, but the Bills to gain approval for such devices had never gone through.

That said, there was a good chance both the Russians and the Americans had items like this.

Time to speak to the American, then, Marlowe thought to himself as he checked Chechik one more time, sitting him up in the seat, and closing the door.

Looking around, Marlowe decided the fields would be his best option for travelling back to the service station. It was a mile by road, but only a quarter the distance as the crow flew. Luckily it'd been a hot month and the ground was dry, so he wouldn't have to worry about muddy shoes giving him away.

Wiping down the handle of the car, Marlowe pulled off his latex gloves, folding them up and placing them into his pocket until he could find a better place to dispose of them, then left the scene, walking across the fields back to the service station.

13

LONG TERM PARKING

THE BIGGEST WORRY MARLOWE NOW HAD WAS THE JAGUAR, AS it would have been seen on too many cameras in Cambridge, and the diner manager would have seen it in the car park, so even if there was no footage, an eyewitness account could link the car from Cambridge with the meeting with Chechik, and therefore the potential assassination.

Marlowe was loath to lose the car, however, as he'd become attached to it. So, rather than leave it to be stolen – his usual plan of choice and a common option for spies that not only gave plausible deniability where and when the car was taken but added a nice cocktail of DNA and fingerprints into the mix – he placed it into a long-term car park, somewhere he could hold it in reserve for when he cleared his name.

Because, if he *didn't* clear his name, the chances were he wouldn't need to worry about the car, anyway.

So, after booking a spot by phone, he'd driven to Maldon, in Essex via Stansted Airport. There were a few options for long-term parking here, and several of them were nothing more than a car park created in a field, around five or ten miles away, where a regular shuttle would take you the fifteen-minute drive to the airport while the car, and many others, was effectively left in the middle of nowhere.

This was fine for Marlowe. Although far from the airport, they still had security, and he knew his car would be all right. And he could drive up to one he knew, explain he'd forgotten to book and pay for the entire month he was "travelling" by cash, using the recently gained twenties from Stepan Chechik to fund the venture. This done, he then caught the shuttle bus to Stansted Airport departures, his two holdalls and rucksack weighing him down, before making his way quickly and quietly to arrivals with the help of a luggage trolley.

He knew very well that here, under the intense security, there was a very strong chance he'd be spotted, but usually the cameras were aimed at the check-in desks, immigration and security, rather than the main doors, so it was worth the gamble. It was also because of this, and the lack of metal detectors at the entrance, that Marlowe felt more comfortable bringing a holdall filled with heavy weapons into the departures lounge, rather than leaving them elsewhere. After all, why would someone come to the airport just to leave again?

Five minutes after he arrived, he was already on a shuttle bus to the aptly named "car rental village", and five minutes after that he was at a hire car desk, using a fake identity he'd held aside for when things really hit the fan. It comprised passport and credit cards, and for at least a week the cards would show as real, until they didn't. And again, by then, Marlowe hoped to have everything sorted because if he didn't, the concern of a hire car company wanting a couple of hundred pounds he owed would be incredibly low on his list of concerns.

'Would you like a saloon or an SUV?' the man behind the counter, blue waistcoat over white shirt asked. 'We have a deal on Peugeots and Skodas today. Or, if you want to upgrade, we can give you a full electric vehicle?'

'Basic model,' Marlowe smiled. 'Just need enough boot space for my luggage.'

The counter assistant looked over the side, peering down at the holdalls.

'I think the Peugeot 3008,' he smiled, already tapping the keyboard. 'Now, Mister Davison, will you be requiring car breakdown?'

Marlowe had fulfilled everything needed on the paperwork and was eventually given the keys to a grey Peugeot, out in the parking bays beside the office.

'Hey, do you have a spare terminal I could use?' Marlowe passed a twenty across as he spoke. 'My phone's not connecting since I landed, and I need to send an email. It's browser based, so all I need is Chrome, or Safari, something like that.'

'Sure, we can sort something out,' the counter assistant smiled as he took the money, making it disappear like a magician. 'There's a computer at the end for business and gold-level members.'

'Thank you,' Marlowe smiled, grabbing the keys and walking over to the computer. It faced away from the counters, so there was a modicum of privacy, but Marlowe was still visible to anyone watching.

Quietly and with minimal fuss, Marlowe took out the USB drive he'd taken from Chechik and inserted it into a USB slot on the monitor.

On the screen, a file appeared.

ЮЛИУС ЦАЕСАР

Marlowe stared at the file for a long moment. His Russian wasn't great, and he was pretty convinced that this Cyrillic wasn't one of the more commonly used words or phrases. Copying them, he opened a browser and pasted it, with "translate" written next to it, into the search field. A spilt second later, the result appeared.

JULIUS CAESAR

Marlowe smiled at this, remembering his conversation with Bridget.

'Apart from the fact it was the river Caesar crossed, hence the phrase "crossing the Rubicon", as in reaching the point of no return.'

Clicking on the file icon, Marlowe opened up a new file box, expecting to see dozens of files within it. Instead, there was only one.

It was a photo, named *caesar.jpg,* and when clicked on, opened up a familiar-looking marble bust of a Roman general in armour and a cloak. His hair was short, he looked to be in his mid-forties, and he wore a breastplate with a screaming Medusa, and a Roman Eagle upon it.

The statue was well known and had been made in the sixteenth century by artist Andrea Ferrucci. Marlowe had even seen it in person, at the Metropolitan Museum of Art in New York City once.

Why Stepan Chechik had a picture of it on a drive, Marlowe had no idea. But he knew someone who would.

Opening up a games forum page on a long-forgotten message board, he typed a message.

Trix hadn't brought Tessa straight to her friend's cottage after they'd left Marlowe at the service station; instead, Trix had driven north, visiting another friend in a lockup in Northampton. There, she'd picked up a black luggage case, the sort of hard case that rock bands carried their equipment in, and loaded it into the back of the van without another word. They'd kept silent for the bulk of this, primarily as both women were tired, and the weight of the previous day was resting heavily on their shoulders.

In fact, it wasn't until the evening when Trix and Tessa finally arrived at a small cottage nestled into the Chiltern Hills. They'd spent the day casually travelling, making sure they weren't being followed while Trix met with people to sort out whatever plans she had next before going to ground, and their only breaks had been in service stations, where they ate unhealthy foods while Trix watched her small electronic tablet, shaking her head and groaning now and then.

She'd almost exploded with anger around lunchtime and had explained to Tessa this was because the Cambridge police chatter had gone crazy after they had reported armed men and explosions all over the centre of the academic quarter.

Marlowe.

Tessa had realised at this point Trix had been killing time until the meeting had finished, possibly because she didn't trust Marlowe not to be caught and give away their destination. But, after she saw he'd made a successful escape, they'd made their way slowly towards the safe house and now, finally there and secure, Trix having spent the last two hours in the garden placing motion detectors and suchlike into the lawn, the two women could finally relax.

'I'm guessing the garden isn't a place to pop out for a smoke right now?' Tessa asked, staring out of the kitchen window. 'You know, when the lights and sirens go off?'

'I haven't set lights and sirens,' Trix replied while rummaging around in a bag she'd brought into the cottage. 'It's claymores and C4 explosive. Sirens don't scare someone off as much as a leg blown off does.'

'Nice,' Tessa said as Trix pulled a Glock and a full magazine out of her bag.

'You know how to use one of these?' Trix asked, tossing gun and magazine across. Tessa caught both in one hand and, in quick, calm motions, slid the magazine home and racked the slide.

'Good,' Trix smiled, taking it from Tessa and walking over to the front door. There, she placed it to the side, easy to grab if anyone knocked. 'I trust you'll not miss if you need to use it.'

'Dad taught me at a very early age,' Tessa smiled. 'Mum, too.'

'I saw your dad's record,' Trix said as she pulled out another claymore device from her bag with an abandon that made Tessa twitch. 'To fall in love with an enemy agent ... that's cool. Romantic and possibly insane, but real cool. Must have been tough, though.'

'You have no idea,' Tessa took a scope, looking through it. 'Dad couldn't visit mum's family, as they thought she was a traitor. So, mum and me, we'd have to go alone. And when we got back, we'd be debriefed by MI5, just in case we'd sold dad out.'

'Harsh.'

'I didn't understand at first, but I got there in the end,' Tessa shrugged. 'It's why I moved into law rather than following them.'

'Wanted to be a solicitor?'

'Wanted to work in politics.' Tessa was walking over to the kitchen area now, opening the fridge. 'I thought I could do well in Parliament. Maybe as an MP.'

'Couldn't do worse than the current lot,' Trix replied. 'So, how did you and Marlowe meet?'

'Through Dad.' Tessa pulled out a bottle of cheap beer, using a bottle opener to pop the top off. 'They worked together about ten years ago and they stayed in touch; he became a friend. Probably one of the few people who'd put up with dad's bullshit stories.'

'You didn't believe them?'

'I believed them, to a point,' Tessa smiled sadly. 'Dad had a bit of a hero complex. He had to be the saviour in every mission, and unfortunately I knew the truth about a couple of them. Anyway, weirdly, Tom was close to my age, and we had the same tastes in music, films, all that. We got on well. And that terrified dad.'

'Didn't want you to fall for him?' Trix was unspooling network cable wires onto the floor.

'I think it was more a case of seeing too much of himself in Tom,' Tessa said. 'And he blamed himself for mum's death, thought I'd have the same problems.'

'Your mum died?' Trix looked up. 'I skipped that part.'

'Committed suicide when I was a teenager.' Tessa stared at the bottle as she talked, as if visualising the scene in the amber liquid. 'Drove off a cliff like *Thelma and Louise*. Left a note, saying she couldn't do it anymore. As I said, she was hated by her family, and distrusted by dad's. It was a tough life.'

Tessa placed the bottle on the table, walking back to the window, staring out of it.

'How about you? How did you and Tom meet?'

'Work,' Trix grinned. 'I was in trouble for screwing up a police enquiry my then bosses wanted closed. I was expecting jail, but Wintergreen liked how I worked. I got stuck in Section D and Marlowe was the first person who didn't treat me like a screwup.'

'And why are you helping him?'

Trix stopped working, straightening up.

'Because he didn't treat me like a screwup,' she repeated. 'I owe him.'

There was a beep and a flash of light, and the hastily erected network station Trix had been building burst into life.

'At last,' she said, forgetting Tessa and the conversation, as she sat at the dining table the computer array had been created on. 'We can now see what we have here.'

'Can you get in?' Tessa asked, avoiding the window now as if worried someone was outside, walking to the front door and staring through the peephole. 'Into Rubicon?'

'Possibly. Looks like Marlowe left me a note on a forum.' Trix read the scraped data, writing numbers on a Post-It note. 'It's a sat-nav set of coordinates. And it looks like there's more in the message, as he says on the forum he's got a fake file that's possibly a NOC list of agents in the UK. We need to download it, open it up and—'

She stopped as the muzzle of the Glock, previously on the table beside the front door, now rested against the back of her head.

'I'd really appreciate it if you didn't do that,' Tessa icily stated, nudging the muzzle against Trix's head. 'I'd appreciate it a lot.'

———

FINDING A SPY WHEN THEY DON'T WANT TO BE FOUND IS ALMOST impossible if the spy is experienced in tradecraft. Finding a spy when they *want* someone to find them, and when they've sent some kind of message, is a different matter.

Marlowe had nothing on Brad, apart from the fact Marshall Kirk had once fought with him on a boat a good twenty years earlier; about what, or even whether they were on the same side at the time, Marlowe didn't have a clue.

What he had, however, was information on the town of Maldon. It was once a significant Saxon port, and even in modern times, Hythe Quay was the mooring location of several Thames sailing barges, the last cargo vessels in the world still operating under sail, and now used mainly for leisure.

Marlowe knew this because Marshall had once taken him to the *Maldon Mud Race*, a charity event where entrants competed to complete a five-hundred-metre dash, in thick mud, over the bed of the River Blackwater. Marlowe had lost a bet and had to run it dressed like a seagull. He'd hated every second, but he'd seen the barges, the Quay, and the docks as they started and finished during the race. He'd also, after changing out of that bloody mud-splattered torture corset, sat in the sun with Marshall and downed a few pints, laughing about the seagull costume, the race, and the whole insane day.

And because of this, he had a solid idea of where Brad

was hiding. Because Marshall Kirk had explained he knew of this event because of a friend. A friend who knew the area well.

It was evening by the time Marlowe pulled up at Hythe Quay; the car parking, usually *one hour only,* had passed by this time of day, and he could find a spot to pull up in with little hassle. And, on the side of the road, with the Thames barges to his left, floating on the River Chelmer's tide, Marlowe stared at the possible location of Brad Haynes.

Grabbing his SIG P226 and hiding it inside his jacket, Marlowe climbed out of the Peugeot, locking the door and walking across to the pub that faced him. His stomach was growling, and the only real food he'd eaten in the last twenty-four hours was a half-eaten sausage and a mixed grill the previous night, so he hoped that if Brad Haynes was here, and he classed Marlowe as a threat, he'd at least wait until he'd eaten before trying to kill him.

The *Jolly Sailor* was actually beside a bed-and-breakfast named *Fish on the Quay,* and Marlowe watched the door to the building as he walked up the road, wondering whether Brad was one of the several men that sat outside, eating their dinner in the warm evening air.

The bar itself was recently redecorated, the walls painted green, while the floors were almost bare wood. A large clock, easily two, maybe three feet in size, was on one wall behind a table, and to its side was a further section of the pub, running into the back with two-person tables lining the far wall.

In front of him, it looked as if the surface of the bar was made from buffed-copper sheeting, and the old timbers had been tidied up and painted black. It was a nice-looking pub, but it felt claustrophobic.

It was a tight space, and this wouldn't help Marlowe if

there was a problem. And he knew the same would have gone through Brad Haynes's head.

But this had to be the place.

Marlowe ordered a cod and chips for the outside dining area and, with a pint of IPA in his hand, walked out into the evening, sitting with his back to the building so he could see all angles. He was in a chokehold, and his car would be behind anyone attacking, which blocked off using anything from his holdalls within it, but he felt safe for the moment. And, when the waitress walked over with his dinner, some cutlery and some condiments, he chanced his luck.

'I'm looking for a friend of mine,' he said before she left. 'Old guy, late sixties, retired, American. Goes by Brad.'

'Sorry,' the waitress pursed her lips as she tried to recall anyone with that description. 'I could ask at the bar, but …'

'Please,' Marlowe smiled. 'He was a friend of my dad. And my dad recently passed.'

'Your dad's name?'

'Marshall.'

The waitress walked off, and Marlowe smiled. When someone mentioned a family member passing, it wasn't usual to ask for the name. Usually, you'd give a small message of condolence, or, more likely, the morbid curiosity section of your brain would pop out and ask how the member died.

For the waitress to ask this could have been normal to her, but far more likely, she'd been coached, or primed. If Marlowe had been the other way around, he'd have booked in with the story of a man caught up in some love triangle, perhaps with a celebrity, a story that hadn't broken yet, but he knew the press were coming. He'd pass some twenty-pound notes around, explaining if anyone came looking for him, they would likely be press hunting a scoop, and he'd appreciate a heads up. The staff would think they were helping an underdog, and he'd have an instant team of assets assisting him.

Brad Haynes had probably done the same, and all Marlowe could do was set the bait and cast the line. With luck, the waitress would contact Brad somehow, and inform him a stranger had arrived asking around. This gave Brad time to watch Marlowe and see who he was. The bed-and-breakfast had rooms that looked out onto the plaza he now sat on, and there was every chance that Brad Haynes had a sniper rifle aimed at Marlowe's chest right now.

Marlowe fought the urge to check for red dots, and instead grabbed his knife and fork, tucking into his dinner with wild abandon. It was good, plentiful, and bloody well needed. And, while he did so, he took a moment to consider his options once more.

Curtis had sounded both tired and irritated when he'd spoken to Marlowe, but there was something off with the tone. He was probably still in pain from when Marlowe had sucker punched him and slammed his shin with the rifle, but that wasn't the thing that bothered Marlowe. It was something different, more subtle somehow. Marlowe knew he wouldn't get it right now, but it was something he needed to consider.

'I understand you're looking for Brad,' an American voice spoke.

With a mouth full of food, Marlowe looked up at a middle-aged man in good condition, a bomber jacket zipped up, and a hand in a pocket, likely holding a gun, trained on the stranger eating dinner. The waitress had done what Marlowe had wanted, and now the man he hunted was in front of him, although likely still considering him a threat.

As Marlowe swallowed his food, patting his mouth with a napkin, he considered Brad Haynes. His hair was still thick, his body stocky but not fat, his jawline strong. He looked like the poster boy for the US Army's *grandfather*, and Marlowe guessed Brad was likely recruited from the military into the CIA.

'I am,' Marlowe said as Brad Haynes slid into the chair opposite. 'I'm Tom Marlowe. I—'

'Are you enjoying the food?' Brad interrupted.

'Yeah, it's okay,' Marlowe frowned. He hadn't expected the question, and for a split second it threw him as Brad leant closer.

'Good,' he said, his body now hiding the gun under the table, aimed at Marlowe, audibly cocking the hammer back as he did so. 'Because you have five seconds to explain how you found me before it becomes your *last meal on Earth*.'

14

SEAGULLS

TRIX RAISED HER HANDS FROM THE KEYBOARD, STILL FACING away from Tessa as she spoke.

'You're on the list, aren't you?' she said matter-of-factly. 'Let me guess, mummy was a double agent?'

'This isn't easy for me,' Tessa stepped back, gun still aimed at Trix. 'Turn around.'

'Looks pretty bloody easy to me,' Trix smiled. 'You working with Harris? Is he a spy too?'

Tessa didn't speak, staring at the hacker with what looked to be disdain, or some kind or inner conflict.

'Did your mum actually love your dad?' Trix continued.

'Not at first,' Tessa admitted. 'I mean, there was some attraction, but she wasn't intending to run off with a guy from the other side. But the Russians saw this as an opportunity. They opened doors, gave an opportunity for dad to escape the Gulag, and mum was there waiting for him. He took her home, and then about a week later the Berlin Wall fell.'

'That must have been inconvenient.'

'To an extent.' Tessa looked down at the gun. 'She stayed

an operative, a double agent, right up to her death. And, when I was a child, around nine, ten years old, she'd bring me to see her family. And by that, I mean—'

'She took you to junior spy training,' Trix chuckled. 'Fighting and guns and all that James Bond shit. Christ, I'd have hated to have you next to me at normal school every time you came back.'

'It wasn't me,' Tessa pleaded. 'I wanted a normal life. However, dad was a spy, mum was a double agent, so I was damned before I even started. But as a teenager, I rebelled. Told mum I wouldn't do it anymore and, if she pushed me, I'd tell dad. Tell everyone.'

'And let me guess, this was when she drove off a cliff?'

'Or was driven, yeah,' Tessa nodded. 'I couldn't tell dad. It would have killed him. And the guilt I felt ... I knew it wasn't my ultimatum that killed her. It was her belief she'd failed with me.'

'That's a lot to throw onto a teenager.'

'It was,' Tessa nodded. 'But at the same time, I knew with mum gone, I'd be left alone. And I was.'

'Until now, with Rubicon being dug up again.' Trix looked back to the screen, where her system had now fully logged on. 'So did they come to you, or did you—'

'Nobody came to anyone,' Tessa spat. 'I've not been contacted by agents on either side. But I know I'm on Rubicon, because I remember my mum and dad fighting about it years ago. Which means the moment it becomes public I'll be ostracised by everyone.'

'Is this what all the gun waving's about?' Trix moved closer now, hands still raised. 'Your own bloody First World problems?'

'How many people do you think get to be in the Government, maybe even a Minister, when they're a double agent? Or a sleeper agent, no matter whether it was done to them without their consent?' Tessa was pacing now, gun tapping at her forehead as she tried to focus. 'Last week, I'm a shoo-in for the next safe Conservative seat. And then dad dies, Tom's on the run and I realised it was all the bloody past, hitting me again!'

'Marlowe saved your life,' Trix said coldly. 'Unless Harris or his friends were bringing you in for the old school reunion.'

'I don't want any part of that world,' Tessa muttered. 'But I'm damned now. It'll be out I'm a sleeper, and I'll be stuffed into a black site. Or, worse, traded to Moscow.'

'You don't want to go there?'

'Christ, no!' Tessa shook her head. 'I hated the bloody place.'

She spun, the gun still raised, facing Trix once more.

'We could delete Rubicon,' she suggested, wide-eyed. 'We could blow it up, stop everyone looking at it.'

'If Marlowe has the list, then others have it. And that means the whole thing's already out there,' Trix said sadly. 'No matter what happens, you're out there on it.'

'I ... I know,' Tessa lowered the gun, sighing. 'I'm screwed, no matter what. Sorry, I didn't mean to use the gun. I'm—'

'Desperate,' Trix took the gun from Tessa now. 'I get it. And now you don't want my silence, you want my help.'

'I wouldn't have shot you,' Tessa said sullenly. 'I just ... I needed to feel in control.'

'And how did that go for you?'

'Badly,' Tessa forced a smile.

Matching the smile, Trix raised the Glock 17 until it was level with Tessa's face – and pulled the trigger.

Click.

Tessa stared in horror at the gun.

'But I loaded it,' she whispered.

'No, you loaded *this* one,' Trix replied, reaching behind, pulling out an identical gun. 'I wanted to test—'

She didn't get further as Tessa grabbed the gun, twisting, and taking hold of it. Trix had never been a field agent, and this reversal was easy for someone like Tessa, trained for this from childhood.

'I'm sorry. I guessed you'd test me,' Tessa replied, backing towards the door, 'I guessed you'd leave a dummy when you placed it by the door, but I couldn't be sure until just then.'

'Yeah, well, I never claimed to be a field agent,' Trix shrugged.

'You didn't trust me,' Tessa realised now. 'This was all a test.'

'Tessa, your mum was an ex-Stasi agent,' Trix dumped the empty gun onto a table. 'There was a pretty good chance it wasn't going to be a happy ending.'

'Then why carry on with the charade?' Tessa was at the door now.

'Because of this,' Trix said, pointing at the gun on the table. 'You didn't fire it, even if you have another aimed at me. I wanted to see where your loyalties lay.'

'With myself, it seems.' Tessa opened the door, nodding. 'Don't worry about your mines and tripwires, I worked out where everything was.'

'So, what are you going to do?' Trix was already walking over to the fridge and pulling her own bottle of beer out. 'Being out only for yourself means you're not buying into anyone else's ideology. You're not leaping up and taking one for the home team, are you?'

'No,' Tessa smiled. 'I'm my own team, and right now I need to do something to stop this coming out. And no offence, but hanging around here, waiting to be outed, isn't helping me.'

And with that, Tessa disappeared through the door, and into the night.

Trix listened in case any of her defences exploded; they didn't. Taking a long draught, she sighed.

'I'm likely burned by now; Marlowe's definitely burned, and politically? You're burned too,' she muttered, aware that Tessa was no longer around to hear, but needing to speak aloud, regardless. Now alone, Trix closed the front door and then returned to her computer. As she started reading through the messages she'd been sent, however, she paused, scanning across the desk. The Post-It note she'd written the sat-nav coordinates on was gone.

'Oh, that was sneaky,' she muttered. 'I hope you know what you're doing.'

There was another beep, as the second part of Marlowe's message appeared, and Trix opened up an image of a bust of Julius Caesar.

Either that or he's got a really strange fetish going on.

The image was probably a cyphered message, and, opening up an app on her computer, she dragged the jpg over to a *drag-and-drop* section. The moment the image settled lines of code appeared on the other side.

Steganography.

Trix had specialised in this, so the idea wasn't new to her as she started scanning the new lines of code. The terminating byte for a jpg file was "FF D9" in hex, so using a hex viewer, she knew she could find out where the image finished. These bytes were sometimes hard to find in a sea of numbers though, so looking at the dump of the hex also helped her find hidden *txt* or *zip* files.

This now done, Trix opened up a Linux app, converting the location of the hidden zip file from hex to decimal, which not only changed the location but allowed her to gain the block size and write it to an output file—

On her screen, a zip file appeared.

'Now we have hidden spy treasure,' Trix spoke to the empty room, leaning closer to the screen as she extracted it. 'Let's see where it leads us.'

The file opened, and Trix's screen brightened as she stared at it.

'Oh shit,' she whispered, pulling out a battered old phone. Staring long and hard at one number, she eventually hit "call".

'It's me,' she said, after the call was answered. 'Yeah, I know I'm not supposed to call, but you're gonna want to hear this.'

RELAXING IN THE EVENING AIR, BRAD LEANT BACK ON HIS CHAIR, hand in pocket.

'I bet you thought you were pretty smart, didn't you?' he asked as, with his other hand he pulled a foldable cloth carrier bag out, tossing it across the table. 'Weapons in there. Quietly and then place to the side. These are nice people. I've known them for years and I don't really want to get blood anywhere.'

Defiantly eating a last chip before opening the bag, Marlowe slipped the SIG P266 and a small folding-blade into the bag, tossing it onto the ground.

'This is how you treat friends?' he muttered.

'I don't know you. So, you ain't my friend,' Brad replied. 'How'd you find me?'

'The porcelain doll,' Marlowe said, already returning to the food, speaking calmly, as if he wasn't in the least worried about the man with the gun facing him. Also, it meant he could hold a knife, as much as a cutlery knife could be called as such, and it reassured him a little. 'The one you sent to Bridget Summers.'

'I didn't send no doll to Bridget,' Brad hissed. 'Goodbye—'

'Wait!' Marlowe half shouted. 'That makes no sense. I saw Raymond Sykes today. He said you sent them a porcelain doll of a clown. Red and white top, blue jacket, and with "Maldon" written on the bottom.'

'I sent Marshall Kirk that,' Brad's voice was emotionless. 'The day after Blanchet was killed in Paris—'

'By Stepan Chechik.'

Brad's eyes widened in surprise.

'You know that for a fact?'

'He told me in person. Before he died.'

'You kill him?'

Marlowe tapped his tooth with the fork.

'Cyanide.'

'Convenient.'

'Look,' Marlowe continued. 'Maybe Marshall passed it to Bridget, and she didn't mention this to Raymond. I don't know, and I can't ask her because she's dead.'

'I heard.' Brad's posture seemed to relax a little. 'So how does a doll bring you here?'

'Blue jacket,' Marlowe replied. 'The clown had one. It's a nickname for a junior enlisted sailor in the United States Navy. It's also used in *The Bluejacket's Manual*, the basic handbook for United States Navy personnel, given to all enlistees. I'm guessing you're US Navy-born-and-bred, as I was told you like to sail.'

'Navy Seal before the CIA,' Brad nodded. 'And the clown?'

'A clown is happy. And this, the Jolly Sailor, using your Americanism, is a *happy bluejacket*.' Marlowe looked around. 'Marshall brought me here once, after a stupid mud race. Mentioned he knew an American, I put two and two—'

'Goddamn!' Brad half rose, his face breaking into a smile. 'You're the bird guy! The flappy-winged idiot who tried the mud run!'

Marlowe ignored the jibe and forced himself to smile.

'Guilty,' he replied. 'Can I finish dinner without dying now?'

Brad brought both hands onto the table.

'Yeah, I reckon so,' he said. 'So, you're really Tom Marlowe? He spoke about you.'

'The bird guy. You said.'

Brad smiled.

'He said you were clever; could think your way out of anything. A good friend to have. I'm sorry you learned about his last case the way you did.'

'So, why don't you tell me what I'm missing?' Marlowe now found his appetite had gone and pushed the plate away. Ignoring this, Brad leant over the table, stealing a chip from the plate.

'MI5's out to clean house,' he said. 'CIA, Russia too. They're all wetting their panties over Rubicon.'

'Why now?'

'Because it shouldn't exist,' Brad replied, munching on a second stolen chip. 'When the wall fell, it was decided that, in the spirit of Perestroika or whatever it was called, that we shred the lists. Russia would stop their sleeper operations, and anyone who wished to stay could do so, and we'd all do the same. Double agents were allowed back home, all that happy-clappy shit.'

'I'm guessing it didn't go as planned?'

'Of course, it didn't,' Brad spat, reaching for Marlowe's pint and taking a mouthful. 'You mind? You used that vinegar crap all over your fries and they taste awful.'

'They're chips and they taste fine,' Marlowe bristled. 'So, it didn't go as planned?'

'No,' Brad admitted. 'We all told each other we'd done it, but we all made sure there were copies. Or, in the Russian's case, they killed our agents before we could extract them, and then held their hands up claiming Mossad did it. So, we started again. And again. Each time claiming we'd done what we'd promised, each time being proved a liar. Until we *had* all done it.'

'Except for MI5.'

Brad smiled.

'Your lot always were sneaky bastards,' he said. 'They kept a list of the survivors. The Russians in America and Britain. The Americans in Russia and Korea. The Brits ... actually, I think they killed all your lot.'

He leant back, stretching as he groaned.

'For twenty years, the Brits claimed there wasn't a list, and we believed them. They had nothing to lose, their assets were gone, and they played the peacemaker. Your man, Blair, great poker face.'

'So, what changed?'

'Someone found the list,' Brad shrugged. 'Somewhere deep in a bunker. Or a scrap of the list. A hint of the list. I don't know. But it was the Russians who learnt of it first.

There was talk the Salisbury poisonings were a distraction while they got in, but I don't believe that. I think they found something on a random hack. Anyway, Primakov, the stupid bastard, heard about it. And he couldn't help opening his stupid Soviet mouth.'

'I don't think he was Soviet anymore,' Marlowe muttered, disliking Brad.

'He's not much of anything anymore,' Brad corrected. 'But the problem was, it wasn't the Russians. They're so busy trying to land-grab back everyone who left them when the USSR fell, they've taken their eye off the ball. This seems to be a new player. Someone corporate.'

'So, what, billionaires are now hunting NOC lists?'

'Makes sense,' Brad nodded. 'Think about it. You get a sleeper, in a position of power, to take out a world leader? You're playing a life-sized version of RISK. You can aim your company towards high profit items, knowing in advance they'll be needed. Weapons dealers, arms manufacturers, anyone can take over the world now. And you no longer need to be a politician to rule a country. Donald Trump showed us that.'

'Jesus,' Marlowe whispered. 'We're literally talking Bond villains here.'

'Ones with the money and the men to take out anyone they want and get away with everything,' Brad nodded.

'You mentioned world leaders.' Marlowe recalled Raymond Sykes from earlier that day. 'I heard a date in September was being bounced around. Apparently that's when the US President is talking to Parliament, as part of his State visit to welcome Charles Baker to the world leader club, when they all come back from summer recess.'

'If he's taken out, or if in a worst-case scenario they're

both taken out, nobody will consider a corporation as the culprit,' Brad shook his head. 'Nobody would look twice at the Jeff Bezos or Elon Musk clones out there. They'd immediately aim at Russia. Korea. Anyone else they wanted a pop at. And America wants a pop at a lot of people right now.'

Marlowe looked around the outside area; even though it was early evening, it felt darker than it should be. 'Chechik called someone after I escaped his men in Cambridge today,' he said. 'I called the number myself later, and it was answered by a man named Curtis. He's an MI5 agent.'

'You think he's a sleeper?'

Marlowe shrugged. 'He was in our Berlin Station, and had connections in the East, so there's a chance he did so,' he replied. 'But Chechik also claimed he loved the motherland, that he did this for her.'

'You think MI5 are bringing in outside contractors?'

'I think Curtis might be,' Marlowe considered. 'If you're right, and the Bill's being funded by corporations, I think MI5 might not even know about it.'

'Christ, I need a drink,' Brad muttered and, before Marlowe could respond, he rose from his chair and walked inside the pub. A moment later, he emerged, a second pint of IPA and what looked to be a neat whisky in his hands.

'Bourbon on the rocks,' he explained as he passed Marlowe his pint. 'Or what I call my thinking juice.'

They sat in silence for a moment, sipping their drinks. Marlowe didn't want to break the spell; he needed Brad to make the first move here. Marlowe already knew what needed to be done, but he had to allow Brad Haynes, ex-CIA agent, to suggest it first.

'The fun we have here,' Brad finally spoke, after placing his drink down, 'is whether this is a case of the motherland bringing back the faithful, or, more likely, somebody finding a list of names and activating them.'

'By someone, you mean a third party?'

Brad nodded. 'Yeah, although how they'd find it is anyone's guess. Last I heard, it wasn't even connected to the internet.'

'Raymond said the same thing,' Marlowe nodded. 'Analogue tape deck, most likely.'

'Well, that was the nineties,' Brad smiled ruefully. 'Makes sense you Brits never bothered converting the damned thing until it was way too late, and then you made a complete hash of it.'

'But if I was one of these sleepers, why would I listen to some corporate suit?' Marlowe frowned. 'I'm a party faithful, or a Queen and Country sort of guy, and then some billionaire wakes me up. I'm more likely to shoot him than work for him.'

'Ah, but there lies the beauty of this,' Brad smiled, leaning closer. 'Think about it, You sit there waiting for years for Russia to call you back, or for the British spooks to call you back. You get the point, right? Whatever country you're a sleeper for, you've waited decades for a nod, a wink, an order. And then suddenly, someone contacts you out of the blue and says they have details, proof that you're a sleeper agent, a traitor to your own country.'

He sipped at his drink as he looked out across the Chelmer River, and at the estuary that led into it.

'Of course, you're gonna do anything to make sure it doesn't come out, aren't you?' he stated. 'I mean, hell, these people aren't fanatics anymore. Maybe thirty, even forty years ago, this was a noble cause for them, but nothing's happened for decades, and now they're in a situation where they have a happy life.'

'One that could be removed with one simple upload.' Marlowe leant back in his own chair, whistling. 'So, you think they're being blackmailed to do this?'

'If I was doing this, it's what I would do.'

Marlow nodded. 'It's a good plan,' he agreed. 'So, what do you suggest?'

'I think somebody out there has got hold of the list, or at least a part of it.' Brad was counting off points on his fingers. 'They've read it and worked out who some of the people are on it they need to use, and they've contacted them, activated them, for their own means.'

'And their own means is something terrible.'

'As I said, if they take out the Prime Minister or the President, you know, someone on that level, they won't be blamed. It'll be countries. You lose your leader, and then find an agent of a foreign country with the weapon in their hand, you've got the start of a war.'

'And if the assassin is dead, they can't protest, either.' Marlowe moved closer to match Brad. 'However, if we get the list as well, then we can work out who's been activated and we can find and stop them before it happens. But to do this, we need to get this tape drive. Which could be where Raymond also is.'

Brad grinned.

'So basically, your plan is to save Raymond, get the list, find the sleepers and stop the President being assassinated, all while being hunted by your own? Damn, man, Marshall wasn't wrong about you.'

He considered this, pursing his lips as he thought.

'I've heard of worse plans,' he smiled. 'But this is just two of us against a country's security.'

'Three, if we include my friend Trix,' Marlowe had pulled out a small notebook and was already noting down thoughts. 'She's a computer hacker, best I know.'

'Trained by your Government, perhaps?'

'I think she was trained by yours,' Marlowe frowned. 'She bounced around a lot before she settled down. But she'll get us in and find us all we need.'

Brad looked around the Quay, as if taking it in for the last time.

'My friends are dead, and I'm sick of running,' he hissed. 'So, when do you wanna start?'

'We already have,' Marlowe smiled, raising his glass in a salute. 'They won't know what hit them. All we need is a way to get into a server room.'

'Actually,' Brad patted Marlowe on the shoulder. 'I might be able to help you with that.'

15

SHOPPING LIST

Marlowe sat in the driver's seat of his hired Peugeot and stared out at the industrial park in front of him with a little confusion visible on his face.

'So, let me get this right,' he said, pulling out his SIG P226 and checking it for likely the third time that hour. 'The second floor of this building is owned by a gunrunner, and he owes you a favour?'

'More owes me, full stop,' Brad nodded, placing rounds into his shotgun. 'It's a long-term debt, but I think it's time to call it in.'

Marlowe leant back in the chair, remembering something he'd been told earlier.

'Tell me about the key?' he asked.

Brad looked at him in surprise.

'Key?'

'Don't bullshit me.' Marlowe shifted in the seat so he was looking at the ex-CIA officer. 'Raymond told me about it. Said Amélie Blanchet died on a ski slope, and that you disappeared the next day with some old key in your hands, one that Primakov reckoned he gave Blanchet.'

'And that's why he went to Marshall?' Brad shook his head as he placed the pieces together. 'The bloody idiot Soviet.'

Marlowe waited, and eventually Brad sighed, reaching into his pocket and pulling out a brass key.

'Primakov got hold of this,' he said, showing it to Marlowe. 'Only Marshall knew where it goes. All we can tell is that it's a new key for an old lock and it could lead anywhere. Primakov took it to Blanchet, as she's an expert in these sorts of things, and she talked to me about it.'

'Why?'

'Because I had a drink with her the following day.'

Marlowe waited, keeping quiet. Brad stayed equally silent but broke after twenty seconds.

'Okay, fine,' he admitted. 'I was following Primakov. I didn't trust him. And when he spoke to Amélie, I turned up on her doorstep and suggested we go for a drink. While there, she explained Primakov's crazy story.'

'And she gave you the key?'

Brad looked out of the window, ashamed.

'I stole it,' he muttered. 'I wanted it to examine, and I knew she wouldn't let me. So, I broke in and took it.'

He leant back against the seat; staring up at the ceiling as he exhaled.

'The next day, she was dead,' he continued. 'She hadn't realised I took it, went to the Pyrenees with a friend, and Chechik got to her. I realised quickly that if she died a couple of days after being given the key, and I was revealed to have stolen it, I'd either be arrested or killed myself, so I went on the run.'

'You've been here for four months?'

Brad shook his head.

'I hid out in the US,' he said. 'Ranch in the middle of Utah. Nobody would find me. And then I heard Marshall was checking into things, so I came back, sent him the doll so he knew to meet. But he never did.'

Marlowe took the key, examining it.

'And you have no idea where it goes, or what it unlocks?'

Brad shrugged.

'What am I, some kind of historian locksmith?' he joked. 'Keep it. You might work it out before I do.'

Placing the brass key in his pocket, Marlowe opened the driver's door and was about to leave when he noticed Brad hadn't moved.

'Problem?' he asked.

'I think if we both walk in, it'll spook him,' Brad suggested. 'You might want to do this alone.'

'But it's you he owes the favour to?'

Brad nodded again, gripping the shotgun.

'I know. And *he* knows. I'll just wait here. In case there are any problems.'

Resisting the urge to ask *what sort of problems required the use of a shotgun when you were supposedly visiting an old friend*, Marlowe sighed, closed the driver door behind him and walked towards the two-storey building in front of him. It had a tall roller-door to the right, most likely for large vehicles and vans to enter and exit through, but there was a normal-looking door to the side. In fact, if it wasn't for the extortionate amount of CCTV cameras, Marlowe might even have passed this Chelmsford building by without a second glance.

The door was frosted glass, with a buzzer to the side.

Marlowe tried the door, unsurprised at the fact it was locked, and so pressed the buzzer.

'What?' a voice asked irritably.

'Well, that's a nice way to speak to a potential client,' Marlowe smiled as he spoke, unable to see a camera aimed at him, but sure there was.

'It's gone ten,' the voice carried on. 'We're closed.'

'And yet you're still there,' Marlowe continued. 'I'm here to see Deacon Brodie.'

There was a pause.

'Dunno that name,' the voice said.

'Yeah, me too,' Marlowe replied. 'Unless you count the eighteenth-century Edinburgh thief. But I was sent here to speak to him, and I know if he's not there you can tell me where to find him, so let's cut the shit, yeah?'

'Who sent you?' the voice continued.

'Why?' Marlowe was enjoying this. 'You just said you don't know Brodie, so why wonder who sent me here?'

'Don't be a dick, mate.' The voice was tiring of the conversation, but this was what Marlowe wanted. You only had one chance to make a first impression, and he wanted to make his as bad as possible, as there was something off with Brad's endorsement, possibly because rather than visit the offices of his so-called asset, he was waiting in a car with a rifle in his lap.

'Look, I'm tired, I don't want to be here and the guy who sent me is a Yank prick,' Marlowe continued. 'If I have to go back empty handed, I won't hear the end of it. Unless I can convince you to go shoot him?'

'Yank, eh?'

There was a long pause, likely as the doorman spoke with Brodie himself, before the door buzzed and unlocked. Taking this as an invitation, Marlowe entered the building and walked up the stairs to the second floor.

Two men with AK-47s stood in the reception area.

One was young, Indian with short spiky hair, while the other looked Middle Eastern, with shoulder-length black hair and an obviously curated stubble. Both were in jeans and dress shirts, but Marlowe could see they were labelled clothing, not cheap.

These weren't simple hired help.

'Need to search you,' the Indian said, and Marlowe recognised the voice as the man he'd spoken to. Pulling his SIG P266 out carefully, he placed it on the table.

'All I got, guys,' he said, holding his hands out. 'But I totally understand. Have at it.'

The two men made quick work of the pat down, and the Indian took Marlowe's gun, dropped the magazine, racked the slide, clearing the chambered round and handed the empty weapon back.

'Looks good,' he said with a hint of admiration. 'You take care of it. That says a lot.'

'It's saved my life several times,' Marlowe replied, placing it back into his waistband, following the two men as they moved either side of him, walking him into an open plan office.

It looked like a call centre, with rows of screens and monitors but, although nobody was working right now, Marlowe could see from the notes at the desks these weren't telemarketers of the normal kind. These were likely arms sellers, dealing in death, a commodity trading of the most fatal degree.

At the end was an office and through the glass window that ran from floor to ceiling was a large black man, with long, braided hair, a thick, bushy beard and sunglasses, leaning back on his chair, feet up on his desk. Marlowe had noted the size, not because the man was fat, but because it was likely to be pure muscle. The man, obviously "Brodie", looked like a wrestler, the effect made more prominent by the tight white T-shirt he wore.

'This is the man,' the Indian stated as he waved Marlowe in.

'So, you were sent here to speak to me?' Deacon Brodie spoke, and Marlowe was surprised to hear a strong Scottish accent within the deep, gravelly voice.

'I was,' Marlowe replied calmly. 'I'm Tom Marlowe—'

'And why do I give a shit about your name?'

Marlowe nodded. He'd been expecting some attitude. He had, after all, made a point of being a pain.

'How about another name then?' he shrugged. 'Brad Haynes sent me.'

Marlowe wasn't sure what he'd expected to happen once he stated the name, but the one thing he *was* expecting, based on Brad's refusal to leave the car, was the two guards to raise their AK-47s, now both aiming at his head. In fact, he'd so been expecting it, he didn't even flinch, something that Brodie noticed.

'Cool customer,' he chuckled. 'Not even a twitch. So, tell me, Tom Marlowe, why should I care about that?'

Marlowe eyed the two rifles.

'You might not care, or at least pretend to me you don't, but these two? They're pissed and they're not clever enough to hide it,' he smiled. 'I'm guessing he lied to me.'

'And how's that?'

'He told me you owe him a long-term debt.'

Brodie laughed at this, a deep, booming one.

'Owe, I owe that Yank prick alright,' he hissed. 'Bastard left me for dead in Venezuela. Claims he saved my life, but the abandonment kinda nullifies it, don't you think?'

Marlowe nodded. He'd expected something like this.

'I do,' he replied as he pointed his thumb behind him. 'He's outside, in a Peugeot, wetting himself with a shotgun in his lap, if that makes you feel better.'

He looked at the Indian.

'If you *are* going to kill him, do it outside the car, yeah? It's a rental.'

Deacon Brodie stared at Marlowe for a long moment.

'MI5 or MI6?' he eventually asked.

'MI5,' Marlowe replied, followed by, 'ex, actually. Probably. I think I've just been fired.'

'And how do you know that?'

'My people tried to kill me.'

Brodie laughed again at the comment.

'That's why you're with Haynes?' he asked, leaning back in his chair, the axle creaking under the weight. 'You don't have anyone else?'

'He has information I need to stop a war.'

'I like wars,' Brodie's smile faded. 'It's the basis of my entire business. "Give a man a fish, and he can eat for a day. Give a man a gun, and he can shoot the man and take his fish." You're not helping yourself here.'

'You don't want this war.' Marlowe shook his head, walking closer. 'It's not going to be fought in conventional terms.'

Deacon Brodie considered this.

'So, what do you want?' he sighed.

'I have a shopping list.' Marlowe relaxed a little; the fact they'd gotten this far was good. 'Brad thought your debt could be covered if you fulfilled it.'

Reaching slowly into his pocket, he pulled out a piece of folded paper, placing it on the desk.

'And now?' Brodie ignored the paper as he spoke.

Marlowe shrugged.

'Rock paper scissors?'

Brodie sat up and, as he rose from his chair, Marlowe realised he was a good foot shorter than the man.

'Actually, you could do *me* a favour,' Brodie said, slowly mulling this over as he spoke, finally picking the paper up, unfolding it and reading the list. 'I've got a place in town, and there are undesirable elements around. Dealer setting up shop, driving the house prices down.'

'So, call the police.'

'They don't do shit.'

Marlowe looked around.

'So, use these guys and shoot them,' he suggested.

'Can't be seen to get involved,' Brodie smiled and, for the first time since meeting, Marlowe felt like he was food, being played with by a shark.

'You want plausible deniability,' he nodded. 'A new player takes them out, you get to keep your hands free.'

Marlowe pursed his lips as he thought this through.

'The items I need are for tomorrow,' he said. 'Day after at the tops. How about I give you an IOU for the work and do it after?'

'You want these items?' Brodie waved the paper. 'I won't be able to get them until tomorrow. So, you have until then to sort my problem out. You see, I can take down the gangs, that's not an issue. However, I have a more time sensitive issue.'

'Go on.'

Brodie shifted on his feet, as if working out how to explain this.

'I have a friend, he went against them,' he explained.

'He was your man for the job, I'm guessing?' Marlowe asked.

'Yeah. Always been a straight shooter, but these guys are mental,' Brodie replied. 'They shot up his house, and told him if he called the police, they'd kill his daughter, slow and painfully.'

'And he didn't call the police?'

'He never would have, so instead he rocked up with some heavy weaponry and started on them,' Brodie sighed. 'Happened last night. Caused a hell of a ruckus but disappeared right after.'

'Thing like that could bring attention,' Marlowe suggested. 'Maybe he's hunkered down somewhere until the police stop looking into it?'

'Yeah, I thought that until lunchtime today,' Brodie waved his phone at Marlowe, as if this explained everything. 'I've got it on good authority they took him down during the fight, but not fatally. Instead, they've kept him alive.'

Marlowe shuddered at this. 'They're making an example of him,' he stated. 'That's not a good way to go. Unless you know something more?'

Brodie nodded.

'They want weapons,' he said. 'They know this guy means something to me, and they're using him as leverage. The ransom for his release is to give them enough firepower to wipe all their rivals out.'

'Which of course stops you from being able to take them

out too,' Marlowe nodded, understanding the situation. 'What's this guy to you?'

'He's my brother Barry.' Brodie sat back down, or, rather, he slumped, resigned, into his chair, the creak of the seat audible. 'He's a bloody fool, but I need to save him.'

'What's the deadline?'

'Tomorrow morning.' Brodie gave a wry, humourless smile. 'They have a shopping list of their own.'

Marlowe considered this.

'Twelve hours to take down a drug gang,' he said. 'I'll need help.'

'Don't worry, you have the mighty Brad Haynes on your side,' Brodie chuckled. 'He's a goddamned American hero, you know. Will you do it?'

'He ain't gonna be able to do this,' the Middle Eastern guard muttered. 'He—'

He didn't finish the statement as Marlowe spun around, grabbing the stock of the AK-47 and pushing up with his right hand while yanking the butt of the rifle away with his left. The speed and force were so instantaneous and unexpected, it took less than a second for Marlowe to take the rifle, spin it, and now aim it at the two guards.

'Go on,' Marlowe smiled. 'Carry on. "He" what?'

The guard stared silently and sullenly at Marlowe as Deacon Brodie laughed again.

'Yeah, you can do this,' he said. 'I'll provide you with the details. Get in early and I'll give you what you need early. Yeah?'

'And if I fail? Or if your brother's already dead?'

Brodie's face darkened.

'Then I'll be starting my own war,' he said. 'And I'll need every weapon I own.'

———

BRAD LOOKED RELIEVED AS MARLOWE WALKED BACK TO the car.

'You saw him then?' he asked, as Marlowe climbed back in. 'He can help us?'

'You're a son of a bitch, you know that, right?' Marlowe snapped. 'You knew he didn't owe you shit, and you sent me in there on a fool's errand.'

Brad considered this.

'So, what was the job he gave you?'

'How did you know there'd be a job?' Marlowe turned to face the American. 'Of course, you'd know there was a job. Goddammit, Brad. I'm not some asset to string along here.'

'I know, and I'm sorry,' Brad nodded sheepishly. 'I also knew Brodie was your best chance of getting what you needed, fast. Sure, he and I have issues, but I don't think he'd come for me or anything—'

'He wouldn't,' Marlowe smiled darkly. 'I told him where you were and what you were armed with. He didn't even consider sending someone to pick you up.'

Marlowe couldn't read Brad's expression in response to this; it seemed to be part relief, but also part professional insult.

'So, what happened?' Brad repeated. 'Apart from the two of you bonding over your mutual hatred for me?'

'We're rescuing Brodie's brother from a drugs lord,' Marlowe started the car. 'He's going to provide the details later tonight, so right now, I'm going to find a pub and grab a drink.'

Brad nodded, knowing this wasn't the moment to break the spell by saying something stupid.

He couldn't help himself.

'If I'd been there, we wouldn't have had to do errands like this,' he said.

Marlowe looked at him once more, before pulling out onto the road, his expression unreadable and cold.

'If you'd been there, I would have had what I needed,' he replied.

'That's what I mean!' Brad exclaimed but stopped as Marlowe shook his head.

'No, because I would have taken that shotgun from you and given you to Deacon Brodie,' he hissed. 'You might be an old friend of Marshall's, but currently you're a bloody pain.'

16

LATE NIGHT / EARLY MORNING

It was gone midnight when Deacon Brodie sent Marlowe the details of where his brother was being held, and by then Marlowe and Brad had made a plan, one which was half genius, half insanity, and guaranteed not to work if anyone went off plan.

The gang that had taken Deacon Brodie's brother – boringly named Barry Brodie – were known by the unoriginal "Chelmsford Crewz" nickname. Already, Marlowe wanted to explain that the "z" gave the impression of multiple crews, but from what he'd found out through a few discussions on the late-night streets of the city, this was definitely not the case. The "Crewz" should have been more aptly named the "Chelmsford Cuckoos", as their modus operandi in the Great Baddow part of the city seemed to be to "Cuckoo" a resident, as in taking over the home of a vulnerable person in order to use it as a base for drug dealing. Through this they could build up an empire of houses that weren't connected to them, and could be discarded at any time, with the hapless resident blamed for everything.

Marlowe hated them the moment he heard about them.

He'd also had feelers put out through Brodie's network, and learned they gained their major supply from a Southend gangland family, who gained theirs from somewhere in Turkey; a chain that, if used, could be utilised nicely. Marlowe had already set the wheels moving before dawn appeared.

A couple of years earlier, Marlowe had worked under-cover for Section D on a heroin smuggling case, in conjunc-tion with Special Branch in Southeast Essex. His legend back then had been *Kieran Lachlan*, ex-Real IRA and now a full-time money launderer. They'd taken down some nasty Saudi buggers, and Kieran had disappeared in the way all spy legends did, hidden away in a Tupperware box until it was needed again.

Like now, for example.

And so, after finding a place to rest up and hide his holdalls filled with weapons, Marlowe, or rather "Kieran" had made calls, demanding to know *which bloody idiot was running the Southend scheme these days,* calling old assets and reminding them exactly why he'd been hiding for the last couple of years. In fact, by one in the morning, he was drinking in a "Bas Vegas" night-club, in nearby Basildon's suburbs, waiting to be met by one of his old "friends".

The friend, although only an unknowing asset, was a woman named Mercedes, surname unknown, who had explained that after the Saudis had left the area, the Turks had slipped in, filling the need with no delay. And, if the Turks didn't do it, there were a dozen other places who would have done so. Marlowe had explained he had issues with the "Crewz", only to gain laughter in response; they weren't seen as players in the industry, and this was why they'd been violently upping their game. Marlowe had then asked to speak to Frank Maguire, the head of the Southend family. Luckily for him, his assets were still solid, and also believed he was the same man he was several years earlier, and an hour later he was waiting in a car park in Battlesbridge, east of Wickford. Brad was in a high location nearby, sniper rifle at the ready while Marlowe, back in what was left of his funeral clothes, waited by the car.

It was almost three in the morning when a white Range Rover pulled up beside him, the rear window slowly sliding down to reveal Maguire.

'You'd better have a bloody good reason to drag me out here,' Maguire snapped.

'I did,' Marlowe adopted a slight Derry twang to his tone, as Kieran was supposed to be a Northern Ireland patriot. 'It's why I'm back.'

'Yeah, I heard you shit off when the Saudis went,' Maguire sneered. 'Back to your bog-trotting Mick homeland.'

Marlowe smiled. This was what he'd said to explain his absence, but now it was time to up the ante and use a little of his own real past.

'You think that's where I went?' he asked, unbuttoning his shirt. 'I spent eighteen months in an MI5 black site after you set me up.'

He pulled the shirt open to reveal his bullet wound. It was only six months old, but it had healed up. And a six-month-old wound's scar looked the same as a vicious two-year-old wound.

'I did nothing of the sort,' Maguire replied, shaken by the change of direction this meeting was taking. And, as he went to say something else, he paused as a red laser shone through the window, resting on his chest.

'Yeah, your windows aren't bulletproof, are they?' Marlowe continued. 'Don't even think about lying to me, or I'll have you plastered all over those nice leather seats.'

He crouched slightly, looking through the window at the driver and passenger, now pulling their guns.

'And don't for one moment think you don't have snipers aiming at you,' he continued. 'Just because there's no pretty red light, don't mean they're not there. I wanted Frank to see it.'

He looked around at Frank once more.

'Some paramilitary friends broke me out, about six months back,' he said, knowing that if they checked into it, they'd find an unnamed prisoner escaping after a truck, the one that Marlowe had driven, was ambushed. 'And for six months, I've been watching you and your little subordinates.'

'And?' Maguire was still unsure where this conversation was going.

'Was it you who brokered the deal?' Marlowe continued. 'Or one of your men?'

'What deal?' Maguire enquired, and Marlowe fought the urge to smile. The easiest way to gain a stranger to your side was to aim him at a mutual enemy, and that was exactly the plan here.

'The one with the Triad!' Marlowe slammed his hand against the Range Rover's roof. 'Don't you go playing with me now! I know your man's trying to cut the Turks out! And they're the ones who sprung me, so I don't want them being pissed at me, yeah?'

'Wait, I work with the Turks too!' Maguire climbed out of the car now, no longer the arrogant one. 'If you think we're double crossing you, you're wrong.'

'So, your man Conor of the Chelmsford Crewz isn't one of yours?'

'Yeah, Conor's one of my—'

Maguire stopped.

'Wait,' he carried on, more cautious now. 'Are you saying this was bloody Conor Clarke?'

'I'd like to believe you didn't know this, but I don't,' Marlowe replied, and raised a finger. At this command, five lasers now appeared from the roofs of warehouses around them; two each targeted on the goons in the car, and one on Maguire, as Marlowe pulled his own gun out.

'You're a bright, ambitious man, Mister Maguire, and I can't believe a thug like Conor wasn't speaking to them without your approval. So, you just go back to your nice, cosy bed and we'll take care of everything now, okay? The family's coming over.'

Marlowe hadn't explained any more about which family he meant, as he knew a Northern Irishman saying the word *family* would do better if it was enigmatic.

It worked.

'*I'll* bloody kill him!' Maguire hissed. 'You don't need to do this!'

'And what if I want to?' Marlowe waved a hand, and the lasers disappeared. Which was easy enough to do, as Brad had a switch beside him that turned a handful of laser pointers, connected to rotating gimbals, and set up around the meeting place on and off.

'If I knew where he was, I'd—' Maguire started, but stopped as Marlowe pulled a piece of paper out, passing it across.

'That's where they're holing up,' he explained. 'A cuckoo's nest. And I'm going there in a couple of hours. You're welcome to tag along, but I wanted you to know I wasn't stepping on your turf.'

'Why are you going?' Maguire frowned. 'You don't need to risk yourself.'

'Because my man on the inside is there, and they're torturing him for the Triad,' Marlowe was walking back to his car now. 'Your call, Maguire. Be at that address at five am or come later to a fire sale.'

Before Frank Maguire or his men could reply, Marlowe drove off, already on the phone to Brad.

'Done, make your way down,' he said.

'Already doing it,' Brad replied. 'Started the moment I turned off the pointers.'

'You picked the pointers up, right?'

There was a long, awkward pause down the line.

'Should I have?'

Marlowe clenched his teeth.

'Let's just hope they don't check any roofs before they go find Conor,' he muttered.

MAGUIRE WAS TRUE TO HIS WORD, AND IT WAS JUST BEFORE FIVE am on the Sunday morning when two SUVs slowly drove through the Great Baddow Estate.

Marlowe had decided not to be visible during this and had instead moved into the bushes to the side of the house he'd aimed Maguire at. For a drugs den, it was quite nice; a detached three-bedroom house, with what likely used to be a pleasant garden in the front and was probably well looked after until Conor and his friends appeared and commandeered it.

It also had a basement. Marlowe's early patrol around the house half an hour earlier had found vents that led into it, but no doorway in. If there'd been a coal hole from the days coal was the primary power source, it was long removed.

There was, however, a side door that, from a look through the frosted glass seemed to provide entrance to the kitchen. But again, Marlowe hadn't wanted to press his luck, and so had kept to the shadows, with Brad once more manning the Peugeot, out of sight a street away for a quick escape.

At five am on a Sunday morning, most of the neighbourhood were asleep, but for Conor's house, the Saturday night's antics had only just finished, and a faint drum and base throb could be heard through the windows as Marlowe positioned himself, feeling sorry for the neighbours who had to put up with this, with no real way to stop it.

The SUVs stopped outside the house, on the front kerb, and Maguire emerged from the first car, his men spreading out either side. Marlowe watched them suspiciously; the last thing he really wanted was Maguire's men flanking the house, because then it made things harder for Marlowe to get out with Deacon Brodie's brother without a gunfight, but knowing the type of gangster Frank Maguire was, Marlowe knew there would be a lot of shouting and posturing before any gunplay began. Maguire had to make sure everyone knew he'd spanked his rogue employees, or else others might go against him.

Marlowe idly wondered, while he waited, at what point Maguire would learn Conor hadn't changed sides at all.

'Conor!' Maguire shouted out, and Marlowe smiled. Maguire wasn't waiting for "Kieran" to turn up, and that was expected. Maguire wanted to be seen sorting his own mess out, not being seen to be helped by the IRA, or ex-IRA, or anything along those lines.

There was a rustle of net curtains in the window above him, and Marlowe hunkered down as a teenage boy in a white vest leaned out of it.

'Oi! Blud!' he hissed. 'Keep 'yer banging down, aye?'

'Get Conor out here now, you little scrote,' Maguire hissed. 'Or we'll drag him out by his balls ourselves.'

'Alright, alright,' the teen sucked air through his teeth, playing it cool but obviously rattled by this. 'Keep your wig on, pops.'

There was shouting heard from inside the house, and Marlowe felt a presence emerge above him. Risking a look, he saw two men standing at the window, rifles in their hands. And, if he knew Conor's mindset, Marlowe suspected there'd be troops at every other window, too. Conor would also need to show force, to prove to his own people he was a force to be reckoned with.

Maguire might have *his* men, but so did Conor.

In fact, the man himself now opened the door to the house, standing relaxed, half-leaning against the frame, gun in his waistband.

'What the hell's going on, Maguire?' he yawned, and Marlowe guessed he'd been rudely awoken by this. 'I was sleeping.'

'Oh, long night?' Maguire was holding back his anger, but Marlowe could see it was only a matter of time.

'What's your problem with me partying?' Conor was tired and irritable and confused, and it was clear in his tone and body language.

'It's the people you're partying with,' Maguire continued. 'Triad, perhaps?'

'Man, you're smoking crack!' Conor laughed now, looking back at his men, who also laughed. 'What kind of fool—'

'Oh, so I'm a *fool* now?' Maguire pulled out his gun, and following this motion, his men raised their own weapons, aiming at the house. 'I'm a fool for letting *you* get away with so much!'

'Lower your guns,' Conor hissed as his own men pulled out their weapons. 'You're old, Maguire, sure, but you have a few more years if you think clever—'

Blam.

The gunshot echoed around the estate. One of Conor's men, from the lower front window, shot at Maguire, winging him. And within seconds, the front of the house had turned into a war zone, with both sides taking defensive positions as they fired blindly at each other.

Marlowe, by now, had moved away. After firing the first shot, making sure it matched the trajectory from the window, he slid away quickly, before anyone realised the two men at the window were as surprised as anyone else, and, as he reached the door, he threw his hood on, running in.

'Get to the front!' he shouted. 'Blood's getting killed out there! Go!'

The chaos in the house was already high, with confusion and panic overtaking common sense, and as the drug dealers and scavengers ran around in fear, Marlowe made his way through the door beside the stairs, heading into the basement.

There was a man down there, secured to a chair with cable ties. He was muscular, and bore a family resemblance to his brother, but instead of long hair and a beard, this man was clean shaven with a short, faded cut. In fact, with his dress shirt and trousers on, he looked respectable, if you avoided the bruised and bloodied face.

'Barry?' Marlowe asked, already cutting the cable ties that were securing the battered brother to the chair. He didn't get an answer, more a groan, but he knew he had the right man. That, and the fact there was a distinct lack of anyone else in such a predicament here.

'I was sent by your brother, Deacon,' Marlowe explained as he pulled Barry to his feet. 'We don't have much time. Can you walk?'

'I'll bloody well walk out of here,' Barry hissed, holding his ribs as they walked up the stairs. 'Did you bring an army?'

'In a way, yes,' Marlowe smiled, but as they reached the top of the stairs, he faced a stunned teenage boy who, seeing the stranger holding up their prisoner, went to shout out to the others—

Only for Marlowe to grab him by the lapel and pull him hard towards him, allowing the momentum to send the teenager past the two men on the top step, and down the stairs at speed, landing with a very nasty crack at the bottom.

Moving quickly, Marlowe led Barry out of the house through the side door, running across the next door's garden and down the road beside it. Brad had parked out of the way, so nobody could catch them before it all kicked off ...

But Brad and the car were gone.

'Bollocks!' Marlowe hissed, looking around. 'What the hell are you playing at, you bastard Yank?'

'Hey!' one of Maguire's men had spied Marlowe and Barry, shouting out so his boss heard. 'Why's Kieran got that fella there?'

'Where are the men you promised, you Mick bastard?' Maguire shouted in anger, and Marlowe knew that within seconds, all enmity would be removed as both Conor and Maguire's men hunted the bastard that set them up.

Who now had no escape vehicle.

Pulling Barry along, Marlowe fired a couple of shots down the road to dissuade the gangsters. He also hoped neighbours would call the police by now, and the concern of being arrested might delay the bloodlust.

Of course, it would also end with being arrested and likely killed in prison, so that wasn't good, he considered as he pushed onwards.

As Maguire's men ran towards Marlowe, he placed Barry to the floor and knelt, holding his SIG P226 in both hands, making every shot count, as he took out the approaching force at the knees, hoping it'd slow them down enough for him to think of a new plan.

Brad had betrayed him. All this for what, to see how well he did? Was the whole rescue a set up?

The slide of his SIG P266 locked back on an empty chamber, and Marlowe pocketed it, reaching for his ankle knife. He didn't need to take them all on with it, just the fastest. Then, taking their gun, he could start all over again if he had to—

There was a screech of brakes, however, and a new player arrived on the scene, as a black SUV turned into the housing estate. For a moment Marlowe thought it was more of Maguire's men, but the rear window dropped, and machine gun fire echoed through the streets as both drug dealers and goons dived for cover. Marlowe wasn't sure if this was a guardian angel or a new execution squad firing from the car, however, as the SUV stopped beside him, and the driver's side window rolled down, revealing Marlowe's third-least-favourite MI5 agent, Shaw.

'Get in the car,' she hissed.

'Look, I know you want me, but this man needs a hospital,' Marlowe said, wincing as something inside the house, likely clipped by a bullet, exploded, breaking a couple of ground-floor windows. 'Save him and—'

'Oh, for God's sake, get in the car, the both of you,' a voice from the back hissed, and Marlowe was surprised to see Bridget Summers, back from the dead, leaning out as she fired another burst from her MP5 in covering fire. 'Before you get us all killed.'

'I'll get him to a hospital,' Shaw promised.

And, trusting his fate to chaos and a woman with a submachine gun, Marlowe threw Barry into the passenger seat and climbed into the back, as the SUV drove off into the Essex morning.

17

BREAKFAST MEETINGS

'I HOPE YOU KNOW HOW BLOODY INCONVENIENT THIS IS,' EMILIA Wintergreen, head of Section D and hard-arse spook muttered with the slightest twinge of an accent, maybe Scouse or Geordie on her lips as she leant back on the faded wooden bench and stared out across the platform at the weeds and foliage at the side of the track, and the battered painted sign on the other side.

Denham Station

In her late sixties, Wintergreen was slim, attractive and wore her white hair short, giving the slightest hint of an incredibly put-out Helen Mirren who'd lived a very hard life.

'Oh, I'm sorry,' Trix, sitting beside her smiled. 'Did I interrupt breakfast plans?'

'It's still too early for breakfast,' Wintergreen hissed. 'I mean, for God's sake, Preston, six in the morning on a bloody Sunday? The first train from Marylebone was empty. And empty trains make you visible.'

'Sorry, boss,' Trix apologised. 'I wouldn't have called if it wasn't important.'

'I know,' Wintergreen grumbled. 'And I wouldn't have come if I didn't rate you.'

Trix grinned.

'Compliments? You must be tired.'

'Get on with it, girl,' Wintergreen's tone became distinctively icy. 'The train back is in seventeen minutes, and I'm catching it.'

Trix opened up her laptop, bringing up the files she'd found the previous night.

'Marlowe sent me a picture,' she said. 'Picked up off Stepan Chechik.'

'I heard they found him dead,' Wintergreen mused. 'Our boy did it?'

'No, it was a cyanide tooth, but Marlowe probably caused it,' Trix replied. 'Anyway, Chechik had a USB drive, and on it was one image. A bust of Julius Caesar.'

She showed the image.

'The image was a clue, but it wasn't the entire show. In it, embedded in the code was a zip file with a couple of documents in.'

Wintergreen took the laptop, sliding it across onto her lap as she read the images on the screen.

'This is a NOC list,' she said. 'Old, though. I'm guessing this is Rubicon?'

'No,' Trix shook her head. 'That is, yes. And no.'

'Make your mind up, child.'

'Look,' Trix scrolled down the list, pointing at a name.

```
Preston, Michael
```

'Do you think my dad was a Russian sleeper agent?' she asked. 'He's a bloody bus driver. How about this one?'

>   Marlowe, Olivia

'Or even this wrong'un?'

>   Wintergreen, Emilia

Wintergreen stared at the page, frowning.

'Well, I know I'm no sleeper agent,' she muttered. 'For a start, I came in from the police, not the old school tie these morons love to go by. And Olivia sure as hell wasn't a sleeper, and by default, neither is Tom.'

'And ...' Trix offered.

'And I suppose you're probably safe, on this at least,' Wintergreen smiled. 'So, it's fake.'

'I thought that, but this is where the yes and no part comes in,' Trix pointed at another line. 'Bryan Higgs. he turned out to be a whistle-blower for the Russians during the second Iraq War. And here, Aysha Hart? She was a defence contractor in the 2000s who was exposed as working for North Korea. Committed suicide shortly afterwards. Also, Juan Lazaro, who was outed as Mikhail Vasenkov during the *2010 Illegals Program,* after living in Peru and America since the Russian SVR sent him there in 1976.'

Trix tapped a last name.

'Angela Weber, the maiden name of Angela Kirk, Marshall's wife,' she said. 'Tessa Kirk as good as admitted she knew her mum was a sleeper agent when we spoke last night. She talked about trips to Moscow as a child, how the Russians tried to train her to follow in her mum's footsteps.

She spent her life suspecting her mum's, and maybe even her own name would be on the list.'

'And where's Tessa Kirk now?'

'I think she's hunting a secret warehouse in Canary Wharf,' Trix looked sheepishly away. 'I may have accidentally given her the details before she left.'

'Of course, you did,' Wintergreen scrolled through the list. 'So, it's false, with truth peppered in to make it plausible. Or it's true, but with some facts altered to fit some narrative. But why add us in?'

She froze, realising the answer.

'This discredits us,' she said. 'We won't gain a fair hearing, as we're possibly corrupted. But surely we can prove the list has been altered?'

'That's the biggest issue,' Trix shook her head. 'Looking at the base coding, the numbers are the same. You can't add a new row to this list. And although you can amend details in the name columns, you can't change the sex of the spy.'

'Me. Olivia. Your dad,' Wintergreen looked at Trix, running the information through her head as she spoke. 'Two women and a man have been taken off this list for us to be placed on.'

'Yeah,' Trix nodded. 'But here's the thing. Marlowe wasn't supposed to have this, he said Chechik had the drive on his person, and he was returning to London. I had a message later, explaining when he dialled the number on Chechik's phone, it was answered by Curtis, the MI5 spook that's been hunting him.'

'Chechik and MI5, us on damning lists, someone's playing Opposite Day,' Wintergreen scrolled through the file. 'Was this the only thing? You mentioned a couple of documents.'

'Yeah, I did,' Trix's voice darkened as she opened the next

document, which seemed to be a scanned PDF of written pages. 'This is a little more gruesome.'

It was a suicide note but phrased as a manifesto. Scanned, but handwritten. In it, over three pages of closely packed text, Marshall Kirk's handwriting explained in great detail not only what was wrong with the Secret Service but also what was wrong with the Government, the Prime Minister, and the world in general. Sprinkled with conspiracy theories, a smidge of QAnon fantasies and effectively a confession that he was turned by his wife in the years they were together, it was just believable enough to explain why Marshall wasn't in the right state of mind when he was investigating his friends deaths. It also stated that Marshall wasn't alone in this belief, and that he would strike a blow for the free world very soon, with his friend Tom Marlowe by his side.

'Ah, damn, I see why this is a problem now,' Wintergreen was reading the note. 'Is it Kirk's writing? Could this have been by him before he died?'

'Well, there lies the next issue,' Trix leant back on the bench, rotating her neck to loosen her tight shoulders. 'There's no proof he died. Apparently Harris told Marlowe he'd been shot in the back of the head by a SIG P266, set fire to and left in a warehouse car park in the middle of the night, and was now in some basement morgue within Thames House while the casket buried at Kirk's funeral two days ago was empty. But, as yet we've seen no body.'

'We don't need to see a body,' Wintergreen noted. 'All we need is an absence of one in the grave. You mentioned on the call you possibly connected this to the US President?'

'Yeah,' Trix took back the laptop, closing the screen. 'There're links to September the fifth, when the President arrives to meet with Prime Minister Baker, and Parliament returns from recess.'

'The fifth. So, you mean tomorrow.'

'Yeah, that's why I wanted to meet as soon as,' Trix nodded at the empty tracks. 'And why you need to be on the next train back, regardless, boss. I don't think Chechik was supposed to give Marlowe the USB. I think he was given it, and they were supposed to place it on Marlowe's dead body, incriminating him, or maybe claim they grabbed it off Marlowe when they arrested him. Hell, they could even have been taking it back to Curtis, or whomever he works for. Harris, maybe.'

'Neither of them are on the list.'

'True, but as I said, they removed a male name off the list to make space for my dad. So perhaps that was one of them?'

'This creates a worrying hypothetical,' Wintergreen ran a hand through her hair, pulling it back from her forehead as she thought. 'The US President is killed on UK soil. The killers are ex-MI5 agent and civil servant Marshall Kirk, and MI5 agent Thomas Marlowe, currently on administrative leave. Files are then released to show both were potential sleeper agents for the Russians, one through marriage, one through his mother. Kirk's grave is dug up, and there's no body to be found. Eventually, he turns up dead, maybe in an explosion, to explain the burnt state of the body. Meanwhile, anyone actively going against this, or trying to decipher the truth is discovered to be dead, or on the list, which nullifies anything they say.'

Wintergreen rose from the bench now, pacing in anger.

'We've been played every step of the way,' she hissed. 'They knew Marlowe would look into this. They planned for it. And, in the process, they've burned our whole department.'

'We could go straight to Baker?'

'And what, paint a target on his chest? He's weak at best. Only way he stays in the role past the next General Election is to win the bloody thing,' Wintergreen spat. 'Where's Marlowe now?'

'Dunno,' Trix admitted. 'He was looking for a Yank, Brad Haynes, and then he sent me this, and then ... well, he's disappeared.'

'Find him,' Wintergreen looked down the line. 'Because my train's arriving and we're shit out of time.'

SHAW HAD KEPT HER PROMISE; WITHIN TEN MINUTES OF LEAVING Great Baddow they'd screeched to a halt outside of Broomfield Hospital's A&E entrance, where Barry had been placed onto the pavement with orders to call his brother, before the SUV drove off, staff running out to the half collapsed and injured man on the floor.

'I did what I said,' Shaw stated as they headed down the A12, already past the M25 junction. 'Maybe that gives me a little trust?'

'Shaw was following you,' Marlowe looked at Bridget. 'We saw her.'

'Of course we bloody saw her,' Bridget sighed. 'She deliberately revealed herself, so I knew to run.'

Marlowe took this in.

'She works with you?'

'With *us*, yes. As close to Harris and Curtis as she could get.'

'She wasn't in the room when they tried to kill me,' Marlowe remembered.

'No, I wasn't,' Shaw replied. 'And, if you recall, they sent me to the front of your house while Curtis went deer hunting in the woods behind, with you as the prey.'

'I recall you clocking me hard with the butt of a pistol.'

'I recall you deserving it.'

Ignoring the jibe, Marlowe stared out of the window for a while, watching the houses pass by, the suburbs waking up.

After a few minutes, he looked over at Bridget again.

'How did you survive the gas explosion?' he asked.

'Shaw gave me a heads up,' Bridget replied. 'I popped into a friend's house, two doors down, saying I'd heard someone in the house, and I was concerned. She allowed me to call the police.'

'So, what happened then?'

'I hadn't realised, but she thought herself a bit of a martial artist, and went to confront the stalker, while telling me she was popping out for some milk. I waited for my extraction, and then the entire street went up in flames when my house exploded.'

She sniffed.

'Dozy cow tripped a wire they set up,' she said. 'Died instantly. Not much left after that, and as they thought it was me, I slipped out the back, ran as fast as I could until I could reach out.'

'To Shaw?'

'No, to Raymond,' Bridget replied. 'Luckily for me, Shaw caught me before I could leave a message.'

Marlowe looked over at Shaw as she pulled into the fast lane.

'Raymond was working for you, wasn't he?'

'Depends on the usage of "you",' Shaw said through clenched teeth. 'He was working with MI5, but with Harris. And, when he spoke with you, Harris was the one that debriefed him on your true nature.'

'He lied.'

'Or he told him what he truly believed,' Shaw kept her eyes on the road as she spoke. 'Your record isn't exactly spotless.'

'And Chechik?'

'I don't know,' Shaw replied honestly. 'But it wouldn't surprise me if Harris brought in mercs because he didn't want MI5 looking too deep into it. And Chechik had previous with Rattlestone, before they were broken up, so Harris could have worked off books with them.'

Marlowe leant back on the seat, considering this.

Raymond was MI5, even if he was just an analyst. He would have worked with spies for decades. *Would a man like that tap his ear?*

Marlowe wanted to scream. They had played him from the moment he arrived. Raymond had probably had men check the area like Marlowe had, working out, like he did, the most obvious ways to escape. And this also explained how Chechik and his men only arrived after the important information had been passed. They wanted him to escape, but probably didn't expect him to return to the source.

He thought back to that moment when he watched Raymond being placed into the SUV. He'd been angry, holding a cloth to his temple, before getting into the car. Marlowe had seen this as the actions of a captive, but it could also have been that of a man whose mission had failed. Could Raymond have been working with them? What was Curtis, on the phone, deciding?

One of Chechik's comments in the diner came back.

'Your insistence has changed the plans, so I will fulfil contract.'

Marlowe wasn't supposed to escape. They didn't realise he'd rigged the garden with gas canister explosives.

Marlowe was nodding to himself as Bridget watched.

'You're working it out, aren't you?' she asked. 'You've been staring off into space for five minutes now.'

'They changed the parameters when I proved to be awkward,' Marlowe nodded. 'They expected me to go by protocol. Go to ground, go off grid. Like the rest of my team. Not abduct their lead hunter.'

He looked back to Shaw.

'But why all the cloak and dagger?' He frowned. 'Raymond aimed me at Brad. Why bother?'

'Because he couldn't find him,' Bridget replied. 'None of us could. The porcelain doll went to Marshall, but Raymond intercepted it.'

'Why hunt Brad in the first place?'

'For the key he took from Amélie Blanchet,' Bridget glanced out of the window. 'Poor woman. Chechik was supposed to get it, but Brad already had it.'

Marlowe felt a shiver of ice slide down his spine; *the brass key they were talking about was currently in his trouser pocket.*

'Where are we going?' he said, noticing they were passing Bow Station.

'London,' Shaw said airily. 'We have a safe house.'

Something niggled at the back of Marlowe's mind, and he played a hunch.

'Chechik was going to London,' he said. 'It was on his satnav.'

'Where?' Bridget asked.

'Westminster,' Marlowe lied. 'I didn't get much though

because Curtis sent some kind of hack down the phone, aimed at detonating explosives.'

'Westminster,' Shaw smiled, visibly relaxing. 'Don't worry, we won't be going anywhere near there. In fact, we'll be following the A12 all the way to the end, and then more.'

Marlowe forced himself to stay relaxed as he casually nodded. He knew where the A12 ended, a little north of Canary Wharf. Where Chechik had been heading.

'So, what do we do about Brad?' he enquired calmly. 'I don't appreciate the son of a bitch deserting me.'

'He's CIA, what do you expect,' Bridget sniffed. 'Never was a reliable source at the best of times. What was your plan?'

'We were going to hack into the MI5 black archive's server,' Marlowe admitted. 'It has a direct link into Thames House, so we could grab the list.'

'And this led you to a Chelmsford crack house how?'

'Favour for an arms dealer who was giving us a way in. Brad was also going to see if he had any contacts who could help with the key.'

At this, he saw both Shaw and Bridget sit up.

'You saw the key?'

Marlowe smiled.

'Yeah. Big iron bugger,' he lied.

'Good to know,' Bridget said, her attitude changing, an element of disbelief sliding into her tone, watching out of the window. 'Look, Tom, I don't know how to say this, and I've been holding off speaking ... but Marshall ... we learned—'

'He was on the list, wasn't he?' Marlowe played a hunch.

Bridget's eyes widened.

'What makes you say that?'

'He was in a Gulag before the end of the Cold War, came

home with an ex-Stasi wife,' Marlowe shrugged. 'I mean, I never met her, but there had to be warning signs.'

Bridget nodded. 'I believed in Marshall, but I've since learned he was up to terrible things,' she said. 'Shaw told me you were in the room when Harris spoke of his actual death?'

Marlowe nodded, watching the road. They'd passed Canary Wharf on the right and were heading towards Millwall. This was where Chechik had been driving to, and this was where Raymond had mentioned an MI5 black archive, the same one Marlowe had talked about breaking into but moments earlier.

He didn't have his gun anymore, but he had a knife in his sock; casually and slowly, he reached to grab it, slipping it up his sleeve.

He didn't yet know who was on whose side, and he was now worried he was about to walk willingly, straight into the lion's den.

'I was,' he said. 'But feel free to update me with anything else.'

18

WAITING ROOM

IT WAS ANOTHER FIVE MINUTES BEFORE THEY PULLED UP outside a warehouse just north of Millwall Docks. It was early, but the area was already buzzing with activity, which was strange for a Sunday morning. That said, Marlowe hadn't been here before, and this could have been completely normal.

Shaw parked in a parking spot beside a warehouse marked 13, and both Bridget and Shaw left the car leaving Marlowe sitting alone, lost in his thoughts until Bridget rapped on the window.

'Are you coming or not?' she asked.

Marlowe smiled, waved and climbed out. He'd been so busy trying to work out the gameplay here, he'd zoned out.

'Sorry,' he said. 'No sleep last night, minimal the night before.'

'You can catch some winks in the break room,' Bridget smiled as they walked towards the entrance. 'We won't be debriefing until noon.'

'Debriefing?' Marlowe raised an eyebrow at this. 'That sounds very "security services".'

Bridget scrunched her face in embarrassment.

'Once a spook, always a spook,' she gave as response.

The warehouse was simple: a wide-open area where three vans were parked, and a rest area behind a large reception. If anything, it looked more like a high-end garage than MI5 location, but that was because everything wasn't as it seemed.

The building was small, but linked to three others, each with graphics on the side revealing them to be printing companies, infrastructure providers, and even a pole dancing school. But the windows of the two floors above were all blacked out, something that seemed cosmetic, but mainly because this was where the magic happened.

Walking to the stairs and away from the entrance, Marlowe noticed the subtle changes in security. Now, CCTV cameras were more prevalent. The doors were steel, rather than wood, the glass bulletproof and at least an inch thick.

More importantly, there was an elevator door: metal, unmoving and out of place in such a location.

'You have people with disabilities?' he asked.

'It's the twenty-first century,' Bridget said humourlessly. 'Of course, we do.'

Marlowe nodded, following the two women, but mentally noting the elevator had two buttons on the outside, one for up, and one for down. Buttons like this on the inside were commonplace, but something here felt off.

Why would a ground floor elevator door have a down button on the outside? This was the lowest it could go. All you could do was go up.

There was a guard, in black combats, an armoured vest

and with no visible weapon in his hand, but Marlowe was pretty sure, should he pull his knife out, he'd be taken down in seconds. And, although he didn't recognise the man, there was a vicious-looking red burn on his cheek, recently attended to.

Could he have been one of Chechik's men?

Marlowe decided not to raise this until he knew more about what was going on. He didn't trust Shaw, but Bridget had seemed sincere when they met. And since she'd worked with Marshall for years, he'd never mentioned her being shifty—

He'd never mentioned her.

Marlowe wanted to punch a wall but forced himself to stay calm. In all the time he knew Marshall Kirk, not once did he mention Bridget Summers. Even Tessa's comments hadn't set off alarm bells.

'Bridget? Woman who used to work with my dad? I haven't heard her name mentioned for years!'

If Tessa was right, Bridget had worked with Marshall, but they weren't close. And if she was connected to all this somehow, within days of Primakov meeting Marshall, the Russian was dead, likely killed by the same people who killed Amélie Blanchet, one of whom looked to be guarding the room he was about to enter.

'Here, rest up,' Bridget smiled as they entered a recreation room. There was a TV, a sofa with a coffee table beside it, and a small kitchen area with a microwave, kettle and tap. 'There's coffee on the counter, it's instant but it works. Toilet and shower through the back. I'll be back in a few.'

'Is there any chance of some breakfast?' he gave a hopeful expression. 'It's been a long day.'

'I bet it has,' Bridget kept smiling, and now, watching her, Marlowe knew it was as fake as her sincerity. 'I'll sort a flapjack and some crisps from the vending machine. We don't have much here, it's not usually manned.'

Marlowe smiled in reply, and Bridget gave him a second, awkward hug, one which felt a little more forced than the one in the Nellie Dean pub a couple of days earlier.

'That'd be great,' he said, slumping onto the sofa. 'I'll grab some sleep.'

Bridget nodded silently and closed the door behind her, and Marlowe was sure he heard the door locking. Without making a show of it, Marlowe lazily scanned the room, looking for the CCTV cameras that were likely to be in here. He knew someone somewhere would be watching him, so he made a show of yawning, stretching his arms and rising from the sofa, walking over to the kitchen counter and grabbing a glass, pouring himself a drink of water from the tap. Sipping it, he leaned back, checking the room from a different angle.

If there was a camera, it was well hidden – he had to say that for them. All he could think was that somewhere, in a shadowed corner of the recreation area, a small Wi-Fi camera was in the room, but at the same time, MI5 might have allowed this area to be the one exception, or maybe he was overthinking what was going on. *Was he sure he was being lied to?* Maybe Shaw and Bridget didn't know who they were working for, either?

Turning back to the counter, he placed the glass down and, holding the front edge, stretched his arms as he bent over, hearing the clicks of his spine as he moved things back into place. He was about to rise and move on when something in the waste bin beside the counter caught his eye.

It was small and had obviously been tossed in without a second thought. It was compressed and solid, nestled into the liner bag and staring up at him. Marlowe wanted to reach down and examine it, but he knew the moment he did, it'd be picked up on a camera, if there even was one in here.

But he didn't need to pick it up. He'd recognise a prawn cocktail crisp packet folded in on itself anywhere.

Marlowe returned to the sofa, his mind spinning. *Could Marshall Kirk be alive?* If what Harris said was true, there was no body in the coffin. And a body, shot and then burned to a crisp, would be hard to identify quickly. Could Kirk have been here, stuck in this room, before him, eating vending machine snacks and working out how to escape?

No, this was too much to ask for. Kirk had to be dead. No matter what the cause was, everyone seemed convinced of this. And Marlowe knew without a doubt that, if Marshall Kirk was still alive, he'd have passed a message to Marlowe, or even Tessa.

Who was currently off the grid, with no way for anyone, apart from Marlowe, to contact.

Dammit. If he was alive, why would he be here? Did he try to stop Rubicon? Was Bridget the one who caught him? Or was he brought here unknowingly, thinking he was with allies, just as they'd tried to do with Marlowe?

One thing was for certain, he had twenty-four hours at most to work things out before the US President touched down in the UK. He'd wanted to break into a black-site archive, and now here he was, smack-bang in the middle of one. All he had to do was work out how to get out of the damned place, with the NOC list, and possibly Marshall Kirk.

Although that said, he was interested in seeing what else would happen if he just stayed here. After all, if they wanted him dead, they could have left him with Maguire. There had to be something—

With a sudden feeling of dread, Marlowe rammed his

hand into his trouser pocket, rooting around for the brass key Brad Haynes had given him the previous night.

It wasn't there.

Now, there was every chance he'd lost it during the night, or even at the house in Chelmsford, but Bridget's questioning of him about the key, and the awkward hug a few moments earlier, made Marlowe question this. Raymond had wanted Brad and the key he'd taken from Amélie Blanchet, and here Marlowe was literally giving it to them.

You goddamned bloody idiot.

There wasn't much in the room to work with so Marlowe walked to the bathroom and opened the door, checking the shower, toilet, and sink. Apart from trying to drown someone in it, he didn't really have many options. He had the knife which had been in his ankle holder still, and that knife was now in the sleeve of his jacket, ready in case they attacked him in any way, but apart from that, his list of usable weaponry was small.

There were sounds of movement from the other side of the door, and as Marlowe walked back to the sofa, he saw Shaw walk in, a flapjack and cup of takeaway coffee resting on a file folder.

'Vending machine doesn't have much, I'm afraid,' she said, placing both onto the coffee table. 'White, no sugar. That's how you take it, right?'

Marlowe picked up the coffee cup; it was the standard plastic-lined paper cup you got from most chain coffee shops, with a cardboard holder around the middle to stop your fingers burning, and a plastic lid on top, with a small hole to drink from. Marlowe pulled off the lid, staring at it.

'You don't trust us?' Shaw asked.

'I was seeing if it was a flat white,' Marlowe bemoaned, sniffing it. 'Italian roast. You have a coffee shop nearby?'

'We have an excellent machine,' Shaw said as Marlowe raised it to his lips to drink, pulling back instantly.

'My tonth!' he hissed. 'I burd my tonth!'

'Yeah, it's hot, I should have warned you,' Shaw smiled maliciously, as Marlowe waved for the water on the counter. Walking over to it, she graciously picked it up, returning to Marlowe, who'd now replaced the lid and placed the coffee back on the table, gratefully dipping his tongue into the water for a second.

'Sorry,' he said. 'That hurt like a bitch.'

Swapping the water for the coffee, he blew into the hole to cool it down.

'So then, what's the file?' he asked.

'News you probably don't want to hear,' Shaw replied. 'Did you take the USB from Stepan Chechik?'

Marlowe knew it was pointless to lie, so nodded.

'It had a picture on it,' he said.

'We believe Raymond gave him that, and he was on his way to MI5.' Shaw opened the folder, pulling out two sheets of paper, stapled at the top and filled with names. 'It held the Rubicon list on it.'

Marlowe mocked surprise, widening his eyes at this. Trix hadn't come back to him yet with what was in the image, or rather, he hadn't had the time to check if she'd sent a message, but he was realising quickly this wasn't a situation where he was going to be told the truth. If Chechik had the list, then there was a different reason here.

'Why are you telling me this?' he watched her suspiciously.

'Because you deserve to know why MI5 doesn't want you

back,' Shaw said, pointing at a name on the list. 'Your mother was on it.'

'Bullshit,' Marlowe leaned back on the chair, raising the cup to his lips as he considered this.

'I'm sorry,' Shaw continued, showing another name. 'And so was Angela Weber, Marshall's wife. And, because of this, both Marshall and Tessa have been compromised.'

'Kirk's no traitor.'

'But his wife was.' Shaw watched Marlowe carefully as he continued sipping at the coffee. 'Raymond intends to use this to take the list and cause an international event.'

'Why don't you go to MI5 with this?' Marlowe asked, his voice slurring slightly. 'Marshall—'

He stopped, staring at the coffee cup.

'What did you do?' he whispered.

'Ah, about time it started working. You've been sipping at a sedative, laced with a little smidge of amobarbital and sodium thiopental,' Shaw smiled, taking the papers and putting them back into the file. 'It makes you a little more suggestible to telling the truth, before putting you to sleep.'

'You ... killed Marshall.'

Shaw's face didn't change as she replied coolly.

'The less you know, the better,' she said. 'Besides, I'm the one asking questions. What did Brad Haynes tell you?'

'Nothing,' Marlowe slumped against the sofa, struggling to rise. 'He was ... nothing but a drunk. Why are you doing this? You're ... MI5 ...'

'So what?' Shaw hissed. 'You think they give a shit about women like me? Curtis will get the promotion I deserved. Curtis, who you bettered twice, I might add.'

'You're ... on the list ...?' Marlowe was struggling to stay conscious now, dropping the cup beside him, the lid falling off and splattering him and the corner of the sofa with the last remnants of the coffee.

'No,' Shaw smiled. 'But I have several friends and mentors who were. That's the problem with Rubicon. When it was analogue, it couldn't be changed. But the moment someone stuck it on a server, it became anyone's, no matter how deep you bury the original.'

'Russia?'

'You think too small,' Shaw shrugged. 'Countries aren't the world powers anymore. And the UK will see that soon.'

'The ... key?'

'Primakov got it from a friend, and tried to keep it from us,' Shaw explained. 'It opens a very important door in Westminster.'

'President ...'

'Presidents come and go,' Shaw rose now. 'I'm sorry, Marlowe, I'd hoped we could convince you to join us.'

She walked over, pulling the blade from his sleeve.

'But as I can see, you were never much of a joiner—'

She stopped as she stared at the coffee stain on the sofa.

'There's too much liquid there,' she frowned. 'You'd finished drinking the cup—'

Marlowe moved fast, grabbing the glass of water and slamming it against Shaw's head, the glass exploding with the impact, sending her stumbling to the floor.

'I poured it away when you went to get this for my burnt tongue,' he said, dropping the broken glass from his bloodied hand, reaching into Shaw's jacket and pulling out her gun. 'Coffee is strong, but it doesn't hide the smell of rotting onions or garlic. Both of which are smells given by sodium thiopental.'

Shaw didn't reply, and Marlowe pulled the dazed agent

up, going through her pockets, pulling out her phone, her ID card and a pair of large cable ties, obviously meant for Marlowe. Quickly, he took the ties and secured Shaw's hands behind her back, placing his knee on her spine to stop her moving as he did so. With the agent now secured, he aimed the screen at Shaw's dazed face, using the phone's facial recognition to open it, scrolling through her call history.

'There,' he said, tapping the screen with the muzzle of the pistol. 'Three calls, all in quick succession, yesterday afternoon, the third answered. Curtis answered your phone, didn't he?'

'Go to hell,' Shaw spat, as Marlowe rolled her over, still using his weight to keep her down while watching the door.

'Stepan phoned you as well, didn't he?' Marlowe insisted. 'Was he telling you he failed to catch me? Or to let you know Raymond had aimed me at Brad Haynes?'

Shaw glared silently at Marlowe.

'How long before they come in?' he asked. 'I'm guessing there's a camera in here?'

'You're dead,' Shaw hissed.

'Yeah, but so was Marshall Kirk, but I'm reckoning he's around here and alive, too,' Marlowe smiled. 'So again, how about explaining to me what's going on?'

'Retribution!' Shaw's voice rose as she looked at the door. 'Guar—'

She didn't finish as Marlowe finally returned the favour from their first meeting, slamming the butt of the gun against her head. And, with Shaw now unconscious, Marlowe rose, gun in hand.

He'd been lucky; if he'd taken in more than a sip of the coffee, he'd be unconscious now. That was probably how they got Kirk when he was here.

Thank God for rotting garlic.

Walking to the door, Marlowe took one last look around, and, with a knife in one hand and gun in the other, he opened it, walking outside.

———

Tessa Kirk had watched Marlowe walk into the building with the MI5 agent who had chased them, and Bridget Summers, who she'd last heard was dead. It was something she hadn't expected, to be honest, and her plan of somehow breaking into the building and stealing the Rubicon file was placed mentally on hold as she reassessed the situation.

It hadn't been hard to find the location from the Post-It note, and she'd stolen a car half a mile down the road from Trix's cottage. She felt bad for doing that, but she didn't know the woman, and with her parents now both gone, she had to control her own narrative.

And besides, the bitch had scared the crap out of her when she pulled the trigger, so Tessa was happy to be as far from that psycho as possible.

But Marlowe, entering with both friend and foe had thrown her. This meant there was an unreliable narrator somewhere, and a story that was being deliberately changed, or – and Tessa didn't want to consider this – Marlowe had thrown his lot in with the enemy.

But that still didn't explain Bridget.

She was about to make her way back out of the car park, using the low wall she was currently behind as a barrier, when she heard the familiar sound of someone moving up behind her. She spun, gun raised, only to find Brad Haynes, smiling, shotgun in hand, watching the same warehouse.

'Uncle Brad?'

'Hey, kiddo,' he said. 'You here to rescue the Brit too?'

'You mean Marlowe?' Tessa was surprised by this. 'I thought he was on their side.'

'That remains to be seen.' Brad looked at Tessa's gun and frowned. 'Come back to my car. The Brit left a ton of toys for us to play with, and I think you need an upgrade.'

19

RESCUE STRANGERS

THE ELEVATOR WAS IN A HALLWAY THAT SEEMED TO BE IGNORED, and Marlowe wondered if this was because nobody believed anyone would be stupid enough to enter it.

He knew he had a couple of minutes before anyone reached Shaw; she wouldn't be waking soon, and it was likely whomever was watching the footage would be the first to attend her. So, he needed to move fast. Pressing the down button, he waited, impatient for a couple of seconds, before peering closer.

The button wasn't lighting up.

Of course, he thought to himself, pulling the plastic card he'd taken from Shaw out of his pocket. *The damn thing needed a security level pass.* Pressing it against the metal plate with one hand as he pressed the button again, he sighed with relief as it lit up, and the faint rumblings of the elevator could be heard from beneath him.

Of course, if the elevator had a guard, this could be over real fast, and as the gun he'd taken didn't have a suppressor on it, he placed it in the back of his waistband, pulling out the knife and hiding it up his forearm. The guard would be suspicious, but it'd give him a second or two for an attack.

What if they were MI5 agents? the voice of his conscience muttered. *Would you kill someone who you'd worked with?*

Marlowe pushed the thought back. The fact they were here meant there was a strong chance they weren't on "his side", which meant they weren't working in the best interests of MI5. He had to consider them as enemies, no matter what he saw.

Luckily for him, though, when the elevator door opened, there was nobody inside. Quickly and quietly, making sure nobody was watching, but aware the security cameras were marking his every move, Marlowe slipped into the elevator, hitting the down button inside, only relaxing when the doors finally closed.

There was a camera in the back left of the elevator, nestled into the top corner, observing everything which happened within. Marlowe knew he couldn't avoid it, but he'd kept his face down as he entered, and now stood directly underneath it, so at best it gained a great shot of the top of his head. He knew it wouldn't work for long, but anything that extended his time down here was a Godsend.

He didn't know if Marshall Kirk or Raymond Sykes were down here, but either agent was a bonus, for different reasons. Marshall would need rescuing, while Raymond would need questioning. But the basement was more likely to be the location of the server farm they had originally created this building for, and somewhere within the servers was the real Rubicon list.

At least, he hoped so.

There was every chance the list Shaw showed him earlier had overwritten the original list, and that could be a major issue down the line, but the server's version of the list was still a digital version of the original one, transcribed in the last twenty years. The original Rubicon list, created by the eighties and nineties *Project Rubicon,* was probably still on a tape drive somewhere, a lost relic of an analogue era. Maybe even down here.

The elevator opened out into a corridor, with doors on either side. The ceiling was low, lit by fluorescent lamps, and it surprised Marlowe to see no visible security. Moving slowly, keeping to the wall, he watched the exit at the end as he stopped at the first door, a black-painted one to his right, trying the lock.

It didn't open.

Marlowe considered trying to pick the lock, to see what was inside, but at the same time there were two more doors, and a chance to check through both. If he had the time, and by that he meant *if he wasn't being shot at*, he could always come back and check it.

The next door was the one on the left; twisting the handle, Marlowe found it opened, the room within bathed in semi-darkness. Quickly, and as quietly as he could, Marlowe moved in, closing his eyes for a moment so he could adjust to the darkened space. Closing the door behind him, he looked around.

The room was unlit by lighting, but filled with a faint shade of electric blue, as LEDs on banks of computer servers flashed on and off rhythmically. Marlowe walked over to the first rack, examining either side, finding nothing but glass-fronted encasements. He walked to the next one and paused, smiling.

In the middle of the third rack was a slim shelf, and as it pulled out on the sliders on the sides, it revealed a folded laptop, connected to the network. Opening it up, he saw the screen flare up, a login command the only text on it.

Tapping quickly, Marlowe entered a name and code. It was one he'd known for a while, but it should still have the priority clearance he needed.

```
WINTERGREEN, EMILIA
028486 - 3HYb^ - DELTA
```

Nothing happened, and for a second, Marlowe wondered if Wintergreen had changed her login details while he was ill, but then a red command flashed up on the screen

ACCESS DENIED

Oh, crap.

Marlowe looked around the room, expecting to be caught at any moment. He was sure he'd just heard gunshots, and a faint klaxon could be heard from the floor above him.

He had another log in, one he'd picked up more recently, more because he was bored than anything else, and so he typed that instead.

```
FENCHURCH, CARRIE
947823 - 8vhW@ - GAMMA
```

He'd learnt the passcode while investigating Doctor Fenchurch when he discovered her connection to Rattlestone and Francine Pearce. He'd never intended to use it, but right now, it sounded like he had a matter of minutes before they found him.

ACCESS GRANTED

The green command screen lit up his face, and Marlowe gratefully searched through the file system of the servers. Anything Thames House had was automatically backed up here, so within reason, Rubicon should be easy to extract.

It was around this point Marlowe realised he didn't have a USB drive on him. But that was fine because he'd found another problem.

There *was* a copy of Rubicon on the server. He could see the details.

Details that were modified two days earlier.

'Shit,' he hissed, stepping away. If this was showing as changed here, then it'd be the same in Thames House. Maybe there was a small, remote and air-gapped server out there which hadn't been caught yet, but Marlowe doubted it.

Opening it up, he read through the list. It was the same one Shaw had shown him, one that didn't name Harris as a traitor, while allowing Trix, Marlowe and Tessa to be damned by parental conspiracies within the list, with Wintergreen named personally. Which was bollocks, because back in the nineties, when this list was created, she was a beat copper in East London and nothing to do with this. She hadn't even met Marlowe's mum at that point, and the connection, and death, that brought her into the fold wouldn't occur for years.

And Olivia Marlowe was no traitor.

Marlowe wanted to scream, punch something, *break* something; he couldn't believe the lies being told here. However, on a second scan, he noticed something else. Only the file codes for *Michael Preston, Olivia Marlowe,* and *Emilia Wintergreen* had been altered recently. And, checking the data cells, he saw someone had changed only the names; the sexes of the traitors hadn't been altered.

More importantly, Angela Weber, the wife of Marshall and mother of Tessa, hadn't been touched. She really was a sleeping soldier.

Did Tessa know?

There was shouting now, faint and through the ceiling, and Marlowe could hear gunfire. Something was definitely happening and possibly not to his advantage, so he needed to move fast. There was no point taking a copy now, as this was the same list Trix now had, if it was from the USB Chechik had owned. Closing the laptop and moving to the door, Marlowe was still running through the scenarios in his head.

The sexes couldn't be changed, which meant three sleepers, two women and a man had been removed. The obvious answers were Bridget and Raymond, as they seemed to work together, but the third name, the second woman, was a curious one. Was it Shaw? It couldn't be, as she was too young to be on the list. A parent, perhaps? Shaw becoming damned like Tessa was. Or was there someone else out there still?

Marlowe couldn't consider this, he needed to move, and fast. Opening the door, he was about to cross to the end of the corridor—

A door opened, and a very surprised guard stood facing him.

'What's all the noise—' the guard started, but stopped as Marlowe moved in, chopping at his throat hard with the edge of his hand, the guard staggered back, grabbing at his neck, unable to shout and his eyes bulging as he struggled to breathe. Marlowe took the moment to step closer again, this time spinning the guard around and placing him in a sleeper hold, dropping him to the floor.

He hated to do this, but if the guard was a friendly, if misguided one, convinced the enemy were on his side, then Marlowe didn't want to have his death on his conscience. Straightening up, Marlowe looked around the room. It was lit, and someone had placed a camp bed in the corner. The room seemed more like a cell, with a padded chair for the guard to sit, a table beside him, an iPad playing something off one of the streaming services beside it.

To have a guard in your cell was quite rare and made Marlowe wonder who'd need such treatment.

'About bloody time,' Marshall Kirk wheezed, sitting up on the camp bed. 'Took you long enough.'

'You're lucky I found you at all.' Marlowe walked over to his mentor, crouching in front of him, and checking him for injuries, smiling widely at the fact his friend was still alive. 'I went to your bloody funeral two days ago.'

Marshall Kirk was exhausted, bruised, and battered. He had a dried cut running down from his forehead, and his nose looked to have been broken at some point and placed back into position, likely by Kirk himself. His clothes looked like he'd been sleeping in them for days, which was likely, and his stubble's length gave a rough timeline of two weeks held.

'They said I died?' Kirk tried to rise, but he was weak, shivering.

'Let me find you something to drink,' Marlowe went to rise, but Kirk grabbed his arm.

'No,' he insisted. 'It's all drugged. I'd rather be dehydrated and awake. Now tell me what the hell happened. Is Tessa all right?'

'Tessa's with a friend, as far as I know,' Marlowe helped Kirk up to a sitting position. 'They tried to bring her in because she's connected to the list.'

He watched Kirk's face.

'Although you knew that already, didn't you?' he asked. 'This was why you got involved, wasn't it?'

'I never wanted to admit it, but I knew her mother was still loyal,' he whispered. 'I hoped she'd grow out of it, like a phase. And when Rubicon was active, I saw her name on it. I couldn't change the details, I didn't have the security level to do that, but I realised if I could control the op, I could make sure her name didn't come out. And, when the Op ended, I made sure Rubicon was buried on a tape drive, deep inside Whitehall.'

'Not deep enough, it seems,' Marlowe nodded. 'But Tessa's safe, as far as I know. Some MI5 guy named Harris brought me in, said they found your body in a car park, burned to a crisp and with two rounds in the skull. I don't know whether or not this was true—'

'Obviously not true!' Kirk exclaimed as Marlowe waved him back down.

'I mean, whether Harris made this up, or believes it because there was a body,' he corrected. 'I had Bridget tell me she worked with you, but she seems to work with Raymond Sykes and a bunch of mercs. Oh, and some rogue MI5 agent named Shaw.'

'Martina Shaw?' Kirk's eyes widened. Marlowe shrugged.

'Never got the name. Why?'

'Martina Shaw was brought in under Raymond Sykes' internship scheme, about ten years back,' Kirk replied. 'I met her a couple of times before I retired. Analyst at GCHQ who moved into Special Branch.'

'That sounds like her,' Marlowe rose now, looking around the makeshift cell. 'She's working with Bridget and Raymond.'

'Bridget was someone I knew, but not that close. And bloody Raymond is a snake,' Kirk groaned as he stood now. 'He has a plan—'

'I know, to kill the US President tomorrow,' Marlowe helped Kirk to the chair where the guard, still unconscious, had once sat. He paused, as the sounds of gunfire could be heard again in the distance.

'Friends of yours?' Kirk smiled.

'Not that I know of,' Marlowe shook his head. 'I came alone.'

'Some things never change,' Kirk smiled weakly. 'Working alone, jumping to conclusions—'

'What do you mean?'

'I mean, Raymond isn't using the list against the President,' Kirk replied. 'He's using it to take down Parliament. Real Guy Fawkes shit. And he's using me as the Oswald.'

Marlowe paused in surprise.

'They made me write a confession,' Kirk looked ashamed as he continued. 'Pages of conspiracy shit. They drugged me up to the nines, writing whatever they told me to, because they told me they had Tessa. Had images of her with guards in MI5's building.'

Marlowe knew how this had been shown; they must have taken them before she was rescued and escaped through the tunnel system.

If only they'd taken the photos an hour later, he thought morosely to himself as Kirk continued.

'They're using the confession to explain why I detonate a dirty bomb under Westminster tomorrow, and in the process reveal the list, starting a war,' he finished. 'I'm sorry, Tom, they made me add your name to it, making out you were helping me. I don't think they intended us to live.'

There was the muffled sound of an explosion above them.

'They got the key from me,' Marlowe muttered. 'I'm sorry.'

'It's okay,' Kirk croaked. 'It was to a secret room in Westminster Palace. They already have a copy, they wanted to make sure nobody else could unlock the door.'

Marlowe felt a small sense of relief at this. Losing the key had been an inconvenience, but not to the level he'd expected.

'We need to get out of here and find the original list,' he said. 'The unaltered one; and use this to prove our innocence.'

'Your innocence,' Kirk replied sadly. 'My wife will still be on there.'

'You good to walk?' Marlowe asked, and Kirk replied by rising unaided and walking to the door. Smiling, Marlowe followed.

'Raymond has the original,' Kirk spoke as he went to open the door. 'It's on a DLT cartridge.'

'What the hell's one of those?' Marlowe continued, pushing Kirk to the side. 'And I'll be going through doors first, thank you.'

'Digital Linear Tape,' Kirk replied. 'It's what we used with computers in the eighties. I'd hid it in the secret room. Nobody even knew of it, I thought it'd be safe there for years, bricked away and hidden, ready to be found when needed. Safest place in the world, and all that. Raymond laughed when he saw me, told me Primakov had given Amélie a key, but the silly cow had copied it. When they killed her, they took the key, but found a receipt saying there was a duplicate, the one Brad had stolen. They didn't know if he knew where the key went—'

He stopped speaking as Marlowe opened the door; there, standing on the other side and looking as surprised to see Marlowe as he was to see them, was the guard with the burn mark on his cheek. This time he was holding a weapon, a HK MP5 and he raised it up, shouting.

'He's here! I repea—'

Marlowe moved in, grabbing the muzzle and yanking it up so it aimed at the ceiling as he placed Shaw's gun to the guard's chest, firing twice, sending him collapsing to the wall.

'That was harsh,' Kirk stared down dispassionately. 'He could have been one of ours, maybe as conned by them as we were.'

'He worked for Chechik, so I'm thinking East European merc.' Marlowe was already kneeling beside the groaning man, pulling items out of his pockets. 'The burn gave it away. And he's wearing Kevlar, so all he got there was bruised ribs and the wind knocked out of him.'

He paused, watching the guard.

'Or maybe a broken rib or two,' he admitted, taking an extendable baton and ramming it into the guard's mouth as a gag, the guard clamping down on it.

'You can't get to your suicide tooth, and I'm not falling for that again,' Marlowe spoke calmly and softly, waving to Kirk to pick up the rifle. 'I'm not here to kill you, and I don't care why you're here. In a minute I'm walking out, and you can live a happy and long life.'

He leant closer.

'I watched Stepan Chechik die,' he said. 'He didn't want to let the motherland down. I get that. But you're not working for the motherland, no matter what you think. You're working for sleeper agent MI5 operatives who want to start a war for their own enjoyment and their corporate masters. Do you really want to die for that?'

The guard, obviously in pain, shook his head, and Marlowe removed the gag.

'Tell me what I need, and I let you walk. You work for Bridget Summers and Raymond Sykes, right?'

A shake of the head. 'The woman, she runs the op. And also Raymond Sykes. The old woman you mentioned works for him.'

'What woman runs the op? Shaw?'

'No. The rich lady, I do not know her name. Very old, was a politician. All I know.'

'Okay, I can look into that. And Raymond has a dirty bomb?'

A second nod.

'And he's escaped already with it?'

'With the old woman,' the guard finally spoke. 'Your friends caused a ruckus, as you say, the police are on their way. Which exposes us.'

'I don't have friends here,' Marlowe frowned.

'The old American, and the young woman,' the guard muttered, wincing as he tried to sit up. 'They are being very obstinate.'

'Brad Haynes?' Marlowe grinned. 'About bloody time. Where's the bomb being set under Parliament?'

The guard chuckled.

'I'm missing something,' aren't I?' Marlowe growled, pressing the muzzle under the guard's chin. 'Please, explain.'

'You British, always so literal,' the guard whispered. 'Not under, but *inside*.'

Marlowe leant in.

'Define "inside" for me and I might let you live.'

'A secret tunnel, from King Charles the Second's time.'

'That's the secret room I hid the tape in,' Marshall groaned. 'They're using it to kill two birds with one stone.'

'And how do they get there?'

'This evening,' the guard, giving up on trying to hide anything, spoke freely now. 'They have people inside Westminster who will make sure this occurs. The old woman controls it all.'

Nodding and rising, Marlowe looked at Kirk.

'Looks like we have until the end of play today to fix this,' he said. 'You up for this?'

'Never more ready,' Kirk replied, and the two of them left the groaning, downed guard as they continued to the elevator, and potential safety.

Marlowe took this momentary pause to reflect on what he'd been told; today was a Sunday, and the Palace of Westminster, what was more commonly known as the Houses of Parliament, would be awash with cleaners and security, preparing the location for the return of the MPs, Ministers and Cabinet after the summer recess.

And, with the US President, Anton McKay arriving to address Parliament, the Westminster Great Hall would likely be packed with workers as they created a stage, halfway up the rear staircase, for him to speak from, with technical rehearsals working through the night. When Barack Obama spoke in 2011, they had a red carpet along the lower stairs break, where he could speak from, with rows either side watching him, and the hall itself filled with chairs, four sets of eight-chair columns, filled to capacity, and a military brass band in the top right.

Traditionally, the speeches had been held in the Royal Gallery, but after Obama, any subsequent President would class a return there to be an insult.

Which meant, unfortunately, two things.

First, the Houses of Parliament didn't have to be destroyed to kill everyone, as every important member would be in Westminster Great Hall. And second, it was easier to get in there than to enter all of Parliament.

And, if this hidden room was part of a secret route to the Great Hall, not only did it provide a secret stashing place for a dirty bomb but it also didn't even need to be that big to do what it needed to do.

Now in the elevator, Marlowe prepared himself for more guards, but when he walked out, the corridor was quiet. And, as he led Kirk out into the open, he found two SUVs at the front, with Brad, Tessa, and a familiar old woman waiting.

'Took your time,' Wintergreen snapped. 'Can we leave now? The real MI5 are on their way, you bloody showboater.'

20

PALACE HALLS

THE SOUNDS OF SIRENS HAD RISEN IN VOLUME FROM THE NORTH as the two SUVs rode south, taking a more scenic route away from the warehouse and the chaos that was about to ensue there, as the collected forces of Special Branch, MI5 and whichever local police had picked up the call all headed to the same place. Marlowe almost wanted to wait, to watch and see the fights kick off as each unit claimed the scene for their own.

Of course, MI5 would win, but the police would get their licks in before that happened. They loved opportunities like this.

The driver of the car was a Section D agent named Moore, and Marlowe had a vague recollection he liked vinyl music, but nothing more. A tall, slim black man with a faded cut, Moore wore stylish clothes, and was probably better in conversations than Marlowe was. Add to this Marlowe's unkempt beard and long, straggly hair, and Marlowe was feeling decidedly underdressed for the occasion.

Wintergreen was in the front, giving directions at break-neck speed as the SUV ran red lights on its way out of the Canary Wharf spur before the roads were closed down, and beside Marlowe, looking out of the window was Brad Haynes, with Marshall and Tessa having taken the second SUV, likely reuniting while daughter told father everything that'd happened.

'Sorry about Maguire,' Brad eventually said as they headed into Whitechapel. 'I didn't mean to leave you hanging, but I saw Shaw and Summers. She was supposed to be dead, and now she turns up with an MI5 spook who, let's face it, has been on this from the start for the wrong reasons. Too many questions. And I knew they'd save you, I just waited until the moment I could step in and save you from them.'

'And how did Tessa turn up there?' Marlowe frowned.

'Trix Preston decoded your photo,' Wintergreen spoke, the tone clipped and, as ever, emotionless. 'Learned Miss Kirk was connected to a sleeper on the list. There was a confrontation, Miss Kirk left, but not before taking the coordinates Stepan Chechik was driving to.'

'Is Trix okay?'

'Oh, she's fine,' Wintergreen half-snapped back. 'You should be grateful, after leaving her with the daughter of an Eastern Bloc sleeper agent.'

'I didn't know,' Marlowe protested. 'I only saw Rubicon when I was interviewed by Shaw.'

'You saw a faked Rubicon,' Wintergreen snapped.

'No shit,' Marlowe muttered. 'I got that the moment I saw my mum on it.'

'Have you forgotten how to speak when talking to a superior?' Wintergreen raised an eyebrow at this.

'No, but as you're as burned as I am, I'm thinking ranks are irrelevant until we fix all this,' Marlowe smiled. 'I saw they changed three names: two women and a man. I'm guessing Trix's dad replaced Raymond Sykes, you replaced Bridget Summers, and my mum replaced Shaw, but I can't see how that works, as she's too young for the list.'

'I think there's someone else at play here,' Brad replied. 'All this talk of getting into Westminster, there has to be an inside man or woman. Surely they'd be removed, just to make sure?'

Marlowe nodded. 'Makes sense, and the guard I spoke to mentioned an old woman controlling everything this evening,' he replied. 'Any idea of who's taking charge of the security tonight? Narrow it down to females in their late fifties upwards?'

'Speak to Preston when we arrive,' Wintergreen turned back to the road in front, pointing at a side road to turn down. 'She should be at the safe house by now.'

Marlowe leant back in the seat, feeling an overpowering edge to shut his eyes and pass out. He fought this, shaking his head to stay awake.

'When did you last sleep?' Brad asked. 'You didn't last night.'

'Couple of days,' Marlowe admitted. 'I could do with a catnap or two.'

'We'll grab it after we've de-briefed,' Wintergreen replied from the front of the car. 'And to show I'm a magnanimous leader, you can have a whole thirty minutes.'

Marlowe chuckled.

'After six months of leave, this feels like home,' he chuckled.

THE SAFE HOUSE TURNED OUT TO BE A BASEMENT FLAT IN Hackney, a true Cockney neighbourhood and within the sound of Bow's Bells, the ringing of them faint on the wind, calling people to Sunday service as the SUV parked up, and Wintergreen, Marlowe and Brad climbed out.

'He'll keep looping until needed,' Wintergreen explained as Moore drove off. 'He'll change the plates too so the ANPR doesn't work. I want them hunting the old car details, and while they do that, they won't be looking for us as hard.'

'And if they catch him?'

'He's not on the list, and he's only part of a group that's been suspended, it's not a personal attack,' Wintergreen said as she walked down the steps to the basement door. 'If they catch him, he'll probably ask for a job.'

'They'll want to know where you are.'

'And he'll tell them,' Wintergreen smiled, and for a moment Marlowe wondered if she was enjoying this cloak and dagger intrigue. 'I've said to do so after six pm if he's caught.'

'I'm guessing we'll be heading to Westminster by then?' Brad asked.

'We will,' Wintergreen replied. 'I'm not sure if you will, Mister Haynes.'

'The hell I'm not!' Brad snapped. 'That's my President you've got standing beside a dirty bomb. I'm not letting you Brits get all the credit.'

'Your call,' Wintergreen opened the door, waving them both through. 'But don't come screaming at me when you spout bumps and sores. I sincerely believe this RDD won't be giving anyone superpowers soon.'

Inside the room, and already working on a laptop connected to an external monitor, Trix glanced around, nodding at the newcomers.

'Brad, meet Trix,' Marlowe said. 'What do we have?'

'Thanks to information given to Marlowe here, it's believed Raymond Sykes and Bridget Summers are planning to deploy a radiological dispersion device inside Westminster Great Hall,' Trix replied. 'Otherwise known as a "dirty bomb", it's a device that combines conventional explosives, such as dynamite, Semtex or C4, with radioactive materials in the solid, liquid or gaseous form.'

She pulled up a map of London, with a red circle around the Houses of Parliament.

'If it's placed there, the device would not only kill anyone in the Great Hall, but it'd also disperse radioactive material into a small, localised area around the explosion area. Basically, it'd destroy the Great Hall and anyone in there—'

'The President of the US, the Prime Minister, and pretty much every member of the Houses of Commons and Lords,' Marlowe muttered.

'Yes,' Trix continued, annoyed at the interruption. 'But it'd also throw enough radioactive material around that it'd contaminate the entire Palace of Westminster, and surrounding buildings. If it disperses in the air, it could even reach Buckingham Palace and St James.'

'Do we have figures of previous RDD attacks?' Brad frowned at this. 'I don't recall the US ever having one.'

'That's because nobody has,' Wintergreen spoke now. 'Outside of film and TV, nobody's been stupid enough to do this.'

'Until now, apparently,' Marlowe sighed. 'Do we know anyone who can help us here?'

'Not conventionally,' Wintergreen walked to the window, looking up. 'Ah, good, the others are here.'

She walked back, pausing as she remembered where she was in the conversation.

'MI5 and the Security Services won't help us, as they currently have us down as unreliable and likely working against them, and the moment we start asking around, they'll take us down. I spoke to people in Whitehall a couple of hours back, and nobody cares. They don't want to be seen as rocking the boat, even if it means multiple deaths.'

'Pilate washes his hands,' Brad hissed.

'Actually, we do have one option,' Marlowe looked back at Brad now. 'Deacon Brodie owes us for his brother.'

'Brodie won't have this kind of firepower,' Brad shook his head, considering the suggestion. 'That said, he might know who would, or might have heard rumours of movement ...'

He looked at Trix.

'Hey, kid, do you have a list of ingredients for one of these things?'

'Yes, and I'm not a kid.'

Brad grinned.

'At my age, everyone's a kid,' he said, looking at Wintergreen. 'Present company excluded, that is.'

The door opened and Marshall and Tessa Kirk walked in.

'I know you told me to stay put, but I couldn't,' she said to Marlowe, almost as if getting the statement in before he could complain to her. Marlowe, in return, shrugged.

'The Tessa I told to wait with Trix wasn't the Tessa I see standing before me,' he said. 'I didn't know you'd been training since childhood, and I feel a little intimidated by you right now.'

Tessa laughed.

'My super spy days were long behind me,' she replied. 'I'd rather not being doing this, believe me.'

She looked over at her father.

'I'm just glad to have you back,' she said.

'What do we know about this tape drive?' Marlowe asked Trix now.

'Makes sense, it fits the analogue equipment of that time,' she tapped on her keyboard. 'It makes it a bastard to read, and it's quite clunky. To be honest, though, you'd have seen it.'

'He had a leather messenger bag when I saw him,' Marlowe remembered. 'Would it fit in that?'

'Yeah,' Trix nodded. 'Possibly. But the old guy said he was keeping it somewhere safe.'

'I'm not that old,' Kirk muttered.

'Tell me about this secret room,' Marlowe asked. 'The one you originally hid it in.'

Marshall Kirk nodded.

'I was working in Westminster a lot in the late nineties,' he explained. 'I was making sure nobody could use Rubicon, but I got shot on a mission and was out of action for a month. During that time, someone in the office found the tape and digitised it. They were doing it to everything back then, and I didn't realise until another couple of months had passed by and Raymond, then up and coming through MI5, started asking questions where the original was.'

'So, you hid it.'

'I realised a clean copy was important, as everyone was talking about "Y2K" and the "Millennium Bug" hitting us when we clicked into the twenty-first century, so I put it somewhere nobody would find it,' Kirk leant back on his chair. 'There was an old guy who talked about putting a light switch in a secret room in Parliament in the fifties, and he still had the only key. When he passed away – natural causes, I add – he bequeathed me the key, as I'd been the only one that gave a shit.'

He shifted in his chair.

'The old guy believed it was built for the procession for Charles the Second's coronation banquet in the seventeenth century. It had been used afterwards to access Parliament by Robert Walpole and William Pitt, before being bricked up and covered by wood panelling. During the restoration work of the Houses of Parliament in the fifties, they rediscovered the passage, a space unused since the mid-nineteenth century rebuilding. It was nothing more than an oddity, and ignored, locked up and forgotten over the next five decades. It was small, but easily large enough to hide a tape drive, especially behind some new brickwork, and I thought it'd stay hidden until I was long gone.'

'And then Raymond gained access to it when Primakov found a key.' Brad rubbed at his chin. 'Or did you give him it?'

'I gave him my key,' Kirk admitted. 'I was being watched, and it was my backup.'

'And Amélie was his backup,' Brad laughed. 'Christ, bloody spies.'

'And this space is beside the wall of the Great Hall?' Marlowe asked, interrupting before they started telling old spy stories.

'Literally the other side of the wall in the middle section of the stairs.'

'Where the President will stand,' Brad muttered.

'And most of our Cabinet,' Wintergreen added.

Brad shrugged at this. 'Yeah, I don't care too much for them.'

'And this space is big enough for a bomb?' Marlowe looked back at Kirk, who nodded.

'It is,' he said. 'However, to get it *into* the space, key or not, would require someone bringing such a weapon literally through the front door.'

'Which, if someone was controlling the event, could be managed.'

'We need the original drive to gain proof of who this is,' Tessa muttered. 'Say Raymond got it, he'd want to do the same as dad, surely? Find a place where nobody would think of looking?'

'He'd have had to hide it in the last week or so,' Marlowe paced now. 'Hold on. Shaw said, "no matter how deep you bury the original." What if it's underground?'

'Are you saying it's in dad's grave?' Tessa looked horrified.

'Raymond works with Bridget, and she turned up to the funeral when she knew Marshall was alive,' Marlowe continued. 'She could have been there just for me, but then she would have moved on, not attended the funeral. Do we even know if anything was left in the coffin? She could have put it inside, or even in the surrounding ground. Pile on some dirt and nobody's going to come looking. Especially when Marshall's found to be a traitor and his body is apparently atomised. At best, they'd remove the headstone. Incredibly secure, and nobody can argue the new list they've created.'

'We need to dig up a grave, then,' Wintergreen nodded. 'Marlowe, you're not cleared for field service, but I don't think that really matters right now. Take the Yank and go see your gunrunner friend, see what he says. In the meantime, the rest of us will work out how they're intending to complete this insanity without being shot.'

'If you don't mind, I'd like to do the digging,' Kirk smiled. 'Kinda like the idea of exhuming my own plot of earth.'

'I'll go with him,' Tessa nodded. 'In case he has a heart attack and actually dies. I mean, he is super old now.'

Marlowe looked over at Wintergreen as across the room, father and daughter began arguing over heart health.

'Can I grab a nap first?' he asked, walking over to the sofa and sitting down on it, sighing as he finally relaxed. 'Brad can arrange the meeting with Brodie, and it won't be for an hour or so, as he'll likely be with his brother.'

'Yeah, you deserve a break,' Wintergreen nodded. 'Why don't you—'

She paused, as Marlowe, already asleep, started snoring.

'Bloody field agents,' she muttered, walking back to Trix and the monitors. 'I've never been able to work out how to do that.'

'SO, WHAT DO YOU KNOW ABOUT WINTERGREEN?' BRAD ASKED as he sat in the passenger seat of Marlowe's rented Peugeot, brought to the safe house by Moore after he'd ditched the SUV. Marlowe had been overjoyed to find Brad hadn't played around too much with his duffel bags, although he seemed to be a little lighter in the dollar bill section than he was earlier, and a couple of weapons were missing.

The latter, however, were probably used in the warehouse assault.

'What do you mean?' Marlowe rubbed at his eyes, still

half asleep. He'd managed forty-five minutes before being awoken by Brad, explaining how Brodie not only wanted to meet asap, but that Marlowe and Brad were his new favourite people because of their rescue of Barry. Marlowe noticed the use of "their" several times, although couldn't for the life of him remember where Brad was exactly during this point. Still, the man saved him, so he wasn't all bad.

'I mean, is she married? Gay?'

Marlowe snorted.

'Oh, you fancy her?' he smiled. 'Oh yeah, she's a keeper. And to my knowledge, she's not seeing anyone. And she's definitely not married.'

Marlowe ignored explaining that, when Emilia Wintergreen took over Olivia Marlowe's role in the department, she'd had to wipe her entire history to do so, including suddenly removing a marriage of several years overnight, something that had pissed her then husband, the City of London DCI Alexander Monroe off something chronic, a slight that even now, years later, rubbed him the wrong way whenever her name was mentioned. And, as Section D and Monroe's team had worked together several times, that was quite a lot.

Brad hadn't taken the implied warning though, and simply smiled in response.

'I might chance things there, then,' he grinned. 'Old Brits love a bit of the American charm. We remind them of Clark Gable.'

Marlowe nodded, looking away, unable to keep the smile from his face. "Old Brits" didn't really watch Clark Gable movies anymore, and anyone who found Brad to be reminiscent of Gable had to be pushing a hundred by now.

'I'll pray for you,' he said, meaning it, but not for the reasons Brad probably thought.

They were in a cul-de-sac near Shoreditch, at an address that looked more like a trendy urban house than an arms depot. But at the same time, it was Shoreditch, where a simple-looking shoe shop could be a trendy concert venue, or a greasy spoon cafe had a fridge that opened into a secret underground speakeasy, so there was every chance there was something bigger and better inside. If a room filled with weapons could be called "better", that was.

They'd watched the house to make sure Deacon Brodie wasn't selling them out, as although he owed them for saving his brother, there was every chance he too had been turned by MI5, Raymond Sykes, or half a dozen other agencies, all with their own agendas. After fifteen minutes of nothing, though, Marlowe had just about considered the location to be safe when his phone went.

'When you're finished pissing about outside, come in,' Brodie's voice was amused as he spoke down the line. 'I'm a busy man, and I'm guessing you're not here for a breakfast.'

Disconnecting the phone and looking at Brad, Marlowe was unsurprised to see the American not moving.

'Staying here again?' he asked.

'Don't want to get the car towed,' Brad explained. 'I'll wait, make sure no traffic wardens come.'

Marlowe sighed, nodded and left the car, walking to the front door. It was a terraced house, opening straight onto the pavement, with a window beside the door, and two above. It was narrow, and likely built in the nineteen hundreds, and when Marlowe rapped the brass knocker, he almost expected the door to collapse in.

The Indian with short spiky hair opened the door, a pistol

in his hand, held down to the ground as he stepped back, allowing Marlowe in.

'No pat down this time?' Marlowe was surprised.

The Indian shrugged.

'What's the point?' he replied, a hint of respect in his voice. 'You'd just take mine, anyway.'

Marlowe grinned as they led him into the backroom of the house, looking out over a narrow, unmaintained garden. Deacon Brodie sat at a dining-room table, waiting. As Marlowe walked in, he rose, walked over, and embraced him.

'You saved my brother,' he said. 'Whatever you need.'

'I might hold you to that,' Marlowe smiled gratefully, pulling out the note Trix had passed him. 'Currently, I need to know who'd have these ingredients to hand, and what we'd be looking at once it was made.'

Brodie read the list, his face darkening.

'You want to make a dirty bomb?' he looked up. 'I owe you, but I won't—'

'No,' Marlowe held his hands up. 'These are ingredients we think have already been purchased. We need to know who sold them, and who bought them, as we need to prove a paper trail.'

'You think there's a dirty bomb in London?' Brodie was appalled, and Marlowe couldn't work out if this was a professional or personal insult here.

'We know there is,' he replied. 'And it's set to go off tomorrow. I need to know what sort of size it could be, and more importantly, how to turn it off.'

'It's possible,' Brodie nodded. 'A year ago I'd have said no, it was too expensive to do anything, but now ...'

'Why now?'

Brodie looked back at the list.

'Chernobyl,' he said. 'Or, as the Ukrainians call it, *Chor*nobyl. When the Russians invaded Ukraine earlier this year, they took over the area where the Nuclear Power Plant is. The power went down for five days sometime in March, and during that time there were reports that looters had raided a radiation monitoring lab in Chernobyl village, making off with radioactive isotopes used to calibrate instruments and pieces of radioactive waste that could be mixed with conventional explosives to make this bloody thing.'

He looked out of the window at the garden.

'The Institute for Safety Problems of Nuclear Power Plants, or ISPNPP, had a separate lab in Chernobyl with even more dangerous materials,' he continued. 'Powerful sources of gamma and neutron radiation, used to test devices, and intensely radioactive samples of material left over from the meltdown. These, too, were looted.'

'So, a Ukrainian with Russian connections could have brought it across?' Marlowe now understood why Stepan Chechik was so adamant about killing himself rather than talk. 'I think I know how that could have happened.'

'What's the target?' Brodie asked.

'Houses of Parliament,' Marlowe didn't bother hiding the answer, as there was no time. 'Although we think it's mainly aimed at the Great Hall.'

Brodie looked at the list, considering this.

'It'd be about the size of a cabin case,' he explained, sketching on a piece of paper. 'Maybe broken into two parts; detonator and timer on one side, the package on the other. They'd still need to be linked, though. It'd set off every bloody detector in the world though, so if you're getting it in there, you'd better have a shit ton of power, because you're walking that damned thing through multiple checkpoints.'

'And do you know who can make such a thing?'

Brodie gave a dark, humourless smile.

'Yeah,' he said. 'I'll make some calls. But I'll tell you now, I've seen some of these components already being sold on the market, so it's pretty much as you said earlier, spook. It's not a case of who could make one, but who's already done it.'

21

EXTRACTION

MARLOWE WALKED BACK TO BRAD AND THE CAR WITH HIS MIND already working through the possibilities here. Raymond Sykes was an analyst with explosives expertise, Bridget Summers was a fanatic with connections to the East, and the late Stepan Chechik had every opportunity to bring the radioactive material over from the Russian-held areas of Ukraine, to finish the ingredients needed. But this would have meant he couldn't have caught a domestic flight; he would have had to bring the radioactive material some other way. It wasn't uncommon to transport radioactive materials though, as many companies and even countries used them for medicine, agriculture, research, manufacturing, non-destructive testing and even minerals exploration. But the paperwork to do so would have been intensive.

There had to be a paper trail here.

Looking at his watch, he realised it was almost noon now. In twelve hours, the bomb would be ready and placed; in around twenty-four, they would detonate it. And even if he spoke to MI5, nobody would believe him. If Emilia Wintergreen was unreliable and a threat, then there was no way loose screw Tom Marlowe would be listened to.

There was no point talking to the CIA, either. Brad had already scuppered that idea. Marlowe wondered what lies the guards had said at the Canary Wharf safe house when the real MI5 arrived? How many of them had been on the list themselves?

There was only one way to know.

'So, what now?' Brad asked as Marlowe sat in the driver's seat, staring blankly out of the window.

'How do you feel about an extraction?' Marlowe replied, completely serious.

'Depends if the target is aware of it?' Brad shrugged. 'Easier that way.'

'And if they're not?'

Brad turned in his chair, now watching Marlowe.

'We're a day before ultimate carnage and destruction,' he said. 'We need to find a friendly to help us, and you're looking to kidnap someone?'

Marlowe smiled.

'More arrange a secret meeting.'

'By kidnapping them.'

'It's a process,' Marlowe was already tapping on his phone, dialling Trix, connecting it to the car's speaker so Brad could also hear.

'It's me,' he said. 'How's it going?'

'We think we have a candidate for the third woman,' Trix's voice spoke through the speaker. 'Baroness Levin. She's a high-level Tory in the House of Lords, she's running point on the event management for tomorrow, she's director of a transport company that could have privately brought

Chechik and his people in by boat and she used to date an East German in the seventies.'

'Dating doesn't mean turning,' Brad muttered. 'Hell, if I add up all the Commie chicks I slept with back then, I'd be in a holding cell for the rest of my life, if that was the case.'

'That's still an option,' Trix, unfazed, continued. 'She was a member of the Communist Party in University and spent a lot of time in East Berlin in the eighties as part of a fact-finding group. It's a reach, I know, but here's another thing, she worked in the seventies with a young Bridget Summers. And, when he worked in Berlin, Harris spent a lot of time in her company.'

'That's our spy,' Marlowe nodded. 'See if you can get proof she brought Chechik in. Good work.'

'So, what stupid thing are you about to do?' Trix asked, and Marlowe knew she had a smile on her face as she asked. 'You never call for updates or catchups.'

'Harris,' Marlowe leant closer to the microphone above the dashboard. 'I need his schedule for today.'

'You thinking of taking him out?'

'Yes, but more taking out for a coffee, than the ... well, you know.'

'Could be dangerous,' Trix warned. 'MI5 could take you. You're still on their wanted list.'

'If we don't do something soon, we'll all be on their most wanted lists,' Marlowe turned the car on. 'I just need something, a gap in the diary where I can extract and question him.'

'Want Marshall and Tessa involved?'

'No,' Marlowe looked at Brad. 'They're too busy grave robbing right now. I think the smaller the team, the better.'

There was a pause, a faint typing the only noise heard, and Marlowe knew Trix was checking through records.

'It's a Sunday, so he's probably at church or something. He's – oh, that's perfect,' she said. 'He's in Canary Wharf.'

'At the warehouse?'

'No, that seems to be emptied now,' Trix was still typing, the faint clacks being heard through the speakers in the background as she spoke. 'He's seeing Doctor Fenchurch, mandatory session time until one pm.'

'On a Sunday?'

'Probably the only time he can meet. Can you get to him by then?'

'It's a fifteen-minute drive, twenty at most,' Marlowe glanced at the clock on the dashboard. 'We can manage that.'

Disconnecting the call, Marlowe smiled at Brad.

'You know,' he said as he pulled the car out from the parking bay and onto the Shoreditch Street. 'I think I could do with some therapy.'

MARLOWE HAD BEEN CORRECT, AS THE DRIVE TO DOCTOR Fenchurch's chrome and glass offices had only taken them fifteen minutes. Marlowe had decided once more this was a solo mission, mainly as he knew the building layout, while Brad didn't even know the streets around there. And with a very limited parking situation in the Wharf, added to a rather twitchy security gatehouse at the entrances that would have some kind of heart attack if they saw the weapons in the boot of Marlowe's car, they decided to play this clever.

First, Marlowe pulled over in a lay-by before they reached

the main road into the Wharf, and pulled back on his suit, shirt, and tie. It was a little crumpled now, but all it had to do was get through a security cordon. This done, he rummaged around for the ID he'd taken from Stepan Chechik; it didn't have a photo on it, and this helped incredibly with the pretence.

Out of the last four times he'd come to Doctor Fenchurch, he hadn't been stopped, but that had also been because he was in a black cab. The gate guards were quite vigilant though, and would stop cars fitting security warnings, sometimes opening the boots of the vehicles, often wiping down the handles of the cars with swabs which were placed into ETD or "Explosive Trace Detector" machines, looking for any explosive residue, left on the handles when bomb-making hands opened the doors.

Marlowe didn't really want the handles of this car wiped, or the boot opened. Both would instantly have him on the floor, hands spread out.

But the ID in his hand was a very good "get out of jail" card.

Driving up to the gate, Marlowe saw them stop the car in front. Often, they'd open the traffic up for a few more cars to pass through, but this was a Sunday lunchtime, and they were probably bored. And, as the car in front could leave, Marlowe felt a sinking sensation in his gut as he saw the barrier rise again, and a fluorescent-jacketed guard walk over, swab in hand.

'Alright, sir?' he asked. 'Mind if we have a look—'

'Actually, yes,' Marlowe smiled, holding up his card. 'Sergeant Peter Bradley, *Counter Terrorist Specialist Firearms Division*.'

The guard took the ID, examining it. Marlowe didn't

expect there to be an issue, as they would have made sure Chechik's papers were immaculate.

'And why are CTSFO coming into the Wharf on a Sunday, sir?' The guard watched, suspicious.

'Because of the visit tomorrow,' Marlowe frowned. 'You know about the visit, right?'

The guard looked at his colleague in the booth.

'You mean the President?'

'Thank God,' Marlowe looked relieved. 'I thought you hadn't been briefed.'

'Briefed on what, sir?'

At this, Marlowe stepped out of the car.

'Who's the superior here?' he asked, looking from the confused guard to the one in the booth as he took his ID from the former, tucking it quickly away.

'I am,' the guard in the booth, an older man with thinning hair combed across his scalp, replied. 'We weren't told anything.'

Marlowe went to argue, but then looked around, as if realising.

'Shit, they haven't considered this,' he said, turning back to the guard in the booth. 'McKay's got a niece in one of the American law firms here. He was planning to pop in quickly before travelling to Parliament. But he was coming in by helicopter, landing in the park area in Canada Square. They wouldn't need to come through here.'

He looked back up the road; a couple of cars were waiting behind him.

'But the terrorists would come this way,' he said ominously. 'By road.'

He turned to the guard by the car, walking to the back of his Peugeot, opening the boot as he spoke.

'You still have HKs, right?'

'Um, yes,' the guard looked at his boss. 'Why?'

Marlowe closed the boot down and passed the guard two magazines of ammo.

'If they come, get down, start firing and don't stop,' he said, tapping the stab vest. 'And get some metal behind that. A couple of baking trays would help. Just in case.'

He walked back to the driver's side, pausing as he climbed back into the car.

'I wasn't here, you never saw me, yeah?'

'Um, yeah,' the booth guard said, lowering the barrier. 'And … thanks?'

'We're on the same side,' Marlowe smiled, gunning the engine as the car headed around the roundabout, away from the security checkpoint and towards Canary Wharf.

'Did you just bribe two guards with ammo?' Brad chuckled. 'And I thought my guys were gung ho.'

'We're in, aren't we?' Marlowe snapped. He hated lying to the guards; they were just doing their jobs. But, the silver lining was they'd worry about attacks all morning, they'd be vigilant, and when nothing happened, they'd be more relieved than any time before this day.

Marlowe pulled up beside a building, nodding to Brad.

'Keep it running, I might be awhile,' he said. 'If anyone comes over—'

'Give them a bag of bullets?'

Marlowe shrugged.

'Can't hurt,' he smiled as he pulled his tie and jacket off, pulled a more casual jacket from the back seat on, and left.

He didn't walk to the building, however; there was every chance that even on a Sunday, there'd be guards waiting. And footage of him walking in would give things away too quickly. Instead, he needed to move in carefully.

And that involved the delicatessen to the side.

There was a set of stairs leading down to the side of a canal, and there, beside a wide plaza was a delicatessen that delivered on a variety of food delivery services. Marlowe had called an order in for collection twenty minutes earlier, knowing they'd close early on a weekend and, grabbing the package, handily placed into a large, paper bag, Marlowe smiled, overpaid, pocketed a baseball cap with the delicatessen's logo on while they were checking the order, and left.

Putting the baseball cap on now and pulling it low over his eyes, Marlowe smiled. He was literally doing the same con as he'd done to save Marshall Kirk a decade earlier, and he still didn't feel any more comfortable doing it.

At least I'm not smoking a joint this time, he considered.

Walking into the main building, he strolled casually up to the counter. A lone, bored security guard was sitting behind the reception desk, reading a sci-fi novel, scowling as Marlowe walked up.

'Delivery for Doctor Fenchurch, fourth floor,' he said.

'She's busy,' the guard looked at his bank of phones; there was a flashing red light in the middle of the bank, likely from where Fenchurch would block calls while working with a patient. 'She's in session.'

'I know, it's an all day one,' Marlowe said. 'I drop these to her all the time. She loves our bagels. I'll call her.'

He pulled out his phone, dialling a number and connecting. Unseen by the guard, however, the moment it connected, and before it rang through, he disconnected, still holding the phone to his ear.

'Miss Fenchurch – sorry *Doctor* Fenchurch – hi, it's Luke, I've got your bagels,' he said, nodding to the guard. 'Want me to leave them at the desk?'

He pretended to listen, raised his eyebrows, and smiled.

'No worries,' he replied to absolutely nobody. 'I'll bring them up. The code is ... ah, great.'

He pulled the phone away.

'She said to take them up,' he said.

'I don't know who you called,' the guard muttered, so Marlowe showed his call list, Fenchurch's number under LAST NUMBER DIALLED, already in his contacts list as ANNOYING SHRINK.

'Yeah, that's the number,' the guard grudgingly admitted, smiling slightly at the name. 'She didn't want to come pick them up?'

Marlowe grimaced, as if caught in an awkward situation.

'She said you'd eat her lunch,' he said, making a *what can I do* expression. 'Shall I just go up?'

'Whatever, man,' the guard returned to his book. 'Don't want her shitty sandwiches, anyway,'

'Bagels,' Marlowe corrected as he walked to the elevators. He didn't need to, but the delicatessen had helped him get past the gatekeeper, and he kind of owed them.

———

EMERGING FROM THE ELEVATOR AT DOCTOR FENCHURCH'S floor, Marlowe kept his disguise; he didn't know if any MI5 agents were around, and he didn't want to walk in cold. Currently, he had the safety net of "delivery agent" for a couple of seconds before all hell broke loose. However, there was nobody beside the doors to the office. Obviously Harris didn't want anyone near him during his therapy sessions in case they heard something.

Pulling his SIG P226 from his waistband, Marlowe walked to Doctor Fenchurch's office, listening against the door for a moment. There was a faint murmuring inside, likely Harris telling Doctor Fenchurch all about his mummy issues. Marlowe actually felt bad about interrupting this, but he needed to move fast.

He knew the door led to a waiting area, and then a door that brought you into the main office. When Marlowe had attended sessions, they were always on weekdays, and trying the door handle and finding it locked, Marlowe assumed the receptionist in the office obviously didn't work Sundays.

The lock wasn't a problem though, as with his lock picks, Marlowe was able to quietly pick the handle in a matter of seconds. Sliding through the door, he could hear Harris speaking on the other side of the wall, deep into his session. He almost wanted to wait, to see if Fenchurch gave Harris the same shit she gave Marlowe, but he also knew there was a guard at reception who, after a few minutes would wonder where the delivery guy got to and might send someone to come and look.

So, with the gun in his hand, he quietly took the sideboard next to the door and carefully, and as softly as he could, pulled it across until it blocked the doorway. It wasn't the best barricade, but it was a good start, giving him a couple of seconds of grace if anyone tried to come through the door. This done, he paused, listening, hearing the conversation continuing.

Good, they hadn't heard him.

Raising the gun, Marlowe took a breath, calmed his nerves and then swiftly walked into Doctor Fenchurch's office, smiling as he saw Harris half-rise from his chair, stopping as Marlowe waved the gun at him to sit back down.

'Man, she gives you the uncomfortable chair to sit on, too?' Marlowe sighed. 'Sorry to see that, sir. I find you need to slump slightly to get any kind of traction.'

'What the hell is going on?' Harris exclaimed. Marlowe, meanwhile, was looking at Doctor Fenchurch, waving the gun.

'Sofa, please,' he said as she rose and reluctantly walked over to the leather sofa at the side of the room, away from any potential desk panic buttons or hidden weapons. She was ex-Rattlestone, and MI5 trained, after all.

'Sorry to interrupt your session,' Marlowe turned back to the red-faced Harris, 'but I really think we should have a chat. You could literally say the state of the world depends on it.'

22

BURKE AND HARE

'You know, I really thought this would be more fun,' Marshall Kirk muttered as he slammed his shovel into the ground and scooped out another pile of freshly turned grave dirt. 'Turns out, it's just manual labour.'

Tessa pulled the shovel from her father and climbed into the hole. They'd been in East Finchley cemetery for two hours now, and they'd only made it down three feet into the grave.

'We need to find a second shovel,' she grumbled, ploughing the shovel back into the ground. 'Or some kind of power tool.'

'I don't think drills work in that respect,' Kirk said as he walked back to their SUV, parked on the verge a few metres from the gravesite. 'But I can use a pickaxe to break the earth up.'

Taking the pickaxe from the back of the SUV and jumping back into the hole, Kirk started breaking up the ground beneath him.

'How long did you know?' Tessa asked as she tossed aside another spade full of earth.

'That your mum was training you to be a Communist ninja?' Kirk considered the question. 'She told me the day she ... well, the day she left us. Asked for forgiveness.'

'And did you?'

Kirk rested on his pickaxe handle.

'I asked for her forgiveness for not being around enough to work it out for myself,' he admitted. 'My work was always more important, and I never even thought she'd want to return to the life she left. I didn't consider it and therefore didn't consider her.'

'She loved you,' Tessa pushed her father aside, scooping up the broken earth. 'This is easier, go do that side too. She loved you, and she still lied to you. It became second nature.'

'When you're a spy, *everything* becomes second nature,' Kirk replied softly. 'She lied to me, and I was lying to her.'

At a raised eyebrow, he raised his hands.

'Not like that,' he continued indignantly. 'I mean I was working for MI5, and I couldn't tell her what I was doing. I wasn't allowed to. The Cold War might have been over, but she was still classed as an enemy to my superiors.'

'You were still an enemy to hers, too,' Tessa smiled. 'Nana utterly hated you. Said you were everything wrong with the West.'

Kirk slammed the pickaxe handle into the packed earth with a little more force than required.

'She did, did she?' he asked a little too conversationally. 'That's nice.'

'You met Nana once, didn't you?'

Kirk nodded, and his face went emotionless.

'After your mum drove off the cliff, there was a funeral, as well you know,' he explained. 'What you might not know is she turned up. With half a dozen Weber relatives.'

Tessa frowned.

'I don't remember seeing her,' she said.

At this, Kirk shook his head.

'You never did,' he replied. 'When they rocked up, all ready for a fight, I was waiting a couple of miles down the road with an SA80 Bullpup in my hands. I suggested they turn around, and when they didn't, I emptied a magazine into their engine and left them. Surprisingly, they waited until we'd all gone before paying their respects.'

Tessa chuckled.

'If you'd known how harsh Nana had been with me, you'd have aimed higher than the engine.'

Kirk stopped, allowing Tessa to move across and work on his recently broken ground.

'I still could,' he said. 'She's still alive over there. The old witch refuses to die.'

'Let's see if we survive this weekend,' Tessa smiled. 'If Rubicon becomes public, then we might ask if we can live with her.'

Kirk shuddered and was about to carry on when he looked up out of the hole. Walking towards them was a man, likely a groundskeeper, a shovel in his hand.

'You shouldn't be doing that,' the groundskeeper said accusatorially.

'It's not what you think it is,' Kirk smiled as he climbed out of the hole. 'I mean, it technically is, I suppose, but it's my grave, you see.'

At this, the groundskeeper paused, and Kirk assumed he'd probably confused the poor fellow.

'Stay here,' the groundskeeper said as he went to turn away.

'Interesting accent,' Tessa climbed out of the hole now, joining her father. 'Eastern European, right?'

'You have a problem with Eastern Europeans?' The groundskeeper's hands shifted grip on the shovel, and now it was held more as a weapon than a gardening tool.

'More with Russian mercs,' Tessa carried on. 'Or are you Ukrainian, but playing for Putin's team? Is Stepan Chechik your leader? Sorry, I mean *was* he?'

The groundskeeper visibly started at this, and Tessa pressed on, moving closer.

'Oh, too soon?' she asked with mock sympathy. 'Does it make you want to take your cyanide capsule too, or are you too unimportant to get one?'

She looked around the cemetery.

'I mean, shit, you pulled guard duty for a graveyard,' she said. 'Do you even know why you're here? What you're guarding?'

'Bitch, I will kill you.' The groundskeeper dropped the shovel now, pulling a pistol from his pocket. However, as he did so, Kirk stepped in front of Tessa.

'You go through me,' he hissed.

'Dad, what are you doing?' Tessa pulled to the side of her father now, glaring at him. 'I've got this! Look at him, I'd take him out in seconds!'

The fake groundskeeper went to reply to this, raising his gun to aim at the two grave robbers, but Kirk spun to face him.

'Wait your turn,' he said irritably. 'I'm having a conversation.'

'No!' the groundskeeper snapped. 'I have the gun here! You—'

He didn't finish as, with his attention diverted for a split second, Tessa swung her shovel at the gun, connecting hard, with the edge biting into his wrist, the force knocking the weapon into the air and deep into the cemetery. This done, she spun the shovel in her hand, taking the handle end and slamming it into the underside of the groundskeeper's jaw, sending him staggering back.

'Hold this,' she said to her father, passing him the shovel. And, moving relentlessly forward, she stalked the groundskeeper, crawling away backwards, looking up at her in surprise.

'Where do you think you're going?' she smiled. 'We've only just started. Where were you trained?'

'Mikhailovskaya,' the groundskeeper spat.

'You were a trainee warrant officer?' Tessa laughed. 'I thought you were a *threat*.'

She leant closer, relaxing as she spoke.

'I was trained as a child by the *spetsial'noe naznacheniya*,' she hissed. 'You know them?'

The groundskeeper nodded. There was no way he wouldn't, if Tessa was honest, as the spetsial'noe naznacheniya, or the Spetsnaz, the "Grey Men" were the bogeymen of the Russian army.

'I spent my holidays in Averkyevo,' Tessa continued. 'I might be rusty, but I'm pretty sure I can take you down. Shall we?'

The groundskeeper, aware of his situation, shook his head.

'Good man,' Tessa smiled. 'Now stand up and turn around so I can tie your wrists together.'

The groundskeeper rose, calmly, and then attacked desperately, swinging his arms wildly as he tried to score a blow. Tessa sidestepped these and, grabbing one of the outstretched arms, twisted and flipped the groundskeeper over her shoulder, slamming him against the ground, immediately dropping to a knee onto his chest as she grabbed the shovel, pushing it down against his throat, cutting his air supply as he struggled to stop her.

'You're going to lose consciousness now,' she hissed. 'Be thankful it's nothing more.'

The groundskeeper struggled for a moment longer, before his eyes rolled up, and he slumped into unconsciousness. After giving it a couple more seconds, Tessa rolled off the body, now pushing it onto its front, and pulling the laces out of the boots. Once freed, these were used to tie the ankles and wrists together tightly and looped together to hogtie the groundskeeper.

'You feel better now?' Kirk asked, a smile on his lips.

'Much,' Tessa grinned, wiping a loose hair from her forehead. 'And we came out on top.'

'How do you work that out?'

Tessa picked up the groundskeeper's shovel.

'We now have two of these,' she said, jumping into the hole and passing it to her father. 'It'll make things much quicker.'

ON A SUNDAY, THE PALACE OF WESTMINSTER WAS USUALLY quiet. The MPs and Lords never came in on weekends, and most of the time the Great Hall was filled with tourists, staring at plaques on the floor explaining where Kings had said their final words, or more recent leaders had spoken to the nation, even where traitors had been sentenced to death, or leaders laid to rest in state. The Great Hall had hundreds of years of history, and everyone wanted to see it.

That, and the cafe attached to the side had a wicked cream tea, with proper clotted cream to place on the scones.

This evening, however, the hall was busier than usual; contractors were in, using trolleys to wheel in stacks of chairs, while others carried rolls of red carpet into the hall. Interspersed between them were backbench MPs, back from their summer holidays and nervously watching the preparation, technical teams arranging speakers and sound desks and caterers preparing for the following day's events. Even the contractors removing the railings on the staircase to gain more space for upper seating were working hard, making sure the metalwork was removed, but also in a state to be returned the following day.

This wasn't a minor event, either; a Presidential Address to Parliament hadn't occurred since Barack Obama, a good decade earlier, and only half of the MPs and guests attending would have been there for that. Even the Speaker of the House had changed. The MPs, the small amount of press allowed in and even the invited guests like the various Archbishops and suchlike would have to arrive a good hour or more before President McKay turned up, and there had been a lot of complaining about that. After all, half the MPs didn't even turn up for their own leaders.

And, amid this stood Baroness Levin, Minister without Portfolio for the Conservative Government and member of the Privy Council. She'd been one of the main organisers of this event since her predecessor, Lord Ashbrown, had suffered a surprise and fatal heart attack two months earlier.

It had been a shock to lose such a prominent spokesperson, but Levin had, over her years in the party, first as MP and Minister, and then as life-Peer, made sure she was at the forefront of every major policy decision.

And tonight, she stood on the steps of Westminster Great Hall, a clipboard in her hand.

There was some kind of commotion at the main entrance, and Levin walked over to the three guards, one of who was wearing the uniform of a black long-tailed coat, white bow tie, and a silver-gilt waist badge of office, who seemed to stop an old man, pushing a trolley of drinks.

'What's the problem?' she asked.

'We don't have a chit for this guy,' the man in the black long-tailed coat replied. 'And as Doorkeeper for the Palace—'

'I know who you are, Sean,' Levin snapped. 'And I know who this is. Raymond Sykes, security services.'

Sean the Doorkeeper frowned.

'Why are the security services bringing in bottles of champagne?' he enquired, confused, pointing at the two crates of bottles, one above the other, and both nestled on the trolley.

'Because bloody Lord Ashbrown made the security clearance impossibly high for the afterparty before he popped off,' Levin explained, 'which means that half the people we'd usually use can't get in, and as MI5 have the grading, I've pulled in all non-essentials to work on this. You'll have a couple of others too; they'll ask for me if they can't get through.'

Raymond smiled at the guards.

'Look at it like this,' he said. 'I don't really want to be doing this either. I work in threat analysis, though. Primarily here to check the security, and the Baroness here decided I could combine roles for the night.'

The guards nodded, feeling sorry for the poor bugger, and glad they were just doing the one job tonight.

'Get him a proper ID,' Sean the Doorkeeper snapped. 'Or he'll keep getting stopped.'

'Oh, don't worry, I'm just delivering this for the party, checking some windows and doors, and then I'm gone,' Raymond made a cross on his chest. 'Scout's honour.'

As they walked through, leaving the others behind them, Levin looked at Raymond.

'Bloody "Scout's honour",' she hissed. 'That's three fingers in the air, not a bloody cross.'

'I wouldn't know,' Raymond shrugged. 'I wasn't a scout.'

Arriving at the end of the hall, and before the staircase that led into the Houses of Parliament themselves, Raymond started pulling the trolley up, a step at a time.

'Is the location secure?' he asked.

'Yes,' Levin nodded, helping him by holding the handle and adding her power to pull it up. 'Should we be bumping this?'

'It's not dangerous until we connect them together,' Raymond said, watching around, making sure they weren't being scrutinised. He didn't need to worry though, because everyone was engrossed in their own jobs, and two people pulling a couple of boxes of champagne bottles up a staircase were incredibly low on the list.

'Hey, over there?' Raymond pointed to a spot on the left of the staircase as they climbed it. 'That's where they believe Guy Fawkes stood as he was sentenced to death. Executed right outside those doors, too.'

'Let's hope we're not sentenced there too,' Levin muttered. 'Where are the others?'

'Keeping their distance unless needed,' Raymond smiled. 'As should you, because when this goes off in a couple of hours, it'll kill you.'

By now they were at the top of the staircase, on what was known as St Stephen's Porch, and, nodding to the guard, Levin led Raymond to the left, and into a corridor that led towards the ornate expanse known as St Stephen's Hall. However, before they entered, Levin used a key to open a heavy wooden door to the side, and the two of them moved into the staircase that led to the walkways around Cloister Court, an ornate stone corridor with marble flooring, and the left side covered with oak panelling. In fact, it was a few paces down the panelling that Raymond stopped, pulling out a rather simple looking key.

'This was taken from Blanchet,' he said, slotting it into a small hole and twisting, hearing the click as the door opened, revealing a small stone and brick chamber. 'Used to hold a tape drive, now about to hold something way more fun.'

There was a small lip, only a few inches in height, but enough to stop the trolley, so Raymond lifted the first box, placing it into the cubbyhole, looking around as he did so.

It was white-walled, apart from old brickwork around the entrance, a light switch installed and forgotten about decades earlier, and a door-shaped hole opposite. This was where King Charles the Second had once placed a door for his 1661 Coronation, in the process reworking the whole of the south-west end of Westminster Hall, creating a now-lost route to the House of Lords, where Charles and his wife would have sat.

On the side wall, a plexiglass covering kept graffiti from

the mid-nineteenth century safe; the names of the men who'd worked on the restoration of the building back then, held for posterity. Raymond smiled as he brought the second box in, placing it down and removing the top of it; the bottles in the box were no more than a fancy lid that, when removed, revealed a squat, metal box.

'What's so funny?' Levin asked nervously, looking around.

'This door's bricked up on the other side, but it's pretty much next to where Guy Fawkes was sentenced,' Raymond removed the box carefully, placing it against the old brick-work before starting on the second box. 'Poetic justice, blowing the place up from here.'

'How long do you need?' Levin asked, checking her watch.

'Not long,' Raymond smiled. 'Close the door. I'll lock it from the inside, and then make my way out through the North Passage when I'm done.'

Baroness Levin stepped back out of the cubbyhole, closing the door and listening as Raymond locked it from the inside. Then, this done, she shifted her clipboard and returned to the chaos of Westminster Great Hall with a sense of regret and sadness.

This had been her home for years, and she didn't want to see it destroyed, but from what she'd learned, this was the best way to do things; the blast would only take out the stair-case and hall, while the building itself would be inhabitable once more after a few years.

A small price for a secret kept, one that if revealed would have had her branded as a traitor and locked away for the rest of her life.

All she had to do now was get out of the blast range before it went off, alerting no one.

She stared at the plaque against the wall, mentally working out who'd be sitting closest. It'd be the Opposition, most likely the lesser parties, like the Greens and the Lib Dems.

Smiling, Levin walked away.

She could live with that.

23

GROUP THERAPY

'IF YOU JUST LET ME FIND A WEAPON, I'LL MAKE IT NICE AND quick,' Harris suggested conversationally as Marlowe walked over, pulling out two pairs of handcuffs.

'Cuff the Doctor, please,' he said, motioning for Harris to sit beside Doctor Fenchurch on the sofa. 'And then get her to cuff you, but only after you link arms.'

As Doctor Fenchurch struggled to do this, Marlowe moved in quickly, checking Harris for weapons. He had none visible, probably because he hadn't expected to need to draw a weapon for a Sunday trip to the psychiatrist, and so Marlowe stepped back.

'If you're going to kill me, you traitor, at least keep the good Doctor out of it,' Harris hissed. In response, Marlowe held up the handcuff keys, placing them on the desk.

'Unlike you, I prefer to look for all options before killing,' he said, glancing at Doctor Fenchurch. 'Has he talked about how he told his subordinate to shoot me in the head? You should get to that in the next session.'

'This is obviously important to you,' Doctor Fenchurch replied calmly. 'So why don't you tell us why you're here?'

'Rubicon,' Marlowe smiled. 'I've seen it.'

'We've all seen it,' Harris snapped. 'And we saw you—'

'My mum wasn't a traitor, and if you ask around, you'd know,' Marlowe raised the gun. 'Also, if you asked around, you'd find that the entries for Trixibelle Preston's father, my mother, and Emilia Wintergreen have all been recently edited, and all digital files overwritten.'

'How convenient for you.'

'Not really,' Marlowe pursed his lips. 'The only version not tampered with is on a data cartridge, being held by a terrorist who intends to kill the US President.'

'The only terrorist I see here is—'

'*Just stop!*' Marlowe screamed; gun raised. 'You're not a stupid man, Harris. You're not blinkered. Just hear me out!'

Harris had gone to reply, but now closed his mouth sullenly as Marlowe paced.

'There's going to be an attack on the President, likely tomorrow,' he started. 'It's being orchestrated by Bridget Summers and Raymond Sykes.'

'Two people you've been seen with,' Harris couldn't help himself. 'Or have you forgotten our last conversation?'

'No, you were right, and I was wrong,' Marlowe admitted. 'They played me, and I thought I was doing the right thing with them. But that aside, they're still doing this, and using Rubicon to aim the blame at the wrong people.'

He looked at Doctor Fenchurch.

'You're a psychiatrist,' he said. 'Do I sound crazy?'

'You definitely believe what you're saying,' she replied. 'That doesn't necessarily mean you're not having some kind of breakdown.'

Marlowe turned his attention to Harris once more.

'Wintergreen. Preston. Marlowe. All added to the Project Rubicon list, replacing actual sleeper agents in high levels of the country, and planning to bomb the President. But the sexes couldn't be changed, so we know the original names were two women and a man. Sykes fits the man's place, and Summers is one female. We thought the third was Shaw, but she's too young.'

'What the hell does Shaw have to do with this?'

'Oh, sorry, I haven't got to that yet,' Marlowe nodded. 'Shaw works for Summers.'

'Bullshit!' Harris half rose, squirming in his chair. 'She's loyal to me!'

'Then why did Stepan Chechik call her phone?' Marlowe replied. 'She picked me up with Summers, took me to Canary Wharf. I'm sure your forensics has found her prints all over the place. As well as mine, and Marshall Kirk, who you told me was dead.'

'Of course, her prints were there,' Harris sighed. 'She led the investigation.'

'Convenient,' Marlowe parroted Harris's original comment. 'Look, I don't expect you to believe me, but I'd like a small amount of trust. This is a conspiracy that goes all the way to Baroness Levin, the third sleeper.'

'Levin?' Harris scoffed. 'She's nothing but a mad old bat in an ermine cloak! What's she got to do with it?'

'We think the Russians also turned her during the Cold War,' Marlowe replied coldly. 'And, considering both Bridget Summers and you worked for her, I think you might want to listen to what I have to say. And, if there's any concern, any moment where you think something could be possible, then—'

'Then what?' Harris shook his head. 'You're deluded, Marlowe. Nobody's detonating a dirty bomb anywhere near the President, this is some kind of God complex you're working through, where you're the only person who can fix this terrible problem, and somehow gain your job back. Well, it's not happening!'

Marlowe went to snap back a reply when the phone in the office rang.

Security checking in, Marlowe realised, waving to Harris and Doctor Fenchurch to stand.

'Say anything or do anything funny, and I start blowing off limbs,' he warned, motioning for them to approach the desk. When Doctor Fenchurch was close enough, he picked up the phone with his spare hand, holding the handset to her ear.

'Hello?' she said calmly. 'Oh, hi Steve. Yes, the lunch arrived a few minutes ago.'

She paused, listening.

'No, I have no idea,' she continued. 'He left right after dropping it off. Maybe he went out the other entrance? No, that's fine. Thanks.'

Marlowe placed the phone back onto the desk.

'I'd hoped you'd be an ally, rather than an enemy,' he sighed. 'There's no back entrance. I've been here enough times to know that. How long do I have?'

'Minutes,' Harris hissed. 'You thought you could walk in here, in the middle of a Sunday, and there'd be no security? You're a known terrorist, a child of a sleeper agent, and I won't listen anymore to your—'

'*Dirty bomb,*' Marlowe said softly.

'What?' asked Harris, caught in mid-sentence.

'You said "nobody's detonating a dirty bomb anywhere

near the President", but I didn't mention it was a dirty bomb. Just a bomb.'

Harris didn't answer this. Instead, he kicked upwards, catching Marlowe unsuspecting between the legs. As Marlowe staggered back, momentarily distracted, Harris grabbed the key to the handcuffs, uncuffing one hand, allowing him free movement.

Marlowe wasn't down, though, and before Harris could move he raised the gun, but Harris used his free hand to swipe the desk, sending paperweights and paper at Marlowe, delaying him a split second. It was enough for Harris to charge the younger agent, spearing him in a tackle, sending him to the floor as the gun clattered across the office.

Doctor Fenchurch, now using the key to remove her own handcuffs, picked up the phone as the two men struggled for possession of the gun.

'Security!' she cried down the handset. 'We have a rogue MI5 agent—'

Marlowe would never know which of the two men she meant, as Harris twisted, grabbing the gun and firing, catching Fenchurch in her side, sending her to the floor, while Marlowe elbowed Harris hard in the chest, forcing the older man to drop the gun. It was now out of reach, and Marlowe was already rising, moving to the back shelf of the office, picking up the Tibetan prayer wheel he'd commented on the last time he'd been here, throwing it at the flailing Harris, stopping him from gaining distance.

Harris pulled a blade from his pocket, slashing at Marlowe, who leant back, allowing the blade to miss him, but overbalancing in the process, staggering backwards.

'Yes, Levin was removed,' Harris snarled, moving closer.

'She needed to be clean for tomorrow. Me? I'm doing this for loyalty to her, and if I'm honest, it's the money. A shitload of it.'

'Betraying your country?'

'This?' Harris laughed. 'This ain't anyone's country anymore! It's owned by corporations and big energy companies. And in companies, it's all about the bonuses—'

Harris didn't finish the comment. As he'd been speaking, Marlowe had watched as, behind him, Doctor Fenchurch, bleeding from a vicious wound in her shoulder rose silently and painfully to her feet, reaching onto the desk and picking up the familiar looking, small bottle of hot sauce Marlowe had given her a couple of days earlier. As Harris reached the "bonuses" part of his statement, she tapped him on the shoulder.

'Hey,' she said as he turned, surprised - and *slammed the open bottle into Harris's face,* the glass shattering on impact. 'Suck on this, *you traitor!*'

Clutching at his burning eyes with his free hand, Harris blindly rammed his blade deep into Doctor Fenchurch's chest, allowing her to fall as he spun back to where Marlowe had been, slashing wildly, half blinded in pain, catching Marlowe's arm as he blocked a thrust, a line of deep, red blood already soaking through the shirt.

But thanks to Doctor Fenchurch, Marlowe had managed to gain his breath and, arm now stinging from the cut. pulled a cardigan off a chair. It was the wrong colour for Harris, so obviously Doctor Fenchurch's, and, flicking it around in circles as he backed away, he twisted it into an effective rope, deflecting the next attack with the cardigan held tight in both hands, wrapping it around Harris's wrist and spinning, yanking the wrist as he did so, slamming it onto the coffee table, trying to dislodge the blade. But Harris had expected this, and flipped as Marlowe did, landing painfully on his back, but able to rise quickly, the cardigan loosed now, slipping his arm out as he slashed again.

'You're too late,' he said. 'The bomb's made, and it's beautiful. And tonight it's going to kill a lot of people.'

'Tonight?' Marlowe almost stopped but lunged to the side to evade a second attack. 'The President isn't there until tomorrow!'

'We don't want the President!' Harris laughed. 'We want McKay alive! When it's revealed the bomb went off early, killing the US Ambassador and everyone inside the Great Hall, McKay will be the first in line to start retaliations!'

'But the Government—'

'This is bigger than Governments,' Harris shook his head. 'Christ, Marlowe, how have you stayed alive so long? This is Shadow Government shit. Corporations, and unlimited expense cheques.'

Marlowe could see the logic of this plan. If McKay was killed by a dirty bomb, believed planted by Russian sleeper agents, the US would want vengeance, but would have to swear in the Vice President first, who might want to look at options before moving to a war footing. However, a near miss, saving Parliament *and* the President? Then everyone had a war in play from the very start. And Harris's comment about "shadow Governments" wasn't a new idea; it'd been a common belief for a long time that behind every leader and his or her Government, was another, secret one that commanded them. Most of the time it was branded as the conspiracies of lunatics, but once in a while, you had to stop and wonder.

But if someone tonight was the target, then this meant they no longer had a day. They now had a matter of hours.

'Yes, you're realising,' Harris grinned. 'Tonight, there's a dress rehearsal. MPs who have scripted readings during the show, ambassadors, all the special people who need to know where to stand, the Privy Council sorting out a spot for some Royalty to sit and watch, doing the make-believe work to look like we all get on great, all that shit. There's a function in the Members Dining Room later in the evening, you see. A little party for after they sort things in the Great Hall. And *these* are the people the press will read about tomorrow. These are the list of the dead, killed by you and Marshall Kirk—'

Harris stopped with a scream; Marlowe had grabbed a pen, the one Doctor Fenchurch always clicked when she took notes, and rammed it into his still hot sauce-blinded left eye. As the older agent pulled at it, dropping the blade, Marlowe grabbed his fallen gun.

The room echoed with two sharp reports. Two shots to the skull, right between the bloodshot, hot sauce-burned eyes of Section Chief Harris as his legs crumpled out from under him, and he fell, very dead, to the floor.

Falling back against the desk and taking a moment to catch his breath, Marlowe considered his options. Security would likely be here in a matter of seconds, and all they'd find were two bodies, both killed by the same gun, a gun Marlowe now held in his hand. There was no way he could talk his way out of this, especially as he'd been seen entering the building, and his blood, caught by a knife slash, was spattered all over the office.

Running to Harris, he started working through the pockets, pulling out car keys, an ID pass, a phone, anything and everything the man had on his person, stuffing his own pockets as he did so. He'd look into what he'd picked up later, but first, the sounds of men arriving in the corridor, and finding his locked and barricaded door, meant he had literally seconds to get out. However, he stopped as he held a small brass key.

Bridget must have met with Harris to pass this on, he thought to himself.

Putting it in his trouser pocket again, Marlowe rose now, walking over to Doctor Fenchurch. She could have survived the gunshot with medical care, but the blade Harris had rammed into her had pierced her chest, and she'd bled out in seconds.

'I'm sorry,' he muttered, the sound of banging building in intensity out by the main door. 'You were a good doctor. And thanks for saving my life.'

Reaching down, he pulled her building pass from her pocket. Moving fast now, Marlowe looked for anything he could use in this situation. Unfortunately, there wasn't much. There was, however, a side door to a closet, where the fuse box for the entire floor was. Marlowe had learned the layout of the building when he first attended his sessions – no good spy didn't – and with this knowledge, he opened the side door, pushing aside some boxes, likely dumped in here months ago when MI5 took over this office for assessments.

There was a toolbox, mainly for minor jobs, but in it was a claw hammer; Marlowe quickly turned to the wall on his left inside the closet and smacked hard at the plasterboard. The building was chrome and glass, built with steel girders and secure enough to stop an earthquake, but the floors were empty, with only pillars to hold the next level up. The offices were all created in the usual manner, with wooden wall frames secured to the floor and ceiling, and plasterboards mounted on either side, skimmed with plaster and then painted. Which was a lot easier to get through at the back than it was at the front, which had likely been reinforced.

Marlowe knew it might have seemed pointless to do this, but MI5 would also have known that, in the event of an attack or political uprising, their operatives needed a way out. It was standard practice anywhere in the world, and as this was an MI5 building of sorts, the same rules should apply.

Looking at the design when he first started attending sessions, Marlowe had seen there was a three-foot discrepancy from the wall to the back of the closet. And now, punching through, he found a small passageway, lined with breeze blocks. On the floor was a coiled length of rope, likely left there from the construction, and Marlowe grabbed it, running into the office. He opened the dividing door, firing a couple of times at the wall to make the security trying to push open the door a little more cautious, and then returned, tying the rope to the chair he hated, firing twice at a window to shatter it, and then placing the chair by the window, the rope now thrown out. There was a small ledge around the lower floor, and with luck, anyone looking out would think he'd used the rope to get onto it.

Marlowe wasn't doing this, though, and pulling the closet door closed behind him, he clambered through his hastily made exit, and ran down the passage, expecting someone to find him at any second. Or, worse, to find this a dead end, with no escape.

As it was, the passage turned, and Marlowe realised it led to a small, rear, fire staircase. Taking the stairs two at a time, Marlowe made as much distance from the office as he could, almost falling frequently, stumbling to a black fire-door on the ground floor. It was locked, but a wireless pad at the side allowed Marlowe access to the exit once he swiped Fenchurch's card across it. Opening the door, he found himself in the ground-floor lobby, further along the wall than the elevators, and with the entrance at the other end of the building.

However, there was noise from that end, and Marlowe knew this was likely the next wave of guards, maybe even agents, preparing to attack.

'There!' the guard who'd been at reception, possibly named Steve, pointed as he walked around the corner. 'That's the guy!'

Marlowe couldn't risk a full-on assault and so turned to the full-length window beside him, firing his last two rounds into it, shattering the glass and jumping out into the Canary Wharf air. As he did so, he saw the two guards who'd let him into the Wharf earlier, standing in confusion outside the main entrance. He felt bad, but this was momentary, as the two of them pulled up their HK MP5s and started firing at him, maybe even with the ammo he'd given them. Marlowe ran for cover but stopped as a familiar blue Peugeot pulled up around the corner, Brad waving for him.

'I don't know what you did, fella, but you've pissed off everyone,' he said as Marlowe leapt gratefully into the back seat, the car already screeching around the corner at speed as Brad made distance from the building. 'You still think giving those guys bullets was a good idea?'

'We were wrong,' Marlowe, out of breath breathed. 'It's not tomorrow, it's today. We need to get to Westminster, and fast.'

'No offence, pal, but you've pretty much just made that impossible,' Brad replied cheerfully, throwing the car into a hard right, and squealing through a red light, into traffic. 'But you seem to do well with impossible, so let's speak to the others.'

24

RETRIBUTION

'You shot and killed Harris,' Wintergreen said dispassionately through the speakers of the car. 'You went to talk to him, and you shot and killed him. I've got that right, yes?'

'In fairness, he tried to kill me first, the moment he realised I'd caught him out.' Marlowe pressed his back into the passenger seat, trying to stretch it out while watching the wing mirror in case they were being followed. 'He knew it was a dirty bomb before I told him. And he confirmed it was Baroness Levin on the list, effectively stating he didn't need to be on it to be a scumbag, and by that, I mean be someone who only did things for the money.'

'Just like Shaw, it seems.'

'Yeah,' Marlowe rubbed at his bruised jaw. 'I'd also assume Curtis is compromised, too. He was happy to follow Harris when he said to kill me, and he answered Shaw's phone, which meant he was with her when she was hunting us.'

'It's a coin toss,' Wintergreen mused. 'He might just be a soldier that follows orders.'

'Well, thank God for soldiers who follow orders,' Brad muttered.

'Christ, isn't the Yank dead yet?' Wintergreen muttered. 'You couldn't put two in his head as well? I mean, by now does one more even matter?'

Brad, currently driving, made a mocking hurt expression and Marlowe smiled. It was the first time in a while he'd felt at ease with the situation, probably because finally there wasn't time to concern themselves with issues and considerations and plans—the rehearsal started in an hour, and currently Westminster Great Hall had hundreds of workers inside, laying out the rows of chairs.

'Do we have anything on the bomb?' he asked.

'Yes, Preston has heard from your arms dealer friend, who's worked out the most likely device,' Wintergreen replied. 'She needs to defuse on site, however, so we're on our way to meet you.'

'Trix is our bomb disposal expert?' Marlowe shook his head in disbelief. 'She's an analyst!'

'She's an expert in all forms of computing tech, and she builds gaming PCs for fun,' Wintergreen replied icily. 'Or, at least that's what she's told me. She reckons once you put together a five grand gaming device, something like this is easy. And before you argue, we don't exactly have that many people lining up to help us here.'

'Wait, you said *we're on our way?*'

'Well, how else do you think the poor girl's going to get in?' Wintergreen seemed irritated by the question. 'I know the quickest and quietest ways into the building.'

'And how do *we* get in?' Marlowe leant his head against the window, feeling the cool glass against his forehead.

'Where are you now?'

Marlowe looked about.

'Coming up to Tower Hill.'

'Then you have the rest of the Embankment to work that out don't you?' Wintergreen could almost be heard smiling. 'Try Portcullis House. We'll leave a light on for you.'

There was a click as the line went dead, and Marlowe uttered some choice, soft expletives.

'Do we have a plan?' Brad asked.

'Pull over,' Marlowe ordered and, as Brad pulled into a side road beside Tower Hill Station, Marlowe climbed out of the car, pulling out all the items he'd taken from Harris.

'Something here must help us,' he said, working through them.

'Tom,' Brad whispered. 'We might need to admit we're not gonna win this one.'

'No,' Marlowe looked over at the American. 'If I do that, then they've won.'

He stopped, rising slowly.

'Farringdon,' he said.

'The station?'

'The man,' Marlowe replied. 'Anthony Farringdon. Used to run security in Westminster. Met him through Marshall Kirk a couple of times, and he was at Marshall's funeral. If anyone knows how to get us in, and where any secret bloody rooms are, it's him.'

'So why didn't we call him earlier?'

'Because the moment he gets involved, he's probably damned by association, and I'd rather not burn all my friends right now,' Marlowe muttered, flicking through the items in front of him. Eventually, pulling a burner phone from his pocket, he dialled a number.

'You know his number off by heart?' Brad was impressed.

'I'm good with numbers,' Marlowe looked around the street as he waited for the call to connect. 'I believe Farringdon lives near Mayfair, but I—'

He stopped as the phone answered.

'I don't know this number,' an elderly voice spoke. 'You have ten seconds before I decide you're an Indian call centre and disconnect.'

'Anthony, it's Tom Marlowe, and I really need your help.'

'Tom Marlowe is on the run from MI5, and is apparently a traitor,' Farringdon's voice replied. 'Why should I believe anything you say?'

'Because you were lied to from the start,' Marlowe said, leaning against the car. 'The coffin you were pallbearer for? Only thing in it was a data drive.'

'Marshall was buried elsewhere?'

'Marshall is alive and well,' Marlowe smiled. 'I rescued him from a rogue agent's hideaway.'

'Well then, you have been busy,' Farringdon's tone hadn't changed. 'So why do I have the pleasure of this call?'

'Because someone's about to detonate a dirty bomb in the Palace of Westminster,' Marlowe glanced at his watch. 'Any time from the next hour, until everything's locked up.'

'Confirmed?'

'Yes.'

'Why not tomorrow?'

'They want it to look like it went off early,' Marlowe wanted to punch the air, as for Farringdon to ask questions, meant he was working through the problem. 'They're blaming me and Marshall. It's all connected to a project called Rubicon back in the day.'

'Never heard of it.'

'You wouldn't have, I don't think it involved Westminster that much. It's a NOC list of sleeper agents, and the digital version has been altered.'

'Let me guess, Marshall's coffin has the original?'

'We think so,' Marlowe nodded before realising Farringdon wouldn't see it. Although, the old man was wily enough to probably guess. 'Look, Anthony, I'm sorry to call. We think Baroness Levin is involved, and she's allowing foreign agents into Westminster right now. We have corrupt MI5 agents and sleepers in high levels of power all being blackmailed by this sodding list—'

'And let me guess, MI5 don't class you as someone worth getting into the place?' Farringdon laughed. 'All I seem to do is help people into the bloody building. So, what do you need from me?'

'Are there any doormen or security guards you trust?' Marlowe asked. 'Maybe they could watch for anything.'

'And if they see something?' Farringdon replied.

'Nothing,' Marlowe grimaced as he said it. 'I don't know who's on what side. The only people I can trust are people barred from attending.'

'So, if my people saw something, raising the alarm could get them killed,' Farringdon's voice was thoughtful, as he worked through the problem. 'So, we'll have to sort this ourselves. How fast can you get to Mayfair?'

'Ten minutes?'

'I'll text an address,' Farringdon was all business now, his military efficiency coming out. 'Come to me. It's

Sunday, the traffic's not bad. We'll go to Parliament together.'

MARLOWE HADN'T KNOWN HOW ANTHONY FARRINGDON WOULD work it, but the man was as good as his word, and by the time Brad and Marlowe arrived at his Mayfair apartment, Farringdon had already spoken to several of his contacts.

'So, Baroness Levin has eight names on her personal list for access, all claimed as diplomatic observers.'

'Let me guess, from Ukraine?' Brad asked, the first time he'd spoken since arriving. Farringdon fixed him with a withering gaze.

'I said the American could come in, but not talk,' he said.

'Hey, I'm just as deep in this as you are,' Brad snapped. 'Deeper, even. You're just a tourist here.'

'Were you a friend of Marshall Kirk?'

'I was.'

'Didn't see you at the funeral.'

'I was in hiding. And the funeral was fake.'

Farringdon nodded, and Marlowe could see from the sparkle in his eyes he was enjoying the verbal sparring.

'Going back to the observers?' he said, guiding the conversation back on track.

'Yes, not Ukrainians as such, but all from Eastern Europe, it seems,' Farringdon checked his notes. 'None of them were checked for weapons, as they had diplomatic privilege, but if they brought a bloody great bomb with them, they would have been searched. Anything larger than a handbag is being looked into, regardless of diplomacy.'

'So, they brought it in another way,' Marlowe nodded.

'As will you be,' Farringdon nodded, opening up a wardrobe. 'You're about the same size as me, although your American friend—'

'I have a name, you know.'

'—won't be able to enter the same way, because of his awful Colonial accent,' Farringdon continued, pulling out a doorkeeper's outfit. 'It's my old one for occasions I had to attend, like the opening of Parliament. You'll be overdressed, but I reckon half the people there will be tonight. It's rare we have such events.'

He stopped.

'*They* have,' he corrected. 'Sometimes I forget I'm retired.'

'So, what do I do?' Brad muttered.

'Keep watch for us,' Marlowe smiled. 'You're good at that. Maybe see if you have any CIA pals who can help?'

Brad brightened at this.

'Actually, that might not be a bad idea,' he said. 'I'll make calls while you get yourself shot.'

Farringdon had been reading something on his phone while they spoke, and now he looked up.

'Bad news, I'm afraid,' he said. 'Seems that before, only MI5 wanted you. But now they've issued a warrant for your capture and arrest, and they seem to be framing you for the murder of some Section Chief named Harris?'

'I'm not being framed,' Marlowe admitted. 'I did kill Harris. He was working with foreign agents.'

'And this therapist you're also being blamed for?'

'He killed her.'

Farringdon pursed his lips as he stared at the phone.

'This makes things difficult,' he sighed. 'We need to move fast. Put the clothes on in the car.'

Marlowe went to reply but stopped as he received a text. Reading it, he smiled.

'Tessa and Marshall found the tape cartridge,' he said. 'They're bringing it in, should be in Westminster in half an hour.'

He held up an image, showing Marshall, Tessa and some tied up third person, standing by a freshly dug grave, smiling and with a black plastic square box, around ten centimetres in length, in their hands.

'That's a DLT cartridge,' Farringdon smiled. 'I used to own those.'

'You wouldn't, by chance still have the drive, would you?' Brad asked.

'You know, my American friend, I think I might.' Now all smiles, Farringdon opened a door, revealing a cupboard filled with boxes. Pulling one out, he pulled a DLT cartridge box from the various cables inside.

'It's definitely here somewhere,' he said. 'But we don't have time.'

Deciding, he threw his apartment keys to Brad.

'Don't break anything,' he said, nodding for Marlowe to follow as he walked out of the apartment.

Picking up the clothes, Marlowe looked at Brad, now holding the cartridge box.

'If you find a drive, get it to Trix,' he said.

And with that, Marlowe followed Farringdon out of the apartment and down to his car.

'Hold on,' Brad said, half to himself as realisation took hold. 'If you're going in the car, how the hell do I get there?'

BRIDGET SUMMERS SAT ON THE BENCH IN PARLIAMENT SQUARE and watched the main gate into New Palace Yard. It wasn't that she didn't trust the people she worked with, but she knew this was the only chance to get everything done. Raymond was the planner, but at the same time he was prone to moments of fancy, *the field agent who never was,* and could easily screw all this up for a taste of adventure.

'I should have gone in with him,' she muttered.

'Who?' the voice of Shaw spoke in her earpiece.

'Sykes,' Bridget muttered. 'I don't trust him. Or Levin. I worked with her years ago and she was a corrupt cow even then.'

'She'll do what needs to be done. She's as in this as we are,' Shaw soothed. 'Just let things work out.'

'Where are you?' Bridget looked around, as if expecting to suddenly see the MI5 agent waving from across the road.

'Portcullis House,' Shaw replied, and Bridget could hear the triumph in her voice. 'And you'll never guess who we caught trying to sneak in.'

Rising, Bridget started walking towards the corner of the park, and the buildings on the other side of the road.

'Marlowe?'

'Even better,' Shaw was gloating now. 'We got his grandma. Wintergreen.'

'Oh, you're right,' Bridget smiled. 'That's indeed better.'

WINTERGREEN SAT ON A CHAIR IN THE PORTCULLIS HOUSE atrium, glaring at the man aiming a Glock 17 at her.

'Did I fire you once?' she asked. 'You look familiar.'

'No, but you turned me down for a promotion,' Curtis smiled. 'Guess I had the last laugh.'

'Sure, if you mean "guess I killed dozens of blameless people",' Wintergreen shrugged. 'So, when does your boss turn up?'

'My boss was killed by—'

'Not Harris,' Wintergreen snapped, half rising. 'I don't mean more important *puppets*; I mean your *actual boss*.'

Curtis stared at Wintergreen for a long moment, confused.

At this, Wintergreen chuckled.

'So, you don't even know who your boss is,' she said, sitting back up. 'Christ, you think you get the last laugh. You don't even know which country you're selling us out to. What corporation's paying your mortgage.'

She stood now, facing Curtis.

'Because know this,' she said. 'They'd better be paying you "mortgage payment" levels of money because you're going to need it when you find yourself hunted across the globe. And you *will* be hunted after what you do tonight.'

'Lies,' Curtis snapped. 'You'll say anything to convince me you're not the traitor I know you to be. I've seen the list, Miss Wintergreen. I saw your name.'

'You've seen *a* list,' Wintergreen sighed. 'A doctored one. The one Shaw and Harris wanted you to see.'

Curtis went to speak again, to shout, but stopped, looking away, and Wintergreen knew he was mentally replaying half a dozen conversations at once.

Christ, he really doesn't know what's going on, she realised.

Eventually he looked back, waving to the chair as he did so.

'Just sit the hell down,' he said. 'It won't be long now until MI5 gets here.'

'My friend, MI5 aren't coming,' Wintergreen smiled, complying. 'Shaw has her own plans.'

Sitting back against the chair, Emilia Wintergreen hoped to God this was worth it, and that Trix had got in while she played bait. Otherwise, this was all for nothing, and she was about to be caught in a radioactive blast radius for her sins.

That said, she had *many* sins.

THE GUARDS ON DUTY AT THE SOUTHERN END OF THE HOUSES of Parliament were surprised when the blue Peugeot pulled up at the gate, and Anthony Farringdon leant out with a smile.

'Sir!' the first one said with delight. 'Been a while.'

'You're looking good, George,' Farringdon said, patting the arm through the window. 'The stripes suit you.'

'What are you doing here?' the guard, now identified as George, looked into the car. 'With …?'

'All hands on deck,' Farringdon said, shrugging. 'And I'm the only one who can remember where everything was the last time we did this. Eidetic memory, remember?'

He nodded at Marlowe, now dressed in the uniform of a doorkeeper.

'Williams here met me at the other gate, he'll be taking me through,' he said calmly. 'All I'm doing is looking over everything, getting in my car and going home.'

George considered this for a long time, and then nodded.

'ID?' he asked. 'Sorry, sir, we need—'

'No, that's fine,' Farringdon's smile faded. 'I thought

loyalty meant a lot here. Looks like the moment you retire, your word's not worth shit.'

'Sir, I didn't mean that—' George looked conflicted now, looking back at the gatehouse.

'Bring it down, they're okay,' he eventually said.

'Thank you,' Farringdon smiled. 'You're good people. Stay safe.'

And, the barrier now lowered into the pavement, the Peugeot drove into the Royal Court, which was mainly a car park for official vehicles.

Farringdon stared back at the guards, his face impassive, and Marlowe could see he regretted lying to them.

'You've done your bit,' Marlowe said. 'I can do the rest from here. Give it ten minutes, then leave. And tell the guards to get the hell out.'

'That doesn't help the people inside,' Farringdon was already unbuckling his seatbelt, but Marlowe placed a hand on Farringdon's.

'I said, I've got it,' he repeated. 'I know where to go, you've helped me in. Now, all I ask is you ...'

He trailed off as his phone beeped.

'Message from Trix,' he said, reading it. 'Wintergreen gave herself up as a distraction. She's at Portcullis House.'

'I'm sure she has a plan,' Farringdon smiled. 'Be safe, Thomas.'

'And you, Anthony,' Marlowe shook the older man's extended hand and climbed out of the car, hastening to a door to his left. This, through the Norman Porch, was the route to the Queen's Robing Room, and the path every monarch took on the way to open Parliament. It was as far from the Westminster Great Hall as you could be, but at least he was inside.

All he had to do now, was make it through the entire Houses of Parliament without being recognised, take down half a dozen foreign mercenaries and a couple of zealot sleeper agents, and disarm a dirty bomb in a locked, secret room before it killed hundreds of people.

So basically Sunday then, he thought to himself as he started up the stairs.

25

ADDRESSED REHEARSAL

Baroness Levin watched the contractors finish up the Great Hall setup with a sense of distinct sadness. That they would work so hard for something doomed to never be seen was a bittersweet honour, but they'd at least have the opportunity to be part of a greater purpose, martyrs to a cause they didn't yet know they believed in.

She knew Raymond Sykes would be done soon, and the bomb primed and ready, he'd unlock himself and scuttle away like the coward he was. Levin, however, wouldn't be leaving. For her to leave would raise flags; people would frown when they scanned the lists of the dead and go *"why would the woman organising this walk out shortly before a horrible terrorist attack"*, and there would be questions, and likely answers; ones she didn't want brought out into the open.

No, she'd had a good life, a fulfilled life, and although many of the people on the Rubicon list had spent years waiting for this call, this moment to effectively destroy their prior lives, she was at peace to move on to the next life. And, with her death, her husband, her children, even her grand-children would mourn without the press demanding answers.

Weirdly, she was even looking forward to it. She wondered what her obituary would say, whether she'd get even a speech from the Prime Minister.

One of the Eastern Europeans she'd brought with her, a request from Sykes she should have ignored, walked over.

'There are crowds of rehearsal invitees building up outside,' he said, his accent showing. 'Do you want them in?'

Levin looked at her watch in surprise. Although tomorrow would be packed out to the rafters, tonight would be a smaller affair, with only a couple of hundred people: ambassadors, minor MPs and civil servants, even a couple of lower-level Royals coming to help; all on the basis they got a ticket to sit at the back the following day.

Poor buggers didn't know there wouldn't be a following day, she thought to herself as she scanned over the chaos in the hall.

'Ten more minutes, and then I'll let them in,' she said. 'And once they're all in lock the doors.'

OUTSIDE, IN NEW PALACE YARD, THE CROWDS OF SUITED visitors were getting irritated at the wait. Many of them probably hadn't had to wait for anything in a long time, and for Trix Preston, currently in the middle of the crowd in a hastily purchased dress, her tablet in her hand, she found it rather amusing to watch their rising anger.

At the same time, it was irritating. She was supposed to have got in a lot earlier, with Wintergreen diverting MI5 over to Portcullis House, but although Trix had got through the underground passageway into the Palace of Westminster's grounds without being searched, she couldn't get into the building itself until they allowed people into the Great Hall.

Which, when they started doing this, meant the rehearsal was almost ready to start, which also meant the bomb would be primed to explode shortly afterwards.

She had a small earpiece lodged in her left ear, and casually she looked around.

'I can't get in,' she whispered. 'Marlowe, can you hear me? I'm stuck here until they allow us through the doors.'

MARLOWE WAS MOVING FAST THROUGH THE PALACE OF Westminster as Trix's voice spoke in his ear.

'I'm just entering the Peer's Lobby,' he replied. 'Once I'm in the Central Lobby, I can—'

He stopped as a suited man walked into the Peers Corridor ahead of him. The man was in his thirties, obviously military, even though he was well dressed, and he seemed as surprised to see Marlowe as Marlowe was to see him.

'You!' he hissed, reaching into his jacket and pulling out a suppressed pistol, firing at Marlowe as Marlowe dived backwards behind a counter beside the double doors to the House of Lords. Marlowe had his own weapon, but unlike the one facing him, his wasn't suppressed, and he knew the moment he fired it, he'd alert everyone in Westminster.

But maybe that was a good thing, he thought to himself. If the doors were closed, even with Trix outside, nobody else would be inside when the bomb went off.

Pulling his SIG P266 out and readying himself, he popped up from behind the counter, firing two rounds in quick succession, the report echoing in the hallway as they both hit their target, the suited assassin falling to the ground, his face now half missing.

But, as Marlowe ran to the body, he could already hear the cries of people echoing up through the Central Hall, only a hundred feet away.

Well, so much for subtly, Marlowe grimaced. *Let's just hope it did the right thing.*

'GUNSHOTS!' SEAN THE DOORKEEPER SHOUTED AS THE CROWDS outside, hearing the faint echoes, panicked. 'Lock it down!'

'Stop!' one of Baroness Levin's observers ran down to the doors from inside. 'It is nothing! You must—'

'We'll do what we're trained for,' Sean said, nodding to the armed police outside. 'Lockdown!'

As the crowds ran from the double doors, Trix walked quickly over to Sean, seeing his uniform, and knowing his likely connection to the man who'd recently helped Marlowe at the other end of the building. It was a hunch, but a calculated one.

'Farringdon sent me,' she hissed, showing her probably blacklisted by now MI5 security pass. 'I need to be inside when you lock things up.'

Sean, not knowing who this woman was, but recognising her ID and Farringdon's name, waved her beside him as she slid through the doors, the bulk of the crowd moving the other way.

'You mustn't send them away!' the observer cried out,

looking back into the building at his friends, who'd spaced out in the Great Hall. And as the door was closed, and Sean the Doorkeeper turned the lock, the observer decided finally to stop this, and, pulling out a gun, shot the armed policeman standing to his side in the temple, grabbing his rifle as he fell to the floor.

'*Zaperét!*' he shouted, firing the gun into the air. At least it sounded like *zaperét* to Trix, who by now was running, using the terrified crowd as cover, towards the other end of the hall. She only had a smattering of Russian in her vocabulary, but she was pretty sure this meant *blockade*, or *block up*. And if this was the case, then the observers, overpowering the unsuspecting armed police, meant to lock down the location, hold the fort until, well, until the bloody bomb went off.

Which meant she'd probably made a terrible mistake pushing her way in.

'Move!' the observer by the door shouted, firing into the ceiling. 'Get into the middle! Sit down!'

'What the hell do you think you're doing?' Baroness Levin said. 'You were supposed to get more people in!'

The observer glared at Levin as, from the Central Lobby, they heard more gunshots.

'*Kill whoever that is!*' Levin shouted to her men, and two of them, standing near the back stairs peeled off, cocking their freshly gained HK weapons.

'Two baddies heading your way,' Trix muttered, hoping the gunshots had been Marlowe, and not the sound of Marlowe being shot.

At Portcullis House, Curtis looked to the main entrance as Shaw and Bridget Summers walked into the building.

'We have reports of shooting in the Houses of Parliament,' he said, 'Do you know anything about this?'

Shaw ignored him, looking at Wintergreen.

'Is it Marlowe?' she asked.

'I asked you a question!' Curtis snapped, looking over at Bridget. 'I don't know what's going on, or why *she's* here, but with Harris gone, I'm leading—'

He stopped abruptly as Shaw pulled a gun, aiming it between his eyes.

'For the love of Christ, just shut the hell up,' she hissed. 'Do your job. Baroness Levin is caught inside, and we need to get her out. If you can't do that, then piss off and let the grownups do it.'

'You keep aiming that gun at me, and I'm going to make you eat it,' Curtis stated coldly, but was distracted by the sound of throaty laughter.

Wintergreen leant back in her chair.

'Told you,' she said. 'You have no clue who you work for.'

'And you can shut up too,' Shaw placed the gun away. 'The whole bloody place is on lockdown thanks to your Boy Scout, and now we need to fix this before he kills everyone inside.'

'Oh, would you rather he killed other people as well?' Wintergreen asked innocently. 'With the nice big bomb you snuck in?'

Shaw was about to reply when there was a commotion at the door, and one of the MI5 agents standing there looked back at them.

'We have a visitor,' he shouted. 'American. Claims he's Wintergreen's boyfriend.'

Shaw looked to the door, seeing Brad Haynes, smiling, a bouquet of hastily grabbed flowers in his hand.

'Tell him to piss off,' she said. 'If he stands outside, he'll just cause attention.'

'I heard that,' Brad smiled, pulling a DLT Cartridge case out from behind his back. 'You're holding my love, and I had gifts for her and everything.'

Bridget stared in horror at the case.

'Get him in here now!' she growled. 'Where did you get that?'

'Went to see a friend, dug it up,' Brad said as he entered the atrium, hands up, one holding the flowers, the other the cartridge case. 'Got the bouquet from there too.'

The MI5 agent grabbed the DLT case, opening it.

'It's empty,' he said.

'Well, of course it's empty!' Brad grinned. 'You think I'd bring you the *actual* goddamned original of Rubicon, the one showing certain people's names where the more recent one says otherwise?'

'Bullshit, you're bluffing us,' Bridget walked over to Brad. 'You always were a chancer, Haynes. Why should we believe you right now?'

'People's lives are in the balance,' Brad shrugged. 'And I want to be the hero for a change.'

Bridget considered this.

'And what do you want from us?'

'Let the woman go, accept your fate, Raymond takes the fall.'

'And your friend Marlowe?'

'Screw him,' Brad shrugged. 'He's probably dead by now,

anyway. And if he's not, let Marlowe kill Sykes, and let MI5 kill Marlowe. No need to kill anyone else, and you can still claim the win, and start your little war.'

He looked over at the MI5 agent.

'Is he loyal to you, or the service?' he asked.

'Me,' Bridget snapped. 'And this is another scam, just like every other time I dealt with you.'

She paused, frowning.

'Why are your flowers smoking?'

'Oh, that's the acid,' Brad smiled. 'In the bouquet's base. You see, I knew you wouldn't take the deal, so I swapped the water.'

And, with that, Brad flicked the bouquet at the turncoat MI5 agent, the "water" held within the paper and plastic wrapping splashing out as the agent clutched his face and screamed.

MARLOWE HAD REACHED THE CENTRAL LOBBY BY THE TIME THE two mercenaries arrived.

He recognised the area well, as often news channels would have reporters speaking to camera here, because this was the very spot where corridors from the Lords, Commons, and Westminster Hall met. It was a wildly ornate location for a gunfight, though; the arches surrounding the tall windows of the Lobby were decorated with statues of Kings and Queens of England and Scotland, while over each of the four exits were large mosaic panels depicting the patron saints of the four constituent countries of the United Kingdom. And this was how, as Marlowe ducked behind a counter, firing wildly at the two attackers, St George of England, St David of

Wales, St Andrew of Scotland and St Patrick of Northern Ireland watched down upon the scene.

Marlowe had two guns, one suppressed; he also had a radio. But, as the mercenary he'd killed hadn't taken weapons from a more armed source, for example an armed policeman like the newer arrivals, he now knew he was outgunned and outnumbered. And so, giving suppressing fire, he sprinted across the open space, heading for the corridor that led to the House of Commons, directly opposite. He needed a distraction, something that could even the odds, as currently they could tear him to shreds. He needed to turn out the lights, or worse.

Looking around, he smiled as he saw a large, red, fire extinguisher against a fire point. There was no fire, but Marlowe knew how the damn thing could still be useful.

The first of the mercenaries, a vicious-looking man with a burned hand, likely from the Cambridge explosion started across the lobby, headed after Marlowe, but stopped as he arrived at the corridor, as Marlowe took this moment to aim and fire at the fire extinguisher, releasing an explosion of smoke and what looked like steam, the previously pressured ammonium phosphate base now released into the atmosphere, filling the space. Marlowe watched through the smoke as the mercenary stopped, staring down at the extinguisher, and then his head snapped back as Marlowe fired a second time, the body falling to the floor, Marlowe's hands reaching through the smoke and dragging him out of sight of his companion, using the smoke to hide him as he blindly searched the dead man's pockets.

There wasn't much, as the suit would have had small pockets, with only a suppressed pistol able to be brought in. The dead man had, however, taken a Kevlar vest from an officer, and also held a HK MP5, so Marlowe quickly slipped it off the body, throwing it onto his own as the smoke cleared, looking for higher ground. The rifle didn't have a suppressor, and the pistol only had a few rounds left. Marlowe couldn't run in firing at everything, because right now, he didn't know how many were out there after him.

'Sergei!' the second mercenary shouted, moving carefully closer, checking his magazine, making sure it was loaded.

Marlowe dived from the plinth he'd been crouching on, slamming into the mercenary and knocking him to the floor, sending his rifle clattering across the marble flooring. As the mercenary moved to grab a smaller weapon from his ankle holster, Marlowe shot him twice in the vest, a similar move to the one he'd done earlier, kneeling on the wheezing mercenary.

'How many?' he hissed.

'Fifteen,' the mercenary replied. Marlowe placed the gun against the mercenary's forehead.

'Again. And this time, the truth.'

'Eight,' the mercenary, deciding this information wasn't worth dying for, corrected himself. Marlowe nodded.

'Five left then,' he said, slamming down with the stock of the rifle, knocking the mercenary out, emptying his pockets of anything that could be classed as a weapon. He'd awaken, but when he did, he'd be unarmed, and hopefully surrounded by police.

The mercenary did, however, own a phone, with one number in. Marlowe dialled.

'What?' an irritated Raymond answered.

'Hey Raymond,' Marlowe smiled. 'Looks like I'm going through Russian mercs to get to you. Almost feels like Cambridge again.'

'Marlowe,' Raymond's voice trembled. 'It's too late. You should run.'

'What, and get blamed for this?' Marlowe tutted. 'We both know who the traitor is.'

'Depends who the traitor has been loyal to from the start,' Raymond replied.

'What's your real name?' Marlowe asked. 'I mean your Russian name?'

'It's my own,' Raymond admitted conversationally. 'I turned in seventy-eight. I didn't know Marshall had worked me out in the late eighties, but luckily Glasnost happened before he could end me, and we were all friends again.'

'You could walk away from this.'

'Nobody's walking away from this now, Tom,' Raymond was almost disappointed as he spoke. 'Your mum was a good woman. I met her a couple of times. I'm sorry we used her to get to you, but we needed a scapegoat, because Marshall wasn't a big enough draw.'

'I'm going to kill you,' Marlowe held the phone out. 'You wait there, okay?'

Already grabbing the discarded rifle and moving on, Marlowe threw the phone against the wall in anger, the smash echoing down the hall as he considered his options. He could continue down St Stephen's Hall, moving into the Great Hall and take down the five remaining armed insurgents, but that wouldn't stop the bomb. The better option was to find the secret room, stop Raymond and defuse the bloody device, while fulfilling the promise he'd just made.

Turning back to the Commons Chamber, Marlowe started down the corridor at a run.

IN A SMALL, HIDDEN ROOM AT THE SIDE OF WESTMINSTER Great Hall, Raymond Sykes sat on the stone floor staring at the disconnected call and tried to stop himself from screaming in anger.

It wasn't supposed to end this way. It was supposed to be glorious, with Westminster either ruined or uninhabitable, with the Government hunting their own, and MI5 blamed for *World War Three.* He was supposed to be a hero, returning to Moscow through back channels, finally able to receive his payment – enough money to buy his own fortified island.

Maybe even two.

But now it had all gone wrong. There was shooting nearby, and the alarms he'd heard meant the whole place was on lockdown. There was no entry or exit anymore, and this meant no way to avoid the bomb when it exploded.

And it had to explode. If they found it intact, Marshall and Marlowe couldn't be blamed for the bombing, and the note wouldn't make sense. People would realise it was a setup.

But if it exploded now, Raymond would be within the blast radius, because the locked-down building *was* the blast radius, if only for the lethal dose of radiation, rather than the explosion itself.

He bit at his lip, chewing, unsure what to do. He *knew* what he had to do, but whether he could do it was a different matter. The list was changed, but if Marshall was out there, they'd find the original. He had no doubt of that. Bloody Tom Marlowe, who should have been stopped half a dozen times by now, was already here, playing at being a one-man army and making prank phone calls.

No, Marlowe couldn't win. MI5 couldn't win.

Nobody could win.

Taking a deep breath and flicking three switches on the top of the arming device in quick succession, Raymond Sykes made his final decision, armed the RDD bomb with a press of the small, rounded button recessed into the top, sat back, and laughed hysterically, staring down at the key that had locked him into his final resting place, as the digital clock on it counted down from five minutes.

It should have been enough time to get to safety.

Now it was just long enough to say a prayer.

26

COUNTDROWN

Marlowe knew he had little time, and he knew Trix would have been planning the same thing, having likely heard the call, if only Marlowe's side, through her earpiece.

'How bad is it there?' he asked, hugging the sides of the corridor, so as not to cast a shadow.

'They're unsure what to do,' Trix said softly through his earpiece. 'But it means I can't get to you. And unless I see the device, I can't tell you how to defuse it.'

'Then you'll have to talk it through,' Marlowe made his way through the Commons Lobby now, heading down stairs that led to the Members Writing Rooms. Once inside, Anthony Farringdon, and his knowledge of all things Westminster had explained how it was a short walk to the secret door, Raymond and the bomb.

Raymond would be waiting. This wouldn't be easy.

'I might not be able to do that,' Trix replied uncertainly.

'Why not?'

'Because I don't know if I can defuse the bloody thing!' she snapped. 'I've never done this before. I'm a hacker!'

'But you said it's as easy as building a gaming PC—'

'Oh, don't give me that shit,' Trix half laughed. 'I told that to Wintergreen to shut her up. She was going to do this. Have you seen her hold a fork? She shakes the food all over the place. Imagine her with a pair of clippers, cutting a wire under a magnifying glass. We both know I'm the best option, but it's out of my wheelhouse. At best, when looking at it I can make a calculated guess. On the phone with you? Impossible. Ah, shit.'

'What now?'

'There's movement at the end of the hall,' Trix whispered. 'They've been sent to guard the door to the room. You won't get past them.'

'I need a diversion,' Marlowe said. 'Delay the mercs from leaving.'

'And how am I supposed to do that?' she hissed. 'Were you not listening just ten seconds ago? I'm a hacker not a spy!'

'Then hack *them*,' Marlowe moved into the corridor that surrounded Cloister Court. 'Go analogue.'

———

TRIX STARED UP AT THE TOP OF THE STAIRCASE, WHERE THE FIVE remaining mercenaries prepared to leave the hall, moving in a group to the exit of St Stephen's Porch. She had to stop them, but how did a twenty-one-year-old woman, who'd spent most of her time since hitting her teenage years sitting in front of a screen, gain attention?

By hacking their thoughts.

'*Stepan Chechik!*' she shouted, standing up now, facing the confused Baroness Levin, who stared down at her.

'What?' Levin asked, confused.

'I wasn't talking to you, I was talking to them,' Trix said, pointing at the five suited mercenaries stopped at the door. 'You worked for Stepan, right? In Cambridge? Working with Raymond Sykes?'

'We never worked for him,' the lead mercenary, who Trix decided was going to be named *Neck Tattoo,* snapped. 'We worked for Stepan.'

'And yet, after Stepan died, you still work for the people who killed him,' Trix shook her head. 'Man, that must suck.'

'We never killed Chechik,' Levin looked back to the mercenaries. 'MI5 killed him.'

'Marlowe killed him, right?' Trix ignored the Baroness, walking towards the staircase now, tablet still in her hand as she continued to speak to the men. 'That's what you were told?'

'You know different?' Neck Tattoo asked.

'I know Stepan Chechik took his own life with a cyanide capsule,' Trix carried on. 'And his last words to Marlowe were that he wouldn't betray the motherland, that he wouldn't betray *her.*'

She emphasised the last word by pointing at Baroness Levin. Trix didn't know if it was true or not, but it was certainly doing the job.

'They blackmailed Chechik into helping because Raymond Sykes found the Project Rubicon list, right?' she continued. 'A list you're maybe on as well. Or you agreed to follow him because he was your leader. An army to stand behind him while he stole radioactive materials for the dirty bomb the other side of that wall.'

At this she pointed to where she'd been told the door once was, nothing but a brass plaque to even hint as to the location. The surrounding people, the ones who heard her words panicked now, moving across the Great Hall, away from the stone wall. However, the mercenaries spoke to each other, nervously.

'Oh, don't tell me they *didn't* mention the large bomb that's going off at any moment? The one that'll irradiate the whole place and kill you all? That's a hell of a sacrifice you're making, for corporation profit.'

'Just who the hell are you?' Levin shouted, and Trix grinned.

Time to split the deck.

'I'm Trix Preston, and according to the Rubicon list in Thames House's basement servers, I'm a sleeper agent who works for Moscow,' she said to the mercenaries. 'Just like Stepan was. But you know who *aren't* on the list?'

She pointed at Levin.

'Baroness Levin, Bridget Summers and Raymond Sykes,' she said, holding up the tablet. 'I have the list here if you want to see. Brought to me by Stepan Chechik himself.'

It wasn't technically a lie, as the list had come from Chechik, even if they had taken it from his corpse.

'*Shut up!*' Levin shouted. 'She's lying!'

'Why don't you go have a look inside the room you've been told to guard?' Trix suggested to Neck Tattoo. 'If there's a bomb there, I think we all know what that means.'

Neck Tattoo glared at Baroness Levin.

'You said you were with us until the end,' he hissed. 'But you removed yourself from the list?'

'I had to!' Levin argued. 'I needed to be prominent for the next stage!'

'The next stage being after we died in this explosion?'

'I wasn't supposed to die in this explosion!'

'See?' Trix gloated. '*I wasn't,* not *we weren't.* She'd already decided you were expendable.'

The mercenaries had forgotten their orders now and stared down the stairs at the now worried Baroness Levin.

'Bought you some time,' Trix muttered into her earpiece. 'Use it.'

MARLOWE HAD REACHED THE DOOR BY THE TIME TRIX SPOKE, and, holding the HK in one hand, he pulled at the wood panelling, hoping it hadn't been re-locked.

It had.

'You can't get in, and you won't be able to break through before the timer hits zero,' Raymond's voice was faint, but defiant as Marlowe rattled the door. 'We took your duplicate key.'

'And I took it back from Harris when I killed him,' Marlowe replied as he quickly unlocked the door, kicking it open. Raymond Sykes, in a black suit and tie, sat against the wall, staring up in horror at him. In front of Raymond were two champagne boxes on a trolley, and beside those were two metal boxes, connected to each other with wires, the smaller of which sat beside Raymond, seemingly only three switches and a button, and a timer that was counting down from three minutes, twenty seconds.

'Oh, you dumb bastard,' Marlowe lowered the rifle. 'You've set the device already?'

'What else could I do?' Raymond muttered. 'Only if we blow the building, can we convince everyone it was a pre-meditated act.'

Marlowe frowned.

'But Marshall Kirk is out there,' he said. 'He's alive, and he's found the original cartridge holding the Rubicon list.'

Raymond took this in, nodding.

'We guessed,' he said. 'But it's not just Marshall who's mentioned in the note, Thomas. It's also you.'

Marlowe considered this for a long moment.

'It's the right play,' he nodded. 'I'm a burned ex-agent who's now on the list. They could blame me for doing what Marshall had planned to do.'

He smiled at this.

'I was always the backup, wasn't I?' he asked. 'You knew if I got in, I'd try to stop you. This way you have a second patsy if I failed to stop it.'

'If?' Raymond pointed at the bomb, now showing two minutes and fifty seconds. 'I think, with us in lockdown, and the Great Hall filled with people, it's very much a case of *when*.'

'Not if I can help it,' Marlowe moved to grab the main bomb, but Raymond lunged forward, slashing with a knife, opening up a deep slash in Marlowe's arm.

'No!' he snarled. 'You won't stop me! I'll die—'

He fell back as Marlowe, finally sick of talking emptied the submachine gun into him, before tossing the rifle aside, gathering the two parts of the RDD device in his hands, stacking them on top of each other, and carrying them out of the cubbyhole.

'Trix!' he shouted into his earpiece. 'Bloody thing's got just over two minutes on the clock. How do I disarm it?'

'You don't,' Trix's voice was calm, but he could hear the resignation within it. 'I've just been told all about it by Baroness Levin, with the help of some rather pissed off mercs. There's no kill switch, and if you want to defuse it, you need to bust in through the outer shell. It'll take more than the time we have.'

'Dammit,' Marlowe looked around the corridor. 'I could get it into a courtyard?'

'That might save the building, but the radiation would still get into the air.'

'I could run to the other side of Parliament?'

'That would save us from the explosion, but not the radiation. And you'd die.'

'I'm dead either way,' Marlowe started towards a staircase. 'You said air, right?'

'Yes,' Trix was confused. 'The stuff we breathe.'

'I might have an idea,' Marlowe said as, with the heavy device in his arms, he started to jog towards the Central Hall once more.

THE MOMENT BRAD HAD ATTACKED THE MI5 AGENT, Wintergreen had kicked out at Bridget, taking her knee out from behind and sending her to the ground, as the elderly head of Section D dived onto her back, throwing her into a chokehold.

'Get back!' Shaw shouted, aiming her weapon at Wintergreen. 'I'm warning you—'

'Drop the gun,' Curtis, finally choosing a side, spun, his Glock 17 now aimed at his partner. 'I'm serious, Shaw. This needs to end. You're talking about killing dozens of people!'

Shaw turned to Curtis, her gun following.

'They're sleeper agents,' she said calmly. 'Here to start a war.'

'They're lying to you,' Brad interrupted.

'We're lying?' Bridget laughed, croaking through the chokehold. 'Curtis, Marlowe took you out twice!'

'But didn't terminate, even though you were about to do that to him,' Brad replied. 'Just took out your shin, which he feels real bad about, by the way.'

'Bullshit!' Shaw hissed. 'Do you even have the real tape?'

'No,' Brad admitted, looking back to the main entrance, where, pulling up on a motorbike were Marshall and Tessa Kirk. 'But they do.'

Shaw turned again, raising her weapon at the new arrivals, but Curtis moved a step closer, the Glock 17 still aimed at her.

'Don't,' he said. 'Don't make me do this.'

Shaw aimed back at Curtis.

'That's the problem,' she replied. 'You're too boring to be made to do anything.'

MARLOWE HAD ALWAYS ENJOYED RUNNING, BUT THAT WAS WITH correct running shoes on, and without bloody heavy bombs in his arms. He'd run in army boots, he'd run in flip-flops, but that he could run in these didn't mean he wanted to, as he crossed the Central Hall, heading to the Lower Waiting Hall, and the staircase that took him to the lower levels of Parliament. It meant he knew there was a point, in any mission, when the ability to run fast, in whatever you were wearing, could save your life.

Mainly, these offices were filled with meeting rooms, libraries and offices, but at the back of the building, recent renovations had given Marlowe a potential way to save the day. The counter was down to ninety seconds now, as Marlowe took the steps two at a time, desperately trying not to lose balance or slip on the stone stairs; the last thing he wanted to do was tumble and set off the bomb through his own clumsiness.

Now on the lower level, Marlowe ran into an ornate, glass-fronted events space; this was the Terrace Pavilion, and for a moment Marlowe had to double-take, as the white drapery that ran across the ceiling and down the back made him feel he was in a wedding venue. Ahead of him, though, through the panoramic glass doors that ran along the southern side was the actual Members Terrace, providing a spectacular, uninterrupted view of the River Thames.

Which was exactly where he needed to be.

He had less than forty seconds now, and with urgency in mind, he ran to a glass door and turned the handle—

It was locked.

Of course, it's locked, you fool, Marlowe chided himself. *It's an external door. Anyone could walk in.* And, glancing at his countdown clock, he saw the digits click down to thirty seconds. No time to pick the lock, so placing the RDD device onto a side table, he pulled out both guns and emptied them into the window in front of him, shattering it, and, as the shards still fell to the floor, he grabbed the device for the last time, running through the broken glass frame and to the edge of the Terrace, hurling both parts of the device as far as he could into the Thames, watching it hit the water below with ten seconds left on the clock.

This done, Marlowe turned and started sprinting back into the building.

He remembered being told once that radiation was diluted quickly in water. Depending on the size of the bomb and the size of the body of water, it was entirely possible the radiation could return to naturally occurring levels within days, although eating anything from the water was probably a no-no.

With an explosion underwater, there was also no dust to contaminate the air, which reduced the effectiveness of a "dirty" bomb. And exploded water vapour didn't really stick to things the way radioactive dust did.

At least, Marlowe *hoped* it didn't as he—

The explosion was underwater and muted, but the shock wave still took him off his feet as he sprawled onto the marble floor of a Westminster corridor. He could hear alarms in nearby buildings go off, but there was no major damage, and thankfully, there didn't seem to be any major fallout.

Still, better safe than sorry, he thought as he rose to his feet and started running back to Westminster Great Hall.

THE EXPLOSION IN THE THAMES WAS UNEXPECTED, AND THE Portcullis House atrium shuddered as the blast force reached them. Curtis, distracted by the event diverted his attention for a microsecond, a momentary lapse, but it was enough for Shaw to fire her weapon, catching him in the shoulder, spinning him around as he fell to the floor, Shaw already running for the tunnel that led under the road and into the Palace of Westminster.

Brad went to go after her, but Tessa, now in the atrium and tossing the cartridge case to him, grabbed Curtis's Block 17 from the ground where it fell.

'I've got this,' she said, running after the rogue agent.

THE JOURNEY BACK TO THE GREAT HALL WASN'T THAT LONG, and Marlowe had picked up a discarded weapon from another of the fallen mercenaries in the Central Lobby before opening the door at St Stephen's Porch. He'd lost the earbud in the explosion, so didn't know what Trix's status was, but he knew there were still five mercenaries in the room.

As it was, there were only three worth worrying about, and they were in a standoff against the other two, with Baroness Levin in the middle, and Trix at the bottom of the steps.

'Stand down!' the Baroness was shouting. 'This isn't your battle anymore!'

'We will be taken and executed for what you tried to do!' one of the two rogue mercenaries was saying. 'We can stop now! This was not supposed to be like this!'

They stopped as they saw Marlowe, who, as the other three turned to face him, held his weapon up in a peace gesture.

'The bomb is gone,' he said. 'And we're still alive. Raymond Sykes is dead. This doesn't have to end badly. Let the people go.'

He noted that, at the other end of the hall, the crowds had moved to the doors. As they did this, though, one of the three mercenaries still keeping to the mission fired into the ceiling.

'Stay where you are!' he cried out. 'We will—'

He didn't finish as, with cool determination, Marlowe shot each of the three arguing mercenaries, catching them all in the torso as they fell to the floor, killing the man who'd been speaking, but winding the other two, both of whom were wearing stolen vests. As the remaining mercenaries ran over, securing their downed colleagues, one of them, a man with a neck tattoo looked at Marlowe.

'We honour Stepan, not these people,' he said, nodding at the now pale Baroness Levin. Marlowe nodded at this, lowering his weapon and holding out his hand for Neck Tattoo's own weapon. Reluctantly, Neck Tattoo and his colleague gave the guns across, as, at the back of the hall, the double doors were finally opened and the crowd of technicians and support staff ran through them into the waiting crowd of police and security services, who came in, guns raised.

'*On the floor! Now!*' they cried, and Marlowe dropped his weapons, clambering onto his knees, hands behind his head.

He hoped to God Marshall and Tessa had found the real cartridge, or this was going to be a very long night.

———

SHAW PAUSED RUNNING AS THE GUN FIRED BEHIND HER, THE bullet ricocheting off the wall to her side.

'Just stop,' Tessa sighed, walking out of the tunnel and into Speaker's Yard. 'It's over.'

'How do you see that?' Shaw turned to face Tessa now. 'You're a sleeper agent for Russia. I'm an MI5 agent who's taking you in.'

'An MI5 agent who shot her partner.'

'I was taking down a sleeper cell,' Shaw smiled. 'Who knows where it ends. I had to be sure, confusions always occur.'

'We have the original Rubicon,' Tessa replied. 'We can

prove Bridget and Raymond were on it, that Wintergreen, Trix, Marlowe, they were all framed.'

'But we can't change yours, though, can we?' Shaw smiled. 'Must suck knowing your mummy's past has effectively burned you.'

Tessa laughed as she placed her borrowed Glock 17 to the floor, holding her hands up.

'Take me in,' she said as Shaw, surprised and a little confused by this turn of events, reached into her pocket for a pair of cable ties. 'But you don't know, do you?'

'Know what?' Shaw asked, moving a hand out towards Tessa, cable ties in it, as she kept her weapon aimed at her opponent.

Tessa took the offered cable ties and then grabbed the arm, pulling to the side as she spun Shaw in a quick motion, kicking out, sending Shaw's gun across the stone floor as she flipped the MI5 agent onto the floor.

'I *am* a sleeper,' Tessa smiled again; a dark, vicious smile. 'Trained by Spetsnaz as a kid. Although, like many others on that list, I never wanted the order to come.'

Shaw rose, rubbing the back of her head.

'You should have joined us,' she said.

'You shouldn't have tried to kill me, or taken my dad hostage,' Tessa moved in now, kicking out as Shaw blocked it with her arm, pushing her backwards, across the green. 'My mum taught me every move MI5 teaches you, by the time I was twelve. You seriously think you have a hope?'

Shaw went to give a pithy reply, but instead made a *whuff* noise as Tessa linked her hands together and swung them into her gut, taking her off the ground for a moment with an explosive force that sent Shaw to her knees.

However, before she could continue, Shaw grabbed a

piece of wood and connected hard with Tessa's cheek, sending her staggering back as Shaw, groaning in pain rose, only to be taken back down again as Tessa, screaming with rage, speared her in the midsection, landing on her, grabbing the wood and slamming it down on her throat as Tessa, blood in her eyes from the head wound, choked the life out of her.

'You're a failure as a traitor,' she hissed. 'You're not even a real one. If I kill you, you know what'll happen to me? They'll thank me and give me a medal. Your bomb failed, your plan failed and now *you've* failed for the last time—'

'Tessa,' Marshall Kirk ran into the garden now. 'Don't do it.'

'She's the reason we're here,' Tessa said. 'She's the reason my life – our lives – are over.'

'No,' Marshall picked up the fallen Glock 17, walking over. 'I'm the reason. I should have acknowledged what your mum did. I should have told MI5, but I was scared to. And it's because of this fear, they were about to use us for terrible things. Don't become like them.'

He placed a hand on Tessa's shoulder.

'Don't be like your *mother*.'

Tessa's eyes clouded with tears, and she backed away, rolling off the now wheezing Shaw as, from around the corner, armed police came running.

'Down on the ground!' they shouted. 'All of you.'

'I'm MI5,' Shaw croaked. 'These traitors tried to kill me—'

'The only traitor here is you,' Curtis, his gunshot wound hastily bound and packed, said from the tunnel, leaning against the side of Wintergreen. 'Take her in, guys. Take everyone in.'

And, this done, Curtis looked at Wintergreen, who helped position him into a sitting position against the wall.

'What now?' he asked.

'You take the credit for stopping a terrorist attack,' Wintergreen smiled. 'I find an old tape machine and prove my innocence, and MI5 will owe Section D.'

'I can live with that,' Curtis replied, wincing at his shoulder. 'But can medical attention be part of this plan, too?'

———

EPILOGUE

MARLOWE HADN'T SEEN THE LIGHT OF DAY FOR A WEEK AFTER they took him down in Westminster.

He hadn't seen the news; he had heard nothing from any of his contacts or friends, instead he'd been kept in a black-site cell, an eight-by-ten world comprising of a bed, toilet and sink, with regular food and a selection of old, dogeared thriller books to pass the time reading.

As cells went, it was surprisingly civil, considering the level of trouble he was currently in.

On the seventh day, Marlowe looked up from his bed as the door opened, and a familiar, suited slim man, his arm in a sling, stood in the doorway, the light shining in from behind him.

'Come on,' Curtis said. 'Time for a debrief.'

'Can I finish my chapter?' Marlowe asked, but then rose, tossing the book to the side. 'Actually, don't worry, I'll pick it up when I get back.'

The interview room was a few yards down the corridor, and when Marlowe entered, he was relieved to see it was more like a police interview room than the basement nightmare he'd last been in with Curtis. For a start, the lights were bright, and not aimed in his face.

'You killed my boss,' Curtis said conversationally as he waved for Marlowe to sit down.

'In fairness, he tried to kill me first,' Marlowe replied. 'And he killed Fenchurch.'

'We know,' Curtis smiled. 'The police that took on the case didn't believe you did it either.'

He sat facing Marlowe.

'They promoted me to Section Chief,' he said.

'Congrats,' Marlowe replied. 'I'm sorry I tasered you. Oh, and took out your shin.'

Curtis tapped his sling.

'You had the draw on me twice, you could have done far worse,' he said. 'Anyway, sorry for the seclusion, but a lot of people were calling for heads, as you can imagine.'

'The list got out?'

'A version,' Curtis nodded. 'One we could prove was doctored. You'll be happy to know Trix Preston and Emilia Wintergreen have been reinstated.'

Marlowe nodded, his stomach dropping. Curtis had said nothing about *him*.

'I'm guessing I'm still a problem?'

'You could say that.' Curtis leant back on the chair, sighing, and Marlowe realised that in the last seven days, he'd probably had more sleep than the new Section Chief. 'USA want to give you a medal, half of MI5 wants to kill you, so the usual thing.'

'Have you decided what to do with me?'

'Well,' Curtis folded his arms as he looked across the table. 'That rather depends on you. We have the original list, and we now know Levin, Summers and Sykes were on it. You sorted out Sykes, so the other two are now … let's just say they've disappeared in the confusion for the moment. Summers is likely never to appear again, but Levin, being a Tory Baroness will be let go, long enough to retire from public life and start a new, quiet existence somewhere small, atoning for what she did.'

His face darkened.

'And, a year from now, when everything's calm, I'll personally shoot her in the back of the head.'

Marlowe smiled.

'I'll bring popcorn,' he said, 'if I'm likely to be out of there by then? I notice you didn't mention me.'

'You. Yes,' Curtis looked uncomfortable. 'Wintergreen said it should be up to you.'

'What should be?

'Your future,' Curtis replied. 'We haven't said who the third name changed was, but it'll get out soon, I'm sure. Unless we give another.'

Marlowe considered the words, and then nodded.

'Tessa.'

Curtis shifted in his seat.

'She's a civilian, no matter what training she had, and her mother's name coming out as a sleeper will likely affect Marshall too, probably stop his pension immediately, if he's not thrown into a cell somewhere,' he said. 'So, we have a choice. We can either say that Bridget Summers placed your mother on the list, or we can say she placed Angela Weber on the list.'

Marlowe nodded. It if came out Tessa's mum was a sleeper, her political career, her future in any way, would be destroyed. Although he wasn't as concerned about her political shenanigans as she probably was, there was something nice about having someone in Parliament, no matter how junior, who had your own interests at heart. But more importantly, as Curtis had said...

Marshall's military pension, and likely his freedom would also be gone.

There would be questions asked.

But Olivia Marlowe was dead, and Marlowe himself had spent enough time in the shadows not to warrant too much scrutiny. He could weather the storm, whether or not it was true, far better than she could.

'It's the clever play,' Marlowe said. 'She's an asset too, can give you information on her training. And if she makes it into Parliament, the Cabinet even, she'd owe you personally. Nice thing to have.'

'She'd owe you too,' Curtis said, as if assuming Marlowe hadn't already considered the option.

Marlowe looked down at the table.

'But if it comes out my mum was a sleeper, I'm burned, aren't I?' he asked. 'I can't get back in.'

'Even if you cleared your name, you'd still be burned,' Curtis stated apologetically. 'Too many ruffled feathers, and too high a body count.'

'So, this is my future?' Marlowe waved around the room, but he meant the black site. 'Next door to Bridget Summers?'

'You saved the world from World War Three,' Curtis shook his head. 'You deserve a medal, not this. You're free to do whatever you want. But remember, we can't look out for you. We've cut your air supply off.'

Marlowe grinned.

'I call that *weekdays*,' he said as he stood up. 'Now, where's my stuff?'

Wintergreen and Trix met with Marlowe at the Heston services on the M4 motorway the next day. They'd explained they had things for him, a desk clear out of sorts, and it wasn't something you could pass on a bridge.

Marlowe arrived in his Jaguar, recently picked up from a long-term parking facility near Stansted.

'You look like crap,' Trix said. 'Thought you'd at least make an effort.'

Marlowe looked around.

'She's not here,' Wintergreen gave a sad expression, the first time Marlowe had ever seen her do so. 'She wanted you to know she appreciated everything, but with the by-election coming up, and the Tories about to name her …

'I get it,' Marlowe chuckled. 'I'm not the type of person you want appearing out of nowhere. You two shouldn't be seen with me either.'

'We won't shy away from you.' Wintergreen reached an arm out, as if she was about to hug Marlowe, and then thought better of it, patting his shoulder. 'And we have some things for you.'

Trix walked him to the van, where she opened the side door, pulling out a duffle bag.

'Three fake identities, best you can get,' she explained. 'One even has a bank account, but I'd suggest you do your own thing there.'

'Any reason I can't stay as me?' Marlowe frowned. 'I've fought bloody hard to sort my real name out.'

'Because you're going on a mission,' Wintergreen replied. 'You might be burned, and some of the nastiest bastards on the planet might be hunting you, all with their own reasons to hate you, but you're the best positioned person to do this.'

'Do what?'

Wintergreen leant closer, making sure they couldn't be overheard.

'Rubicon,' she said. 'You think Primakov just found it by accident?'

'Go on.'

'It was Trisha Hawkins and Phoenix,' Trix replied. 'Their grubby fingers are all over it. We just don't know who they were doing it for.'

'And that's where you come in,' Wintergreen continued. 'We can—'

'No,' Marlowe shook his head. 'I'm sorry, but I can't.'

He pulled the bag out of the van, slinging it over his shoulder.

'I need to work out who I am before I do anything else,' he explained. 'I spent my whole working life saving people. And doing that cast me to the gutter. I need to climb out, have a look around, and decide what I want to do with my life before I talk to anyone about what *they* want to do with it.'

Wintergreen sniffed, and then nodded.

'You've earned that right,' she said. 'Call us when you've decided.'

Before Marlowe could reply, she waved for Trix to join her. Trix mimed a "call me" sign as she clambered into the driver's seat, and the van left; Marlowe now alone in the car park.

Walking over to the Jaguar, he placed the duffle into the boot. For a few IDs, it seemed quite heavy, so he opened it up.

It was filled with banknotes. Easily a hundred grand's worth.

'So, this is what the private sector feels like, eh?' Marlowe smiled to himself as he pulled out a wad of notes, riffled it beside his ear for no other reason than to say he'd done it, and then slipped it into his jacket. 'Could be worse.'

With the sun now going down, Marlowe climbed into his Jaguar, turned the engine on, and drove out of the service station, heading away from London. He was free of all commitments now, and he could travel the world, do the backpacking trip he'd always promised himself, even visit his bootneck mates from his days in the Royal Marines.

He had a lot of thinking, of re-evaluating to do with his life, and apparently all the time in the world to do it in.

Bring it on, he thought, grinning as he gunned the engine, turning on the radio and twisting the volume up.

I wonder how much trouble I can get into by the weekend?

———

ACKNOWLEDGEMENTS

When you write a series of books, you find that there are a ton of people out there who help you, sometimes without even realising, and so I wanted to do a little acknowledgement to some of them.

There are people I need to thank, and they know who they are.

People who patiently gave advice when I started this back in 2020, the people on various Facebook groups who encouraged me when I didn't know if I could even do this, the designers who gave advice on cover design and on book formatting, all the way to my friends and family, who saw what I was doing not as mad folly, but as something good.

Editing wise, I owe a ton of thanks to my brother Chris Lee, who I truly believe could make a fortune as a post-retirement copy editor, if not a solid writing career of his own, Jacqueline Beard MBE, who has copyedited all my books since the very beginning, and our new editorial addition Sian Phillips, all of which have made my books way better than they have every right to be.

Also, I couldn't have done this without my growing army of ARC and beta readers, who not only show me where I falter, but also raise awareness of me in the social media world, ensuring that other people learn of my books, and Eben M. Atwater, who helped me fix my rookie weapon mistakes.

But mainly, I tip my hat and thank you. *The reader.* Who took a chance on an unknown author in a pile of Kindle books, and thought you'd give them a go.

I write these books for you. And with luck, I'll keep on writing them for a very long time.

Jack Gatland / Tony Lee,
  London, August 2022

ABOUT THE AUTHOR

Jack Gatland is the pen name of *#1 New York Times Bestselling Author* Tony Lee, who has been writing in all media for thirty-five years, including comics, graphic novels, middle grade books, audio drama, TV and film for *DC Comics, Marvel, BBC, ITV, Random House, Penguin USA, Hachette* and a ton of other publishers and broadcasters.

These have included licenses such as *Doctor Who, Spider Man, X-Men, Star Trek, Battlestar Galactica, MacGyver,* BBC's *Doctors, Wallace and Gromit* and *Shrek*, as well as work created with musicians such as *Ozzy Osbourne, Joe Satriani, Beartooth* and *Megadeth.*

As Tony, he's toured the world talking to reluctant readers with his 'Change The Channel' school tours, and lectures on screenwriting and comic scripting for *Raindance* in London.

An introvert West Londoner by heart, he lives with his wife Tracy and dog Fosco, just outside London.

Locations In The Book

The locations and items I use in my books are real, if altered slightly for dramatic intent. Here's some more information about a few of them...

Thames House is the home of MI5, as the building often seen in *James Bond* movies in Vauxhall is the home of MI6. It's a standard looking building, but it you've seen *Spooks* (or *MI5: Spooks* in the US), they use Freemasons Hall off Covent Garden to portray the outside of it.

Q-Whitehall exists, and was investigated in the *New Statesman* by journalist Duncan Campbell in 1980, as stated in the book. In fact all the tunnels I mention are real, and there really is an exit from one of the tunnels underneath the Bouddica statue beside the Thames!

The bunker under Marlowe's house is fictional, but they do exist in the UK, and inspiration for this was taken by the excellent Colin Furze underground bunker project on YouTube.

Caxton Gibbet exists, and there are tales of murderers being hanged and displayed at the nearby village of Caxton in the 1670s, and records in a court case that the gibbet was still there in 1745. It was apparently a gruesome example of the cage variation of the gibbet, into which live victims were allegedly placed until they died from starvation, dehydration or exposure. After execution, dead bodies were certainly suspended in cages as a warning, and this may have happened here. Now, however, it's a Shell petrol station, with a Costa and McDonalds drive-thru beside it.

There is a replica gibbet at the entrance.

The *Jolly Sailor* pub in Maldon, off Hythe Quay has been recently rebranded as *Fish on the Quay*, and is a grade II listed building, in which some parts date back to the 15th century.

It was used in an episode of *Lovejoy*, so is no stranger to mysterious goings on and strange meetings!

The Maldon Mud Race is also real, in which entrants compete to complete a 500 metres (550 yd) dash, in thick mud, over the bed of the River Blackwater. The race is organised by the Lions & Rotary clubs of Maldon and Maldon District Council, and raises money for charity.

Started in 1972, the text race (as of writing) will be in May 2023.

Finally, the secret room in Westminster, amazingly, is true! Historians working on the renovation of the House of Commons found the lost 360-year-old passageway, hidden in a secret chamber. The doorway was created for the coronation of Charles II, in 1660, to allow guests access to a celebratory banquet in Westminster Hall, the building next to the modern day Commons chamber.

It was used by MPs and political notables, such as the diarist Samuel Pepys, as the main entrance to the Commons, but was eventually blocked up. It was briefly rediscovered in 1950, during repairs to bomb damage, but then sealed off again and forgotten about until 2020, when a key was made for a mysterious lock in the wood panelling.

A brass plaque, erected in Westminster Hall in 1895, marks the spot where the doorway once was, and it matches exactly where I place it in the novel.

If you're interested in seeing what the *real* locations look like, I often post 'behind the scenes' location images on my Instagram feed and in my Facebook Readers Group. This will continue through all the books, and I suggest you follow them.

In fact, feel free to follow me on all my social media by clicking on the links below. Over time these can be places where we can engage, discuss Declan and put the world to rights.

www.jackgatland.com
www.hoodemanmedia.com

Visit my Reader's Group Page
(Mainly for fans to discuss my books):
https://www.facebook.com/groups/jackgatland

Subscribe to my Readers List:
www.subscribepage.com/jackgatland

www.facebook.com/jackgatlandbooks

www.twitter.com/jackgatlandbook
ww.instagram.com/jackgatland

Want more books by Jack Gatland? Turn the page...

Tom Marlowe will return in his next thriller

TARGET LOCKED

Order Now at Amazon:

My book.to/targetlocked

Released January 2023

Gain up-to-the-moment information on the release by signing up to the Jack Gatland VIP Reader's Club!

Join at www.subscribepage.com/jackgatland

LETTER FROM THE DEAD

"BY THE TIME YOU READ THIS, I WILL BE DEAD..."

A TWENTY YEAR OLD MURDER...
A PRIME MINISTER LEADERSHIP BATTLE...
A PARANOID, HOMELESS EX-MINISTER...
AN EVANGELICAL PREACHER WITH A SECRET...

DI DECLAN WALSH HAS HAD BETTER FIRST DAYS...

AVAILABLE ON AMAZON / KINDLEUNLIMITED

EIGHT PEOPLE. EIGHT SECRETS.
ONE SNIPER.

THE
BOARD
ROOM

HOW FAR WOULD YOU GO TO GAIN JUSTICE?

NEW YORK TIMES #1 BESTSELLER TONY LEE WRITING AS

JACK GATLAND

A NEW STANDALONE THRILLER WITH
A TWIST - FROM THE CREATOR OF THE
BESTSELLING 'DI DECLAN WALSH' SERIES

AVAILABLE ON AMAZON / KINDLE UNLIMITED

THE THEFT OF A **PRICELESS** PAINTING...
A GANGSTER WITH A **CRIPPLING DEBT**...
A **BODY COUNT** RISING BY THE HOUR...

AND ELLIE RECKLESS IS CAUGHT IN THE MIDDLE.

JACK GATLAND

PAINT
— THE —
DEAD

A 'COP FOR CRIMINALS' ELLIE RECKLESS NOVEL

A NEW PROCEDURAL CRIME SERIES WITH
A TWIST - FROM THE CREATOR OF THE
BESTSELLING 'DI DECLAN WALSH' SERIES

AVAILABLE ON AMAZON / KINDLE UNLIMITED

" ★★★★★ AN EXCELLENT 'INDIANA JONES' STYLE FAST PACED
CHARGE AROUND ENGLAND THAT WAS RIVETING AND CAPTIVATING."

" ★★★★★ AN ACTION-PACKED YARN... I REALLY ENJOYED
THIS AND LOOK FORWARD TO THE NEXT BOOK IN THE SERIES."

JACK GATLAND

THE
LIONHEART
CURSE

HUNT THE GREATEST TREASURES
PAY THE GREATEST PRICE

BOOK 1 IN A NEW SERIES OF ADVENTURES
IN THE STYLE OF 'THE DA VINCI CODE'
FROM THE CREATOR OF DECLAN WALSH

AVAILABLE ON AMAZON / KINDLEUNLIMITED

Printed in Great Britain
by Amazon